Deadly Risks

March 5, 2008

For Davy –

Who knows all the risks – deadly + otherwise – about the publishing world – and a great friend to boot.

Lew

Deadly Risks

a novel by Lew Paper

Seven Locks Press
Santa Ana, California

Books may be ordered through booksellers or from:

Seven Locks Press
PO Box 25689
Santa Ana, CA 92799
(800) 354-5348

This book is a work of fiction. Names, characters, places and incidents, including references to historical figures and events, are products of the author's imagination or are used fictitiously. Any resemblance to actual events or locales or persons, living or dead, including historical figures and events, is entirely coincidental.

Photo Credit on Dust Jacket Cover: Cecil Stoughton, White House/John Fitzgerald Kennedy Library, Boston

ISBN 1-931643-96-2

Library of Congress Cataloging-in-Publication Data
is available from the publisher

Printed in the United States of America

Other Books by Lew Paper

John F. Kennedy: The Promise and the Performance

Brandeis: An Intimate Biography

Empire: William S. Paley and the Making of CBS

To Jan, my partner in crime

Chapter 1

It was, thought Jeff Roberts, exactly as he had imagined. Africa. He could remember all those *National Geographic* specials he had watched on television as a kid, wishing that some day he could see for himself the beauty of the African landscape, and most especially the animals in the flesh. And here he was, sitting on a wooden chair outside a tent on a small plateau near the Tsavo River in southern Kenya, looking out over plains and feathery acacia trees and watching the sun set behind Mount Kilimanjaro. Yes, he reminded himself, taking a four-week photographic safari was, in a very real sense, a dream come true.

Then why, he asked himself, was he not more relaxed? He knew the answer even as he asked the question. He could not escape the grip of his father's letter. He had read it countless times in the weeks since his father's untimely death and could probably recite it by heart. No matter. The letter's contents still haunted him. And more than that, he had a sense that his mere possession of the letter had placed his life in jeopardy. He could not shake the feeling that people were following him, that his telephone was tapped, and that his every move was being watched by people whose identities remained a mystery to him. And then there was the large white sedan that had forced him off an isolated country road late one night as he was driving back from his sister's home. The experience had frightened him, so much so that he had taken the letter and his concerns to his law firm's senior partner the next morning.

Bill Blackhorn looked up from the papers on his desk when Jeff Roberts knocked on the door to his office.

"Yes, Jeff," the senior lawyer said pleasantly. "Come in, come in."

Blackhorn motioned for Jeff to sit down in one of the expensive chairs in front of his desk. Jeff did so but continued to hold the envelope tightly in his left hand. From the troubled look on his face, Blackhorn realized that the young attorney was not there to discuss legal business.

"What's on your mind? Is something wrong?"

Jeff took the letter out of the envelope and handed it to Blackhorn. Jeff felt awkward, in part because he had never shown the letter to anyone, not even his sister, with whom he shared almost everything. Blackhorn, a seasoned lawyer, read the letter without saying a word, but Jeff could see that he too was taken aback.

"I understand," the senior lawyer said when he had finished reading and had handed the letter back to Jeff. "It's a terrible burden for a son to bear."

"I wish that were the end of it."

Blackhorn looked at Jeff with arched eyebrows. "There's more?"

Jeff then told him about his fears, his suspicions, and the encounter with the white sedan.

Blackhorn knew Jeff Roberts to be serious-minded and highly intelligent. So he was not prepared to dismiss the young lawyer's concerns as mere imagination. But Blackhorn was not sure what he could or should do to help his young colleague—only that there did not seem to be any need for immediate action.

Blackhorn remained deep in thought for a few moments, then got up, walked around the desk, and settled into the chair across from Jeff. He leaned over and put his hand on Jeff's shoulder.

"The trauma of a father's death is always tough. Couple that with this letter and the kind of hours you work...." He shook his head again and looked at Jeff with compassion. "I think that you're stressed out. You need a vacation. A long vacation. Let's put the letter in the firm's safe, and you go somewhere for a few weeks. Somewhere far away where you can let your mind unwind and put things in perspective. When you return, we'll decide what to do."

It was then that Jeff thought of Africa.

"Want some company?"

Jeff's reverie was interrupted by Nicole as she strolled up the slight incline toward the tent they were sharing.

"I can't think of a better time or place for it," he said with a smile.

Jeff watched Nicole as she climbed the small hill, her petite but striking figure evident even in the loose-fitting safari shorts and shirt she wore. His mind raced back to the first time he had seen Nicole. The tight black pants, the beige wool crewneck sweater with the sleeves rolled up to the elbows. But the clothes were secondary. He loved looking at Nicole regardless of what she was wearing—or not wearing. She aroused emotions that surpassed anything he had previously known.

"This sure beats practicing law, doesn't it?" Nicole said with a grin as she settled into the wooden chair next to Jeff.

Jeff looked intently at her. She knew nothing about his father's letter, and Jeff wondered if he would tell her. He did not know the answer to that question, but there was no doubt about his feelings for her.

"From this perspective, anything beats practicing law. In fact, I can't believe I'm really here. And I still have to pinch myself that you agreed to come."

"You deserved an affirmative response," Nicole replied as she looked at Jeff with blue eyes.

He knew what she meant. He had pursued Nicole relentlessly almost from the moment he had met her two years earlier in the reception area of Senator Geoffrey Gimble's offices on Capitol Hill. He had gone there for a luncheon appointment with a law school friend who worked on Gimble's staff, and Nicole was leaving her job as a legislative correspondent to work in Gimble's re-election campaign. Until that moment, he had never believed in love at first sight. Nicole changed all that. There was something electric about her personality. He couldn't take his eyes off her, and even she began to sense his keen interest.

There were complications, however. To begin with, he was married. And so was she. But none of that could change how he felt.

At first he made seemingly innocent offers to help her with her schoolwork. She was attending law school at George Washington University, and what better tutor could she have than a Harvard Law School graduate who worked at Chase and Blackhorn, one of Washington, DC's most prestigious law firms? But she quickly saw through that ploy and tried to deflect his pursuit. The problem was that she felt the same about him.

They began to see each other periodically, and at first there was nothing sexual. There were meetings at the GW Law Library, lunches at Luigi's on 19th Street, and dinners at Union Station down the street from the Capitol. Soon enough it evolved into something more, until that one night almost a year later when they found themselves at the party to celebrate Senator Gimble's re-election. They decided to have their own celebration by getting a room at the J.W. Marriott Hotel around the corner from the White House. It was a wonderful night, now forever etched in Jeff's memory. After that, Jeff knew he could not maintain the pretense of his marriage. The separation from his wife was quick and clean.

Nicole was tempted to follow Jeff's lead, but she was more risk averse and could not make the same kind of quick decision. She feared that Jeff might go back to his wife and was not sure in any event that she could, or even should, leave her husband.

Jeff looked at Nicole now, sitting across from him under a tall acacia tree outside their tent on the African plains.

"I bet you never thought you'd be here either."

"No," she said quietly. "I never thought I would have the courage to end my marriage. And I never thought you'd still be there if I did."

"Hello there."

The loud cheerful voice with the British accent was the unmistakable sign that their safari guide, Mike Remington, was back from his early evening trip to the river. Jeff and Nicole watched as he maneuvered through the long yellow grass and the low-lying bushes that surrounded the campsite. Remington then flopped his lean six-foot frame into one of the other wooden chairs in front of the tent.

"How was the bath?" inquired Jeff.

"Well, it would have been a lot more relaxing if I didn't have to worry about all those crocs staring at me with hungry eyes. Thankfully, Happy was there with his rifle," Remington added with a reference to the well-muscled Masai gun bearer who was his steady companion on these safaris.

"Come on," said Nicole, "you're not going to tell me in this day and age that sophisticated hunters like you have to worry about being eaten by one of Africa's finest."

"To the contrary, my dear Ms. Landow," Remington said with feigned formality. "Man-eating is still an unfortunate habit of many African animals, and the last thing you want to do is take for granted that old habits *don't* die hard."

"Come on," Jeff said with obvious disbelief. "I know that cougars and bears sometimes attack people, but that's a rare event and, as far as I know, only occurs when the person is unsuspecting and alone. I can't imagine that an animal could sneak up on someone like you."

"You can never be too careful, Jeff. That goes for me and especially you. Americans come out on these photographic safaris and start to think that these animals are cuddly creatures that are, well, almost civilized. Siegfried and Roy certainly contributed to that mentality with their Las Vegas show and those home movies with all their tigers. The reality in the wild is far different. Cats like those are merciless predators, and they quickly recognize that people make a far easier catch than most other animals when they're looking for their next meal."

"You've got to be kidding me," said Jeff. "This man-eating stuff still occurs with regularity out here?"

"For sure. It's a danger well known to the locals. And, sad to say, there are still many visitors who learn the hard way and never make it home."

It was then that Jeff looked beyond the plateau where they were sitting and caught the form of a lioness in the distance slinking through the tall grass, obviously stalking a herd of zebras that were upwind and plainly unaware of her presence.

Remington's comment about man-eating lions made Jeff think about the people who had stalked him back home. Could they use a lion to plan some kind of "accident" that would turn him into prey like those zebras and bring an ugly end to his vacation? It seemed bizarre, but who could say for sure? Siegfried and Roy had demonstrated that these big cats were capable of being trained.

"This clearly calls for a drink," Jeff said, his hands trembling slightly as he reached into the nearby cooler to pull out a chilled bottle of white wine. He tried to convey a joking manner, but the fright he felt was hardly humorous. He uncorked the bottle and poured the white wine into nearby glasses for the three of them.

Remington took a long sip of wine and then picked up where he had left off.

"In fact, we're located near one of the greatest disasters in the recorded history of man-eaters. Have you ever heard of the Tsavo lions?"

When Nicole and Jeff shook their heads, Remington proceeded with the enthusiasm of a good storyteller.

"At the end of the nineteenth century, the Brits sent one of their finest engineers, a Colonel John Henry Patterson, to British East Africa to supervise the construction of a bridge over the River Tsavo. It was part of a railway that would extend from Mombasa on the east coast of what is now Kenya and wind its way through five hundred miles of wilderness to Lake Victoria in Central Africa. Many regarded it at the time as a preposterous proposal. And for good reason. You must remember," Remington said, leaning forward in his chair, "that the state of communications and technology at the time was rather primitive. And then of course there was the vast expanse of dense and uninhabited jungle that confronted the railway company. The British press aptly dubbed the new railway the 'Lunatic Line.'"

"God," said Nicole, "it's hard to imagine what that must have been like. Building a railroad in the middle of a jungle."

"If that wasn't enough," Remington continued, "two large lions were making a daily meal of at least one or two of the Indian coolies who constituted most of the workforce. Needless to say, the Indian coolies who had not been eaten did not feel very secure about their future, and Patterson quickly realized that the coolies couldn't keep their mind on work when they had to worry about some large cat turning them into lunch. So he had to utilize a lot of time, energy, and ingenuity to stop the rampage."

As he took a sip of wine, Jeff took another look at the lioness in the tall grass, a tawny silhouette in a crouched position, obviously waiting for the right moment to attack. Even from his distant vantage point, he could see that the lioness was larger than any dog or other animal he had encountered anywhere else. She had to be hundreds of pounds of muscle that probably stood up to his chest on all fours. Not something to be trifled with.

"I take it that they eventually killed these Tsavo lions," Jeff said, turning back to Remington.

"Oh, yes, but Patterson had a bloody hard time doing it, and not before dozens of other Indians landed in the lions' stomachs." Remington paused and took a long sip of wine. "If you want to see the Tsavo lions today, they're enshrined at the Chicago Museum of Natural History."

"And you're telling us," said Nicole incredulously, "that this kind of thing still goes on?"

"For sure. Lions haven't changed much in the last hundred years, and they still like a good meal."

By now, the last tentacles of the brilliant sunset were fading amidst the sweet swirling smells of animals and vegetation. As if on cue, porters in white coats seemingly emerged from nowhere to prepare dinner for Jeff, Nicole, and Remington as well as the other travelers and guides seated around the nine tents that were enclosed in a ring of large fires.

The three of them sat quietly while the porters set up tables with white tablecloths and then served a gourmet dinner of grilled impala with roasted vegetables. Remington was as hungry as Jeff and Nicole, and there was little conversation as they plunged into the meal.

After he had cleaned his plate, Jeff put down his fork, wiped his mouth with the cloth napkin, and took a quick glance in the distance, but he could no longer see the lioness or the herd of zebra. He looked at Remington across the table, the fear evident in his eyes.

"I'm still blown away by this man-eating stuff. You certainly never read about it in the brochures these safari companies give you."

Remington's countenance suddenly became somber, and there was an awkward pause in the conversation as he put down his utensils and stared at his dinner companions. Jeff had a sense that something was wrong. Had his comment about the safari company offended their guide in some way? Remington broke the silence after a few seconds, but his response left the question unanswered.

"That's hardly surprising." His words had a tense, almost angry, tone that Jeff found unsettling. "It wouldn't be good for business. But it's very real and well documented." Remington paused again to let his anger subside and then resumed with a tutorial air. "My favorite writer on the subject is Peter Capstick. He was an investment banker on Wall Street who became a professional hunter and one of the best outdoor writers of the African scene. He told of many incidents in more modern times where people like you and me had the rather frightening experience of seeing a lion's fangs at close range. And when I say close, I do mean close. A lion's mouth is incredibly large, and his jaws can easily wrap around a man's head."

"I think I'll pass," said Jeff with a nervous laugh and a look at Nicole.

Remington ignored Jeff's attempt at humor and plunged ahead. "The problem is, lions can be awfully smart about it. They can sneak up when you least suspect it and suddenly they're in your tent having dinner. Patterson himself told of how the Tsavo lions somehow knew where he was waiting with his rifle and found Indian workers located elsewhere who believed—wrongly—that they were adequately protected. The only possible saving grace is that most lions will growl before they make their charge. But that's small consolation if you're asleep at the time."

"I'm beginning to wonder," Nicole interjected with a glance at Jeff, "whether we made a mistake by booking this private tented tour. I think I would've felt a little more secure spending my nights in one of those lodges built on stilts."

Jeff was also beginning to wonder whether they had made a mistake.

"What do you think, Mike?" he asked, only half-jokingly. "Do we have to stay up all night with rifles in our laps?"

"Oh, no. The fires should keep out any lion or other predator that has malevolent intentions and, as you know, one of the guides is on watch all night. So I think you should regard this whole business as nothing more than the kind of stories you heard at summer camp when the counselors tried to scare the bejesus out of you. And with that," he said with a final flourish, "I will bid you good night. The wine was wonderful, the food was marvelous, and your attention very much appreciated. Tomorrow I promise a good shot of a pride of lions—but, I assure you, at a respectable distance."

Remington rose from his chair and turned toward his own tent on the other side of the grassy plateau.

Nicole turned to Jeff, eyes wide.

"Can you believe that?"

"Given where we are, and the fact that you're here, I'm ready to believe anything." He paused and looked at Nicole intently, his eyes reflecting the emotional energy she so easily triggered. "But let's not talk about lions anymore. Let's find a safer subject."

Jeff pulled out another bottle of white wine from the cooler and poured each of them some wine. He then moved his chair closer to Nicole's and leaned over to kiss her. Nicole returned the kiss without a word. Totally engrossed in each other, they did not see the eyes that peered at them from the long grass, eyes that had an eerie glow in the growing darkness.

They continued like that for what seemed hours, talking, kissing, and gently stroking each other from their chairs. The night, still suffused with the aromas of animals and vegetation, became black, punctuated only by the murmured conversations of other travelers and the nightly sounds of the jungle that remained a mystery to them.

"I think we should relocate to more comfortable quarters," Jeff suggested.

Nicole responded by rising from her chair and walking into the tent, where they had the luxury of a small double cot on a raised wooden floor. Jeff followed right behind, closing the tent flap as they moved inside. As they did so, the eyes in the long grass moved closer to the tent.

Jeff and Nicole stood facing each other in the darkness of the tent, peeling away each other's clothes. Jeff slowly moved down Nicole's body, kissing and gently stroking her and then easing her onto the cot. He felt the heat of his excitement and thought to himself that he wanted that rush to last for hours.

And then Jeff heard the crack of a twig. It caught his attention, but he did not want to be distracted. Not now. But the unexpected noise was followed by a low, deep-throated growl, and everything else suddenly became secondary.

CHAPTER 2

As Jim Roth walked back from the bathroom, the noise among the cluttered cubicles in Suite 223 of the Russell Senate Office Building somehow seemed louder than usual. But that couldn't be, he told himself. It's just that he was so used to blocking it out when he sat in his cubicle by the door, focused on whatever speech, testimony, or other legislative matter he happened to be working on. Maybe, he thought, I'm finally succumbing to the pressures of working in the United States Senate.

By the time he reached his desk, all the lights on his phone were blinking, and the intercom was ringing.

"Jim Roth," he answered.

"Jim," said the soft voice, "I have the senator on line one and Kelly Roberts on line three."

"Becky," he said, referring to the tall blonde who handled the reception area, "tell Kelly I'll call her back in a few minutes."

Becky's response caught Jim by surprise.

"I think you better take Kelly's call. She's hysterical, and it sounds like she needs you more than the senator."

Jim placed great faith in Becky's judgment on social matters, a trust that had evolved from the short time they had dated when Becky first joined the senator's staff. The romance fizzled quickly but then turned into a friendship that they both found more comfortable in an office with close quarters and irrepressible gossip.

"Okay. Tell the senator you can't get me. Tell him I'm in the bathroom."

"I already told him that, and he said he wanted to wait. So I'll just tell him to keep waiting, and you talk to Kelly. But keep it short."

Jim pushed the button on line three.

"Hi, Kelly."

He could hear the sobbing, and he knew immediately that something traumatic had happened. Kelly always seemed to be in control of her emotions. In fact, in that one instant, he could not recall if he had ever seen her cry.

"Oh, God, Jim," she moaned between sobs. "Jeff's dead. He's dead."

Although he heard the words, Jim could not accept the reality of the message about Kelly's brother—and his best friend. He could only remember the envy he had felt when Jeff had told him he was taking a four-week vacation in Africa.

"What're you talking about?" said Jim, his voice rising. "Isn't he still in Africa on the safari?"

"He's been killed," Kelly said, her voice cracking with emotion.

"Killed? Who killed him?"

"It's not a who. It was a lion. He was killed by a lion."

"Holy shit," Jim cried out, drawing stares from colleagues in the nearby cubicles. "How can that be? What happened?"

Jim then realized the senator was still holding and that this conversation was not going to end quickly.

"Hold on, Kelly."

Jim punched in the other line.

"I'm sorry, Senator. I had a little crisis coming back from the bathroom."

"I know what you mean," said Senator Geoffrey Gimble, not understanding Roth's reference. "It happens to all of us from time to time, even senators."

Jim did not want to take the time to correct the senator's misconception.

"In any case, Jim," Gimble said, "I hope you're well enough to walk over to the Senate floor. I need you here when I give this speech on the Middle East situation. Senator Stahl is bound to challenge me on some of these matters, and your research may come in handy. So hustle over here. And make sure you bring that notebook of materials we got from the State Department."

"I'll be there in a flash."

Jim punched back the line on which Kelly was holding.

"Listen, Kelly, I hate to get off, but I've got to go down to the Senate floor and I'll have to be there for a couple of hours or so. Where are you?"

"I'm at the house."

"I'll be there as soon as I can."

Chapter 3

The sun remained bright and the humidity dense as Jim maneuvered his red Mazda Miata convertible through the late-afternoon traffic toward Kelly's house in the Maryland suburb of Potomac twelve miles from downtown Washington. The traffic was predictably light for that hour, and Jim found himself on River Road, the main road into Potomac, within thirty minutes of leaving the Capitol.

Jim had been to Potomac many times. On some occasions he had gone to visit Jeff at the house that Kelly now occupied. On other times he had gone there to play tennis at the Potomac Tennis Club. And on each of those trips he had always marveled at the beauty of the ride along River Road into Potomac. The large, stately homes with long driveways, white split-rail fences, expansive lawns, and majestic trees. Some of the larger homes even hosted grazing horses. It was indeed impressive. Especially if you liked the country. But being a city person, Jim had often wondered what would bring a person to live in a suburb, no matter how attractive.

Jim could not indulge any of those customary thoughts now as he made his way up River Road. His mind was totally preoccupied with his earlier conversation with Kelly. It was difficult to accept the notion that Jeff was dead. And he could not even begin to imagine the horror Jeff must have experienced. It was, Jim said over and over to himself, beyond comprehension.

While his mind grappled with Jeff's death, Jim's car passed through Potomac Village, a small assortment of upscale shops and stores, and continued traveling along River Road, which took on a more pastoral character, with open fields, the fragrance of freshly-cut grass, and horses interspersed among developments of large homes. Totally distracted by thoughts of Jeff, Jim did not notice the large white sedan that had been tailing him for almost the entire trip.

Jim then saw the unmarked and almost hidden driveway on his left and turned into it. The white sedan continued past the driveway for a hundred yards and then pulled onto the shoulder and left the engine idling.

As he drove down the long driveway bordered by the large pin oaks, Jim tried to imagine what it must have been like for Jeff to grow up in the house that Kelly now occupied. She had moved back into the house several months ago, but their father had purchased it in the early 1960s when Potomac had been little more than a few country stores with a small-town atmosphere—hardly the image one would have associated with the high-powered government jobs that Kelly's father had held. Like many Washington, DC suburbs, the area soon experienced an explosion of growth and development, but Jim assumed it must have retained much of its rural character while Jeff was a young boy. And now, Jim said to himself, it's a sad reminder of a person no longer here.

Jim passed the white stables on the left and saw the horses slowly moving about in the pasture with the natural split-rail fence. The Potomac River, which separates Maryland from Virginia, lay just beyond the south end of the stables and down a steep ridge, but the river's rushing waters and gorges were well hidden by the foliage on the massive trees behind the stables.

Jim parked the car in front of the house and walked up the stairs to the porch and knocked gently on the front door. It was not the kind of house one saw in Potomac's new developments. It defied definition but seemed to be a Cape Cod style with dormers that projected both age and a certain intimacy. Kelly had maintained the house well since her father's death. The white paint looked fresh, the landscaping well manicured, and the large dogwood trees surrounding the house carefully pruned.

As he stood there waiting, Jim's thoughts were suddenly flooded with memories of Jeff. The first time they had met in front of Harvard Law School's Langdell Hall, one of the school's main buildings. A casual conversation. An instant rapport. Followed by lunches. Study groups. The house they later shared near the Radcliff campus. The parties and the girls. The laughs. The heartaches. And Kelly, who was attending school at nearby Wellesley College. How proud Jeff was when he introduced her to Jim. "This is my kid sister," he had said, his face beaming with warmth. Despite the age difference, Kelly soon became a frequent presence at their house.

He and Jeff had stayed in touch after law school even though they had followed very different paths, Jeff to a high-powered Washington law firm and Jim to the Navy to honor a three-year commitment he had made to the Judge Advocate General's Corps when he first entered law school. He was supposed to be a lawyer in the Navy JAG program but soon decided that he was too young and, as a dedicated athlete, too interested in physical activity to spend all his time chained to a desk. He laughed to himself as he recalled Jeff's constant ribbing whenever they later talked about his military career, Jeff saying that Jim was probably the first and only Jew to become a Navy SEAL.

Jim's recollections were interrupted by the sound of footsteps from inside the house. Within seconds, Kelly opened the door and, as always, Jim was caught by her good looks, with her shoulder-length brown hair and oval face. And then there was that body. It was something he had always taken note of in Cambridge and elsewhere, but nothing he would ever discuss with Jeff. In other circumstances, Jim would have jumped at the chance to date Kelly. But dating your best friend's sister seemed to be one of those taboos that Jim could never shake. Still, as he looked at her now, her eyes red from crying and her cheeks stained with tears, Kelly looked as attractive as ever, even though she was only wearing a large, navy blue T-shirt and the beige jodhpurs she wore for horseback riding. Jim said nothing. He just put his arms around her and held her close.

They maintained the embrace for several minutes without exchanging a word. At long last, Kelly pulled away and looked up at Jim with tears running down her cheeks.

"I can't believe he's not here anymore." She started to say something more, but the words got trapped in sobs.

Jim gave no immediate response. What could he say? He had never experienced a death in his immediate family, but he could easily imagine the pain Kelly felt. She had already lost her mother and her father. Losing the last member of her immediate family had to be overwhelming, especially since she and Jeff had been so close.

Kelly sat down on the front porch and locked her arms around her knees. Jim sat opposite her, leaning against the rail.

"What happened?" he finally asked.

Kelly took a deep breath and looked down at the stairs.

"I don't know all the details, but he was with Nicole when this huge lion ripped into their tent in the middle of the night. They were able to kill the lion pretty quickly, but it was too late for Jeff."

Jim shook his head in disbelief. He wanted to say something, but the words would not come.

"How's Nicole?" he asked after a few minutes.

"I don't know for sure, but I think she's okay. The guy from the safari company said that she had been scratched up pretty badly but that she was resting comfortably in a Nairobi hospital. At least that's what he said. Apparently the lion only went after Jeff. Anyway, she'll probably be in the hospital for at least a few more days."

Jim put a hand on Kelly's knee.

"Life sure is strange," he sighed, talking to himself as much as to Kelly. "Who would have believed that lion attacks happen in this day and age?"

Kelly was only half listening to Jim at this point. She was looking out over the pasture with the grazing horses, obviously adrift in another world. Jim moved over to her and put his arm around her shoulders. Kelly turned and looked at him with red-stained eyes.

"We'll get through it," he said. "We'll get through it."

Chapter 4

The morning sun shined brightly as the throng of people drifted slowly out of the small white church with the tall steeple set on top of the hill at the corner of Falls Road and South Glen Road in Potomac. The tall trees hovering over the church provided some needed shade in the searing summer heat and gave the church a pastoral appearance. But everyone's attention was focused on the closed casket that remained in front of the altar inside the church. The conversations were hushed as people stood in small groups, shaking their heads in obvious disbelief.

A tall, slender man with silver hair and a serious demeanor approached Kelly and Jim, who were shaking hands and talking with people as they departed.

"Kelly," he said with his hand extended, "I'm Bill Blackhorn. I'm one of the attorneys at Chase and Blackhorn. And I just want to tell you how sorry we all are. Jeff was not only one of our rising stars. He was also a great guy, and we're all going to miss him terribly. He had such a bright future, and it's horrible to think that it could have ended like this."

"Thank you so much, Mr. Blackhorn. Jeff never tired of telling me what a smart decision he had made in choosing your firm, and I really appreciate your coming out here today."

"Not at all. It was the least we could do."

Kelly turned to Jim.

"By the way," she said, "this is Jim Roth. He was Jeff's best friend at law school."

Jim then felt a hand on his shoulder. He instinctively turned and saw a tall gangly man of some twenty-some years with long curly black hair.

"Dave!" Jim exclaimed quietly. "I didn't know you'd be down here. Why didn't you tell me you were coming?"

"Well," the friend responded with a shrug, "I actually didn't think I was going to make it, but after all the time you, Jeff, and I spent in Cambridge, I decided I just had to work it out. Ironically, I had talked to Jeff right before he left on his safari to tell him that I was re-locating to my firm's Washington office."

Jim introduced his friend to Kelly and Blackhorn and then asked to be excused while the two of them caught up with each other.

"You go ahead," Kelly said, "I'm sure Mr. Blackhorn will take good care of me."

As Jim and his friend walked down the driveway toward the small cemetery next to the church, Kelly turned back to Blackhorn.

"I must confess," he said, pulling a sealed business envelope from the inside pocket of his gray pinstriped suit, "that I have another mission in coming here. Jeff had this envelope placed in our firm's safe, and he gave me instructions to give it to you if anything should happen to him."

"What is it?" Kelly asked, holding up the envelope.

"It's a letter from your father that Jeff thought was sufficiently important to keep in a safe. But," and now Blackhorn lowered his head ever so slightly to emphasize the point he was about to make, "he made it clear to me that you were to discuss its contents with no one."

Blackhorn then gently gripped Kelly's arm, his large fingers completely encircling her bicep. It was not painful, but the pressure made Kelly focus on Blackhorn's determined look.

"And I mean no one," he repeated slowly. "If you have any questions, you should call me. And me only."

As Blackhorn released his grip on her arm, Kelly caught a quick movement out of the corner of her eye. She glanced to the left to see a stocky man in a dark suit walking briskly down the driveway past Jim and Dave and the other mourners. She could only see the man's back and had no way of knowing who he was. She dismissed the matter from her mind and turned back to Blackhorn, who was still standing in front of her, stone-faced, with his hands clasped in front of him.

Kelly stared in silence at the envelope she now held. Blackhorn's words had stunned her and had raised a torrent of questions that cried out for answers. Talk to no one? Was there some dark secret in their father's past that Jeff never dared to reveal? What could it be? She wanted to pursue all of those matters, but Blackhorn's demeanor made it clear that no further discussion would be tolerated. At least not now.

"I understand," was all she could say.

Blackhorn shifted slightly.

"I would like to add something else," he continued. "This is not the time or place, but at some point you should consider taking action against the safari company. What happened to Jeff is unconscionable, and our firm would like to assist you in obtaining whatever justice may be left to the situation. It's not something we have to discuss now. But I would like to pursue that with you as soon as you're feeling up to it."

Kelly sighed as her mind drifted from the envelope in her hand to her brother's fate.

"That's so kind of you, and I may want to take you up on that. Every time I think about it, it makes me so angry. People should not have to put their lives on the line to go on a photographic safari. And if they are, then they should be told that up-front. Although I doubt that would be something a safari company would want to advertise."

Kelly paused, as though she needed to let the anger pass. After a few seconds, she looked up at Blackhorn.

"I'll let you know if I need any help with this," she said, holding up the envelope. The senior lawyer nodded slightly and gently shook Kelly's hand.

"Remember," he instructed with arched eyebrows as he turned to leave.

After Blackhorn left, Kelly placed the envelope in her purse. She was still standing there, mesmerized by Blackhorn's warning, when Jim returned by himself.

"How was your conversation with Blackhorn?"

Kelly said nothing. She took a deep breath and stared straight ahead. And then the tears started to stream down her cheeks.

"I still can't believe all this," she murmured.

"I understand," Jim said as he put his arm around her shoulders. Kelly looked up at him, her brown eyes filled with sadness, and they turned to go back inside the church.

Chapter 5

The phone was ringing as Jim stepped out of the shower. He wrapped a towel around his lean six-foot frame and moved quickly into the bedroom, which was bathed in the morning sunlight. He picked up the cordless phone on the nightstand by his bed.

"Hello," he said, but all he heard was the dial tone. Another missed call. Probably his father, Jim said to himself. He often called before Jim left for work. Or maybe it was Kelly.

The thought of Kelly reminded Jim that he hadn't talked with her in the two days since the funeral. Not that he didn't want to call her. In fact, he had been thinking of her constantly and had talked to himself repeatedly about calling her. But he was not sure what he should say or how he should handle the situation. So he had put off making the call.

He stood there motionless in the middle of his bedroom, wearing only the towel, pondering his dilemma. This hardly compares, he scolded himself, with the dangers he was trained to handle as a Navy SEAL. He could certainly deal with this. For better or worse, Jeff is gone, and life must go on. Although it was getting late, he decided to call Kelly right then and there. No more delays.

He punched in the number. After five or six rings, he heard her familiar voice at the other end of the line.

"Where are you?" he asked. "It sounds like you're in a rain barrel."

"Not really. I'm in the barn."

"You have a phone in the barn?"

"Sure. If I didn't, I'd probably never talk to anyone."

"So how're you doing?"

"I'm fine," said Kelly in a matter-of-fact tone. "I'm getting there. I decided the best medicine for all this was work. So I started giving riding lessons again, and it really has made me feel better. It really helps take my mind off things."

"That sounds right to me." There was a pause, and Jim decided to take the plunge. "Hey, listen, I'd love to get together. What about this weekend?"

"Sure. How about Saturday night? I know you're a man about town, but if you're free, that would be good."

"You're on. I'll be there around eight o'clock and we'll take it from there."

CHAPTER 6

By the weekend the weather had turned cloudy and humid, and there was a warm drizzle as Jim pulled his convertible up to Kelly's front porch. Absorbed with thoughts of Kelly, Jim had again remained oblivious to the white sedan that had followed him almost the entire trip from his condominium in Washington. As before, the sedan continued past Kelly's driveway after Jim made the turn, pulled onto the shoulder, and left the engine idling.

Jim walked up the steps with a bottle of red wine in one hand and used the other to knock on the front door. Kelly opened the door wearing loose-fitting khaki shorts and a light blue work shirt with the sleeves rolled up. Her informality only seemed to accentuate her good looks.

"Well," she said, with obvious reference to Jim's faded jeans and polo shirt, "I can see we're not going to any fancy restaurant tonight."

Jim smiled as he stepped inside.

"You know how it is. A jacket and tie gets old by the end of the week."

He then followed Kelly into the large country kitchen at the back of the house. The two of them settled onto the tall stools on one side of the butcher table in the middle of the room, and Jim pulled a corkscrew out of one of the drawers to open the wine he had brought. As he did so, he tried to think of some topic that would take them away from Jeff's death.

"So," he finally asked as he attended to the wine, "how are all your horses?"

Kelly's eyes seemed to light up. Good choice, Jim complimented himself.

"It's funny you ask. For a while this week I was really concerned about Grant," Kelly said, referring to her favorite horse, a chestnut thoroughbred that her father had bought for her shortly before he died. "He appeared lame again, and I was worried that he might have some form of navicular disease, but the vet discovered that it was only a nail that went into his hoof the wrong way."

"I don't know much about navicular disease," Jim replied as he poured wine into glasses for each of them, "but I presume that it's not good."

"Not at all. It's one of those mysterious conditions that produces constant and sometimes incurable lameness, which would probably mean the end of our riding relationship. And that would be bad for me, because I just love that horse. I can't imagine what it would be like not to be able to ride him."

As she finished speaking, Kelly walked into the pantry and pulled out a jar of salsa and a bag of tortilla chips.

"I thought we'd munch on some of this stuff before dinner."

Jim dove into the chips and salsa immediately. He was hungry. And eager to raise the question that had lingered in his mind for a long time.

"I want to ask you something that's always puzzled me. Why did you quit your job on the Hill and move back here? I know you like horseback riding, but it just doesn't make sense that you'd give up a job in Congress and trade a life in Washington for one out here. I had asked Jeff, but he never wanted to talk about it."

Jim saw immediately that he had touched a raw nerve. Kelly stared at Jim for a few moments, her eyes full of anger. Jim wished he could recall the question, but it was too late.

"I decided I had had enough of all the macho bullshit that politicians hand out. There may be more women in Congress than there used to be, but it's still a man's world. And I realized there's a high price to pay if a woman, especially a young legislative aide like I was, wants to succeed in that world. I just wasn't willing to pay that price. So I decided to come out here where people are a little nicer and less devious."

Jim could not resist asking the obvious question.

"What happened? Did somebody do something to you?"

The question hung in the air, and it was clear that Kelly was not eager to respond.

"Let's just say this is the right place for me right now. Maybe I'll change my mind down the road, but for the moment I'm comfortable with my decision. I grew up here. It's secure and full of good memories. And more than that, I do love horses and horseback riding. I love waking up in the morning, smelling the grass, hearing the rapids on the river, and knowing that I only have to get dressed and walk a short distance to get on a horse any time I want. And there's no prettier place to ride. All the trees. The views of the Potomac River. It's tough to beat."

"Okay, okay," Jim said, anxious to bring the conversation to a close. "You've convinced me." He poured each of them some more wine. "Well, here's to you," he said to Kelly as he held up his glass. "I hope this is a new beginning that will see things go a little better for you."

Kelly sat down on the stool next to Jim.

"What about you? Don't you find working on the Hill a lot different than being in the Navy?"

"For sure. The Navy can be exhilarating, but it's also a tight bureaucracy. The Hill's a lot more freewheeling. In fact, it gets kind of crazy sometimes. You put out one fire and another quickly erupts. On the one hand, it's exciting, almost addictive, and you can't imagine working anywhere else. On other days, and yesterday was one of them, you just look for some escape from the unrelenting pressure and start to count the days until Congress recesses or adjourns."

"I hear you. Jeff used to talk about those kinds of pressures at the firm."

Kelly paused to take a long sip of wine. Jim could see that she was gathering the strength to say something.

"Speaking of Jeff," she said hesitatingly, "would you do me a big favor?"

"Sure."

Kelly moved over to the desk on the other side of the kitchen and opened the top drawer, pulling out the envelope that Blackhorn had given her at Jeff's funeral. It was still sealed.

"I was wondering if you would keep me company while I opened this."

"What is it?"

"Blackhorn gave it to me at the funeral. He said Jeff had it locked away in the firm's safe."

"Why would it be locked away in the firm's safe?"

Kelly could not help but smile at Jim. He's such a fucking lawyer. Always asking questions. Then she remembered Blackhorn's warning and the smile disappeared.

"I don't know why it was locked in the firm's safe. All Blackhorn told me was that I should not discuss it with anyone. Except him."

"Okay," said Jim, putting his wineglass back on the table. "If that's the way you feel," he added with mock solemnity. "So what do we do now?"

"Blackhorn really scared me. And I just didn't have the guts to open it. Certainly not by myself. So I want you to sit here while I read it. Even if I can't show it to you, I think I'll feel a little more secure knowing you're here."

She then signaled him to take a seat at the oak kitchen table. Jim did as he was told, and Kelly took a seat across from him, holding the envelope in her left hand. She sat there for a few moments just looking at the gold seal on the envelope flap. She looked up at Jim.

"So? What do you think it is?"

Jim shrugged his shoulders.

Without adding another word, Kelly gently opened the seal and the flap to avoid ripping it. She then pulled out three pages. The top sheet was much whiter than the bottom two. She read the first page to herself and then looked at the other pages. As her eyes moved down the pages, Jim saw Kelly's mouth drop slightly. There was the look of surprise and perhaps disbelief. He leaned forward and rested his chin on his clasped hands as Kelly read the letter again.

Dear Kelly,

If you're reading this letter, it means something has happened to me and you're the last one left in our family. After Dad died, his lawyer gave this letter to me with the instructions that no one else, not even you, was supposed to see it while I was alive, and that Dad did not want it disclosed publicly while either of us was alive. But he did want it disclosed after that, as you can see, to make his contribution, sad as it is, to history.

Before I left for Africa, I gave the letter to Bill Blackhorn at my firm with the instruction that it should be given to you if anything happened to me. I had already made separate arrangements to have the letter given to the JFK Library in Boston if neither of us was here.

It's not something that will make you happy. But it doesn't take away anything Dad was to us or how much he loved us.

As you'll see, Dad warned us about disclosing the letter's contents to other people. I took Dad's warnings seriously, and so should you. I don't want to scare you, but I had my own suspicions that people were watching me and prepared to do me harm. You should place the letter in a safe or give it to a lawyer as I did and leave it to be disclosed at some distant time when its disclosure will not cause you any discomfort or danger.

Take care. And remember all the good times.

Love,

Jeff

Kelly then turned to the next two pages, which were showing the yellow tint of age.

April 10, 1998

My Dearest Jeff and Kelly,

This letter is one of the most difficult tasks I have ever undertaken. You can only imagine the love and joy the two of you have brought into my life, and I hope you will accept as true that I would never want to do anything that would cause you pain. However, I feel it is my obligation to you, and perhaps more importantly, to history, to disclose something that has weighed on my mind more and more as the years go on.

The sad truth is that I had a role in the assassination of President Kennedy. I do not know who killed the president, but I do know something about the sequence of events that led to it. I believe that future generations must ultimately know the truth and that I have a duty to do what I can to make sure that the truth does become known—although at a time when it cannot hurt you.

I know this will come as a terrible shock to you, and I hope you will not judge me too harshly. At the time I was a young government employee who had, in retrospect, risen too far too fast and had assumed responsibilities that were beyond my youthful capabilities. In any event, I was convinced that President Kennedy's continued occupation of the White House would place the survival of our country in jeopardy and that the democratic process could not be relied upon to protect us. With the hindsight of more experience and greater wisdom, I can now see that my views were the misguided and overzealous perspective of a young man who was too self-assured to accept the possibility of error. And so I assisted others with similar goals.

I want to try, in some way, to make amends for my horrific error by pointing historians in the right direction. But I only want to do that after what I hope will be many years, when neither of you will be around to suffer the embarrassment and ostracism that would surely follow. And beyond that, I cannot emphasize too strongly that there are people out there who will not be happy if the truth is disclosed and who will do anything, and I mean anything, to prevent that. In short, disclosure could pose a grave danger to your safety, and that is certainly not something I want to risk. God willing, each of you will lead long and fruitful lives, but history is entitled to know the truth after you're gone.

With that in mind, please prepare wills to require that the following information be given to the JFK Assassination Records Review Board, or whatever government agency may be the repository for records on Kennedy's assassination:

5412/de Mohrenschildt/P0ATPWJWTJ.

I don't mean to be coy about this, but I don't want you to know the full truth now. You might inadvertently say something to the wrong person and place yourself in danger. But a resourceful and knowledgeable investigator in the future will ultimately be able to use the information to find the answers to the most terrible and unnecessary tragedy of my generation.

May God be with you and bless you as you certainly deserve. And may you find it in your hearts to forgive me, as I have been unable to forgive myself.

With much love,

Dad

"Oh, my God," Kelly murmured.

She turned to Jim, who was staring at her intently.

"This is unbelievable. Just unbelievable."

"I'd like to say something helpful here. But I'm obviously in the dark as to what's going on."

"I know, I know," Kelly responded, reaching for Jim's hand. "You've been so good and patient, and I hate to shut you out like this. But I think I'm going to follow Mr. Blackhorn's suggestion for the time being and keep this to myself. I hope you understand."

Although he was gripped by curiosity, Jim knew there was no way for him to protest.

"Sure. I understand."

They sat there for several minutes, Kelly holding on to Jim's hand, and Jim watching her with a mixture of intensity and curiosity.

"Jim," Kelly finally said, "I think I need to be alone. I'm not in the mood for conversation. I'm sorry. Please forgive me."

"Are you sure? I'd be happy just to sit and keep you company."

Kelly just shook her head slowly.

"No. No thanks. I'll be fine. I just need some time to let this settle in."

They got up from the kitchen table and walked to the front door. The thick humidity and the sound of crickets surrounded them as Kelly opened the door. Jim pulled Kelly toward him.

"I'll talk to you tomorrow."

He kissed Kelly softly on the forehead and walked down the steps of the porch to his car. As his car moved slowly down the driveway, he looked up in the rear-view mirror and saw Kelly standing on the porch, her figure silhouetted by the light emanating from the house. He had a sudden urge to turn around and rush up to her and embrace her and hold her tight. But something told him to keep driving, and he let the car continue down the driveway. As he made the turn onto River Road and the drive back to Washington, the white sedan's lights came on and it slowly pulled out from the shoulder and onto River Road, staying a short distance behind Jim's car.

Chapter 7

Kelly placed the half-empty glass of red wine on the butcher-block table in her kitchen and looked up at the clock. Eleven-thirty. She picked up her brother's note and her father's letter and read them again for what must have been the tenth time. The constant re-reading had not helped. She had not yet adjusted to the reality that lay behind the written words.

A skeleton in her family's closet. That's what it was. But one of historic dimensions. Could she simply put her father's letter in a safe somewhere and forget about it? She was not sure. Jeff did, and God knows, he had more courage and insight into human affairs than she did. He had taken their father's warning to heart, and Kelly was in no position to challenge the wisdom of that decision. Her father surely knew what he was talking about and would not have instilled fear in his children without good cause.

Still, Kelly did not think that she could simply tuck her father's letter away and move on with her life. She could hide it from the eyes of others, but she could never hide it from herself. It would always be there. A cloud that tarnished her father's memory. And it would not go away unless she knew exactly what her father had done and why he had done it.

Kelly settled onto one of the stools and took another sip of wine.

That's where she differed from her brother. Jeff, she reminded herself, had had a greater capacity for detachment. Maybe it was part of his legal training. Whatever. He had that ability to insulate himself from troubling events and thoughts. She had seen it when their father died. It had come so soon after their mother's horrible death from cancer. Kelly had been immobilized by the loss, but Jeff got lost in the new responsibilities as the head of their shrinking family. He had comforted his sister, taken charge of the funeral arrangements, and supervised the thousand and one tasks that seemed to arise in handling her father's financial affairs. It had seemed to energize him and certainly had allowed him to focus on the future instead of on the past.

Kelly knew she was not cut from the same cloth. She was more passionate and far more prone to follow her instincts. So where does that get me? she asked herself.

She understood her father's concern about inadvertent comments that might reach the wrong people. But that danger would have to pass at some point. In fact, maybe it had already passed. After all, her father was now gone, and maybe some of those he had feared had also passed on. Jeff suspected that he was being watched, but she wondered whether that was just the guilt he felt in knowing their father's secret. Anyway, she could be circumspect in choosing the people she talked to and in deciding what to tell them. And if there was some danger, it might be something that she would have to accept. As her father used to say, no guts, no glory.

She began to wonder whether she should show her father's letter to Jim. He was her brother's best friend, and no one had been more helpful since Jeff's death. She knew she would draw great comfort from his involvement. He would keep her confidence and provide the sounding board she desperately needed. Sure, she said to herself, but there was always the possibility that Jim might inadvertently say something to the wrong person.

God, what a dilemma. Maybe the best course of action would be to take Bill Blackhorn's advice and call him. As she thought back to their conversation at Jeff's funeral, Kelly now knew that Bill Blackhorn knew something. Why else would he tell her to talk to only him? She would try to find his home telephone number and call him tomorrow. She was sure he would understand why she wouldn't want to wait until Monday.

Kelly's eyes were getting heavy from the wine and the drain on her emotions. She suddenly felt very fatigued. She put the wineglass in the sink and picked up Jeff's note and her father's letter and placed them back in the envelope. Where should I put them? she asked herself. Someplace where they could never be found by accident or, perish the thought, intruders.

Her eyes scanned the kitchen where she now stood until she mentally selected the hiding place. Of course, she said to herself. No one would look there for a letter. She walked over to the spot and carefully placed the envelope in her chosen location. Satisfied with her ingenuity, Kelly walked out of the kitchen and up the stairs to her bedroom on the second floor. Finding a place to hide her father's letter was easy. Deciding what to do about it was a whole other story.

CHAPTER 8

April 1998

Ted Roberts sat behind the large walnut desk in the library of his Potomac home, his hand running nervously through his salt-and-pepper hair, and stared out the large cathedral window. The trees had just begun to bud in the early April warmth, but he could still see the outlines of the Potomac River below the sloping property. A light but steady rain continued to fall and seemed to reflect his somber mood.

He remembered when he treasured these mornings in the house. Those were days when he knew who he was and what he was about. No longer. He could not shake the sense of dread and guilt that had slowly engulfed him and had now made him a prisoner of his own mind.

He had hoped that his retirement from government would have freed him from those troubling thoughts. But that had proved to be a false hope. Things had gotten worse instead of better. Distant memories now emerged with greater frequency and growing strength. It seemed that he could do nothing to prevent or control them, and even now, as he sat in his leather chair and looked at the treasured photographs and books that surrounded him, he could not help but think back to that time when everything seemed so clear.

Even though it was now more than thirty-five years ago, he could recall vividly the first time the suggestion was made. It came obliquely in a luncheon conversation with Dale in the White House mess. It was well past two o'clock and, because of the lateness of the hour, there were few other people in the room. It was December 1962 and President Kennedy was still basking in the warm glow of the accolades he had received in his handling of the Cuban missile crisis. Like Roberts, Dale was a CIA case officer who worked in the White House. From a physical perspective, he and Roberts were a study in contrasts—Roberts being tall and thin. Dale was much shorter, on the heavy side, and, although still young, starting to show signs of baldness. The physical differ-

ences had no effect on their relationship. The two worked closely together and, like Roberts, Dale had seen close-up the dangers that had escaped the attention of the general public.

"What would you think," Dale inquired over his Navy bean soup, "if someone assassinated the president?"

"What?" Roberts gasped in astonishment.

"Oh, I'm not saying we should do it. But, I mean, do you think it would be good or bad for the country?"

Roberts did not reply right away. On the one hand, he had great admiration for the president. He was a highly intelligent man of many talents and great wit. But he had his failings, and, in Roberts's mind at least, some of those shortcomings had become of considerable concern.

"It's funny you mention that," Roberts finally responded. "I've actually given some thought to whether the president's actions are making us less secure and not, as much of the press seems to think, more secure from the communists. You know what I've seen here. You can't help but think about it."

"Tell me about it."

"Here's something else to think about," Roberts added, as he took a bite of his turkey sandwich. "I was reading something the other day which pointed out that every president elected every twenty years since 1840 has died in office through assassination or natural causes. If that historical pattern continues, your question may not be as academic as it sounds."

"Well," said Dale, breaking off a piece of his French roll to dip into his soup, "in each of those cases the country survived. Even prospered."

"Maybe so, Dale. But I don't know if that answers your question. Sometimes I think the president has really elevated the presidency in the public mind and made government the exciting adventure we want it to be. At other times," Roberts added with a shake of his head, "I really do wonder if that sense of excitement masks a real and mortal danger to our country."

As Roberts took another bite of his sandwich, Dale put down his spoon, took a napkin to wipe his mouth, and picked up the lead.

"I, for one, am becoming concerned. I can't help but believe that the Russian setback in Cuba was only temporary and that they know our weakness. And I'm not just talking about missiles."

"I know. But there's nothing for us to do about it."

Dale looked coldly into Roberts's eyes. It was a look Ted had never seen before. And one he would never forget.

"I don't know about that," Dale said with great deliberation. "Bruce raised the matter with me the other day, and I couldn't tell whether he was just raising an idle thought or making a suggestion."

Dale's comment caught Roberts by surprise and gave credence to his concern about the president. Bruce Lord was their mentor at the Company, as the CIA was then known to its employees. A Yale graduate, Lord's contacts and achievements had enabled him to scale the bureaucratic ladder quickly. He was also the one who had recruited them to the agency, and he continued to guide them through the maze of government procedures and protocol. His word commanded great respect.

"You're kidding," was all Roberts could muster.

"No, I'm not kidding. In fact, a bunch of us are going to meet at Bruce's house tomorrow night to discuss the current state of the presidency and what, if anything, can or should be done about it."

"What time?"

"Nine o'clock."

"Count me in. I'll be there."

"Let me discuss it with Bruce," Dale said. "As you can imagine, he is pretty particular about who should be included. But I'm sure he would want you there. In fact, I wouldn't have raised the matter with you if I hadn't been sure of that."

And so, as Ted Roberts now remembered in the library of his Potomac home, it had begun. An innocent but telling conversation. A noble purpose. Where had they gone wrong?

CHAPTER 9

Bill Blackhorn pulled the silver Mercedes sedan into the driveway of his Chevy Chase home, picked up his dinner jacket from the empty passenger seat, and exited the car. His mind skipped past the Sunday evening's events, another boring dinner, this one sponsored by the District of Columbia Bar Association, and focused on the pleasant weather. He decided to forgo putting the car in the garage at the back of the house. He wanted to smell the grass, gaze up through the large oak and poplar trees, and enjoy the warmth of the summer air before going to bed.

As he trudged up the brick walkway to the front door, he looked up at the white facade of the house. The construction was common to this Washington neighborhood. Although the house was larger than some, it had the same colonial structure that was popular when the house was built in the 1920s. How much this house has seen, he mused. It was home to other families before he and his wife purchased it in the late 1960s. They then raised their three children, all now grown to adulthood, and soon it would be home to another family. Because Bill Blackhorn had decided that the house should be sold. When his beloved wife Nancy died nine months earlier, he had thought about selling the house immediately. But his children pleaded with him to keep it, saying that it would be comfortable for him and make it easy for them to visit with their children, his grandchildren.

For a time he had believed his children were right. Like them, he had loved the house, and who could resist the notion of frequent visits from cherished grandchildren? But he could no longer ignore the reality of his life. He was, he confessed to himself, lonely. His neighbors were mostly married couples, and his social interaction with them was generally confined to a waved hello from a car or a casual conversation on a Saturday afternoon of raking leaves. And while he had always treasured his time in the house, the memories were now a mournful prison. He saw his wife in every room.

After looking at condominiums off New Mexico Avenue in the District, he had decided that apartment life would be better suited to his new lifestyle. He could meet other single people his age. Perhaps another woman who could give him a new lease on life.

Blackhorn walked through the front door and placed his dinner jacket gently on the rosewood table just inside the foyer. As he closed the front door, he thought he heard the echo of another door closing at the back of the house. He stood still and listened carefully. Nothing. Maybe he should have put the alarm on before he left for the evening. He remembered that his wife had always chided him about being forgetful and assuming that the neighborhood was always safe. Another memory of Nancy that brought vivid and sad images to the fore. He pushed it out of his mind and tried to think about something else.

What to do now? He slowly looked around. The only light emanated from a small lamp on a glass table in the living room to the left and cast shadows over the foyer and the large dining room on the right side of the house. Blackhorn loosened his black bowtie and stood there for a moment, lost in thoughts of the new life he would soon begin. It was then that he decided to have something to eat before going to bed. After all, it was the end of the weekend, and he deserved a treat. He then remembered the freshly baked chocolate-chip cookies that he had bought that afternoon. When he had seen them, the cookies had reminded him of his boyhood, when having milk and cookies was a nightly ritual.

Blackhorn ambled down the hardwood floor of the center hallway to the darkened kitchen in the back of the house. His thoughts turned, as they often did these past few days, to Jeff Roberts and the horror of his death. Such a sad and bizarre tragedy. Blackhorn could not help but wonder whether there was something more to it than just a random lion attack. Could someone have orchestrated the whole event to make it look like an accident? Unlikely perhaps, but Blackhorn was not prepared to dismiss the possibility. Which was why he was anxious to pursue a lawsuit against the safari company. The litigation could turn up information that might resolve the issue. In the meantime, he had to decide what he should tell Jeff's sister. She had called that afternoon, understandably disturbed by the father's letter.

"Mr. Blackhorn?"

"Yes."

"This is Kelly. Kelly Roberts. Jeff's sister."

"Yes, Kelly. How are you doing?"

"As well as can be expected, I guess. But..."

He could sense the trepidation in her voice. Not that he was surprised. Nor was he surprised that she had called him. He would've been surprised if she hadn't.

"Yes, Kelly. Tell me. What can I do for you?"

"I'm sorry to trouble you on a Sunday afternoon, Mr. Blackhorn, but I would like to talk to you about my father's letter. I don't know if you've read it, but, even if you haven't, I think it might be good for me to discuss it with you."

Blackhorn did not respond immediately. Although he had anticipated her call, Blackhorn was not sure how he would answer Kelly's inevitable questions. He had not yet decided whether he should tell Kelly about her brother's fears and the incident with the white sedan. He did not want to scare her needlessly and add more trauma to a situation that was already unsettling. But he had his own concerns that Jeff may have been right, and he certainly did not want Kelly unwittingly to endanger her life. And beyond that, there might be something more that should be done to bring the letter to the attention of proper authorities. All of which he had hoped to discuss with Jeff. And all of which he would discuss with Kelly. But not now. Not on the telephone. It was a conversation, he decided, that had to take place in person. Especially if Jeff was right about his telephone being tapped. Who knew if his phone was tapped? All of that shaped his response to Kelly.

"Kelly, I do know something about the letter. But nothing needs to be done today, and I think it would be best if you give me a call at the office tomorrow morning, and we'll set up a time for you to come in."

Blackhorn flipped on the kitchen light as he entered from the hallway, his mind still engrossed on what advice he should give Kelly. In his state of concentration, he did not see the silhouette of a man standing in the dark sunroom off the kitchen. Blackhorn opened the refrigerator, his back to the silent figure, and pulled out the plastic container of milk. He then walked into the pantry to get the bag of cookies, and, as he did so, the figure moved quickly and quietly near the doorway to the kitchen.

Blackhorn emerged from the pantry and placed the bag on the kitchen counter. He pulled a tall glass from the overhead cabinet, took out a plate, and placed one of the large chocolate-chip cookies on it. He stood there savoring the moment.

It was then that he sensed something strange. He picked his head up and tried to listen for unusual sounds. He turned around and tried to see if his anxiety was based on anything real or just a figment of his imagination. This is ridiculous, he scolded himself. I'm too old to be afraid of the dark.

Still, he could not resist the impulse to walk back to the front of the house, leaving the milk and cookies in place, a waiting reward for his return to the kitchen. He walked through the hallway, looking from side to side, and then checked the bolt lock on the front door.

Satisfied that nothing was amiss, Blackhorn returned to the kitchen and his nighttime snack. He stood at the counter and started to pick up the glass of milk, but he could not shake the feeling that something was wrong. He felt the presence of another person. Someone staring at him. He put down the glass of milk and looked down at the counter, trying to concentrate, hoping to hear something. He picked up his head to turn around, but he never completed the motion. There was only the sense of a whirling dark figure and then the feeling of helplessness as the light quickly turned to darkness. It was over before he knew what happened.

Within minutes, a man draped in shadows silently opened the kitchen door and walked unseen through the backyard to his car.

Chapter 10

"What's happening here?" Jim asked Becky as he rushed into Geoffrey Gimble's Senate suite, weighted down by a large black three-ring briefing notebook and an assortment of loose papers.

"Where have you been all day?" Becky demanded. "People have been calling left and right. I didn't know what to tell them, and I couldn't reach you on your pager."

"The senator came under attack from Senator Stahl on the Middle East again. Some very tense moments, especially for a Monday when the Senate wasn't supposed to be in session. I just didn't have time to respond to the page," Jim explained as he stood in front of Becky's desk, waiting for his telephone messages. "But thanks for your concern," he added with a small smile.

"Well," said Becky, handing the messages to Jim, "here they are. And make sure you call Kelly Roberts. She's called at least three times."

Jim went to his cubicle in the inner offices. He quickly flipped through the messages and then turned to the e-mail on his computer. There was a message from Kelly.

> Jim—please call ASAP. I need to talk with you. Kelly

Jim looked at his watch. It was after five o'clock. He picked up the phone and punched in Kelly's number. It rang for a long time before she picked up.

"Hey, Kelly, it's Jim."

"Thank God. I need to talk with you."

"I gathered. I got your e-mail message. And your telephone messages."

"Oh, Jim," Kelly exclaimed. "Blackhorn's dead."

"How can that be? We just saw him at the funeral and he looked fine. What happened?"

"Heart attack. At least that's what his office said when I called this morning. But I don't know. Anyway, I don't want to talk about this over the phone. I'm meeting a friend for dinner at Galileo's," she said, referring to the pricey Italian restaurant downtown, "and I was wondering if I could stop by your office first."

"Absolutely. When?"

"I'll be there in an hour."

As he put the phone down, Jim had a sense of dread. He didn't know what was in the letter that Blackhorn had given to Kelly, but it was obviously something troubling. Blackhorn's death added to the mystery. Maybe it was nothing out of the ordinary. Still, Jim began to sense some kind of lurking danger.

Jim threw on his jacket and met Kelly in the reception area in the senator's suite and immediately felt a rush of excitement. But he knew that his growing feelings for her would have to wait for another time on another day. More immediate business waited. He gave her a quick hello and ushered her out of the suite and over to the elevators near the marble rotunda with its high ceilings, telling her that they needed to go someplace where they could avoid interruptions from the telephone and his colleagues.

"Someplace very private," Kelly added.

Although nothing was said on the short elevator ride to the basement, Jim could sense the tension. Kelly had a tight grip on her purse and a determined look in her eyes.

Jim led the way after they disembarked from the elevator into an underground passageway of cinderblock walls and exposed pipes. They went into a small cafeteria where Jim bought a black coffee for himself and a bottle of water for Kelly. He then took her to a small windowless room with a wooden desk and some metal chairs. Kelly sat in one the chairs while Jim closed the door and took a seat on the other side of the table. They sipped their drinks in silence for a few seconds, Jim keeping his eyes locked on Kelly, hoping that she would soon reveal the purpose of the visit. He did not have to wait long.

Kelly took a long swallow of water and a deep breath and told him everything. The note from her brother. The letter from her father. The probable reasons why Blackhorn warned her to talk with no one except him. Her conversation with

Blackhorn on Sunday afternoon and her call to his office that morning, only to find out that he had died unexpectedly on Sunday night, the victim of an apparent heart attack. And her recollection of the mysterious man who had caught her eye when Blackhorn had given her the envelope at Jeff's funeral. Was there some connection between that man and Blackhorn's death? she wondered. As she retraced the events and possibilities, Kelly said she had come to two basic conclusions: she needed to talk to someone, and Jim was that someone.

"I'm flattered."

"I'm not sure if you should be flattered or scared. Because I'm scared. Very scared. At the same time, I don't know that I can just walk away from my father's letter and leave it to posterity to know what happened. And besides, although Blackhorn's death does seem coincidental, it may be just that: a coincidence. He was in his sixties, after all, and people in that age bracket sometimes do die unexpectedly."

"So now what?"

"Here's Jeff's letter and my father's letter. Read them and see what you think."

Kelly watched as Jim read the letters, his eyes widening as he read.

"Holy shit," was all he said.

He looked up at Kelly and handed her the letters. She placed them back in the envelope and then returned the envelope to her purse.

"What can we do now?" Jim finally asked. "I'm not sure it's wise to run around blindly asking questions about your father's past. That could place you in the very danger he wanted to avoid."

"I know, I know. But there is one thing we could do that would be safe."

"And that is...?"

"Talk to Bud Stamford. He was close to my father and my family. He was like an uncle. And he worked with my father in the government."

Jim picked up his coffee cup and took a long sip.

"What do you make of the cryptic information you're supposed to turn over to the JFK Records Board?" he asked, trying to sidestep Kelly's suggestion. "By the way," he added before Kelly could answer, "that board was abolished. Congress only gave it a limited life. Which is why, I guess, Jeff was going to give the letter to the JFK Library. Seems like the logical alternative."

"Hey, Jim," Kelly responded with annoyance, "I don't know what to make of the clues my father left. That's why I think we should talk to Bud. And then we can decide whether we should do anything further or just put this thing back to bed for a hundred years. But if you don't want to get involved, I'll certainly understand. It could put your life at risk."

Jim shook his head. "That's not it. Count me in to do whatever I can to help you. I just don't know whether we should be rushing off to talk to someone about this. No matter how well you know him."

They went back and forth like that for an hour, exploring the alternatives and trying to assess the risks. Before long, Kelly looked at her watch.

"Oh, my God," she blurted out. "It's seven-thirty. I'm going to be late. I've got to go. I'll call Bud and you'll come with me. And then we'll see."

Before Jim could argue, Kelly was pulling him out the door.

CHAPTER 11

It was dark by the time Jim pulled the car into the garage of his condominium on L Street near Washington Circle in the Northwest section of Washington. He had returned to his office after Kelly left to make a few telephone calls and read correspondence that had been put off by the day's unexpected events on the Senate floor. By the time he left, it was after nine, and he guessed that Kelly was probably ordering dessert at Galileo's.

As he walked through the door of his top-floor apartment, Jim threw his jacket on the couch and thought again about Kelly's father's letter. It was certainly frightening. Assassinations of political figures were common to the Middle East and other faraway places. Not the United States. And here he was, reading about conspirators who had killed John Kennedy and who might be prepared to kill again to protect their secret. And although their identity was not disclosed in Ted Roberts's letter, the clear implication was that the killers could still be in circulation.

He moved through the apartment, turning on the kitchen light and traipsing into the bedroom, where he changed into jeans and a T-shirt. It was easy to understand Kelly's desire for some answers. Frightening as it was, the importance of her father's letter could not be ignored. The Kennedy assassination was the greatest mystery of the twentieth century, perhaps in American history. No one—least of all a participant's daughter—could easily disregard clues that might unravel the mystery.

But what did all those clues mean? Jim went to his briefcase and pulled out his notes of the clues in the letter. He had written them down as soon as he had left Kelly and returned to the office. The number 5412 held no meaning for him.

And he certainly had no idea what the ten letters signified. He studied the third clue. De Mohrenschildt. A name no doubt. A co-conspirator perhaps? He walked over to the computer in his small den. Someone on the Internet had to know something about de Mohrenschildt.

While the computer booted up, Jim went back to the kitchen and retrieved the meatball sub he had bought at a pizza take-out place on the way home. He placed the sub on the table next to the computer desk, opened a Lowenbrau, and looked out the window. The top of the Washington Monument was visible from his chair.

As he stared at the tall spindle of gleaming white stone with blinking red lights at the pinnacle, Jim began to ask himself why he had so readily agreed to help Kelly in her search. Sure, he was attracted to her, and his growing desire to build a relationship no doubt played a role. But was that enough to justify a risk that could prove deadly? No, Jim said to himself, the reasons lay deeper. In a way, it was not much different than the decision he had made to leave a desk job and become a Navy SEAL. Colleagues in the JAG corps told him he was crazy to leave the security of a legal job for the rigors of a soldier trained to work undercover in inherently dangerous situations. But he knew that being a Navy SEAL would give him a sense of pride and an indefinable feeling of accomplishment. Few people could pass the rigorous physical tests that were required. And once there, he would be part of an elite group that could make a real contribution to his country. Corny as it sounded, maybe there was some of that here. Maybe he could make a contribution of a different kind by helping to solve a mystery of historic significance.

Enough day-dreaming, he finally said to himself. He took a swallow of beer, pushed back his long dark brown hair, signed on to his Internet service, and wrote in "de Mohrenschildt" on Google's search engine. Within seconds Jim was looking at a 1979 staff report by a special committee of the House of Representatives that had investigated JFK's assassination. De Mohrenschildt, it turned out, was indeed a person—and a very strange one at that. Jim read the report's references to de Mohrenschildt carefully, totally captivated by the story that unfolded.

After he finished reading, Jim took a bite of the sub and another swig of beer. He leaned back in his chair, bottle of beer in hand, and thought about what he had just read. He had solved one of the clues in the letter from Kelly's father. Or had he? There was something troubling about how easy it had been. Google was not available when Kelly's father had written his letter, and maybe he did not appreciate how easy it would become to use the Internet for research. Still, Jim could not help but wonder whether there was something more to it than just learning de Mohrenschildt's identity. Even without the Internet, there had to be dozens of books about the Kennedy assassination that would have had some reference to the man. If Kelly's father was trying to create some challenge to finding the information he possessed, the de Mohrenschildt reference had to require something more than what anyone could find in a history book.

By now the sub was half gone and the beer was almost finished. Jim stared out the window and again focused on the Washington Monument in the distance. He now knew something about de Mohrenschildt, but he knew that he did not know enough. He needed to know the connection to the other two clues. There was no way to figure that out tonight, but a starting point was to make sure they knew everything there was to know about de Mohrenschildt. That would not be a problem. He would give the assignment the next morning to the Congressional Research Service, one of the country's premier research facilities. They could provide the kind of detail that was needed.

As his mind swirled with possibilities and challenges, the phone rang, and it startled him. Jim looked at his watch. It was almost ten-thirty. He instinctively thought of his father, caught in the throes of a serious heart condition. It could be his mother calling to give bad news. So he was relieved to hear Kelly's voice.

"Jim," she said excitedly, "it's all set up. We're meeting with Bud tomorrow at eight. I'll pick you up at your apartment."

Jim realized that Kelly was now a woman obsessed with uncovering the truth behind her father's letter and that further argument would be pointless. He agreed to be ready and, after a short conversation, hung up. For better or worse, they were about to embark on a journey that could, he knew, be fraught with danger.

CHAPTER 12

Jim was standing outside his condominium building on L Street at eight o'clock the following evening when he saw Kelly's black Cherokee Jeep turn down the one-way street.

Jim always liked to dress in jeans and a T-shirt after work, but Kelly had explained that Bud Stamford's first name was really Winthrop and that he was the scion of a wealthy Manhattan family that traced its roots back to colonial America. Jim decided that jeans and a T-shirt might be a little too casual for a man with that kind of lineage. So he changed into beige khakis and a navy blue polo shirt when he got home from work.

When he got into Kelly's Jeep, he knew he had made the right decision. Kelly was dressed in a skirt and blouse—a far cry from the jodhpurs and T-shirts she always seemed to wear at the house.

"So, how are you?" Jim asked as he closed the passenger door.

"To tell the truth, I'm nervous. I have no idea what to expect. And I'm not sure where we're going with this or what impact it will have. I'm just hopeful that Bud can tell us something that will be useful. But who knows? Maybe he'll know nothing."

As much as he wanted to help Kelly, Jim could not resist reminding her of the possible dangers.

"Those are all the reasons why this is probably the wrong thing to do. We have no reason to believe that Bud knows anything. And if he does, how do we know it's not because he's one of the conspirators your father warned you about?"

"I know that you feel that way. But I can't just do nothing. I'm not that kind of person. And it's inconceivable that Bud was one of the conspirators or that he would do me any harm. He was too close to my father and the rest of us. He used to come over to the house for dinner all the time, and we often spent spring vacations at his home in Palm Beach. So I can't imagine," she added with obvious sarcasm, "that he's going to greet us at the door with a knife in his hand."

Jim switched subjects and started to tell Kelly about de Mohrenschildt just as the Jeep pulled in front of the Watergate condominiums on Virginia Avenue. Jim kept talking as they stepped out into the warm, sticky air. Kelly was intrigued by Jim's story and glad to hear that he had given the research project to the Congressional Research Service. But her mind was plainly focused on the meeting they were about to have.

Within minutes they were standing in front of a door on the eighth floor of the luxury condominium complex. Kelly knocked on the door, and it was soon opened by a large man with short-cropped white hair, dressed impeccably in a short-sleeved black Tattersall shirt with black slacks and well-polished Bally loafers.

"Hello, Kelly," the man said as he embraced Kelly. "It's so good to see you."

"Oh, Bud," said Kelly as she reached up to plant a kiss on his cheek. "I couldn't agree more. It has been too long."

Stamford then took Kelly's hands in his and gave her a long look.

"I was devastated to hear about Jeff. He was a remarkable young man. And I'm so sorry I couldn't be with you at the funeral."

Kelly sighed.

"I'm sorry you weren't there too. It really has been tough. I can't get over it either. It's so overwhelming."

Kelly then introduced Jim, and the three of them walked into a spacious living room with plush white carpeting and a clear view of the Kennedy Center for the Performing Arts, a mammoth white structure situated on the banks of the Potomac River. The walls held large oil paintings and prints of various kinds. One painting Jim knew to be by Claude Monet, whose distinctive impressionist style appealed to him. The other art was unfamiliar to Jim's untrained eye but, like the Monet, it all appeared to be expensive. Bud's obviously a man with class and money, Jim said to himself.

Before long they were sitting in comfortable leather chairs, sipping Bloody Marys, and talking aimlessly of many things, from horses to family vacations in Florida to restaurants. Stamford's diction was slow and precise, and his remarks reflected the careful thought of a seasoned professional. In fact, as Jim thought about it, Stamford appeared to be the only person he knew who spoke in complete sentences.

Stamford's warm feelings for Kelly were also evident. He was plainly enjoying her presence as well as the conversation—although it was clear to Jim that Stamford had no notion of the purpose of the visit.

After about half an hour, Kelly placed her drink on the black marble coffee table and looked directly at Bud. Here it comes, Jim said to himself.

"I have to confess, Bud, that I had an ulterior motive in coming here tonight."

Kelly lifted her father's letter out of her purse and handed it to Stamford.

"You'll see that I'm not supposed to show this to anyone. But I can't just put it away and forget about it. It would haunt me forever. So I need your help in understanding it and trying to figure out what to do."

Stamford took the letter and read it. The impact was immediate. His eyes widened and his facial expression became tense. When he had finished reading, he got up from his chair, the letter clutched in his left hand, and walked to the large window that overlooked the Kennedy Center in the fading sunset of purple and pink hues.

Jim was not sure how to read Stamford's reaction. Was he devastated to learn that a close friend had been involved in the Kennedy assassination? Or was he angry with a co-conspirator for disclosing something that was supposed to be locked away forever?

Those and other questions crowded Jim's mind as Stamford finally turned around after several minutes of staring and slowly walked back to his chair.

"I am completely mystified by this," he said in his deliberate manner as he settled into the chair and handed the letter back to Kelly. "I could never have believed that your father would have participated in anything like this. He was not that kind of man. I really am at a loss for words or explanation."

Kelly decided to push for an answer.

"Tell me something about my father's early career. What was he doing, and how could he have been in a position to participate? And what about this reference to de Mohrenschildt, who turns out to be the name of a man who knew Lee Harvey Oswald—did you know him?"

The questions tumbled out of Kelly's mouth in rapid-fire succession, clearly reflecting her desperate need for information.

Stamford took a sip of his Bloody Mary and locked eyes with Kelly. Jim tried to read something, anything, in Stamford's demeanor. The truth about Stamford's mindset was hidden in there somewhere. But all he could see was the man's seemingly innocent interest in Kelly's questions.

"I don't know that I can give you any satisfactory answers. Everything in your father's letter is beyond belief. Nor is there anything I can tell you about the information to be given to the government. Neither the numbers nor the letters mean anything to me. And I certainly never heard of a man named de Mohrenschildt. But I do have some sense of what your father means when he says he rose too far too fast."

Kelly leaned forward in her chair, her curiosity piqued.

"Tell me."

"Ted Roberts was a brilliant and highly-motivated fellow. When we were at Princeton, he was driven to succeed in every endeavor—whether it was academics, sports, or girls. And succeed he did in all those fields. He was one of those students who seemed to have the magic touch. Everything he did always seemed right."

"I know what you mean," Jim interjected. "A lot of those guys went to law school with me."

Stamford gave Jim a knowing smile and then continued.

"Ted and I became close friends in our sophomore year at Princeton because we were members of the same eating club. And I must admit that I was a little envious of how easy success came to him. I had to struggle to be half as successful. But there was nothing pretentious about your father," Stamford quickly added. "And that was perhaps his greatest virtue. He never flaunted his many talents. He was charming and down-to-earth, the kind of person who could establish a quick rapport with almost anyone—professor, friend, or a date. And I knew those qualities would serve him well in whatever he did after college."

Jim took some comfort in the warmth reflected in Stamford's description of Ted Roberts. There had obviously been a strong emotional bond between the two men. But who could say, Jim said to himself, what that really meant. Was part of the bond their participation in Kennedy's assassination? Jim wanted to blurt out that question but knew that he couldn't. He would let Kelly keep the lead, and she did so without hesitation.

"Didn't you and Dad go into government together after Princeton?"

"We started out together. We were both intrigued by foreign policy, and both of us took the Foreign Service exams for the State Department. We both had visions of traveling to faraway places that we had only read about and utilizing our position to advance the lofty ideals that we both regarded as very important at the time. After all," he said with a small smile, "you must remember that those were the days of the 'ugly American,' when foreigners believed that Americans were too spoiled and too arrogant and, not incidentally, too soft to defend ourselves against the advance of communism."

"So where did you and Dad go after Princeton?"

"I went to the State Department and your father went to the Central Intelligence Agency."

As he was finishing his answer, Stamford rose from his chair and walked into the small kitchen. Jim and Kelly watched as he returned with a small tray of cheese and crackers. He filled their almost empty glasses with more Bloody Marys from the large decanter on the coffee table and offered the food tray to each of them.

"I've got a question," said Jim as he munched on a cracker with cheddar cheese. "Why didn't you and Mr. Roberts go into the CIA together?"

"A good question, Jim. During the interview process Ted met a CIA recruiter, Bruce Lord was his name I think, who took an immediate liking to Ted and convinced him that the CIA was the best avenue to what he wanted. Ted in fact tried to persuade me to join him."

"But you didn't," said Jim.

"No, I didn't. To me, the State Department had a certain stature that the CIA could not match. After all, you must remember, this was the 1950s, and things were much different then. The CIA was not nearly as well known as the State Department, and that troubled me. To be candid, when I was young, the idea of being in the public limelight had much more appeal."

Kelly shifted in her chair, kicked off her shoes, and tucked her legs under her skirt.

"So," she inquired, "was I wrong in assuming that you and Dad worked together in those early years?"

"Actually not. Ted became a case officer, and so we sometimes found ourselves working together in the same embassies."

"What's a case officer?" Kelly asked.

"Someone who makes political analyses and provides advice on intelligence received from the field. A case officer might work in an embassy with a fictitious title from another agency, but he is not an undercover operative who uses binoculars or wiretaps to spy on people. In any case, Ted's analytical skills quickly became evident, and he soon caught the eye of Allen Dulles, the director of the Central Intelligence Agency. And that's how we got separated. I continued to receive assignments over the next few years to work at embassies in such far-flung places as Port-au-Prince, New Delhi, Seoul, and Cairo, all interspersed with periodic visits to Washington. Ted, on the other hand, was given assignments that required him to stay in Washington."

"What year are we talking about?" asked Jim.

"This must have been sometime late in 1959."

"But I assume," said Kelly, "that you guys still stayed in touch. Because I remember all those dinners with you at the house, the vacations in Florida, and the other times we spent together."

"Quite right. Although we had different agencies as employers, I still talked to Ted by phone periodically, and I always saw him when I returned to Washington. I wasn't entirely clear what Ted was doing. He was always discreet when it came to his official duties. But," Stamford said with a twinkle in his eye, "Ted would often tell me amusing stories about Eisenhower, the Kennedys, and other people who made important decisions. And he was clearly energized by his work. You could see that he felt that he was on a mission. And very determined to succeed the same way he had succeeded in everything else."

Jim's suspicions flared again as Stamford denied knowing the details of Roberts's activities. Was he being honest or cagey? Jim wasn't sure, but something didn't feel right. How could he be so close to Roberts and know so little about what his good friend was doing? Jim shifted in his chair and glanced over at Kelly, who seemed oblivious to Jim's growing concerns.

"It doesn't make sense to me," she said. "Given all that, why would Dad have any interest in seeing President Kennedy assassinated? How could he work with these people and yet be interested in hurting them?"

Stamford put his glass back on the coffee table and looked up at Kelly.

"That's the big question, and one that gives me great pause. I can't imagine that he would want to do anything to hurt the Kennedys."

"So where does that leave us?" Kelly asked, almost to herself as much as to Stamford.

"What we should do is hook you up with someone Ted worked closely with in those early Kennedy years. He could give you better insight on what Ted was thinking at the time and what might have triggered these thoughts."

"Sounds good," said Kelly.

Jim could feel the anger rising within him. He believed they had made a mistake in showing Ted Roberts's letter to Stamford in the first place, and now Stamford was suggesting that they discuss it with someone else. He could stand on ceremony no longer. He had to speak up.

"Wait a minute, Kelly. This is potentially dangerous stuff. We can't just be going around talking to people. This is Washington. It won't take many conversations before lots of people know about this, and we can't forget what your father said. There are people out there who won't take kindly to you trying to dredge up the truth. I'm just as curious as you are, but no amount of information is worth putting your life at risk."

To Jim's surprise, Stamford seemed to agree.

"Jim's point is well taken. You must be extremely careful. Washington can be a tough town. Having said that, I do know one person who could be very helpful and who I am sure would guard your confidences: Harvey Teasdale. He was a colleague of Ted's who worked at the CIA and who might be able to tell you something. And even if he can't be helpful, he is as close-mouthed and as loyal as they come. He won't betray your trust."

"I'm placing my fate in your hands," Kelly responded. "If you think that well of him, then I'm game. What do you think, Jim?"

"I disagree. I think it's a mistake to expand the number of people who know about this," he said, looking at Stamford, hoping, maybe expecting, that Stamford would change his mind. It was a false hope.

"I understand and, indeed, share your concern, Jim. But I can't imagine Harvey doing or saying anything that would place Kelly in danger. On the other hand, I do agree that you can't be too careful in this business. So," he continued, turning back to face Kelly, "I won't tell Teasdale anything about your father's letter. I'll simply say that you want to talk about your father's career and let it go at that."

"That's certainly better," said Jim with some relief, knowing it was the best he could get under the circumstances.

Kelly nodded in agreement.

"Good," said Stamford. "Then it's settled. I'll give Harvey a call tomorrow and let him know you'll be calling, Kelly. I haven't talked to him much since he retired from the government, but I believe he still maintains a consulting business in the Washington area. I'll try to reach him and let you know."

"That would be great."

Kelly looked at Jim and then turned back to Stamford.

"It's getting late, and Jim and I both have to get up early. So why don't we talk in the next few days, and you'll let me know about Harvey Teasdale."

They all rose from their chairs, and Stamford walked the two of them to the door. Kelly gave Bud a long hug, and then she and Jim left to return home. As they rode down in the elevator, Kelly looked at Jim.

"What was that all about?" she asked.

"What?"

"You were obviously upset about something."

Jim looked at the floor and then at Kelly.

"You sure you can trust this guy?"

"Oh, Jim," she laughed. "You really are getting paranoid."

"Well, just because you're paranoid doesn't mean they're not after you."

Chapter 13

Kelly lay awake in her second-story bedroom. She lifted her head from the pillow and looked at the red numbers on the digital radio clock by her bed. Three forty-five.

Sleep had not come easily since she had read her father's letter. A thousand emotions swept over her at unexpected moments day and night. Her father had been such a loving and caring parent. Someone who also seemed to have the highest principles. Now everything was clouded by his role in the Kennedy assassination. What exactly did he do? Why did he do it? Would she be able to find out? And where would it all lead?

Kelly kept asking herself that last question over and over. But thinking about it didn't help much. Her mind just drew a blank. And so she continued to lie there, staring at the ceiling and feeling tense, confused, and very afraid. Everything now seemed so sinister, and she worried that she would have difficulty trusting anyone—because anyone could represent the danger that her father feared.

Everyone, that is, except Bud Stamford. She did draw some comfort from his involvement. He conveyed the same kind of strength that her father had. Nobody could replace her father. But Bud was the next best thing.

Kelly wondered whether Harvey Teasdale could be trusted—and whether he would really be able to help. Bud had called to say that he had talked to him and had told him that Kelly would be calling. She had called Teasdale immediately but never got past the secretary. In one sense, she hoped Teasdale would call back soon so she could talk to him. And then there was that sixth sense that told her that she might be better off if Teasdale never called.

A soft summer breeze, nestled in the sweet smells of pasture and trees, gently pushed through the open blinds on her window. The warm air felt good on her face and made her realize that, when all was said and done, she had made the right decision in leaving the Hill. She was in the house she loved. She could ride when she wanted and enjoy life without the pressures of that political cesspool. Sooner or later everything would work out with her father's letter. It had to. The anxiety she felt was becoming unbearable.

It was then that she heard the sound of the front door slowly opening downstairs. That unmistakable creaking sound. Or was it? She had bolted the door lock—hadn't she? She listened carefully, and there were no more sounds. She must have been mistaken. It was probably the trees rustling in the light summer breeze.

She turned over and tried to go back to sleep. But then she heard a stair creak. At least she thought she did. She sat up in bed and tried to listen more closely, turning her head toward the open door of the bedroom. She looked through the door but could see nothing other than the darkness that no longer frightened her. This is Potomac for chrissake, she said to herself. People don't break into homes out here.

But then she heard another creak, and she was not so sure. Maybe someone had broken into the house. What should she do?

She instantly recalled what her father always said. The biggest mistake people made in these situations was to walk downstairs to investigate a possible burglary. If something was afoot, walking in on a burglar in the act was the worst thing. Burglars often did unintended and harmful things, he would say, when caught in the act. Her father never tired of telling them about the Clutter family, whose plight was captured with poignancy and drama in Truman Capote's best-selling book, *In Cold Blood.* The father hears some burglars downstairs in the library of his Kansas farmhouse and, instead of calling the police, goes downstairs to investigate. He walks in on two burglars who tie up the father and the rest of the family and then shoot all of them—in cold blood.

No, Kelly said to herself, she was not going to make that mistake. Better the embarrassment of the police telling her it was nothing than finding herself confronting a burglar.

She picked up the phone to call the police.

There was no dial tone. She clicked it again. The phone was dead.

She heard another creak. Someone was clearly in the house, and he was obviously walking up the stairs.

What could she do? The only way out was through the bedroom door, and that was not a viable option. She looked out the open window to the large dogwood tree that grew beside the house. Maybe she should climb out the window and down the tree. It was certainly strong enough to support her 105-pound frame. And then what? She had nothing on but underwear and an extra-long gray Warner Bros. T-shirt—her favorite sleeping garb. Where would she go? How would she escape?

The answer came from nowhere. Grant. Thank God it was the summertime. If it had been winter, the horses would have been inside the barn at night. But now, with the Washington heat at its peak, Grant was out in the pasture, grazing with the other horses. She would ride him into the woods. Riding bareback would not be a problem. She had done it a thousand times. Of course, she had always had a bridle before, but no matter. She could hold onto Grant's mane. Yes, she tried to reassure herself, riding Grant was the obvious solution. No one could follow her through the woods along the Potomac River, and she could wind her way through the trails to the Andrews's home, her closest neighbor.

She sat up straight, put her right hand on the bed, and eased herself off the bed to minimize the sound. When she put her right foot down on the hardwood floor, it creaked ever so slightly—but in the stillness of the night it sounded like a loud alarm. She slowly put her other foot on the floor and slid toward the window.

There was another creak on the stairs. Whoever it was, he was getting closer. Too much noise and he might rush in and foil her plan.

Kelly's heart was beating so hard and so rapidly she felt as though it would burst out of her skin. So be it. There was no going back now. This was her only chance.

She carefully pulled up the blinds and lifted the screen on the window— which, due to the careful workmanship of the house, was accomplished without a sound. She looked down. The house never looked so tall. But the tree was old and sturdy, and she slowly put her right leg out while holding on to the windowsill with her left hand. The branches barely moved, and, in the summer breeze, with the leaves rustling ever so slightly, there did not appear to be any noise.

She leaned up against the windowsill from the outside and slowly pulled the window screen down with both hands. And then she quickly moved down the tree, moving from branch to branch with relative ease until she could jump the four or five feet from the bottom branch onto the ground.

She looked up at the window. Nothing was moving. There was no sound.

She quickly ran in her bare feet down the dirt road to the split-rail fence and climbed through. In the fullness of the almost-white moon, she could see the outlines of the four horses in the pasture. Even with the light of the moon, it was too dark to see clearly. Still, she could pick out Grant's form about thirty yards away.

It was then that she heard the noises from her bedroom and realized that the intruder was pushing furniture around, opening doors, desperately looking for her—or perhaps something else. It was only a matter of time before the intruder saw her.

She looked up to her window and saw the dark figure now looking directly at her. She had been seen, and she could hear the rapid and loud footsteps as the intruder raced down the stairs to get her.

Kelly ran to Grant who, amazingly enough, stood still, watching her approach. She grabbed hard on his mane and jerked herself up on the first try—something she was not always able to do in the serenity of daylight. She instinctively thought of the little things that can make a difference in critical moments—in this case, the lack of nerves in a horse's mane that enabled her to pull as hard as she could without causing Grant any pain. He would not have stood still otherwise.

Kelly squeezed Grant's belly with her legs and leaned over his neck, holding tightly onto his mane for support and balance. Grant responded to the pressure and slowly cantered to the gate. Kelly pulled up the latch, opened the gate, and nudged Grant through to the other side.

She now heard the intruder running down the dirt road toward the barn, the heavy footsteps signaling a man of substantial weight. Kelly looked backward over her shoulder and saw the man standing on the dirt road, a good forty or fifty yards away. And then she saw him pull his arms up and point a handgun at her. Oh my God, she muttered to herself. The guy wants to kill me! And then she saw a red laser beam emanate from the gun. She had seen enough movies to know that the beam somehow enhanced the accuracy of a bullet's trajectory. This guy's not taking any chances, she said to herself as she sensed the beam on her back. He's determined to kill me. She leaned over to the far side of Grant's massive neck as the horse picked up the gait, and it was none too soon. She heard the explosion of gunfire as a bullet whizzed right over her head.

She then squeezed Grant's belly as hard as she could with her thighs and again leaned over his mane. The horse responded by cantering with greater speed down the trails that they had traveled so many times before and that the two of them knew so well. The sound of another shot rang out, but Kelly knew that, in the dark woods that surrounded the trail, it would be a miracle for the bullet to find her on a moving horse. Not that she was taking any chances. She kept pressing

Grant to canter faster and faster. Within minutes the house and the barn were well behind her, and Kelly was surrounded by dense woodlands, her only companions being the staccato noise of the pervasive crickets and the rushing river below.

After a few minutes the rough terrain and thick woods forced her to slow Grant down to a trot. She kept looking over her shoulder as she did so. Had her assailant given up? Or was he silently pursuing her through the dark woods? There was no way to know. She tightened her grip on Grant's mane and continued to meander as fast as she could through the trails until she reached the open field behind the Andrews's home, which was completely dark except for the floodlights on each of the roof's corners.

Kelly quickly cantered past the Andrews's small barn and rode Grant up to the side of the house. She slipped off the horse and ran onto the deck that wrapped around the back of the house and knocked on the doors, calling out Don and Arlene's names in a loud whisper. Finally a light came on in the bedroom above the deck, and Don yelled down, "Who's there?"

"It's me, Don. Kelly," Kelly responded in an excited whisper. "Please. Come down and open the door as fast as you can. Someone's trying to kill me!"

Within seconds, Don Andrews, a balding man with the paunch of middle age and wearing a white terry-cloth bathrobe, turned on the family-room lights and opened the deck door. Kelly burst through and shut the door.

"Lock it, Don. Lock it as fast as you can."

Kelly then ran to the phone and dialed 911 for the Montgomery County police.

By the time the police arrived at the Andrews's home, Kelly had breathlessly related the evening's events to Don and Arlene, who had joined her husband and Kelly in the family room within minutes after Don had opened the deck door. The police told Kelly that separate police cars had gone to her house to investigate, but those police officers eventually reported back that nothing seemed to be amiss. There was no sign of a forced entry, and there were no spent casings or other signs of bullets being fired. Was she sure it was gunfire?

"I'm sure," Kelly told the police officer. "I'm very sure. Someone was after me."

"Whatever," said Don. "The bottom line is that you're not leaving here tonight. Grant's happily grazing with our horses in the corral, and I'm sure," Don added, looking at one of the police officers, "that the police will be glad to leave someone in front of our house until morning."

The police sergeant nodded in agreement, and Kelly, exhausted by the ordeal, allowed Don and Arlene to lead her to the spare bedroom on the second floor for a few hours' rest.

Chapter 14

About an hour after Kelly reached the Andrews's home, a late-model white Chrysler sedan pulled up on the shoulder of Seneca Road in Darnestown, a few miles from Kelly's house. There was no traffic in either direction. The driver, a large man in black pants and a black T-shirt, took a cell phone from his pocket and placed a call. After one ring, a man answered and, in a very slow, measured tone, said only, "Yes."

"It's me."

"Yes, Leonard."

"I didn't find the letter. And the girl got away."

"What do you mean, 'the girl got away'?"

"She climbed out the window and down a fuckin' tree," he said excitedly. "I tried to get her, but she got on a horse and rode into the woods. Can you believe that? She got on a horse and rode into the woods. I couldn't follow her."

"Leonard, I'm very disappointed. You're supposed to be a professional. These things are not supposed to happen to professionals."

"I am a professional. I took care of that lawyer guy, didn't I?" There was no response and Leonard felt the need to continue. "Anyway, don't worry," he said in a more modulated tone. "I left the house just the way I found it. No one will know I was there—except her of course."

"I just hope that you did not try to kill the girl as she fled. Remember," the voice instructed, "nothing is to happen to that girl until we find the letter." There was a long pause. "You did remember that, didn't you?"

Leonard realized at once that, in the heat of the moment, he had forgotten the admonition. But he was no fool. He would not admit to a lapse in memory about his instructions. He was a professional.

"Of course I remembered," he lied.

"Well, Leonard," the voice continued with condescension, "at least you know how to do some things right."

"What should I do now?"

"There's nothing to do for now. There will be much excitement and police surveillance. I'll be in touch."

Leonard knew enough not to challenge his superior's decision.

"Yes, I understand," was all he said.

Leonard closed the phone, put it back in his pocket, and quietly drove into the night.

Chapter 15

Jim Roth's office phone was ringing in his small cubicle, but he would not answer it. He needed to finish Senator Gimble's speech on a new American policy initiative toward Cuba. He had come in early to get it done, but it was to no avail. The constant telephone calls had prevented him from getting beyond the opening paragraph, and it was already ten o'clock. He couldn't tolerate any more interruptions. At least not for a little while.

After an hour or so the phone rang again and startled Jim out of his concentration. He decided he could take a break and answer it.

"Jim," Kelly said, her voice trembling with emotion, "someone tried to kill me last night."

Jim immediately felt a mixture of fear, curiosity, and anger. A multitude of questions erupted in his mind, but all he could ask was the obvious one: "What happened?"

"I don't know where to begin. Someone broke into the house last night and started shooting at me."

Even without knowing the details, Jim had the same sense of dread he had experienced earlier—except now the danger was real. He could not help but believe that her father's fears were well founded and that someone was trying to prevent Kelly from delving into her father's past. Were they now going to be subject to assault at any moment? And who was behind it? As he pondered these and other questions, Kelly began to review the horror she had endured.

"Yes, I'm okay, I'm okay," she repeated in response to Jim's interruptions. "But it was the scare of my life. You're not going to believe what I did. I climbed down the tree next to my bedroom and escaped on Grant into the woods."

"Any idea who it was?"

"Not a clue."

Jim leaned forward in his chair, his elbows on his desk and the phone cradled in his shoulder. He could feel the adrenaline flowing through his body.

"Goddammit, Kelly, this is exactly what your father warned might happen. What are you going to do now? You can't go back to the house."

"The hell I can't. Nobody is forcing me from that house. I've had a good night's sleep, and the more I thought about it, the angrier I became. I don't think it has anything to do with my father's letter. You and Bud and I are the only ones who know about it. So I'm sure it's just a random crime. Having said that, I have to admit I never thought I would have to worry about crime in Potomac. But I'm no ostrich. I'm not going to ignore reality. I've already ordered an alarm system, and I'm putting in floodlights on the house and the barn."

Jim shook his head slightly as he listened to Kelly describe her plan.

"Kelly, don't you get it? Somehow somebody's already learned about the questions you're starting to ask about your father. And now your life's in danger. I'm as interested as you are in pursuing this thing. But I don't think it's worth risking your life."

"I agree. I don't want to risk my life for this either. And I'm not going to do anything more about it. Except talk to Harvey Teasdale. And then maybe I'll call it a day."

"I don't think you should do even that."

"Oh, Jim. I can't believe it would hurt. Especially since Bud promised that he wouldn't tell Teasdale about my father's letter."

"I'm not sure you're right. Can't we talk about this rationally?"

"So what's your proposal?" Although his mind was focused on the danger that Kelly, and maybe he, faced, Jim detected a slight change in Kelly's tone. He sensed a small smile on her lips. His thoughts suddenly shifted to his growing feelings for her, and he began to wonder whether the feeling was mutual. The possibility encouraged him to be bolder than he otherwise might have been.

"Here's an alternative for you. Maybe not the one you had in mind but an alternative nonetheless."

"You caught me in a weak moment," Kelly replied with a forced laugh. "I don't think I'm going to be very picky."

"My mother called last night and almost begged me to come to New Jersey. And if you knew my mother, you'd know how unusual that was. She's such a stoic, she never asks for anything. I'm sure it's because things have gotten really bad for my dad."

"Why? What's going on?"

"His heart condition has worsened, and the doctors are telling my mother and the rest of the family—but not Dad—that he can't go on much longer. He can't walk more than twenty-five yards without feeling pain or shortness of breath."

"Oh, Jim, I'm so sorry."

"Me, too," he replied with a tone of resignation. "Anyway, I was thinking of leaving tomorrow afternoon after the Senate recesses. How would you like to see beautiful New Jersey?"

"That could be a problem. Tomorrow is Thursday, and I'm supposed to meet with the attorneys at Jeff's firm about the lawsuit against the safari company. You think it can wait until Friday morning?"

"I'm sure it can. I'll pick you up Friday morning at eight."

"That sounds good. I'll need the escape. Pick me up at the house. I'll go over there in the early morning, take care of the horses, and pack some clothes."

"You got a deal."

CHAPTER 16

On Thursday afternoon Kelly pulled her Jeep into the parking lot on 6th Street around the corner from the Navy Memorial on Pennsylvania Avenue. She told the attendant she would return in a couple of hours and walked briskly down the street and past the white Chrysler sedan without taking any notice.

She turned onto the sidewalk next to the broad expanse of Pennsylvania Avenue, walked past the fountain with the multitude of pedestrians and tourists, entered the large white-stone office building that surrounded the Memorial, took the elevator to the ninth floor, and stepped into the mahogany-paneled reception area of Chase and Blackhorn, LLP. The room had the pleasant fragrance of fresh flowers and polished wood. To other visitors it would have all been impressive, but for Kelly it evoked sad reminders of her recent visit to the firm with Jim to pick up Jeff's personal effects.

An attractive young woman with long brunette hair politely asked if she could help, and Kelly explained that she had an appointment with Mr. Neal at four o'clock. The receptionist deftly pushed some buttons on the large console in front of her and told a woman named Grace that Ms. Roberts was here for her appointment with Mr. Neal.

As she waited, Kelly's thoughts drifted unconsciously to the intruder who had forced her to escape down a tree and onto Grant. She could not help but wonder whether Jim was right. Maybe the intruder really *was* after her father's letter. And if so, what did that say about Jeff's death? It sounded like a freak accident, but who could really say? Trained animals were nothing new, and Jeff himself said that he feared he was being watched. Could they have tracked him down in Africa and found an easy way to kill him?

While Kelly pondered those troubling questions, a tall bald man with a cleft chin emerged from a side door and approached her. Although not wearing a jacket, the man still looked remarkably formal in his blue-striped shirt with the white collar and white French cuffs, all complemented by a yellow silk tie.

"Hello, Kelly," he said, extending his right hand. "I'm Gus Neal. I'm sorry it's not Bill Blackhorn greeting you, but, as I explained on the phone, I'm the one who's going to try to fill Bill's shoes as managing partner, and there's no better place to start than helping you."

"Thanks, Mr. Neal. I certainly was sorry to hear about Mr. Blackhorn. Did they ever figure out what happened?"

"Not sure. He apparently collapsed at home on Sunday night, and he wasn't discovered until the next morning when his daughter's calls went unanswered. Bill's family had a history of heart disease, so the thinking is that it was a heart attack."

"That's so sad. I didn't know him well, but he seemed to be a compassionate man."

"Indeed, he was. But we're just as sorry about Jeff. That was certainly a tragic loss for you, and for us as well. And, although we can't bring him back, I'm hopeful that we can do something to rectify the situation."

"I know. And I do appreciate your willingness to help out."

"Not at all, Kelly. Not at all." Neal motioned toward a side door and led Kelly to the inner sanctum of the firm's offices. Kelly followed Neal down a wide hallway past offices with young attorneys walking quickly or talking rapidly to each other or their secretaries. Neal then opened a door and ushered her into a conference room dominated by a large rosewood table with black leather chairs and a magnificent view of the Capitol building located only six blocks up the street on Pennsylvania Avenue.

As Kelly walked in, two men who had been sitting at the conference table rose to meet her.

"Kelly," Neal said, "I'd like you to meet George Kruger."

Kelly looked at Kruger. A young attorney, probably in his late twenties, with light brown hair and a quick smile.

"Hi, George," she said, extending her right hand.

"Nice to meet you, Kelly," he said, shaking her hand.

"And this," Neal said, turning to the other man, "is Caleb Butler."

Butler was not much taller than Kelly, perhaps five foot seven inches, with thinning black hair combed straight back and a very large girth. Kelly guessed that he was younger than he looked, which was around fifty or fifty-five. Even before she knew anything about him, Kelly sensed something comforting about Butler's demeanor.

"Pleased to meet you, ma'am," said Butler with a slight drawl. "I'm sure you don't remember me from the funeral, but I know I'm not the first in this firm to tell you how sad we all were about Jeff. A first-class guy with a great future. He will be sorely missed around here."

Kelly nodded her head in appreciation. Butler's remarks seemed heartfelt and touched a raw nerve that Neal's comments had, for some reason, failed to penetrate. The doubts and fears she felt about her brother's death only moments ago were suddenly replaced by anger. Even if someone had followed Jeff to Africa, the safari company certainly could have done more than it did to protect him. And she desperately wanted them to pay for that lapse.

"I do appreciate your thoughts," she said, trying to control her emotions. "Everyone at the firm has been simply terrific. And I'm hopeful that something can be done here." She then paused and gave Butler a small smile. "But before we start marching down that road, tell me where that accent is from? I know it's not Boston."

"You're quite right, ma'am. Covington, Kentucky. That's where I'm from. Home of the country's best barbecued ribs."

"I never knew that. But it's something I'll want to remember, because I'm a big fan of barbecued ribs."

Kelly then turned back to Neal, who asked each of them to sit down at the table. He wasted no time in getting to the purpose of the meeting.

"Caleb is the head of our litigation department, Kelly, and one of the finest trial lawyers in the city. George is one of our young associates who has been second chair in quite a few trials, and together they make quite a team."

Kelly had never previously heard the "second chair" expression, but she assumed it meant that Kruger played second fiddle to a more senior lawyer.

"Our thought," Neal continued, "is that we would approach the safari company, see if we can reach a quick settlement, and, if not, institute litigation. I think it's highly likely that they will want to settle, if for no other reason than to avoid publicity. But you never know."

"When you say 'settle,'" Kelly asked, "what exactly do you mean?"

"Ma'am," Butler interjected, "he means a check written out to you with a number and a lot of zeros after that number."

"That sounds great, but I'm not in it just for the money. I also want some kind of apology or confession or whatever you call it."

"We will represent you," Butler responded, "and, although we will counsel you about the wisdom and probability of different results, at the end of the day, you call the shots. We won't settle unless you're satisfied with the results and authorize us to settle."

"How much will this cost?" Kelly asked.

"Nothing," said Neal. "We'll take the case on a complete contingency basis. We'll even cover the expenses. If we lose, you don't owe us a dime. If we win, you'll pay our expenses out of the money received at settlement and one-third of the remainder to cover our fees. How does that sound to you?"

"That sounds fine. When do we start?"

"How 'bout right now, ma'am," said Butler. "Did you bring Jeff's brochures and other materials?"

"Yes, I did."

"Well," Neal interrupted, "I've now outlived my usefulness. I will say goodbye, Kelly, knowing you're in the most capable hands you could find in the city."

Neal rose, shook Kelly's hand, and left the room.

Kelly handed Butler a manila envelope with the brochures and other documents on the safari that she had found in Jeff's apartment. Butler pulled out the Barrington and Stone, Limited brochure. It was a high-quality, glossy document of more than 125 pages detailing the various kinds of safaris that the company offered, all illustrated by color photographs of animals, landscapes, and beaches. He leafed through it while Kelly and Kruger looked on.

"Isn't this a pretty clear case?" asked Kelly. "I mean, after all, how can they deny that they're liable when Jeff was killed on *their* safari?"

"If I may say so, ma'am," Butler said in his slow cadence, "nothing in the law is ever that simple. The First Amendment to the Constitution clearly says that Congress shall pass no law abridging freedom of speech, and Congress has been passing such laws almost since the day our country was founded. Now, they always try to justify it by reference to a war, espionage, or some other important public interest, but it happens nonetheless. And I'm sure that Barrington and Stone will have lots of explanations as to why they're not liable for Jeff's death."

As Kelly listened to Butler, she began to wonder whether she should tell him about her father's letter and her growing suspicions about her brother's death. But something inside told her to hold back. She really didn't know if she could trust Butler completely. He might be a lawyer, but who knew what he knew or what he would do if she disclosed everything she knew. So Kelly decided to be cautious. There would always be time to tell him something later.

"What can I do to help?" she finally asked the attorney.

"I know enough now to know that I am interested in speaking with Ms. Landow. So I would be most grateful if you could have her call me to schedule a meeting."

"Consider it done."

"For the rest, I think it best if you allow George and me to review these materials. I would expect we could then be in touch with you in a few days about the letter we plan to write to Barrington and Stone."

"That's great. I'll look forward to hearing from you."

With that Kelly rose from her chair, and, as she did, Butler and Kruger rose from their seats and escorted her to the reception area. They exchanged handshakes and smiles, and Kelly left, satisfied that Jeff's former colleagues were the right ones to vindicate her loss and wondering whether her new lawyers might be getting a case far more sinister than they realized.

CHAPTER 17

Jim pulled his car, the top down, into the familiar driveway of Kelly's house and slowly coasted up to the front. Although early in the morning, the sun was already high and intense. It was going to be another hot, humid summer day.

Jim gave a couple of quick taps on the horn, and Kelly soon walked out the front door wearing cutoff jean shorts and a large white T-shirt but carrying a solemn look on her face. She threw a small duffel bag in the back and was about to get into the passenger seat when she noticed the small white bag.

"What's this?"

"I thought you might be hungry, so I stopped off at Potomac Village and got us a couple of large, and I might add, hot blueberry muffins along with some coffee."

Kelly noticed the two coffee containers in the cup holders in the console.

"Wow. Aren't you the thoughtful one. I'm going to take more trips to New Jersey with you."

"You won't say that after the first two hours."

"Why? How long will it take?"

"Oh, I don't know. Three, three-and-a-half hours. It'll depend on how closely the police are watching the Jersey Turnpike."

Within minutes they were on the Capital Beltway that surrounds Washington, DC and then on Interstate 95 up to New Jersey.

"Well," Kelly said after she had finished half of her muffin and most of the coffee, "I met with the attorneys at Chase and Blackhorn yesterday to talk about Jeff's case."

"So? Don't keep me in suspense. What did they say?"

"They hope the safari company will settle, if only to avoid the publicity. But the trial attorney they assigned to the case said it may not be that simple."

"Nothing is in the law."

"Funny. That's what he said too."

"He's obviously a smart guy."

Jim then raised the question that had troubled him ever since Kelly had described the break-in at her house.

"Hey, I meant to ask what Stamford thinks of what happened the other night." Jim glanced over at Kelly, her hair whipping in the wind. "He's a man wise in the ways of Washington, and I would think he would find it a little suspicious that someone tries to kill you right after we show him your father's letter."

"I don't know what Bud thinks. I've called him a couple of times to tell him about it, but all I get is his answering machine. Maybe he's traveling. Anyway, I'm hoping I'll catch up with him soon."

Kelly looked over at Jim and caught the suspicious gleam in his eyes. She knew what he was thinking. And she had already considered the possibility Jim might be right—at least about the intruder being connected to her father's letter. But she refused to yield. She wanted to believe, really had to believe, that there was no hidden meaning behind the break-in. And, as much as she wanted to talk with Bud, she felt compelled to deny that the break-in had anything to do with her father's letter or their meeting with Stamford.

"Listen," she said, her eyes locked on Jim's face, "I'm telling you, the incident had nothing to do with my father's letter."

"Oh, come on, Kelly. Most burglars would have been happy to see you leave. They could take your things in peace. And no ordinary burglar would be so interested in chasing you down and trying to kill you. I don't buy any other explanation."

Jim's intransigence only made Kelly that much more determined.

"But how would anyone know anything? The only people who know about my father's letter are you and me and Bud."

"Maybe," Jim responded as diplomatically as he could, "Bud's not the sweet guy you thought you knew. Like I told you, I'm not sure you can trust the guy. Maybe he's one of the conspirators your father feared."

Jim turned slightly, caught the angry glare in Kelly's eyes, and realized that impugning Bud's intentions was not a productive line of inquiry with her.

"Let's talk about something else," Kelly suddenly said. "Tell me about your father."

"He calls me often, usually in the morning before I go to work. And he always ends the calls the same way—telling me that he wants to talk to me about some things the next time he sees me."

"What are they?"

"I don't know. He won't tell me over the phone, and when I do see him, we somehow never get around to it."

"A father and son who have difficulty communicating. What a shock," Kelly said with feigned surprise. "But it is clear to me from the little I've seen and what you've said that he does care about you. Deeply."

"I guess."

Neither one said anything to the other for a few minutes, and when Jim next turned to look at Kelly, she was asleep with the wind swirling around her in the open convertible. Even curled up in the car seat, she made his adrenalin flow. But he wasn't going to rush into anything. That much he had already decided. He would let events take their natural course. He had learned that much from experience. Patience was the key.

Shortly before eleven-thirty, Jim pulled the car into a long brick driveway and drove past a wide expanse of lawn to the front of a one-story ranch house with a gray stone facade.

"We're here," he said gently to Kelly. "Time to wake up."

Jim and Kelly exited the car and walked up to the front door, where they were greeted by Jim's father, a tall thin man with wispy white hair who was leaning on a wooden cane and sporting a broad smile.

"Hello, Jimmy boy, hello," he said, giving Jim a warm embrace. "It's so good to see you." He then turned to Kelly. "And how are you? I was so sorry to learn about Jeff. I'm sure it hasn't been easy for you."

Kelly was only half listening. She could not stop thinking of the man who had chased her out of the house and her overwhelming desire to reach Bud. But she wanted to put on a good face for Jim's family and—who knew—perhaps find some refuge from the questions that plagued her.

"That's kind of you, Mr. Roth. It has been tough. But Jim has been helping me through it, and I'm just glad he asked me to join him on his visit here. I needed the break."

As they walked into the living room, Jim's mother emerged from the kitchen. A woman of medium height with short dark hair and intense green eyes, she was far more reserved than her husband. She gave Jim a small kiss on his cheek and extended a hand to Kelly, saying how glad she was that Kelly could join them for the weekend.

She then escorted them into a screened-in porch that looked out over a large rectangular pool surrounded by tall oak trees. The table on the porch had a white tablecloth with a basket of freshly cut bagels in the center.

"I knew you must be hungry from your trip," said Jim's mother, "and I've got a mountain of food to make sure you don't stay hungry for long."

"My mother," Jim said to Kelly, "wrote the book on how to be a Jewish mother. There's no such thing as a time of day when you shouldn't be eating."

"Now, Jimmy," his mother said with slight annoyance, "you know that's not true."

She then disappeared into the kitchen and soon emerged with plates of whitefish salad, nova lox, kippered salmon, tomatoes, red onions, and cream cheese to go with the bagels. And while the others began putting the food on their plates, she poured steaming coffee into large mugs for each of them.

As they devoured the food, Jim's father led the conversation. And while her mind could not let go of her father's letter and all that had happened afterward, Kelly could not help but be touched by Jim's father. He wanted nothing more than to reminisce about his son's accomplishments when he lived at home.

"Kelly," he said between mouthfuls of a bagel sandwich, "did Jimmy ever tell you about the state championship he won for the Toms River baseball team in high school? People still talk about that home run."

"Come on, Dad," Jim said with obvious embarrassment. "Kelly doesn't want to hear about that stuff."

Kelly leaned forward and cut Jim off.

"Yes, I do, Mr. Roth. Tell me more."

And on and on it went. Jim's father took time to recount many other memories, taking particular pleasure in describing various events from his son's childhood. But when the meal was finished, he needed several minutes to get up from the table, and succeeded only with help from Jim.

The rest of the weekend was spent in long drives around Toms River, meals on the porch or in the dining room, and long conversations with Jim's parents that focused on family history. As Kelly had hoped, the distance from Washington seemed to insulate her from the events of the past week and the choices she would face upon her return. But before she knew it, she and Jim were driving back to Washington the following Sunday. They were silent on the first hour of the trip, and Jim could tell that Kelly was deep in thought. As they were crossing the Delaware Memorial Bridge, she turned to him.

"Did you and your father ever have that conversation to discuss the things he wanted to talk about?"

"No. I asked him a few times, and his only response was, 'We'll talk about it later.' But 'later' never came."

"You know what I think? It's his way of trying to reach out to you, to somehow connect with you again. But he's not sure how to do it or what to say. He just knows he wants to say something that will bring you closer to him. He wants to recapture some of the magic that the two of you shared when you were much younger."

Jim reflected on Kelly's comment. It made sense. And it made him sad.

CHAPTER 18

Kelly finished her evening chores in the barn and dialed Stamford's number again. It had gotten to the point where she was extremely concerned. She didn't know if anything had happened to Bud or—and she hardly dared think this—that maybe there was some truth to Jim's comment that Bud was one of those who did not want the truth disclosed about the Kennedy assassination. Her father had always said that everyone had their secrets and that you could never really know what motivated people. In retrospect, his words had a tragic irony.

She was about to hang up when an unfamiliar male voice answered.

"Is Bud there?" she asked.

"Who may I say is calling?"

"This is Kelly. Kelly Roberts."

"And can I ask how you know Mr. Stamford?"

Fear gripped Kelly. Something was wrong.

"I'm a friend. A very close friend."

"I'm sorry to inform you," the voice said, "that Mr. Stamford has died."

Kelly gasped. How could this be? Bud seemed to be in perfect health when they visited him. Bill Blackhorn suddenly came to mind. Was it just a coincidence that he too died unexpectedly? Or was there some connection? Other questions popped into her mind, but Kelly suddenly realized that she had no idea who was on the other end of the telephone line.

"May I ask your name?"

"This is Lieutenant Soggs from the Metropolitan Police Department. I'm a detective with the Homicide Division."

"Homicide?"

"Yes, ma'am."

"You mean somebody killed Bud?"

"No, I'm not saying that, ma'am. At least not yet. We got a call from a sister in California who'd been trying to reach Mr. Stamford for some time and was concerned that something had gone wrong. We just arrived a short time ago and found Mr. Stamford. We're checking out the situation, but we haven't reached any conclusions yet."

"Oh my God," Kelly sighed. "I can't believe it. I just can't believe it."

"When did you last see Mr. Stamford?"

"I don't know," said Kelly, not entirely listening to the detective's questions. "Last week sometime."

"How was he then? His health, I mean."

Kelly was almost too stunned to think coherently.

"I'm not sure. I guess he was okay. He seemed fine to me."

"Ms. Roberts, if it's all right with you, I'd like to take your name and number and call you later if I have any more questions, which is probably likely."

Kelly gave Lieutenant Soggs her name and number and hung up. She stood motionless in the barn for a few minutes and then dialed Jim's number at the Senate.

Chapter 19

Jim walked into the empty reception area in Gimble's Senate suite and looked at his watch. It was almost six-thirty. Becky rarely stayed past six, but there were still several legislative assistants and other staff members moving about the suite.

Jim meandered back to his cubicle and saw the mail and messages piled high on his desk. He sat down and started sifting through the mounds of paper when he saw the envelope from the Congressional Research Service. He opened the envelope quickly and saw that it contained what he expected: the detailed report on George de Mohrenschildt. He leafed through the twenty-two pages of single-spaced type. The CRS certainly was thorough. He began reading and was quickly mesmerized by the analysis. De Mohrenschildt was worthy of a book by himself.

By the time Jim finished the CRS report, it was past seven. His immediate impulse was to call Kelly and tell her about the report, but he decided that he was too tired to have a long conversation. And in any case, he thought it would be best if they could talk about it in person. Maybe he would call her later that night after dinner. But for now he had to take a break.

He saw that he had telephone messages on his voice mail and persuaded himself to plow through them before quitting for the evening. The fifth message was an urgent one from Kelly.

"Jim, it's Kelly. Bud's dead! The police think he may have been murdered. Please call me as soon as you can."

Jim closed out the voice mail and stared at the phone. They were in a tailspin of some kind. Maybe Stamford was a conspirator. Maybe not. But it was all a little too coincidental. Blackhorn's heart attack, if that's what it really was. The attempted assault on Kelly. Stamford's death. He could not help but wonder whether Stamford was murdered, and, if so, was he an innocent victim or a conspirator who finally received his just reward? And what kind of danger was Kelly in? And was he in it with her?

He dialed Kelly's phone. She picked up after one ring.

"Oh God, Jim. I'm so glad you called. I assume you got my message."

"Yeah, I did. I really am sorry to hear about Bud. I know how much you cared for him. And with everything else going on, it's got to be tough on you."

"I know. I just can't believe this."

"So what did you find out? Did someone kill him?"

"I don't know. I don't think they know. But some detective from the Homicide Division was at the apartment when I called, and I presume they wouldn't send someone from the Homicide Division unless they thought there was foul play."

"Maybe. Maybe not."

Goddamn Jim, Kelly thought. He's always such a fucking lawyer. He won't commit to anything until he knows all the facts. But she didn't want to get bogged down in analyzing Jim. She was more interested in finding out what happened to Bud.

"What should we do?" she asked. "I've thought of nothing else since I talked to that detective."

"One thing's for sure. We've got to be very careful. We can call the police and see if they have an update. But in the meantime, I'm very concerned about you being out at the house by yourself."

Kelly was taken aback by the emotional conviction in Jim's voice. It conveyed a sentiment she hadn't picked up on before, and it stopped her short. Maybe he wasn't the cautious lawyer she thought he was. At least not where she was concerned.

"Kelly, are you still there?"

"Yeah, yeah," she said softly. "I was just thinking."

"Look. Why don't I stop by my condo, pick up some things, and come out to the house and stay there tonight? I know you've got plenty of bedrooms, and I'll sleep a lot better knowing that I'm near you."

"God, you're pushy." She then paused. "Have you eaten?"

"No. I'm still at the office. That's the other thing I wanted to tell you. I just read the Congressional Research Report on de Mohrenschildt. I'm still not sure how he figures in with your father, but this guy really was one hell of a character. I can tell you about it when I get there."

"You're on," she said, the relief evident in her voice. "I'll pull something together for dinner."

Chapter 20

It was almost nine o'clock by the time Jim made the turn into Kelly's driveway, and again he remained totally oblivious to the white sedan that followed him almost the entire ride from Washington and then pulled over to the shoulder as Jim made the turn. Jim brought the car to a stop in front of the house and saw Kelly sitting on the front porch, dressed in running shorts and one of her large trademark T-shirts. She walked up to the car door and opened it for Jim.

"I'm glad you're here," was all she said.

They said little more as they walked into the house and moved to the kitchen in the back. As Jim settled onto one of the stools by the butcher-block table, Kelly pulled a bottle of white wine from the refrigerator.

"You do the honors," she said to Jim, handing him the corkscrew.

Jim opened the wine and poured some into the wineglasses Kelly had taken out for them.

"I can't stop thinking of Bud," she began, looking down at her wineglass. "It almost takes my breath away." She picked her head up and looked at Jim with resignation. "And although I hate to admit it, I can't help but wonder whether there's any connection to my father's letter." Jim nodded in agreement. "Anyway," Kelly continued, "I'm glad you got that report on de Mohrenschildt. I need to focus on something else. Maybe a different piece of the same puzzle." She paused to take a long sip of wine. "Let's skip the foreplay and get right to the heart of the matter. What'd you find out?"

"The report really expands on the information I got off the Web. And it confirms that the man was a bundle of contradictions. He was born in 1911 in Russia and told people that he was entitled to be called 'Baron de Mohrenschildt' because he claimed to be the son of some nobleman."

"Interesting, but hardly intriguing."

"There's much more to it," Jim responded. He took another sip of wine and continued. "The guy arrives in the United States in 1938 with a Belgian passport under a slightly different name. He tells people that he was a member of the Polish cavalry and over time claims that he has done a variety of things—from insurance salesman to newspaper correspondent to film producer. No one can verify any of those claims, but de Mohrenschildt always seems to have a lot of money."

"What does any of this have to do with the Kennedy assassination?" Kelly asked as she got up from the stool and moved over to the refrigerator again. She pulled out a large wooden bowl filled with a chef's salad and placed it on the kitchen table.

"You have to be patient. Trust me. It gets more interesting."

They put their wineglasses on the table, sat down, and began helping themselves to the salad and then tearing pieces of the French baguette that Kelly had placed in a basket by the salad bowl. She ate in silence while Jim resumed the story.

"The guy spends World War II in the United States and is reported to have ties with the French counterintelligence, the British counterintelligence, and the Nazi underground. The CIA and the FBI tried to nail down later whether he was a good guy or a bad guy, but it seems they could never reach any definitive conclusions. Anyway," Jim continued in between mouthfuls of salad, "he gets a master's degree in petroleum engineering at the University of Texas and then takes various jobs in the oil business in Texas."

"All of which is starting to make him sound very boring."

Jim ignored Kelly's comment. He took another sip of wine and continued.

"Along the way he marries and divorces different women, and then it really starts to get interesting."

"Thank God."

"The United States government asks de Mohrenschildt to go to Yugoslavia on some geology mission in 1957, and that begins a long connection with—you guessed it—the CIA.

He travels around the Caribbean and then finds his way back to Dallas and somehow meets up with Lee Harvey Oswald in 1962."

"How'd that happen?"

"No one seems to know. De Mohrenschildt later claimed that some friend of his, an oil speculator named Orlov, was with him when he met Oswald, but

Orlov says de Mohrenschildt already knew Oswald before they all met at some gathering. De Mohrenschildt tells another friend that he met Oswald through the Dallas Aid Society, but no such organization ever existed. And beyond all the particulars is the obvious question: why would an aristocratic guy with a master's degree in petroleum engineering and lots of money have any interest in a loser like Oswald?"

"Wait a minute. Didn't Oswald defect to Russia and then come back to the United States? Maybe they wanted to talk about old times in Mother Russia."

"You obviously paid attention in history class." Jim took another forkful of salad and pushed on. "Oswald was a twenty-year-old ex-Marine who defected in 1959, married a Russian woman named Marina, and then returned in 1962. But it's hard to believe that would be enough to interest a guy like de Mohrenschildt. At least not for very long. Because Oswald was a loser in every other way. He had no money, he had little formal education, he couldn't hold a job, and he was apparently very abusive to his wife."

"When you say he was interested in Oswald, what do you mean?"

"De Mohrenschildt was not only giving Oswald money and trying to help him with jobs. He also took Oswald to parties with his friends and tried to introduce him to various political and literary contacts. It's one thing to give money to somebody down on his luck. But de Mohrenschildt seemed to be constantly socializing with Oswald and his wife."

"Go on. I'm sure this is going somewhere."

"I'm not sure where, but it starts to get a little sinister. Oswald gets it in his head that he has to help protect the United States against fascism. So he decides to assassinate General Edwin Walker, a right-wing activist in the early 1960s who was forced to resign from the United States Army because of his political activities. Oswald cases out Walker's house in a wealthy part of Dallas and then, one evening in April 1963, fires at him with the same rifle he later used to kill Kennedy. If, of course, you believe that Oswald killed Kennedy."

"What happened to Walker?" asked Kelly, wiping her mouth with a napkin and pushing her almost-empty salad bowl away from her.

"Oswald missed. But he didn't wait to find out. As soon as he fired the gun, he made a quick exit and buried the rifle. But here's the interesting part. A neighbor kid hears the shot and looks over the fence to see two men jump into two different cars and race away. So it appears that Oswald was not acting alone. And a few days after the incident, de Mohrenschildt visits Oswald at his home and asks how he could have missed Walker. The obvious question is how de Mohrenschildt knew about the assassination attempt."

"How does the CIA figure into all of this?"

Jim had now finished his salad and had placed his napkin on the table. He picked up his wineglass, took another sip, and then put the glass back on the table.

"De Mohrenschildt had apparently been in touch with the CIA the entire time he was dealing with Oswald. So you have to wonder whether de Mohrenschildt told someone in the CIA about Oswald's abortive attempt to assassinate Walker and whether that someone in the CIA stored the information away for later use."

"And then what?"

"Then nothing. After the Walker assassination attempt, de Mohrenschildt goes to Haiti or somewhere, and he never sees Oswald again."

"And that's it?" said Kelly with evident disappointment.

"No, there's more."

Kelly stood up and began clearing away the dishes. Jim stood up too and started to help, but Kelly motioned for him to continue the story.

"After Kennedy is killed, de Mohrenschildt is questioned by the Warren Commission in 1964, but the commission is plainly interested in getting out a quick report that says that Oswald did it alone so that President Johnson can tell the country they found the killer and there's no grand conspiracy."

"So what did de Mohrenschildt tell them about Oswald?"

"In 1964 he really bad-mouthed Oswald. But de Mohrenschildt sings a slightly different tune years later when he was questioned about his relationship with Oswald. Because now people are starting to look at conspiracy theories. There are now dozens of people writing articles and books that challenge the Warren Commission's finding…"

"That Oswald killed Kennedy?"

"And that he acted alone," Jim responded, chewing on a last remnant of the baguette. "Anyway, one of the Kennedy assassination writers, Edward Jay Epstein, interviews de Mohrenschildt in March 1977, and on that very day de Mohrenschildt is also contacted by an investigator from the House of Representative's Select Committee on Assassinations, which is looking into the Kennedy assassination. Within hours of getting that phone call, de Mohrenschildt kills himself."

"Oh my God," said Kelly, standing by the dishwasher. "That does look suspicious."

"And what's more, shortly after de Mohrenschildt commits suicide, his wife sends the House Committee her husband's unpublished memoir of his relationship with Oswald. The book is entitled, *I Am a Patsy,* which is what Oswald said when he was caught. And in the memoir, de Mohrenschildt suggests that Oswald was in fact a patsy and not the assassin."

"Now that's something. It sounds like de Mohrenschildt knew that Oswald didn't do it. But how would de Mohrenschildt know that unless he knew more than he told the Warren Commission."

"Exactly."

They were both silent for a few moments as Jim helped Kelly put the last of the dishes in the dishwasher. They both returned to the kitchen table and just looked at each other.

"So what do you think?" Kelly asked after a few minutes.

"I'm wondering whether your father knew de Mohrenschildt, or at least knew of him. And more than that, whether your father or one of the other conspirators used that connection in some way. Why else would your father have put de Mohrenschildt's name down as one of the clues? There has to be some connection here with the Kennedy assassination."

Kelly sat back on her chair and slowly drank the last of her wine.

"What'd this guy de Mohrenschildt look like anyway?"

"He was apparently a good-looking guy from all accounts. About six-two with dark blond hair, thick eyebrows, very athletic-looking, and apparently a charming demeanor. At least sometimes. At other times he acted very strangely. People reported seeing him and his wife riding around Dallas in a convertible in their bathing suits."

"That sounds more like California than Texas," said Kelly with a laugh.

"California or Texas, it doesn't sound like the behavior of a wealthy baron."

"So where do we go from here?"

As Kelly asked the question, an unexpected sound filtered through the screens on the open windows in the living room in the front of the house. Jim and Kelly stared at each other in silence. And waited. And then they heard another sound. The sound of someone walking carefully up the front steps—someone trying to make sure that no one heard the approach. Or so it seemed. Jim and Kelly continued to stare at each other and then stood up slowly. As they did, Kelly moved over to one of the kitchen drawers. She opened it up quietly and pulled out a large bread knife.

"Stay here," said Jim in a low voice.

Kelly watched in silence as he moved almost stealth-like toward the front door. He stood there, his hands in front of him, perhaps ready for combat, Kelly thought. They waited like that for a few seconds. And then they heard a loud knock on the door.

"Who's there?" Jim said forcefully.

"Montgomery County Police."

Jim moved over to the window, looked out, and saw the white Ford sedan with the Montgomery County emblem and supporting lights on the car's roof.

Jim opened the door, with Kelly right behind him, to find a tall police officer sporting a crew cut and a flashlight.

"Sorry to bother you," he said. "But I know about the break-in that occurred here last week, and we just had a report of a burglary not too far away. So I thought it might be worthwhile to just come by and make sure everything was okay here. I saw the lights on and thought that someone was up. I hope I didn't frighten you by knocking on the door so late."

Jim looked at Kelly, who was still holding the bread knife behind her back. "Not at all, Officer," he said. "But everything is fine."

"Very good. Just make sure to keep all your doors locked and those floodlights on."

The policeman then returned to his car, and Jim closed the door. As he turned around, his eyes caught Kelly's. He instinctively put his hands on Kelly's waist and tried to draw her close. But as he leaned over to kiss her, he could feel her body become tense.

"Please, Jim," she said with lowered eyes. "I can't do this. Not now."

She then picked up her head and locked eyes with him.

"I'm sorry. I just think we should call it a day."

There was a long pause as they looked at each other. Kelly broke the silence.

"I've already set up Jeff's old room on the first floor for you. I hope that's okay."

Jim wanted to talk to Kelly. Had he been too aggressive? Or was she still feeling the aftermath of some terrible experience? He wasn't sure, but he knew there would be no conversation about it. At least not now. So he said goodnight, picked up his suit bag, and walked to the bedroom. Kelly watched for a moment and then walked up the stairs.

CHAPTER 21

"Here's your morning mail, Caleb. There's a few Federal Express packages, including one from Barrington and Stone."

Caleb Butler finished taking a sip of coffee and placed his coffee mug on the coaster on the right-hand corner of his desk. He then took the mail from his secretary and pulled out the letter from Barrington and Stone.

"Thank you much, Laci."

As the secretary left his office, Butler put on his glasses and read the two-page letter. He then pushed a button on his phone. Laci answered immediately.

"Could you please ask George Kruger to come to my office?"

When Kruger walked into Butler's office, the senior attorney handed him the two-page letter.

"See what you think of this."

Kruger took the letter and looked up at Butler after he finished reading it.

"Not entirely a surprise. We knew they might say that Jeff had to know that private tent safaris are inherently dangerous and that they should not be liable for his death."

"No," Butler replied in his slow drawl. "There's no surprise in that. But I did harbor some hope that Barrington and Stone would recognize that the company had some obligation to advise its clientele of the risks that they're now so willing to acknowledge. And then there's the question of the armed guides that they claim were guarding the camp all night long."

"What do you mean?"

Butler leaned back in his chair, his eyes narrowed in concentration.

"I've been thinking about it, and I'm more than a little curious to know where those armed guides were when the lion attacked. If there were armed guards around all night, why didn't they see it coming and stop it? They apparently materialized the instant *after* the lion attack occurred. Shouldn't they have seen it *before* it occurred?"

"What're you saying, Caleb? You think this attack was planned and that the guides let it happen?" Kruger folded his arms in front of his chest and looked at the senior attorney. "I don't get it. Why would anyone want to see Jeff Roberts killed?"

"I don't know. But something in my gut tells me something is missing here. I can't put my finger on it, but something doesn't smell right."

"So what do we do about it? File the complaint?"

Butler got up from his chair and walked over to the large window and stared at the Capitol, which was resplendent in the bright sunlight.

"I'm not sure," he said, turning back to face his younger colleague. "Maybe there's a quicker way to do this."

"What did you have in mind?"

"I thought I would call Barrington and Stone and suggest that we take a few depositions before filing the complaint."

"Take depositions *before* filing the complaint?" Kruger asked, the skepticism evident in his voice. "That's a little unusual, don't you think?"

"Absolutely. But there's no reason we can't be a little creative here. I am sure Kelly would not like to be re-living her brother's death over and over again for years while the lawsuit drags on. We've got to find some way to accelerate the process. If we take depositions now, maybe we'll get some information on where those guards were when the attack occurred. Maybe we can demonstrate they were negligent in not providing that protection. Or maybe we will find something more sinister. After all," he continued, "people are not always what they seem to be. To us, Jeff Roberts was a great guy and a terrific lawyer. But who knows? Maybe he was involved in some drug activity. Or maybe he made somebody angry enough to kill him. Depositions may give us a little window into knowing where the guards were and why they didn't provide the protection they promised."

"But why would Barrington and Stone agree to depositions at this point?"

"To avoid a lawsuit. We tell him we're going to file the lawsuit in any case, and maybe this will give us an opportunity to explore settlement before anyone has to confront the cost—and publicity—of a lawsuit. And make no mistake about it, George. We would make sure it received a lot of publicity."

"So whose depositions should be taken at this point?"

"Nicole Landow for one. After our meeting with her, I am convinced that her testimony would prove detrimental to the continued success of Barrington and Stone. Many people, I'm sure, would think twice about signing up for the tent safari after listening to her recitation of events. And then of course I'd like to take the deposition of that lead safari guide. Remington. I think that's his name." Butler looked over at Kruger. "What's your take on that strategy, George?"

"It certainly is creative. But what about documents? Wouldn't it be necessary to get documents from Barrington and Stone to make the depositions effective? I for one would be very interested in knowing whether they've had any lawsuits or other claims made against them. We can check Lexis or Westlaw, but those services may not have any record of claims or lawsuits that were settled before they reached the point of decision."

"Excellent point. We'll ask for some documents. They may resist that in the absence of a formal lawsuit, but it's worth a shot."

"In any case, I'm game," said Kruger. "Give him a call."

"Good. I'll call Kelly and advise her of our strategy. Assuming she agrees, I'll call Barrington and Stone immediately. And there's one other thing I think I may do."

"And that is…?"

"Call Jerry Kraft."

"The private investigator we used on the Swanson murder case?"

"The one and the same. I'm going to ask him to nose around and see what he can find out about Jeff Roberts. Kraft used to work on the Metropolitan Police Department, and he can keep his ear to the ground without much effort. And who knows? If Jeff Roberts was in some kind of trouble, Kelly may be facing some kind of risk as well."

Kruger nodded in agreement, and Butler picked up the phone to call Kelly.

Chapter 22

Dwayne Soggs sat at his desk in the second district headquarters of the Metropolitan Police in Washington, DC's northwest section and picked up the autopsy report that the chief medical examiner had prepared on Winthrop Ashford Stamford. Soggs lit a Marlboro and took a long drag. Quitting was certainly the right thing to do, but that first cigarette of the morning sure did taste good. Maybe he could limit his smoking to the morning hours.

Soggs leafed through the eleven-page report with its diagrams and medical terms. Having reviewed hundreds of autopsy reports, he knew how to read them quickly—and well. Over the years he had learned to concentrate on command, blocking out the sounds of other police officers, criminals, and visitors who often created a constant din.

Soggs put the report down, crushed out his cigarette, and picked up the phone. After several rings, he heard the receptionist announce the District of Columbia's Office of the Chief Medical Examiner.

"George Nogasaki, please. This is Dwayne Soggs."

After a few minutes, Soggs heard Nogasaki's familiar voice.

"What's up, Dwayne? I bet you're calling about that Stamford report."

"You always were a mind reader, George."

"I pride myself in having many talents. A man has to find some outlet other than cutting up cadavers."

"I'm not sure you did such a good job cutting up this one. What the fuck am I supposed to make of this report?"

"I don't know," said Nogasaki in a more serious tone. "It's a little puzzling."

"Puzzling ain't the right word. According to this report, the guy was in almost perfect health and should be out on some tennis court instead of in the morgue."

"I know, I know."

"You mean you don't have a clue as to how he died?"

"None whatsoever. He's got the normal hardening of the arteries for a man of his age, but nothing that would've killed him. Everything else came up negative. Nothing toxic in the blood. No external abrasions or trauma of sufficient magnitude to indicate foul play, and nothing internal to suggest that something in his body stopped working. I just don't know what happened here," the examiner repeated.

"Well, we do know that he died. And while I'm no doctor, I've got to believe there was some cause."

"That's a fair assumption."

"We've got to find that cause, George. We've got to find it. There was no forced entry or other signs of burglary at his condo. That doesn't mean the guy wasn't assaulted, but I can't rule that out unless I know he died of natural causes."

"I'll give it some more thought, but sometimes God works in mysterious ways."

"Let's not interject religion into this. Just find out how he died."

"I'll give it my best shot, Dwayne. That much I can promise."

"Okay. I'll talk to you later."

Soggs hung up and looked at the report again. There was something unsettling about Stamford's death, and he meant to find out what it was. He hated loose ends.

CHAPTER 23

Jim was lying on the couch in his condominium watching Denzel Washington in *Training Day* for probably the tenth time, drinking a beer, and feeling very relaxed. He enjoyed these evenings after a long day of work, and there was no better reward than a couple of hours watching a good movie. As much as he liked government and politics, he could see the joys of being involved in the movie business. It generated excitement and fun. Maybe he could switch careers and become a screenwriter. It wouldn't be easy, though. His older brother Jason had banged around the Hollywood scene for years and often recounted the obstacles facing would-be screenwriters. The competition was fierce, said Jason. Everyone in Los Angeles wanted to be a screenwriter, and everyone had a script. Even the attendant at the gas station had a script he wanted to peddle.

The ring of the telephone interrupted Jim's meandering.

"Hi, Jim."

Kelly's voice sounded troubled.

"What's up?"

"I'm not sure. I talked to the police detective about Bud this afternoon. They still don't know what killed him. He said Bud appeared to be in good health. He wouldn't tell me what he thought, but it's pretty obvious the detective thinks there's a possibility Bud was murdered."

"So what now? Are they going to conduct some kind of investigation?"

"I guess so. But that's not why I called. I finally hooked up with Teasdale."

"I guess that's good," Jim said with obvious reservations. "But I confess that I had hoped that he might have disappeared into the night."

"No such luck. He's apparently alive and well, and I made an appointment to see him tomorrow afternoon at his office. I was hoping you could meet me there."

"What time and where?"

"Three o'clock. He's got a consulting business on Jefferson Place. Do you know where that is?"

"Sure. It's one of the best little streets in town. Why don't I meet you at the corner of Connecticut and Jefferson a little before three."

"Great. I really do appreciate your helping me out."

"Don't be ridiculous. We're in this together. But more importantly, what did you tell Teasdale? Why does he think you want to see him?"

"Just like we discussed. I said I'm trying to learn more about my father and what he did in his career, and that Bud had suggested I call him."

"Good."

"So I'll see you tomorrow."

"Great. Kelly…"

Jim's voice trailed off. He wanted to say something more to keep Kelly on the line but the words just wouldn't leave his lips.

"What?"

"Nothing. I'll see you tomorrow."

Chapter 24

Kelly was waiting for Jim at the designated corner when he got out of the cab the following afternoon. As they walked down Jefferson Place, Kelly understood why Jim had called it one of Washington's best streets. In contrast to the major avenues that adjoined it in the city's Northwest quadrant—all with large and often modern office buildings—Jefferson Place, a narrow thoroughfare of one short block, consisted primarily of small three- and four-story townhouses with shutters and wrought-iron stairwells, all of which were bordered by tall trees. The street had charm and a sense of intimacy.

"You certainly know your streets," she remarked.

"Hey, after all these years in Washington, you're bound to learn something."

They stopped at a white townhouse with black shutters midway down the street and walked up the stairs. A brass plaque to the side of the front door identified the building as the offices for Global Consulting Group. Kelly pressed the front door bell and a buzzer released the lock so that they could enter through the narrow hallway and into the front room, which operated as a reception area. A middle-aged woman with short gray hair looked up from her seat at the desk and asked if she could help. Kelly explained that she had a three o'clock appointment with Mr. Teasdale. The receptionist picked up the phone, pushed some buttons, and talked to someone in an inaudible whisper.

"He's ready for you now," she said to Jim and Kelly as she hung up the phone.

The receptionist then led Jim and Kelly up a narrow stairway to the second floor and into an expansive office with a large bay window that overlooked Jefferson Place. A brown leather couch occupied an adjoining wall, and two oak chairs were arranged in front of a very large black desk framed by an American flag on one side and a blue flag on the other side that neither Kelly nor Jim recognized. The desk dominated the room, which had innumerable photographs, documents, and other memorabilia covering the walls.

Harvey Teasdale put down his reading glasses and walked from behind the desk to greet Kelly and Jim. His closely cropped hair was turning gray, but he gave the impression of being very fit. Jim guessed that Teasdale looked years younger than he actually was.

"Welcome," said Teasdale with a smile and an extended right hand. After they exchanged greetings, Teasdale turned to Kelly.

"I'm so glad to see you again after all these years. I was a great fan of your father's, and I remember seeing you many years ago when you were a small girl and the light of his life. I'm sure he must have been very proud of the woman you've become."

He then turned to Jim.

"Kelly tells me you're working for Senator Gimble." As Jim nodded, Teasdale continued, "Good man, Gimble. One of the few people on the Hill with some integrity. So that must be a good experience for you."

"It certainly is. But I have to say that I'm intrigued by the photos and documents you have on the walls. It looks like you've had some good experiences as well."

"Indeed I have. And if you're a history buff, you may find some of them to be rather interesting."

Teasdale then walked the two of them around the office, providing some history and identifying the people in the photos. Many figures were easily recognized. John Kennedy. Richard Nixon. Barry Goldwater. Lyndon Johnson. But the photograph that caught Jim and Kelly's attention was the one showing Teasdale and Kelly's father. The two men, dressed in casual clothes and looking much younger, had their arms around each other.

"Where was this taken?" Kelly asked Teasdale.

"That was when your father and I were involved in a project in the Caribbean. It was many years ago." He then paused as if trying to recall the moment. "More than I care to remember."

Jim looked at the photograph closely. Ted Roberts was a handsome man. A little taller than Teasdale with an angular face and short dark hair. But Jim was drawn most of all to the smile. A radiant smile. The smile of a confident man, someone who enjoyed life and could master its changing fortunes.

"So what brings you to Jefferson Place?" Teasdale said to Kelly as they returned to their seats. "You had mentioned trying to learn something more about your father's career."

Kelly paused for a moment, caught in the grip of nagging uncertainty. She was already beginning to wonder whether they had made a mistake in coming to see Teasdale. Was he truly a good friend of her father's? Or another conspirator—and perhaps one of the participants who represented the danger that had so concerned her father? Whatever her doubts, it was too late now. She had to play out the hand.

"Well, Jim and I were going through some old family pictures and letters, and he kept asking questions about my father that I couldn't answer. It made me realize how little I know about what he actually did in government."

"That doesn't surprise me at all," said Teasdale. "Your father tried very hard to keep his professional life separate from his family life. And beyond that, he spent a good part of his career working for or with the CIA, and years ago people working at the CIA were very secretive about their employment, much more so than today. Unless of course you're in the intelligence business. Which is to say spies. Those people are still pretty secretive."

"I thought my father was a case officer, or something like that, in his early days."

"He was,"said Teasdale. "But he did work with other people in government who were in the undercover business."

Jim decided to jump into the conversation. He had to know more about how Ted Roberts had moved up the ladder of government service. Something in that progression might hold the key to what he did later.

"Kelly's house has a lot of pictures of her father with Bobby Kennedy and other government leaders who were not in the CIA. How would he have gotten to know all those people, especially at such a young age?"

"Ted Roberts was an extraordinary guy. People were very attracted to him. He was not only brilliant but also had an engaging personality, and people, even people in lofty positions, were drawn to him. So Ted found himself involved in some very high profile projects that brought him into close contact with decision-makers at the highest levels of government—including the President of the United States."

"You mean Eisenhower?" Jim asked.

"Yes. Ted spent a fair amount of time in the White House in the closing days of the Eisenhower administration. But he was also seen as a rising star in the Kennedy administration as well."

"How'd he engineer that?" Jim asked. "It's not like Eisenhower and Kennedy were close."

"Not at all. But one of the people Ted impressed at the very beginning of his career was Richard Bissell, the deputy director of the CIA. President Kennedy regarded Bissell as one of the brightest people he knew in government. So it was only natural for Ted to stay immersed in those high-profile projects."

As he finished, Teasdale's secretary brought him some coffee, with the steam rising from the cup. Jim and Kelly deflected the secretary's inquiry as to whether they wanted anything to drink. Kelly shifted in her chair. Although still nervous about the decision to see Teasdale, she wanted, really needed, to learn more about her father—or at least whatever Teasdale would acknowledge knowing.

"Is there anything you can tell us about those high-profile projects my father worked on?"

"There were many," said Teasdale as he sipped the hot coffee. "One was the crisis over the Berlin wall in 1961. Another was Laos and our policy in Southeast Asia. And, of course, your father was very much involved in our policy toward Cuba, and there were few matters in the late 1950s and early 1960s that were viewed as more important. I'm not saying that your father was running the show, but he was often at the elbow of the people who were."

"When you say Cuba policy," Jim asked, "does that include the Bay of Pigs fiasco?"

"Yes, it does. Ted and I periodically went to Guatemala to oversee the training of the Cuban refugees who formed the invading brigade. As a matter of fact, that picture we looked at a few minutes ago was taken in Guatemala in early 1961. It was an incredible experience. It was hot, it was uncomfortable, it was arduous. But we were part of a mission," Teasdale said with conviction, "and we believed our sacrifice was more than justified by our goals. It was all part of that 'can do' spirit that John Kennedy had inspired in all of us by his inaugural address. But things turned out quite differently than we had anticipated."

Kelly got up and walked over to the photograph of Teasdale and her father in Guatemala. Jim and Teasdale watched in silence. When she turned around, she had, at least so Jim thought, a wistful look on her face.

"I confess," she said, "that my history background is not what it should be. Tell me again about that Bay of Pigs invasion"

Jim could not resist the opportunity to respond.

"That was the invasion of Cuba that took place in April 1961. The planning for the invasion actually began in the Eisenhower administration. But Kennedy remained committed to it after he was inaugurated in January 1961. The invading force consisted of Cuban exiles trained and armed by the United States. It was supposed to lead to an uprising in Cuba that would result in Fidel Castro's ouster, but at the last minute President Kennedy called off American air support that was deemed critical, and all the invaders were either killed or captured."

"Precisely," said Teasdale.

"You must have been very disappointed when Kennedy called off the air strikes," Jim said to Teasdale, who had turned slightly in his chair and was now staring out the large window behind his desk.

It is April 1961, and he is leaning on the rail at the stern of the large transport ship, his mind mesmerized by the gentle roll of the waves of the Caribbean waters off the southern coast of Cuba. They have been on the ship for several days, all in the hope, even expectation, that they would witness the long-planned invasion and the restoration of democracy in Cuba. He looks down at his watch. It is almost two-thirty in the morning. The sky is black and aglow with stars.

"Harvey, Harvey." The words ring out clearly in the stillness of the night.

He picks up his head. Ted Roberts, wearing a troubled expression, is walking, almost trotting, hurriedly down the passageway.

"Harvey, Harvey," Roberts repeats as he nears his colleague. "I just got a call from Dick."

He did not have to ask who Dick was. Roberts was referring to Richard Bissell, the CIA deputy director, the Company man with oversight responsibility for the invasion.

He focuses on Roberts's face. It is filled with disappointment.

"Oh, no. Don't give me any bad news," he says. "We can't afford any fuck-ups at this point."

"It's too late, Harv. The president's canceled the air strikes."

He is almost numb with fatigue from the grueling hours and the unyielding tension. He cannot respond immediately. But he can already feel the pit-in-the stomach sensation when you know that your worst fears have materialized. Without the air strikes, the invasion is doomed.

"I don't understand," is all he musters at this point. "I just don't understand."

Roberts paces around him, obviously filled with anger and resentment.

"Dick said he got a call from Rusk a few hours ago," Roberts snaps, referring to Kennedy's secretary of state. "Rusk asked him to come to the State Department, where he told him that he had recommended to the president that the air strikes be canceled. Says it would be bad politics. The president agreed. Can you believe that? After all this, the president agreed."

He finally explodes.

"God fucking dammit. Don't they get it? They're throwing those men and this whole thing to the wolves if they cancel that air support. Didn't Bissell tell the president that?"

Roberts stops pacing and slowly shakes his head.

"Dick said that Rusk offered to let him talk to the president directly and plead our case."

"And...?"

"Dick said it wasn't necessary. He thought it was hopeless. So he never told the president that he disagreed with Rusk."

"Oh my God," he moans, looking up at the endless darkness. "How could the president do this to us? How could he sell us down the river? What kind of gutless leader do we have?"

Teasdale turned back to the young visitor sitting across from him.

"You could say," he finally said in response to Jim's question, "that we were greatly disappointed with the president's decision to cancel the air strikes."

As Teasdale recounted his disappointment, Kelly instantly recalled the comments in her father's note that Kennedy had been killed to protect the country's survival. Was the Bay of Pigs an isolated situation or the tip of the iceberg for Teasdale? Kelly had to know. The answer might indicate whether he was a conspirator and not a friend.

"What else did President Kennedy do—or not do—that bothered you and my dad?"

Teasdale leaned back in his chair and titled his head toward the ceiling, recalling other moments of that long-ago time.

"It's hard to remember all the details. We're talking of things that happened decades ago. But neither Ted nor I were happy with Kennedy's handling of the Cuban missile crisis in October 1962. Kennedy knew that the Russians had lied to him about the offensive nature of the missiles in Cuba and then let them off the hook. Then—knowing full well the Russians' incurable habit of lying—Kennedy signed a test ban treaty in 1963 that, in our view at least, seemed to neutralize the advantage America had in the nuclear arms race. And, if that wasn't enough, when the Russians couldn't grow enough wheat to feed their vast population in the fall of 1963, Kennedy stepped in and sold them wheat to help them camouflage the failures of their system."

As Teasdale finished, Kelly pulled a small piece of paper from her pocketbook and handed it to Teasdale. She was going for broke now.

"I don't mean to change the subject, but I saw this series of ten letters written on one of my father's papers," she explained with reference to her father's letter about the Kennedy assassination. "Do you know what they represent or stand for?"

Teasdale took the paper and studied the letters. He then read them aloud: "P-O-A-T-R-W-J-W-T-J." He shook his head and handed the paper back to Kelly.

"I have no idea what those letters mean. They don't appear to be anything I recognize."

"What about a man named George de Mohrenschildt?" Kelly asked. "His name popped up in some of my father's papers as well."

Jim and Kelly watched Teasdale closely to see if there was any sign of recognition. But Teasdale just stared blankly at Kelly.

"That doesn't sound familiar either. How are you spelling that?"

"D-e-M-o-h-r-e-n-s-c-h-i-l-d-t."

Teasdale shook his head again.

"No, I'm sorry. I don't know the gentleman."

"What about the number 5412?" Kelly asked. "Does that have any significance to you?"

"Yes, it does."

Jim and Kelly sat up.

"Ironically, it ties in with our earlier discussion about Kennedy. The 5412 Committee was created in 1955 by Eisenhower as a vehicle to help plan and oversee covert actions by the CIA."

"That certainly is an odd name for a committee," said Jim.

"Not entirely. The committee was authorized by a National Security Council directive that had the number 5412. So it was only natural to identify the committee by that NSC directive number. But the committee was often referred to inside the CIA as the Special Group. It included representatives of the State Department, the Defense Department, and the CIA. Although the committee went through various reorganizations during the years, it basically remained intact through the early part of the Kennedy administration and was a principal vehicle for the planning of the Bay of Pigs invasion."

"Did any of this have anything to do with my father?" Kelly chimed in.

"It did. He was very much involved with the Special Group's activities. And that's how Ted got to know Bobby Kennedy. Bobby was the president's alter ego, and he took a great interest in looking out for his brother, especially in intelligence matters after the Bay of Pigs fiasco. Both of the Kennedys thought the CIA and the Special Group had failed to provide accurate intelligence about the true state of affairs in Cuba."

"You would've thought," Jim ruminated, "that all that contact in those troubled times would have drawn Mr. Roberts closer to the Kennedys and not created any ill feelings."

"You've no doubt heard that old saying, 'familiarity breeds contempt?' In this case, we could see firsthand, close-up, how disappointing the Kennedys were in making executive decisions. Their rhetoric was great, but it was quite another thing when it came to action."

As Teasdale finished his comment, the phone rang. There was a whispered conversation, and, after hanging up the phone, Teasdale folded his hands and placed them in front of him on the desk and looked at Jim and Kelly.

"I'd love to talk some more about what Ted and I did after the Kennedy administration, but unfortunately that was a client with an emergency that I must attend to. If it's all right with you, I would like to pick up our conversation at some later time. Would that be okay?"

"Sure," said Kelly. "We've already been here over an hour, and you've been very generous with your time. We can cover those other matters at a later time. There's no rush about any of this."

"I appreciate your understanding."

They all rose from their seats and walked toward the door. Teasdale shook Jim's hand and then took Kelly's hand in both of his and looked directly at her.

"No one was more saddened by your father's passing than me. We were great buddies. And I hope you find what you're looking for. But I do have a word of caution. I don't want to be presumptuous, and it's none of my business, but I can't help but get the feeling that you're looking for something specific, and, if you are, there's no need to tell me what it is. But please be careful. Your father and I worked in a world where people were not always kind to each other, and even now, bitter feelings may still persist."

Perhaps, Kelly said to herself, he is talking about himself. But she played dumb.

"You mean there are people out there who would have been interested in hurting my father?"

"I don't know. Maybe. But be careful who you talk to and who you think you can trust. And never assume that your conversations will be kept confidential. Even when you think you're alone, you may not be. Surveillance techniques are very sophisticated these days."

"Thanks for the words of caution," Kelly responded innocently. "I will take them to heart. And thanks again for all your time."

"Not at all. And if there's anything I can do, please call. There's nothing I wouldn't do for Ted Roberts's daughter."

As Jim and Kelly walked down the stairs, they gave each other a knowing glance. When they reached the landing on the stairs outside the townhouse, Jim expressed their common fear.

"Maybe Bud wasn't the only one who learned about your father's letter and what we were looking for that night we met him. And maybe we should give careful thought to whether we should continue this search. It may involve a much greater risk than we realize."

Chapter 25

Kelly leaned on the fence outside her barn and looked at Grant and the other horses grazing in the early evening sunset. A warm breeze drifted through the trees and took the edge off the high humidity. Everything seemed so tranquil.

Kelly loved these moments, and she thought back to how her father had loved them too. She remembered how, as a young girl, she had often found him outside by the fence in the early evening, staring intently at nothing, as though looking for something far away. When she found him, he would always pick her up and sit her on top of the fence. And when she asked what he was looking for, her father would invariably say with a big grin that he had already found what he was looking for and that it was right here.

Memories of her father triggered thoughts about the meeting with Teasdale earlier that afternoon. She had had second thoughts about going to see Teasdale and could not help wondering during the meeting whether he was friend or foe. But the more she thought about the meeting, the more she thought Teasdale was being sincere in expressing his affection for her father and his eagerness to help. Reaching that conclusion was made that much easier because Jim liked him, saying that Teasdale seemed more forthright than Bud. She didn't share Jim's suspicions about Bud, but she was now ready to agree with his view of Teasdale. Still, accepting Teasdale as a friend did not ease the mounting anxiety she continued to feel.

The shrill ring of her mobile phone interrupted Kelly's reverie. She picked the phone out of her nearby backpack and said hello.

"Hi, Kelly."

"Hey, Nicole. How are you? I've been meaning to call you these last couple of days, and somehow the time just kept getting away from me."

"Not to worry. We all have those problems. But I do need to talk to you again."

"Why? What's going on? Did you talk to Butler about the deposition?"

"I did. I called him shortly after we talked, and I've given a lot of thought to his proposal. I want to help you, Kelly, I really do, but I don't know if I can do this. It's too soon. I just don't know if I can handle some lawyer picking over the details of what happened."

"I certainly understand your reluctance. Is there any way Butler can do this with just Remington's deposition?"

There was a pause, and Kelly walked over to the shade of the barn, the mobile phone held tight against her ear.

"I'm not sure. If there's any chance of settling this before a complaint's filed, I can see where my testimony might be critical."

"Why? Do you think this Remington guy will lie about what happened?" Kelly asked as she sat down cross-legged against the open barn door.

"It's always possible. But even if Remington tells the truth, I can see where my deposition would be needed to convey the terror of that night. That's what sells to juries, and my guess is that Butler hopes it'll convince the safari company that settling the case is better than going to court."

"Listen, Nicole, I'd much prefer to talk about this in person. And besides, it would be great to see you again. What about getting together for dinner?"

"Sure. I'd always love to see you."

"How about tonight."

"Fine. Where?"

"Would you mind driving out from the District and meeting me at a restaurant out here. I know a great Italian place in Potomac Village."

"Okay."

"Meet me at Renato at eight o'clock. It's in Potomac Village tucked in a corner between the liquor store and the Starbucks."

"I'll see you there."

Kelly hung up the phone with a tremendous sense of guilt. She really did not want to do anything to hurt Nicole. But she didn't want the safari company to get away with murder either. She wondered what her father would've recommended. He always had a knack for solving knotty problems.

At least some problems. Because there was one knotty problem he could not solve—how do deal with his role in JFK's assassination. That lingered in her mind and now placed a cloud over everything she thought and everything she did. There was no escape.

It was, she decided, time to go for a ride. She stood up, walked into the barn, grabbed her saddle, and then returned to the pasture to find Grant.

CHAPTER 26

When Kelly got to the Village later that evening, she was already fifteen minutes late and worried about the raging thunderstorm that was moving through Potomac as she parked her Jeep in the expansive parking lot that sat between River Road and the Village stores and shops. The crack of thunder and the bolts of lightning seemed to be everywhere, and Kelly was frustrated that she could not find a spot close to the restaurant.

She parked near the gazebo at the edge of the parking lot that was used as a bus stop and bolted for shelter. As she ran toward the restaurant, Kelly pulled her wide-brimmed hat over her eyes and didn't see the man leaning against the wall under the covered area of a nearby Safeway.

Nicole and Kelly emerged from the restaurant shortly before eleven o'clock. The storm had passed and the sky was clear, with a full moon that illuminated puffy clouds moving quickly to the east. They hugged each other, waved good-bye, and moved in opposite directions toward their cars.

The large parking lot was now deserted except for a few cars and a few people standing in small groups by Renato and Flaps, the other nearby restaurant. All the vehicles that had surrounded her Jeep when Kelly had arrived hours earlier were now gone, and the Jeep sat alone, facing her as she walked away from the restaurant.

As she moved toward the Jeep, Kelly noticed that the parking lot light by the gazebo was out, shrouding the entire area in darkness. With the memory of the intruder at the house still fresh in her mind, Kelly started walking quickly, pulled out the remote key from her pocketbook, and punched the "unlock" button. She heard the Jeep doors unlock and immediately felt more secure.

As she moved to open the driver's side door, Kelly was surprised by a shout from across the parking lot. She looked up and saw a man standing about seventy-five yards away by a large black sport-utility vehicle and waving his arm. Kelly was not about to wait to hear what the man had to say. She quickly got into the Jeep, pulled the door closed, pushed the automatic lock button, and turned the ignition on in what seemed like record speed. She then turned the Jeep around quickly, almost causing the vehicle to tilt on its side. When she felt the Jeep stabilize, Kelly pushed the gas pedal down hard to move quickly onto River Road and toward her house.

There were no cars traveling in either direction as Kelly drove through the green traffic light in the center of the Village and past the deserted gas stations on either side. She felt secure in the Jeep, and she could feel the tension ease as the vehicle moved quietly in the darkness down the familiar curves of River Road.

Kelly hadn't gone more than a mile when she noticed in the rear-view mirror that another vehicle was speeding down River Road and closing in on her very quickly. She pushed her foot down harder on the gas pedal and kept glancing up at the rear-view mirror.

Within seconds Kelly could discern the outlines of the large black sport-utility vehicle she had seen in the Village. She could feel her body tense and her heartbeat accelerate. She tightened her grip on the steering wheel and drove faster.

The black SUV was now tailgating her.

What could she do? Her mind raced over the options and settled on the obvious one. She would call the police. Kelly looked at the car phone sitting in its cradle to her lower right. The familiar READY in the window display was not present to signify that the phone was operational. She punched the power button but nothing happened. She punched it again, harder, with similar results.

She was now getting nearer to the driveway of her house, but she did not dare make the turn. There was no one there to help her, and she couldn't escape this time on Grant. What could she do?

The black SUV was now bumping her slightly and flashing its brights on and off.

Oh my God, Kelly thought. This guy is brazen.

Her only hope was to find a house with lights on, turn into the driveway, honk her horn, and hope that someone would come out and frighten her stalker away.

The plan sounded simple, but execution would be difficult. She was now traveling more than sixty miles an hour on a winding, hilly road. Making sharp turns, especially in the Jeep, would not be easy.

She focused her mind on the streets that lay ahead and the ones that would provide the easiest turns. Before she could sort through the logistics, she saw a familiar street fast approaching. It was a long street with new houses. She instinctively turned sharply to the right. The Jeep tilted slightly on its side but quickly stabilized.

The black SUV matched her turn and caught up quickly. It was now honking its horn.

This guy, Kelly thought, is really crazed.

Her Jeep charged up the winding road. Although she wanted to stay calm, Kelly was feeling frantic. Her palms, still gripped tightly around the steering wheel, were moist, and she could feel beads of sweat gathering on her forehead.

Kelly saw the lights in a house about fifty yards down a side street on the right. She went to make a sharp right-hand turn, but on the rain-slicked road the Jeep made a U-turn and sped down a hill on the left side and into the muddy entrance of an abandoned barn.

She jammed on the brakes hard. The Jeep twisted in the mud and stalled. She turned the ignition key to restart the engine, but all she heard was the sputtering sound of a choking engine. She tried again without success.

The black SUV had driven to the top of the barn entrance with its bright lights on. As Kelly was frantically trying to restart the engine, she saw the man get out of the SUV. He was tall and dressed in jeans and a denim shirt. None of that was of any significance. Kelly's attention was instead focused on the large handgun that the man held in his two hands and had pointed directly at her.

"Get out of the Jeep," he yelled. "Get out of the Jeep now!"

I'm not going to let it end like this, Kelly kept telling herself. I won't let it end like this. I have to think of something.

She sat there, frozen in the unreality of the moment. What choices did she have? Could she just sit there in her locked Jeep? Getting out was almost certain death. Maybe she could talk to the guy with the gun and promise not to pursue the Kennedy assassination. She was a woman, after all. Maybe she could charm him into changing his mind about killing her. Oh God, she chided herself. Don't be ridiculous.

The man's loud and gravelly voice brought Kelly back to the cold reality that confronted her.

"Get out of the Jeep *now*! Don't fuck with me!"

She slowly opened the door, stepped into the mud, and turned to face her tormentor. She started to speak, but the man cut her off quickly.

"Get over to the side and move away from the Jeep," he commanded in a soothing voice that startled Kelly. Bewildered, Kelly did as she was told and saw that the man continued to point the handgun at her Jeep.

His voice took on a more sinister tone when he spoke again.

"Get out of the goddamn car now or I'll blow your fucking brains out."

Kelly almost fell over backward as she saw the hatch at the back of her Jeep slowly open and a man gingerly step out.

"Get your hands up and don't move," the gunman ordered the new arrival.

The gunman then looked at Kelly and, with a nod of his head, directed her to move to the top of the hill and get behind him. Kelly did as she was told and took a closer look at the man who had just emerged from her Jeep. He was dressed in a black T-shirt and black pants. He had short dark hair and a full dark mustache.

"I saw this man slip into the back of your Jeep right before you got in," the gunman explained, "and that's why I yelled at you in the parking lot. I could tell that you were totally unaware of what was happening, but it was clear that this creep," he said with a wave of the handgun toward the man with the outstretched hands, "was up to no good. That's why I kept following you. I was trying to get you to stop."

"Thank God for the mud," said Kelly with a sigh of relief. "I never would've believed it."

The gunman turned his attention to the man dressed in black.

"What's your name?"

"None of your fuckin' business."

"That's an unusual name," said the gunman. He turned to Kelly. "Go down to the house with the lights on and call the police. I'll keep this guy company."

"Wait," said the man dressed in black. "There's been a terrible misunderstanding. Don't get the police. I need to show you something."

The man then lowered his right hand as though he were going to pull something from his pants pocket, but before Kelly realized what was happening, the man snapped his right arm upward and a stiletto knife was flying through the air directly at the gunman. He deftly dodged the flying knife and simultaneously fired the handgun with a resounding flash and a loud clap that echoed in the stillness of the night.

The man in black fell backward on the ground and lay motionless.

The gunman turned to Kelly.

"I don't think he'll bother you anymore—or anyone else. I never miss."

"What do you mean, 'you never miss'?" Kelly yelled at him in shock. "Do you often go around killing people?"

"No. But I am a Montgomery County policeman, and we're trained for this kind of situation."

"I don't understand. Where's your uniform?"

"I don't work all the time, you know. I had just eaten at Flaps and was getting ready to return home when I saw you. Fortunately for you, I had my gun in the car."

The gunman then extended his right hand to Kelly.

"Bill Vecchio at your service."

He paused for a few seconds and looked into Kelly's eyes. "And your name is?"

"Kelly. Kelly Roberts."

"Well, Ms. Roberts, I guess tonight was your lucky night."

Within half an hour, the area was flooded with Montgomery County Police cars, both marked and unmarked, as well as an ambulance. The flashing red and blue lights, coupled with the bright headlights of the various vehicles, gave the muddy and previously desolate barn entrance the surreal appearance of an amusement park. As the ambulance attendants rolled the body into the ambulance, a heavy-set, balding man in a dark, rumpled suit approached Kelly and Vecchio, who were standing off to the side. As the man came closer, he could see that Kelly was trembling and staring off into space, obviously trying to cope with the reality that someone had again tried to do her harm.

The heavy-set man seemed to recognize Vecchio and gave him a knowing nod. He then turned his attention to Kelly.

"My name is Detective Hanson," he said in a low monotone. "Montgomery County Police Homicide Division."

Detective Hanson took out a small spiral pad and started reading from notes without looking at Kelly or Vecchio.

"Your friend over there is dead from a bullet through the heart," he said in a matter-of-fact manner. "Obviously a professional. No ID, nothing that would reveal his identity. He did have a thirty-eight handgun strapped around his ankle and a very sophisticated device on his right arm where he housed that knife. My guess is that he was around thirty, thirty-five."

He looked up at Kelly with inquisitive eyes.

"Any notion as to who he was or why he would want to hurt you?"

Kelly shook her head without saying anything.

Detective Hanson proceeded in his low-key manner.

"Our records show, Ms. Roberts, that you were assaulted, or chased at least, in your home not too long ago. Does the deceased bear any resemblance to that assailant?"

"I don't know," Kelly murmured. "I just don't know."

"Look," said Detective Hanson with obvious sympathy, "it's been a long night for you. Why don't I have one of the officers take you home and we can pursue this in a little more detail tomorrow when you're feeling more up to it. We'll also have someone tow your Jeep over to the gas station in the Village, and you can arrange to pick it up tomorrow."

"That would be great. I'd really appreciate that."

She turned to Vecchio and held out her hand.

"It's not often that I get a chance to see a policeman in action, let alone be saved by one. But thanks. I'll never forget it."

"Not at all. I'm glad I was there for you."

Vecchio nodded and smiled slightly at Kelly as a Montgomery County Police officer led her away to his patrol car.

Chapter 27

The digital clock radio showed that it was 1:33 A.M. when Jim heard his phone ring. At first he thought it was part of his dream, and then he realized that it was reality. He finally rolled over in his bed and jerked the phone off the hook.

"Hello," he mumbled, his eyes half shut.

"Jim. It's me."

"Kelly! What's wrong? Where are you? What's going on?"

"Oh, Jim. I've had the most horrendous experience tonight. Someone tried to kill me again."

"Holy shit! I can't believe this. What happened?"

"I want to tell you but not now. Can I ask a big favor?"

"Sure. Whatever you want."

"Can you come out to the house? I'm scared, and I don't want to be alone."

"I'm on my way."

Forty-five minutes later, Jim's Mazda Miata was careening into the driveway of Kelly's house at high speed. The car screeched to a stop in front of her porch. Jim jumped out and bounded up the steps to the front door. Kelly opened it just as he was about to knock. She was dressed in her long Warner Bros. T-shirt and still trembling from the experience. Before she could say anything, he instinctively wrapped his arms around her and held her tight. They stood like that in the open doorway for minutes without saying a word. Finally, Kelly released herself from Jim's grip, closed the door, and led him into the house.

She took him to her father's library, with its walls of books and memorabilia. The light from a single lamp gave the room a warm glow. They settled into the old and very comfortable leather couch that sat under a wall of framed photos.

Kelly retraced each event of the tumultuous evening, with Jim, ever the lawyer, peppering her with questions to garner all the details. When she had finally completed the story, he asked the obvious question.

"Do you think we should tell the police everything? I mean, about your father's letter and how there might be a connection between these two attempts? We're playing with fire here, and I don't know that you should be taking any more risks."

"I've thought about that, but I can't do it. Not yet at least. Because to tell the police would be to tell the world. And even if it removes me from danger, I would have to face the prospect of my father being exposed. And I don't know if that's fair to him, and I don't know whether I could deal with it myself, because even now I'm not sure exactly what it is he did. And then, of course, there's always the possibility that I could tell the police and it would only increase the danger that these people, whoever they are, would step up their efforts to kill me and squelch the whole thing."

Jim paused to think through the alternatives.

"What about going back to Teasdale?" he asked. "He seems pretty knowledgeable, and I think he really cares about you. But the bottom line is, I think we need some guidance from someone who knows about this world your father lived in."

"It's funny you mention Teasdale, because I've thought of him too. And I think maybe we should come clean with him. He may have some way of helping us figure out what my father did, or didn't do. And more than that, maybe he could tell me what to do, or not to do, to protect myself."

As she made that last comment, Kelly leaned back on the couch with her feet tucked underneath her buttocks. Jim could feel the excitement rise within him. And he began to sense that this could be the moment when they would connect. In some indefinable way, he felt they had crossed the barrier that had foiled his earlier attempt.

Kelly looked at Jim with soulful eyes.

"You've been wonderful," she said softly. "I don't know what I would've done without you."

"I don't know what I would do without *you.*"

She held out her hand for his. Jim looked at her intently with her eyes locked on his and her mouth half-opened. He took her hand gently in his and leaned over to kiss her, and as he did, she closed her eyes in anticipation.

It was then that the phone rang.

Jim and Kelly opened their eyes wide and stared at each other.

"Who could that be?" Jim asked blankly.

"I can't imagine."

Kelly picked up the cordless phone that was lying on the adjoining table.

"Hello." She then paused.

Jim could tell from her facial expression that it was something serious.

"Oh, I'm so, so sorry," Jim heard her say. She then turned to him and handed him the phone.

"It's your mother. She thought I might know where you are."

Jim put the phone to his ear.

"Hi, Mom. What's the matter?"

"Jimmy, I'm sorry to track you down like this, but I've called everywhere, and I need you."

"Is it Dad?" he asked anxiously.

"We almost lost him tonight," his mother continued with apparent exhaustion. "He got up in the middle of the night to get a glass of orange juice, like he always does, and he just collapsed. Thank God I was awake and heard him. I don't know what would've happened if the ambulance hadn't come right away. Anyway, he's in the hospital now, but it doesn't look good, Jimmy. It doesn't look good."

"Why? What are the doctors saying?"

"They said his arteries are almost completely blocked and that he could go at any time. They're amazed that he's lasted this long."

"I'm on my way now, Mom."

"Do you know where the hospital is?"

"Of course. I'll be there in three hours."

He hung up the phone and looked at Kelly.

"I can't believe this. I don't want to leave. But I can't let my father go. I've got to go see him. I hate to leave, but I've got to go." Tears started to well up in his eyes.

"Well, you're not going alone. There are two seats in your car, you know. And I sure as hell don't want to stay here alone."

"What about the police? You agreed to meet them tomorrow."

"I'll call them and postpone it. Nothing I can tell them tomorrow is going to change anything, and I can't believe a day or two would make a difference in anything."

Jim looked at Kelly and smiled.

Chapter 28

The man picked up the telephone in his well-furnished study in the Virginia countryside and punched in the number.

"Yes," said the voice at the other end of the line.

"Leonard's dead and we don't have the letter."

"You told me Leonard was a professional and that he would get it done."

"Nobody's perfect."

"In this game, we can't afford not to be perfect."

"It's only a temporary setback. In the meantime, the police have no idea who Leonard is. There's no way he can be traced to us. Or to anyone for that matter."

"You better hope that's true," said the voice. "For both our sakes. Anyway, what happens now?"

"Back to the drawing board. But nothing needs to be done right away. The girl hasn't figured anything out, and I doubt she'll go to the authorities."

There was a long pause. The silence was finally broken from the other end of the line.

"Like I said, you better hope that's true. And you've got to figure out some way to get that letter."

"Thanks for the suggestion," the caller responded sarcastically. "I'll keep you posted."

The caller placed the phone back in its cradle and stared at the darkness outside the window. He did not like to be in situations where he wasn't in control. And he resented Kelly Roberts for putting him in that situation.

Chapter 29

April 1998

Ted Roberts walked to his kitchen, made himself a cup of coffee, and then retreated to his library. He stood at the doorway in his jeans and work shirt, glanced out the cathedral window to the unrelenting rain, and turned to scan the room. He focused on the photographs on the walls. The people, the events, the different locales. All part of the story of his life.

He remembered when he first started his career in government in the 1950s. He thought the story of his life would be a good one. Something to be proud of. Something that would give him pleasure, and appropriate rewards, in his later years. And there was, to be sure, much of that. But there had been a turning point when things went sideways. Not that he realized it at the time. He was too young, too inexperienced, to appreciate the long-term consequences of what he was doing.

His thoughts drifted back to the meeting in Bruce Lord's Georgetown home on that evening in December 1962. He recalled parking his car sometime around nine o'clock and walking down the street with its gas lamps and colonial townhouses, most with red brick facades and shutters painted black or white. The snow had started to come down heavily, and he remembered how serene and pretty it all looked. A stark contrast with the somber mission of the meeting.

Lord's housekeeper ushered Ted into the dining room of the elegant but modestly furnished townhouse and closed the door behind him. Seven men were seated around the table. Ted knew all of them. He was the youngest one there. None of that troubled him, though. His position at the White House had given him a stature that far exceeded what might be expected of someone with his relatively short tenure.

Ted nodded greetings and sat down at the far end of the table. Several animated conversations were in progress, all being observed in silence by Bruce, who sat stone-faced at the other end of the table. A small, wiry man with thinning black hair,

Bruce exuded an explosive energy. His size belied a strong will and a talent for skullduggery that was almost legendary inside the Company.

After a short interlude, Bruce asked for everyone's attention and initiated the inquiry, as it later became known.

"We all know why we're here," he said solemnly. "We're all trained professionals and all dedicated to preserving our country's security. The question is whether we should take a back seat and sit idly by while the danger grows around us."

"I think," interjected one of the older men, "that we all recognize that our first duty is to our country, not to any particular man. But our president is our country's chief executive, and the law limits what we can, or cannot do, to fulfill our duty."

"Oh, come on, Jerry," said Dale with some annoyance. "We all know that the Company operates at a different level. There are all kinds of laws that don't apply to us. Wiretapping, break-ins, even assassination. If we worried about the laws that apply to everyone else, we could never do our jobs."

Dale's comment triggered a torrent of discussion, with several men speaking at the same time. Bruce allowed the discussion to proceed in its chaotic state for a few minutes and then held up his hand to restore order.

"Dale's observation is certainly true," he said. "The question is how far we can pursue that line of thinking. The president is no Hitler, but we all recognize, I hope, that we would have been well justified in eliminating Hitler if we had been part of Germany's intelligence service and in a position to take that action. At what point do we cross the threshold to do something here? How bad does it have to get before the need to act supercedes whatever restraints the law and common morality place on us? That's the essential question we have to address."

Ted Roberts settled back into the comfort of the leather chair in his library as he recalled Bruce's question. He remembered thinking at the time that the threshold for action was close at hand—if it had not already been surpassed. He had given much thought to the matter after his conversation with Dale in the White House mess, and he had come to the conclusion that they were sitting on the brink of a disaster.

Many of those seated at Bruce's dining room table agreed with Ted when he expressed that thought. The discussion proceeded aimlessly for another hour before they adjourned. It was agreed, however, that they would reconvene at Bruce's direction after the New Year to re-assess the matter. At that time, Bruce said, they would consider whether their concerns had been alleviated and, if not, what specific actions could or should be taken to remedy the situation.

Ted remembered walking back to his car in the soft snow that now covered the brick sidewalk. He felt good about himself. He was part of an elite corps of men who could control the country's destiny, men who would use that power to do good. It was a heady feeling.

Roberts took another sip of the hot coffee in his library and shook his head slightly. How arrogant he had been. If only he had known. If only…

Chapter 30

The morning sun was starting to pour through the hospital windows as Jim and Kelly walked toward the room where Jim's father had been placed. Although the room was part of the intensive care unit where visitors were strictly limited, the supervising nurse had disregarded the rules so that Jim could see his father.

As they approached the room, Jim and Kelly could see the door slightly ajar with rays of sunlight from the room illuminating the corridor at a sharp angle. Jim pushed the door open a little more and saw his mother sitting in a chair beside the bed where his father lay. His mother, her hands folded in her lap and looking exhausted, lifted her head as Jim and Kelly entered the room. She immediately rose from her chair and moved toward her son and grabbed both his hands.

"Oh, Jimmy, Jimmy, I'm so glad you're here."

"Come on," Kelly quietly implored her, "you need a break. Let's get you some breakfast and leave Jim with Mr. Roth."

As Kelly and his mother left the room, Jim sat down in his mother's chair and surveyed the scene. His father was propped up slightly on a pillow with tubes in his nose and tubes emanating from both of his arms. He looked thinner than the last time Jim had seen him, and his hair seemed to be whiter.

Jim touched his father's wrist, and the elder Roth immediately opened his eyes slightly and looked at his son.

"Jimmy. What the hell are you doing here?"

"Come on, Dad. Mom called, and I just wanted to be here with you."

"You know, Jimmy, I always love to see you, but under the circumstances it makes me feel a little bad. Like you're thinking I'm about to take a permanent leave of absence, and I promise you, that's not going to happen. At least not for a while."

"No, Dad, nothing like that. It's just that when you're sick, I want to be there. Just like you were always there for me when I was a kid."

"That's different. You were my son and you needed to be taken care of. I'm still your father and I'm doing just fine. My heart just had a little hiccup. But I'll recover."

"I know you will, Dad, but, still, I just wanted to come by and satisfy myself and know that you're okay. It's just that, Dad…"

Jim's voice trailed off. He wanted to tell his father how much he loved him, but the words got stuck in his throat. And it hit him that he always had a difficult time expressing his emotions, especially to his father.

"I know, I know," his father said. He paused, gently wrapped his hand around his son's wrist, and looked at Jim with obvious affection. "Outside of your mom, nothing's more important to me than you and Jason. If it were up to me, I'd have you back in New Jersey living in the house. But everything's going to be okay, Jimmy, so I'm going to take a little snooze and you go back to Washington. That senator you work for…"

"Gimble," Jim interrupted, "Geoffrey Gimble."

"Yeah, Gimble. He needs you more than I do right now, so you go back to Washington, and I'll let you know if I need your help."

As he finished, the elder Roth laughed, and Jim laughed too.

"You're the best, Dad."

With that, Jim got up from the chair and kissed his father on the forehead and squeezed his hand.

"You're the best, Dad," he repeated.

The drive back to Washington, DC the next morning was more relaxed—at least for Jim. He was glad to have seen his father and relieved that he seemed to be making progress. Although his condition was serious, the doctors assured Jim and his mother that he would recover and that it was unnecessary for Jason to come back from California.

Kelly was a different story. She had tried to push her anxieties aside and to focus on Jim's situation, but it was not easy. The trauma of the Jeep incident, coupled with everything else that had happened, had taken a toll. She was weary, scared, and exhausted—but still very determined. She would not, really could not, give up. Her father—and his memory—were too important.

Jim kept looking at Kelly through the corner of his eye as he drove. The blank look in her eyes said it all.

"Listen," he finally said after a long silence, "you can't go back to the house alone. I won't let you do that."

Kelly was not biting.

"Look, Jim, if someone wants to kill me, there's nowhere I can hide. Even if I stayed with you or at a hotel or with some friends like the Andrews, there would have to be times when I would be alone, times when I would go outside, times when I would be vulnerable. So I don't think there's any safe place to hide. Unless I want to give up my life and become a recluse somewhere. And I'm not prepared to do that. Besides, my guess is that the police will watch my house more closely and the conspirators, whoever they are, will probably be more cautious before trying something again in Potomac."

Jim persisted, saying that some protection and company was better than none. But Kelly could not be moved, and he realized again that she was going to have her way no matter what he said.

Chapter 31

Caleb Butler's intercom buzzed just as he was putting down his morning coffee.

"Yes, Laci."

"Kelly Roberts is on line one."

Butler punched in line one.

"Mornin', Kelly. How're y'all doin' today?"

"I'm just fine, Caleb. I was away in New Jersey for a couple of days, and I was calling to make sure the depositions were still on for this morning."

"Yes, indeed. Ten o'clock. Are you going to be able to make it?"

"I sure am. I'll be there a little before ten."

The large conference room at Chase and Blackhorn was crowded with people by the time Laci ushered Kelly into the room. Butler rose from his seat at the far end of the long table and moved toward Kelly. He did not know this young woman well, but he immediately sensed a change from the last time he had seen her. Fatigue? Anxiety? Or was it something she knew but didn't want to tell him? He was not sure, but something was different. He wanted to ask her what it was, but he knew this was not the time or place. So he pushed his inner thoughts aside and brought Kelly over to a group of men in suits of various shades of blue and gray.

"Hal," Butler said to a tall man in a navy blue double-breasted suit with white chalk lines and a red tie, "I'd like you to meet Kelly Roberts. Kelly, this is H. Cartwell McDonald, otherwise known as Hal, the general counsel of Barrington and Stone."

Kelly looked at McDonald closely. He looked the part of a British lawyer. Tall, relatively thin, gray hair combed straight back, a very straight nose, and other angular facial features. He might look elegant, Kelly said to herself, but that could not change who he really was. He was the enemy. And she was the avenger.

"Pleased to meet you, Ms. Roberts," McDonald said with an extended right hand. "I'm just sorry it had to be under these circumstances."

Kelly nodded impassively and made it clear she was not interested in small talk.

"And this," Butler continued, "is Darren Feldstone, Barrington and Stone's litigation counsel. Mr. Feldstone is a practitioner here in Washington, and I'm sure," Butler said with a wink at Feldstone, "that Darren is going to advise his client to do the right thing at the end of the day."

"No need to worry there, Caleb," said Feldstone, a small man in a gray suit with an intense glare. He turned to Kelly. "I always advise my client to do the right thing. It's just that there are many times when Caleb and I are on opposite sides, and he fails to appreciate what the right course of action really is."

Butler then walked Kelly around the room, introducing her to the other lawyers until she saw George Kruger. Butler's young associate smiled and said how glad he was to see her and, for some reason, that gesture made Kelly feel good.

After all the introductions and the small talk, Kelly moved to a chair along the wall behind Butler's leather chair at the table. The stenographer, an older woman with shoulder-length dyed brunette hair, sat in a straight-back chair immediately to Butler's left at the far end of the table. She had her fingertips on the stenography machine and appeared anxious to begin the depositions. Diagonally to her left and across the table from Butler was an empty chair, with Feldstone and McDonald seated immediately next to it.

As the other attorneys settled into their chairs, the room took on an eerie silence. Kelly could feel the tension that pervaded the room. But, for her, the tension was not simply a product of the litigation—it was the hope, and perhaps the fear, that the depositions might shed light on whether Jeff was the victim of something more sinister than a hungry lion.

Butler broke the silence.

"I think we should begin," he said in his slow drawl with his eyes moving across the row of adversaries on the other side of the table. "I also think it might be useful to put on the record why we are here today. We are going to take the depositions of Mike Remington and Nicole Landow. These depositions are being taken, for the moment at least, to see whether there are any grounds for settlement. But if no settlement is reached and a complaint is filed, these depositions can be used for any purpose that a deposition could be used in litigation." Butler then turned to Feldstone. "Do you want to add anything, Darren?"

"No. I think you've accurately characterized the state of affairs."

Feldstone then stood up and left the room, only to return moments later with Remington. Despite all the tension and anger that consumed her, Kelly almost started to laugh when she cast her eyes on Remington. She had never met a big-game hunter, but somehow she expected to see a handsome, debonair, and well-dressed man who exuded confidence. Remington was anything but well dressed and was clearly out of his element. He was wearing an ill-fitting dark green suit that was in desperate need of a pressing and a blue tie that was badly askew. He also seemed to lack the confidence that Kelly had anticipated. As he sat down in the chair across from Butler and next to the stenographer, Remington nodded at Kelly, but it was clear that he felt ill at ease and very much wanted to be somewhere other than in Caleb Butler's conference room.

The stenographer asked Remington to raise his right hand and to swear that he would tell the truth. As soon as Remington gave his affirmative response, Butler waited in silence for almost a minute before he commenced the interrogation. To Kelly, it appeared that Butler was trying to heighten the tension, and, if so, the ploy seemed to be working. Remington looked at Butler expectantly, rubbing his hands together on the table in front of him.

"Now, Mr. Remington," Butler began slowly, "tell me your address and your age."

"I'm thirty-four and live mostly on the plains of Kenya. But I do maintain an apartment in Nairobi."

"And what is your occupation?"

"I'm a guide for safaris sponsored by Barrington and Stone. Some of them are photographic safaris, and some are for hunting."

"Tell me something about your background. How'd you become a safari guide?"

"I was born in Cape Town, South Africa, and grew up there. I went to college for a short time at the University of Colorado, but I was not made for the academic life, and I left after a couple of years. I returned to South Africa and took on various jobs at the national parks there, Kruger and all that. Over time I migrated north to Kenya, again taking jobs with various outfits that conducted hunts or safaris."

"What kind of experiences have you had with lions in your hunting excursions?"

"Almost every client on a hunting safari wants a lion," Remington responded with mounting assurance. It was clear to Kelly that he was starting to relax and feeling more in his element as he talked about his life and his experiences. "And so," he continued, "I've been on dozens and dozens of safaris where we've tracked down and killed lions."

"Have you ever been involved in a situation where a lion attacked a human being?"

"Numerous times," said Remington without hesitation. "If you're close enough and they get your scent, a lion is as likely to charge as not. And I will tell you," he added with great deliberation, "those are heart-pounding moments when you're confronted by an animal of that size bearing down on you."

"We've been talking about hunters. What about people who aren't hunters? Prior to Jeff Roberts's death, had you experienced or were you aware of situations where lions had attacked people who were not hunters?"

"Absolutely. Africa's history is full of stories of man-eating lions."

"In fact," Butler interjected, "one of the more famous stories involves John Henry Patterson and the Tsavo lions. Correct?"

"That's right," Remington responded with a nod.

"And you mentioned that particular story to Jeff Roberts and Nicole Landow the night of Jeff Roberts's death, did you not?"

Remington was obviously starting to feel uncomfortable at the mention of Jeff Roberts's death. He hesitated a moment, and then replied, "I believe I did."

"And you knew then, did you not," Butler continued, his eyes locked on Remington's, "that man-eating lions continue to be a part of life in Kenya?"

Remington paused again and shifted uneasily in his chair.

"Yes. Yes, that's true."

"And you knew at the time of Jeff Roberts's death, didn't you, that a lion could attack someone asleep in a tent at night without provocation? That's true, isn't it?"

Remington looked down at the table and nodded his head.

"The stenographer can't record nods of the head," Butler chimed in after a few seconds. "You have to answer the question audibly. You knew about the possibility of a lion attacking a person sleeping in a tent, correct?"

"Yes."

"But you didn't tell that to Jeff Roberts or Nicole Landow, did you?"

"I'm not sure that's right. I did explain to them that lion attacks on people continued to be a part of the animal culture in Africa, that it was not a thing of the past."

"But you didn't tell them to be on their guard, did you?"

"I'm not sure I know what you mean," said Remington.

"Let me state it another way," said Butler, putting his elbows on the table and leaning forward in Remington's direction. "You assured them on the night of Jeff Roberts's death that there was nothing to worry about, that they had no reason to fear an attack by a lion. Isn't that true?"

"Yes, I do believe I said something like that to them."

"But that was a lie, wasn't it, Mr. Remington?"

"I object." Darren Feldstone's loud voice shattered the dialogue between Butler and Remington. "The witness should not be asked to characterize his answers. That's for you and me to argue about at a later time, Caleb. He's here just to tell you what he knows."

Butler watched Feldstone as he spoke but did not respond. Instead, he turned his attention back to Remington after Feldstone had finished speaking. His eyes narrowed. He was honing in on his target.

"It's also true, is it not, Mr. Remington, that someone could provoke a lion attack on another person?"

Remington gave Butler a puzzled look, but the attorney was not sure whether the hunter was truly baffled or just being disingenuous.

"Is there something about my question you don't understand, Mr. Remington?"

"I'm not sure. I don't understand what you're driving at."

"It's not for you to worry about what I'm driving at. Just answer the question."

Remington's lips tightened, and he looked at Butler with an intensity that surprised Kelly.

"Sure. There are things you can do to provoke an attack by a lion. But I don't have any reason to believe that this lion attack on Jeff Roberts was provoked. I think it was just one of those random acts of nature."

Butler sat in silence for a few seconds, pondering Remington's response.

"How can you be so sure that this attack was not provoked, Mr. Remington? It's possible that someone, maybe someone you never saw, did something to attract that lion to Jeff Roberts's tent. That is a possibility, is it not?"

"Yeah. I guess so. But I don't think that's what happened."

"Let me ask you this, Mr. Remington. In all of your experience in conducting photographic safaris for Barrington and Stone, had you ever witnessed or learned about a lion attacking one of the company's clients?"

"You mean when they were asleep?"

"Whenever. When they were asleep, when they were eating, when they were sitting in a chair watching the sunset or picking their nose. Whenever."

Remington's eyes started to blink rapidly, and it was clear that he was trying to decide how to respond to Butler's question. It looks like he's trying to be truthful, Kelly said to herself. Or was he trying to figure out how to hide the truth? As she thought about it in that instant, she was not sure.

After a minute, Butler broke the silence.

"Did you understand my question, Mr. Remington?"

"Yes, I understand the question. But no," Remington finally said. "I don't believe any of my clients on a safari has been attacked by a lion."

"Or any large cat?"

"No, or any large cat."

"But you knew at the time of Jeff Roberts's death, did you not, that lions are cunning creatures that can attack without warning?"

"Yes, every big-game hunter in Africa knows that."

"And you knew, didn't you, that, even without human provocation, there was a possibility of that happening while Jeff Roberts was sleeping in a tent on the African plains. Isn't that true?"

"Yes, if we're talking about possibilities," Remington shot back with unexpected anger. "But we did take precautions. We had large campfires around the tent area, and we had people with rifles who kept a watch all through the night."

Butler waited a few seconds to let Remington's anger subside. And then the Kentucky lawyer started again, almost in a whisper, in his slow drawl.

"That's an interesting point, Mr. Remington. Where were you and the other guards, if you want to call them that, when this lion broke into Jeff Roberts's tent? Why did you not see it—and prevent it?"

There was another awkward silence while Remington digested the question.

"I'm not sure," he finally said in a defiant tone, "but I resent the insinuation that I could have or should have done something more than I did. I was the only one on duty, and I think I was at the other end of the campsite. I just didn't see it. I wish I had, but I didn't."

Butler followed with a series of questions relating to the evening of Jeff Roberts's death, and Remington recounted the details of his last meal and his last conversations with Roberts. Butler then turned his attention to the screams and the pandemonium that, according to Remington at least, alerted him to the attack.

Butler paused in his questions and turned around to Kelly.

"I'm not sure y'all want to hear this, Kelly," he said in a whisper. "I have to get into the details of Jeff's death. Maybe you want to visit the ladies' room."

Kelly had no interest in leaving.

"Not on your life. Listening to this is nothing compared to what Jeff and Nicole had to endure. I can take it."

Butler then turned around and faced Remington.

"And what did you see," asked Butler, "when you raced from the other end of the campsite after hearing all that noise?"

"I saw a large male lion dragging Jeff Roberts from his tent."

"How was he dragging him?"

Remington started rubbing his hands together again and looked down at the table.

"He had his mouth around Jeff Roberts's head."

"How was Jeff Roberts dressed?"

"He wasn't."

"What did you do you then?"

"I had my .458 Winchester rifle with me. I ran to within thirty yards or so of the animal. I took aim and fired and brought him down with a shot through the brain."

The room became silent again as Butler decided to wait and let Remington's answers sink into the assembled crowd.

"Did you have occasion afterward to find out exactly how large that lion was?" Butler asked.

"Yes. He was about ten-and-a-half feet long from nose to the end of his tail, and he weighed about five hundred twenty-five pounds."

"Was Jeff Roberts still alive at that point?"

Remington shook his head.

"I'm afraid he was long gone by that point," he said quietly.

Butler leaned over and had a whispered conversation with Kruger. He then turned to Feldstone and said, "I'm done with this witness."

"Thanks, Caleb. We have no questions for Mike. We can take a short break and eat the sandwiches that have been brought in. But we'd like to keep moving along as quickly as possible."

Butler nodded, rose from his seat, and walked toward the door. Remington stood at the same time, shook hands with the Barrington and Stone attorneys, and reached the door as Butler was opening it.

"That," the African guide whispered to the Washington lawyer, "is an experience I hope I never have to repeat."

"If your employer does the right thing," Butler responded, "you won't have to worry about it."

There was light conversation in the conference room while everyone picked at the sandwiches and condiments that had been placed on a credenza along the side of the conference room. Kelly sipped on a ginger ale and chatted aimlessly with Kruger, but her mind was focused on the next deposition.

After about fifteen minutes, the conference room door opened, and Nicole walked in with Butler right behind her. As they entered the room and moved toward the table, all conversation stopped. Nicole's petite figure and almost regal bearing gave her an arresting look. But the attention of everyone in the room immediately gravitated toward the large scar across her right cheek. It was long and narrow, stretching from the corner of her mouth to her right eye.

The Barrington and Stone attorneys stood up to introduce themselves. They said nothing about the scar, but it was a vivid reminder of why they were all there.

After the introductions, Kelly walked over to Nicole and squeezed her hand. The emotional bond between the women was clear, and the brief exchange appeared to energize Nicole. She settled into the chair next to Butler and took the same oath that the stenographer had requested of Remington. She then looked directly at Feldstone with her hands folded in her lap.

"The witness is yours," Butler said to Feldstone.

"Good afternoon, Ms. Landow," the attorney began without emotion. "Can you give me your address?"

"I live in an apartment on Wisconsin Avenue in Washington, DC."

"Do you have a street number?"

"I don't think that's necessary," Nicole said curtly. "Do you?"

"No, I guess not," said Feldstone in a matter-of-fact tone. "You are a lawyer, though, are you not? You don't mind answering that question, do you?"

"No, I don't mind responding to that. Yes, I am a lawyer."

"And what is your occupation?"

"I'm an attorney with the Environmental Protection Agency here in Washington."

"Well, Ms. Landow, why don't we move to the events at issue here. You knew Jeff Roberts, correct?"

"Yes."

Feldstone then asked a number of questions to establish how Nicole and Jeff had met and the nature of their relationship.

"And not too long ago the two of you decided to take a photographic safari to Africa, correct?"

"Yes, that's right."

"And you ultimately decided to engage the services of Barrington and Stone, correct?"

"Yes."

"And the two of you decided to share a tent on the photographic safari, correct?"

"You've done your homework."

"Please. Just answer the question, Ms. Landow."

"Yes, you're correct."

"And on the evening of Mr. Roberts's death, you had a long conversation and dinner with Mike Remington, the safari tour guide, correct?"

"Yes, we did."

"And he told you then, didn't he, that lion attacks on people remained a fact of everyday life in Africa? You remember that, don't you?"

"Yes, I do remember that. And one of the reasons I remember it so clearly is because I was shocked to learn that that kind of thing still happened with regularity in this day and age."

"Well, Ms. Landow," Feldstone said with feigned surprise, "you're not telling me that you were shocked to learn that lion attacks are commonplace in Africa. You're not saying that, are you?"

"Yes, that's exactly what I'm saying."

"Ms. Landow," Feldstone continued in a patronizing voice, "you're obviously a highly educated woman, and you certainly knew that lions are wild animals and that they can attack people. That's almost common sense, isn't it?"

"It may seem like common sense to you, but I didn't think I was putting my life at risk when I went on this photographic safari. And if the safari did have that kind of risk, I would've thought your client would have had the decency, if not the legal obligation, to let me know that so that I could make an informed decision as to whether I wanted to take that risk."

Score one for Nicole, Kelly said to herself. She glanced over at Butler, who always seemed in control of his emotions, and it appeared to her that he had a smirk on his face. But Feldstone pushed on without any indication that he had lost ground.

"Come now, Ms. Landow, you don't need anyone to tell you that lions and other wild animals are beyond a safari company's control, do you? I know this is an emotional time for you, but you must remember that you are under oath."

"I don't need you to remind me to tell the truth," Nicole shot back. "And whatever you may like to believe now, Mr. Feldstone, I thought I was going on a vacation to take some pictures of these animals. I did not expect to test wills with them."

Feldstone then leaned over his chair and pulled a Barrington and Stone brochure from his briefcase. He handed the brochure to Nicole.

"Have you ever seen this brochure before?" he asked.

"Yes, I believe I have."

"In fact, Ms. Landow, this is the brochure that was sent to you when you booked the safari. Isn't that correct?"

"Yes, I believe so."

"I'd like you to turn to the page that is marked with a paper clip."

After Nicole opened to the particular page, Feldstone resumed his questioning.

"You will see in the area that I have highlighted that Barrington and Stone says, in effect, that it is not liable for events that are beyond its control. Isn't that the import of that highlighted language?"

Nicole slowly read the highlighted passage and then looked up at Feldstone.

"Yes, that appears to be what it says."

"And that document meant that you had been warned that things could happen—including attacks by these wild animals you wanted to photograph—that would be beyond Barrington and Stone's control. Isn't that true, Ms. Landow?"

There was a pause as Nicole considered Feldstone's question. Kelly could sense that Nicole was searching for some answer that would be different from the one Feldstone expected, or at least wanted.

"There's nothing in here," she said after a minute or so, "that makes any mention of attacks by wild animals. And I can tell you that the possibility of that kind of attack never crossed my mind when I read this document."

Kelly gave a big sigh of relief. The answer was as good as she could have hoped for.

"Well, Ms. Landow," Feldstone retorted, "Barrington and Stone didn't have to give you a catalogue of things that could happen. You knew that these wild animals are dangerous—isn't that in part why you wanted to photograph them?"

"Come on, Darren." Butler's slow drawl interrupted the cadence of the questioning. "You're just arguing with the witness, and you've been around the block enough times to know you shouldn't do that."

"Is that an objection, Caleb?"

"Yes, I guess it is. So why don't we move on to something factual."

Feldstone turned back to Nicole and asked her to recount the events leading up to Jeff's death. Nicole took longer and longer to respond as the questions moved to the climactic moment.

"And what happened," Feldstone asked, "after you heard that growl outside the tent?"

Nicole's expression went blank and she appeared to be staring right through Feldstone. After a minute or so, Feldstone tried to elicit a response.

"Ms. Landow? I know this is painful, but we have to know the facts if we are to have any chance of assessing this matter."

"I really don't remember much except an awful smell and blood and screaming. And claws and teeth that seemed to be everywhere."

"I don't want to, but I'm forced to ask, Ms. Landow. Is that scar on your face the aftermath of this attack?"

Nicole looked down at the table top in front of her and nodded her head. "Yes. I later learned that some of that blood was mine."

There was a pause as Nicole's answer settled over the group. Feldstone broke the silence.

"I want to pick up on something Mr. Butler alluded to in his questioning of Mr. Remington." Feldstone glanced over at Butler, who sat impassively on the other side of the table. The Barrington and Stone attorney then turned back to Nicole. "Do you have any reason to believe, Ms. Landow, that this attack was provoked by Mr. Remington or anyone else employed by Barrington and Stone?"

"Not really," Nicole shot back. "But I don't have enough expertise to know what would provoke an attack by a lion."

The firm response took Feldstone aback. But he could see that no use would come from challenging Nicole. He turned toward Butler.

"I think we've asked all we need to at this point, Caleb."

After everyone had left the conference room, Kruger and Butler took some coffee back to Butler's office and sat down to review the day's events.

"So what's your take, Caleb?"

"I'm still a little puzzled about why this lion attack occurred and where Remington was when it happened. Something about Remington's responses left me unsatisfied. But we'll have an opportunity to pursue that further in court. Feldstone took a pretty hard line with me right before he left. He said they all felt sorry for Nicole and Jeff, but they weren't convinced that the company had any legal liability. So I guess we'll have to file the complaint."

"That's certainly disappointing. Is there anything more we can do to push them to settle?"

"I'm not sure." Butler then paused to give the question further thought. "It would certainly help to know whether they had had at least one similar experience with a lion attack before Jeff Roberts's death. On the one hand, that might reduce my concern that this attack was provoked. But it would also mean that Barrington and Stone was on notice that they had to do more than they did to warn their clients about the possibility of a lion attack."

"Yeah, but Remington said nothing like that had ever happened before. And it seemed like he was telling the truth."

Caleb turned in his chair and looked at the Capitol a few blocks away.

"I wonder…."

CHAPTER 32

Kelly squeezed harder with her legs on Grant's belly to make him canter faster. In earlier times she had always loved these early evening rides in the summer. The trees were in full bloom with a honeyed aroma, the sun was still bright, and the tall trees that surrounded the trails kept the humidity under control. And beyond the scenic beauty of the Potomac River, the ride had always allowed her to relax and escape the pressures of daily life.

None of that was possible now. The pressure she felt was unrelenting. Even in the middle of the Potomac woods, she could not avoid the tension that she continually felt day and night.

Her thoughts drifted back to the depositions that had been taken earlier that day. Although she was committed to pursuing legal action against the safari company, she knew that the matter was compounding her anxieties. She wanted so much to vindicate Jeff's loss. Nicole was certainly a big help. She had really put that creep Feldstone in his place. But the matter was not as clear as Kelly would have liked. Butler said that Barrington and Stone would not settle because, in their view at least, everyone knows about the dangers of wild animals. That left them no choice. Butler would have to file the lawsuit.

She wondered whether the lawsuit would shed any light on whether the lion attack had been provoked. Butler seemed to have the same suspicions, and it had forced her to ask herself again whether she should tell him about her father's letter. If the attack was provoked, she knew enough to know the letter might provide the motive. At the same time, she had a lingering concern about expanding the circle of people who knew about the letter. I'll try to make a decision on that later, Kelly said to herself.

Her mind shifted gears without any conscious decision, and she began to dwell on the break-ins of her house and Jeep. She had tried to push it all out of her mind, but it was hard to ignore two attempts on her life. Especially since the police had still been unable to identify the jerk who had crawled into her car. A professional was all the police had said. He was dead, but would there be others?

Life was so unpredictable. Who could have anticipated that Jeff's death would have generated all this turmoil—and danger—in her life? There was one incidental benefit—Jim. Until the last week, she had wondered when, if ever, she could have a normal relationship with a man again. She could feel the walls starting to come down, and she knew it was all Jim's doing. She was not entirely sure how she felt about him, but he made her feel warm and good. And it never would have happened, Kelly reminded herself, without her father's letter.

Still, she was not sure she should continue the pursuit of her father's past. She could give the letter to a lawyer, like Jeff did, and put the whole thing out of her mind. As bad as it might be, why did she have to know what her father did? He had been the most wonderful person in her life, and nothing she could learn would change those memories. They were hers forever.

It might not be that simple, though. Someone knew she had the letter with her father's cryptic clues, and they were obviously prepared to do anything to prevent their disclosure. It might be too late to put the genie back in the bottle. How would that someone know she had given up?

Going to the police was a different question. That option was beginning to look more and more attractive. Her father had warned her against telling anybody, but now that she had already told Jim and Bud, the cat was out of the bag to some extent. But going to the police might expose her father's role in a more public way, and she was not sure she wanted to confront that kind of publicity. People, even friends, might treat her differently.

On the other hand, going to the police had one great benefit: saving her life. She couldn't ignore the danger that confronted her. Someone out there didn't like her, or at least what she might do. And if that someone succeeded in his deadly pursuit, everything else became irrelevant. If you lose your life, Kelly said to herself, nothing else matters.

The last thought coincided with her turning into the barn entrance. Grant was sweating and panting hard, and Kelly brought him down to a slow walk. She stopped just outside the barn entrance and slid off the saddle. She pulled the saddle off Grant, tied him up so that she could hose him down, and carried the tack into the barn.

It caught her eye as she walked through the door and started to put the saddle away. A paper of some kind nailed to the door on Grant's stall. She placed the saddle on the wooden block and moved toward the stall warily. As she approached it, she could see that the paper was a folded page from the *Washington Post* affixed to the stall door with a nail. Even without knowing why it was there, Kelly sensed danger. Her steps became slower.

As she drew within a few feet of the door, she could see that the page had some words circled in red marker. Blood red, Kelly thought to herself. She walked up to it and just looked at the folded newspaper page, unsure of what she could or should do. She turned around to see if there was anyone near her but saw only Grant, standing still and waiting for his hosing. She turned back and fixed her gaze on the newspaper page. After a few seconds, she slowly walked up to it, pulled out the nail, and unfolded the page.

At first she could make no sense of it. Random words from various stories were circled in the red marker. "Covered." "Police." "You." "Too." "Watched." And others. Somebody, thought Kelly, is playing games with my mind. Dangerous games.

It did not take long to piece the words together into a chilling message: "You are being watched. Police covered too."

Kelly continued to stare at the open newspaper page in her hand, her heartbeat accelerating and her hands becoming moist. She picked up her head and again surveyed the barn interior and the pasture just outside the barn door. She was scared. So scared she started to feel nauseous. It was not just the message. It was her vulnerability. That same sense of dread she had felt when that guy broke into her house. Now someone had walked into her barn, obviously unnoticed, and left unnoticed. Someone who was watching her. And the police too. As she thought about it, there was one saving grace. The person could have waited in hiding for her and done her harm. Instead, he only left a warning. Why?

Kelly stood there in the middle of the barn with the newspaper page in her hand for what seemed like hours, trying to make sense of it all. I can't do this by myself, she finally said to herself. She walked over to the phone on the barn post and punched in Jim's number.

Becky answered after a few rings. Kelly tried to sound calm, but it was difficult.

"Becky, this is Kelly. Is Jim around?"

"Hold on, Kelly."

After a minute or so Jim picked up.

"Hey, what's up? Becky said you sounded frantic. Is everything okay?"

"No, everything's not okay," Kelly replied, her voice trembling with fear. She then recounted her discovery of the folded newspaper and its frightening message. Jim listened in silence, plainly disturbed by the discovery.

"What should we do?" Kelly asked. "I'm scared. Very scared."

"I've got to think, Kelly. I've got to think it through. Not that it's ever been far from my mind."

"I think we should go to Teasdale again. He was my father's friend, he likes us, and he would certainly understand the dangers we face."

"I think you're right. But I don't think we should meet in his office. Remember what he said about sophisticated surveillance techniques? So I think we should find someplace else. Someplace very public."

"Like where?"

There was a pause, and Kelly could sense that Jim was struggling to think of the right place. It did not take long.

"Cosi's on Connecticut Avenue in Dupont Circle. It's walking distance from Teasdale's office. And it's quiet and dark. See if we can meet him there for a drink. Say around five o'clock. The restaurant should be pretty empty by then."

"Sounds good. I'll let you know."

CHAPTER 33

Dwayne Soggs lifted the yellow police tape in front of Bud Stamford's condo and used the key he had retrieved from the evidence storage to open the door. Stamford's death still nagged at him, and Soggs was disappointed when Nogasaki had called back to say that he had come up empty-handed in trying to figure out how or why Stamford had died.

Soggs walked through the foyer of the luxurious apartment. Although the manager had maintained the air conditioning, the condo had the musty smell of death. Soggs had smelled it a hundred times before. In his early days in homicide it had bothered him, but he had become inured to it. Now it was just another part of the job.

Soggs walked slowly though the various rooms. He passed though the living room and the dining room and looked at the various sculptures and paintings. Soggs didn't know much about art, but it appeared that Stamford did—and that he had spent a lot of money collecting it.

Soggs looked down at the plush white carpeting as he passed though the living room and dining room. Everything appeared to be spotless. Stamford obviously didn't have young kids or pets. So what kept him busy? Soggs wondered. The detective had done some background checks, and he had learned that Stamford had had a long and distinguished career in the State Department's Foreign Service, with stints in capitals all over the world—Paris, London, Buenos Aires, and other places that Soggs couldn't even pronounce. But Stamford was pretty much a loner, with no family in the area, and Soggs was not sure who his friends were or how he spent his time after retiring from government service a year or so ago.

Soggs squatted on his haunches and inspected the carpet at various spots. He was not sure what he was looking for, but he was hoping there might be something that had been overlooked in the earlier sweeps, something that would give him some clue as to how Stamford died and, more importantly, whether he was the victim of foul play.

He moved into the bedroom, which had a large circular bed. He glanced at the walls. There were large paintings and framed photographs showing Stamford at different points in his career.

Soggs looked at each photo carefully. If Stamford had been murdered, it had probably been at the hands of someone he knew, someone Stamford would open the door for without question. Maybe there was something in the photos. A relationship that had gone sour, or an emotional interest that had turned deadly.

Soggs squatted again and looked at the plush carpeting around and under the bed. It was extremely thick, and Soggs was not sure that he could see everything with the naked eye. He pulled a pair of latex gloves from his back pocket, stretched them over his hands, and then brushed his hands around the carpet, pushing the threads gently to the side. Nothing. He moved to a different location near the bed and repeated the exercise. And then his hand felt something.

It was a small plastic tip, something that might fit over a hypodermic needle used for injections. Soggs picked up the plastic tip. He turned it over in his fingers. There was nothing extraordinary about it and he was not sure it meant anything. If Stamford had been injected with a poison or some other toxic substance, that surely would have shown up in the pathology report. Still, Soggs was seasoned enough to know that it could be something.

He pulled out the small plastic bag he always carried, placed the tip in the bag, and then zipped it up. He would give it to the guys back at the lab. Maybe there were fingerprints, although he doubted that. The lab had not found any fingerprints of consequence when they dusted the entire condo the day they found Stamford's body, and it would be highly unlikely that the murderer, if there was one, had left the only fingerprint on this little plastic tip. Still, maybe there was something else. Perhaps the residue of some substance. Or maybe some other feature that would help him figure this thing out. If that plastic tip had any significance, Soggs would find out what it was. Because he was tenacious. And he hated loose ends.

Chapter 34

By five o'clock Kelly and Jim were seated at a corner table in the back of Cosi's, each nursing a beer. Although there was a constant stream of people and cars outside the restaurant on Connecticut Avenue, the restaurant itself was, as Jim predicted, quiet at that early evening hour, with only a few patrons sitting at tables or picking up orders at the counter. Jim could feel the tension emanating from Kelly as he looked carefully at each of the patrons, trying to guess whether they were really just innocent customers—or whether one of them might be an agent of the conspirators trying to observe, and perhaps record, their conversation with Teasdale.

It was not long before the former CIA case officer walked through the door, glanced around, and, seeing Jim and Kelly, walked toward them briskly. A man with little time to waste, Jim thought. Teasdale smiled in greeting and sat down in the chair opposite Jim and Kelly.

In that moment Jim knew that he and Kelly had made the right decision in meeting with her father's friend again. It was clear that Teasdale was genuinely fond of Kelly. And beyond that, Teasdale conveyed a self-confidence that was contagious, as though any problem could be managed. It wasn't anything in particular that he had said or done. It was his appearance and manner. He looked and acted as though everything were under control. Jim tried to imagine Teasdale in his younger days, participating in covert actions where a wrong move could mean instant death. He must have been quite the swashbuckler, Jim thought. Whatever. Jim was sure that all that background had served Teasdale well and that he would have a sense as to how he and Kelly should proceed.

"We took the liberty of getting you a beer," Jim commented. "I hope it's to your liking."

"Absolutely," he said as he picked up the beer and took a long swallow.

Kelly initiated the conversation.

"First of all, Mr. Teasdale…"

"Come on, Kelly," Teasdale interjected good-naturedly. "You can't call me 'Mr. Teasdale.' We're friends drinking beer now. It's gotta be Harvey. I don't want to have to call you Ms. Roberts," he said with a wink.

"Fair enough. Well—Harvey—I want to begin with a confession."

"Oh?"

"Yes. We weren't entirely forthright with you last time. I, we, were very interested in trying to find out about my father's professional history, that much is true. But it was not idle curiosity. You obviously noticed that, I guess, but we had a purpose in trying to find out what my father did, and, as you suspected, it hasn't been an entirely pleasant, or should I say, safe experience."

Teasdale looked closely at Kelly.

"What do you mean, 'it hasn't been a safe experience'?"

"Somebody's already tried to kill me twice."

Teasdale folded his hands on the table and leaned forward, his eyes locked on Kelly's.

"Please," he said with apparent concern. "Tell me what happened."

"Just that. I know it sounds bizarre, but I've had two encounters where some guy, maybe the same guy, tried to do me in, and I have to believe it's because I'm asking these questions about my father. And then yesterday someone left me a threatening message."

"Many questions come to mind, but why don't you continue."

Kelly then described the letter from her father, the break-in at her house, the car chase along River Road, and the marked-up newspaper page she had found the previous day.

"I also think," she added, "that someone made a thorough search of my house yesterday, because certain things appeared to have been moved after I came in from the barn. And so, I'm not sure what I should do. I certainly want to know what my father did, but I don't want to die in the process. What I need is some guidance of how to protect myself without giving up the search into my father's past."

"I agree," said Teasdale. "It is a tough dilemma."

"Maybe," Kelly continued, "it would be useful if you actually read my father's letter."

She looked around to see if anyone was watching, then pulled the letter from her purse and handed it to Teasdale. Jim and Kelly saw his eyes narrow and his jaw tighten as he read it. After he finished, Teasdale shook his head and returned the letter to Kelly.

"Given the sensitivity of this, I can't help but wonder why we're meeting here and not in my office."

"My idea," said Jim. "I took to heart your warning about sophisticated surveillance techniques and thought we should meet in some public place where surveillance might be more difficult."

Teasdale nodded. "I understand but I'm not sure I agree. Anyway," he continued in a softer voice, "this is shocking stuff, Kelly. Who else knows about this letter?"

"Just you and Jim. And there are no copies. It seemed to be an easy way for me to keep matters under control. Anyway, I had discussed it with Bud Stamford, and that's why Bud called you. He thought you would be the right person to talk to. But Bud, as you know, died shortly after we talked to him."

"Yes, I know. Terrible tragedy about Bud. But I do of course recall that he had first told me that you might be calling. But he never mentioned the letter or the Kennedy assassination."

"We thought it best at the time," Kelly replied, "to be very careful and try to limit the number of people we talked to about this. I hope you understand."

"Of course. That's actually very smart on your part, and I am glad to hear that we are the only three who know about this. The more people there are in the loop, the more difficult it is to control what happens to the information. I learned that long ago from hard experience."

As he said that, Jim surveyed the other patrons, trying to determine whether any of them were looking at their table or trying to overhear their conversation. Nothing seemed out of the ordinary, but, knowing Teasdale's disagreement, he began to wonder whether he had made a mistake by suggesting a meeting in a public restaurant. But it was too late to change that now, and Jim turned his attention back to Teasdale.

"So what do you think of those three references in Mr. Roberts's letter? They are somewhat puzzling. Look at this guy de Mohrenschildt, for example. Here's a European aristocrat who befriends Oswald, an unemployed defector with a high school degree. On its face, it looks a little strange, except that we also know that de Mohrenschildt was in touch with the CIA. And so you have to wonder if there's anything in de Mohrenschildt's relationship with the CIA that explains his interest in Oswald."

"That's certainly possible. In any event, we may be able to clarify de Mohrenschildt's precise role with the CIA. I still have a lot of friends at the agency."

"As long as we're talking about the CIA," said Kelly, "I have a few questions of my own."

"Such as?"

"I read that the CIA used the Mafia in the 1960s to try to assassinate Fidel Castro. They tried, or thought about trying, poison pens, poison food, and other things that seem almost laughable in retrospect. And you told us last time, Harvey, how disillusioned you and my father were with Kennedy's conduct in handling the Bay of Pigs invasion. So I'm just wondering whether some people in the CIA, perhaps including my father, were so upset with Kennedy and his Cuban policy that they tried to enlist the mob to assassinate him. Maybe they thought, however foolishly, that they were doing the country a service. And, if that was their motivation, using Oswald makes sense. He seemed to be someone who wanted to help the communist regime in Cuba. Remember, he was handing out those leaflets in New Orleans for the Fair Play for Cuba committee shortly before Kennedy died."

"Oh, I don't know. I don't believe for a minute that Kennedy died because of Oswald's commitment to communism or his love for Cuba. From what I've read, Oswald was an anarchist. He defected to the Soviet Union in 1959 because he thought the American system was a failure. He was given a job in a factory and came face to face with the hard and meager lifestyle of the Russians. Not surprisingly, he became disillusioned and left the Soviet Union within two years. So it's hard to believe Oswald would've killed anybody because of his commitment to communism or to Cuba."

"Maybe you're right," Jim interjected, "and Oswald had no commitment to Cuba and was nothing more than an anarchist. But even as an anarchist, he would probably have loved the opportunity to participate in the assassination of Kennedy. In his mind, it might have been the best way to throw the world into turmoil. The United States thinks the Soviet Union did it, the Russians get paranoid, and—boom!—before you know it, nuclear missiles are flying through the air and World War Three has started."

"I certainly agree that someone with malevolent intentions may have tried to use Oswald, but it's hard to believe anyone would have given him any kind of important role. The guy was a misfit, and I can't imagine anyone would have trusted him to keep his mouth shut afterward. So if Oswald had anything to do with the assassination, I for one have to believe that he did it alone."

"All of that sounds logical," Jim responded, "but I've been doing a lot of reading about the Kennedy assassination, and I find Oswald's behavior somewhat inconsistent with the notion that he did it alone—or even that he did it at all."

"How so?" Teasdale asked.

Jim took another swig of beer and responded.

"Oswald was interrogated mercilessly after his arrest. He never had an attorney and was brought down for questioning by the police and dragged in front of the press at all hours of the day and night. And never once during his many hours of interrogation did Oswald ever admit—let alone brag—that he had killed Kennedy. Instead, he insisted throughout those hours of interrogation by the police and the press that he had never killed anybody and that he was nothing more than a patsy."

"I guess that's where Jack Ruby comes in," Kelly said. "Here's a guy with underworld associations who owns a strip club, and he decides that he's got to kill Oswald because, as he later claimed, he feels sorry for Jackie Kennedy and didn't want her to have to testify at any trial. That hardly passes the laugh test. It seems to me that the more likely explanation is that he had to kill Oswald because Oswald kept saying on national television that he had been used."

"And there's one other thing," added Jim. "Ruby's first visitor in jail is Joseph Campisi, a major figure in the New Orleans Mafia family of Carlos Marcello, one of the mob's most powerful leaders. That by itself looks a little suspicious."

Teasdale shook his head. "I don't know about the significance of that visit. It could actually cut the other way. I mean, why would a major Mafia figure visit Ruby in jail and force people to raise the kind of questions you're asking now?"

"I'm not sure either," Jim said. "But I have read that when somebody in the mob is arrested, one of the first visitors is a member of the 'family' who reminds the guy that he's being watched and that harm will come to him or his family if he doesn't keep his mouth shut. Ruby certainly seemed to sense the danger he was in if he talked. When Earl Warren and the other members of the Warren Commission came to Dallas to interview him in jail, Ruby said he couldn't talk freely in Dallas and he begged them—several times—to take him back to Washington so he could tell them what really happened. And for some reason, they refused."

"This is all very interesting," Teasdale remarked while leaning forward in his chair again, "but I'm afraid we've gotten a little off-track. The question is whether Ted Roberts had anything to do with this and what you should do right now."

"That's it in a nutshell," said Kelly. "What *should* we do?"

"On the one hand, I'm a big believer in law enforcement and in not trying to take things into your own hands. I guess," Teasdale said, turning to Jim, "it's like that old saw that says that the lawyer who defends himself has a fool for a client. But I'm concerned that the police will not be able to provide the kind of protection you may need. Especially in light of the threatening message delivered yesterday. These people you're dealing with, Kelly, are obviously professionals, and no amount of police protection is going to safeguard you from harm, if that's their goal."

"So where does that leave us?" Jim asked.

"I think you want to lie low and not to do anything for now. Maybe that'll buy us more time to figure this thing out. That message you got yesterday, Kelly, leads me to believe that whoever is out there will bide their time if you appear to be doing nothing. And in the meantime, I'll discreetly check my sources at the CIA and elsewhere to see if I can find anything more about de Mohrenschildt and any contact he may have had with your father."

"Sounds good to me," Jim replied. "What about you, Kelly? What do you think?"

"I guess that sounds right. It'll certainly make it easier for me to go back to the house. How long do you think it will take, Harvey?"

"I really can't tell you. But I'll do it as quickly as possible. This is going to be my number one priority tomorrow."

They finished their beers, rose from their chairs, and walked out of the restaurant just as the sky was starting to clear from a short thunderstorm, with brilliant rays of sunlight emanating from fast-moving clouds. After watching Teasdale cross a rain-slicked Connecticut Avenue toward Jefferson Street, Kelly turned to Jim with a puzzled look.

"What do you think? Are we doing the right thing?"

"For sure. I like Teasdale. He's a good man. And he's definitely in a position to help us. So let's let it ride for a little bit and see what happens."

Kelly then watched as Jim tried to hail a cab back to the Capitol. She was still unsettled by the whole experience.

"So what do you have planned tonight? Do you want to get together?"

"I would love to, but my mom called, and I'm going to drive up to New Jersey right after work."

"How's your dad doing since he got back from the hospital?"

"Better. But he still can't move around much. He basically either sits in a wheelchair or lies in bed. It's not much of a life, but he doesn't have much choice now. And at least he's still with us."

"Well, that much is good, I guess."

"Hey," Jim said. "Why don't you come with me for another look at New Jersey? It would be good for you to get away, and I'm sure my parents would love it."

Kelly shook her head.

"No good. I've got to give some riding lessons tomorrow, and there are some things I have to do around the barn."

"Okay. How's this? I'm just going up for the day and driving back tomorrow afternoon. Why don't I meet you for dinner tomorrow night?"

"Great. Where?"

"J. Paul's in Georgetown. Eight o'clock."

"You're on."

A beige-colored cab finally pulled along the curb. As Jim got into the backseat, he took one long look at Kelly. And then the cab sped away.

CHAPTER 35

Dear Dad,

I'm in such turmoil, and I know it'll make me feel better to get my thoughts down on paper. You always said that writing helps to crystallize your thoughts, and I need a lot of crystallizing right now.

Your letter really has thrown me for a loop. It's so hard for me to believe you really participated in the assassination of President Kennedy. I know this will sound stupid, but it's just not like you. I just can't square the loving and compassionate father I knew so well with a person involved in one of the most tragic murders of our country's history. And I can't believe that Mom would have loved you as much as she did unless you were the person you always seemed to be.

I think I like your friend Harvey Teasdale. I had my suspicions at first, but I'm glad he's going to help us. Maybe he'll find out something to resolve these questions about you that nag me day and night.

But what do I do in the meantime? I guess Harvey's right about not telling the police. At least for now. I recently read how Kennedy once said that there was no way to provide complete protection for a president and that a determined assassin, especially one ready to give his life, could always find some opening. I think Kennedy was right, and if you can't protect a president with all those Secret Service guys and all that security, how could the police protect me? I wouldn't provide nearly the same challenge to a determined assassin.

I do like Jim, though. I don't know what I would've done without him. And he's helped me, without knowing it, to deal with some other problems that have troubled me. It's funny. In a way, I wish I had never gotten your letter and that none of this had happened to Jeff. But—and don't take this the wrong way, Dad—if none of those things had happened to you or Jeff, I'm sure I never would've gotten to know Jim the way I do. Life sure is strange that way. One door closes and another one opens.

Anyway, I'm going to bide my time for now and see what Harvey turns up. But you know me, Dad. In my own way, I'm just as driven as you were. I won't rest until I know the full truth. But thanks for listening. That always was one of your great qualities. And remember how much I love you.

Lots of love,

Kelly

Chapter 36

Although located in the heart of Georgetown, J. Paul's was unusually busy for a weekday night in the summer. The crowd at the long wooden bar was three or four people deep, consisting mostly of young professionals in their twenties and thirties. The tables and booths on the other side of the restaurant were equally crowded, with couples and groups lingering in the small entranceway and on the sidewalk outside while cars moved slowly up and down M Street. An eclectic mix of music could be heard above the din, all conveying an atmosphere of high energy and informality.

Jim was taking another swallow of his beer in one of the wooden booths when he saw Kelly striding in the front door a little after eight o'clock. Jim's heartbeat accelerated. Her shoulder-length brown hair, seemingly iridescent in the restaurant's subdued lighting, lifted lightly behind her as she walked toward the booth. She eased into the booth with a solemn look.

"Hi," was all she said, but Jim could detect the tension in her voice. The visit to Teasdale had obviously done little to ease her anxiety. Jim wanted, more than anything, to relieve the pressure she obviously felt, but there was no easy solution.

"You sound troubled. Tell me what you're thinking."

"I don't know. My mind's a jumble. I'd rather talk about you. How was the trip to New Jersey? How's your father doing?"

As Kelly asked the question, Jim was momentarily distracted by the stare of someone at the bar. He turned his head slightly and saw a young black man holding a drink and looking directly at him and Kelly. It was a strange look, one that made Jim feel uncomfortable. Maybe because the man did not avert his eyes, as most people would, when Jim returned the stare. But so what? he said to himself. He dismissed the matter from his mind and turned back to Kelly.

"Dad's doing okay. His spirit is really beyond belief. His optimism seems boundless. But I guess that's what keeps him young—and alive."

"He really is a great guy. And his love for you is something to behold. I know my father loved Jeff, but your father's devotion to you is something special."

A young waiter wearing a white shirt and black pants and a big smile suddenly materialized and took Kelly's order for a glass of white wine. As the waiter left, Jim looked over to the bar and again saw the young black man holding his drink and staring at him and Kelly. This time, however, the man turned his back when Jim returned the stare. That reaction eased the tension Jim was beginning to feel. He took a long swallow from his bottle of beer, settled back into the booth, and looked at Kelly. She appeared pensive.

"So?" he asked. "Come on. Tell me. What're you thinking about?"

"Oh, I don't know. Talking about your father made me think of mine."

"You miss him, huh."

Kelly looked down at the wine that the waiter had quickly brought her.

"I sure do. Even when I was in college he remained an integral part of my life. There were certain things I could only discuss with my mom, but when she passed on in my sophomore year, Dad became a surrogate mom as well as a father. There was something about him that always made me feel secure, even if we were miles apart. I always knew he was there and could somehow make everything right. And, boy, could I use that now."

"Did they ever figure out why your father died? I have a vague recollection of Jeff telling me that he just collapsed or something."

"I guess that's right. Jeff and I came back one day after doing errands, and he was slumped over the desk in the library. He wasn't that old and he seemed to be in great health. We called the ambulance, but they couldn't do anything. They assumed it was probably a heart attack, but I don't know. There didn't seem to be any point in an autopsy. It wasn't going to bring him back."

Kelly picked up her wine and took a sip. She put the glass back on the table and looked up at Jim.

"This whole thing has really got me down. I've always missed my father since he left us, and now I have to worry about staying alive. It really does keep me up at nights—even with the new alarm system and the spotlights on the house. You've got to do something to divert my mind."

Jim continued to look at Kelly, still unsure of what to say. She sensed the affection in his eyes but said nothing. They remained silent for a few moments, taking comfort in each other's presence.

"I would like to divert your mind," Jim finally said, "but I have to tell you. I'm no different from you. The only thing I can think about these days is your father's letter and the attempts on your life. To be honest, I'm intrigued by the letter and trying to understand who was behind Kennedy's assassination. But I'm also scared. I find myself constantly looking over my shoulder, checking the locks on my apartment, and doing all kinds of weird stuff to make sure I'm safe. And I worry about you in the same way."

Kelly felt the tug of emotion and stretched her hand across the table. Jim instinctively took her hand in his, and the two of them sat there, reliving the attempts on Kelly's life and trying to guess the identity of the people behind it all.

"By the way," Kelly said after a while, "Teasdale called me this afternoon, and I want to tell you about it. But we have to order first. I'm really hungry."

As if on cue, the waiter walked by their table and took their orders. As the waiter departed, Jim looked over at the bar, expecting to see the young black man still staring at them. He was momentarily relieved not to see him. And then, as he started to turn back to Kelly, he saw the man looking at them from a different position farther from the bar. What gives? Jim asked himself. He wanted to get up and tell the guy to mind his own business, but he knew it was something he would never do.

Kelly caught his distraction.

"What're you looking at?"

"Nothing. Really nothing. I thought I saw someone I knew. Anyway, let's get back to Teasdale. Tell me what he said."

Kelly nodded her thanks as the waiter brought her another glass of wine. She took a long sip and picked up the conversation.

"He said that he was able to check on de Mohrenschildt's records with the CIA. It seems that de Mohrenschildt may have given Oswald the money to buy the rifle that he used to try to assassinate that right-wing leader…"

"General Walker."

"Yeah. Which is also the same rifle they found in the Book Depository in Dallas. But—and here's the interesting point—Teasdale said that the CIA contact reports with de Mohrenschildt for the spring of 1963 are missing. He had hoped the reports would have referenced Oswald's attempt to assassinate Walker as well as a circulation list. But no such luck. And without the reports, there's no way to know who in the CIA knew that Oswald may have been a potential assassin."

"So," said Jim, finishing Kelly's logic, "there's also no way to know whether your father knew about Oswald's attempt to assassinate Walker."

"Right. Nor is there any evidence, Harvey said, that my father knew de Mohrenschildt or that he ever saw any of de Mohrenschildt's reports to the CIA. But some CIA records are still classified, and Harvey didn't know whether my father was given access to those."

As Kelly was finishing, Jim glanced at the bar and was relieved not to see the young black man. God, he said to himself, I really am getting paranoid.

"Here's what I think," he said to Kelly after taking a long drink from the second beer that the waiter had brought. "To me, it seems that the key to this whole thing may be those ten letters included in your father's letter."

"Why do you say that?"

"I can't help but think that, if we could figure out what those letters stand for, it'll pull together the other two items—de Mohrenschildt and the 5412 Committee. As your father said in the letter, he could have made it much simpler. And he's obviously a man of his word. This stuff is not easy to figure out. Especially those letters. But let's leave that aside for the moment. How does this leave us with Teasdale?"

"He promised to check more sources. But the bottom line is we don't know any more now than we did before. Except those missing CIA records for de Mohrenschildt do sound suspicious."

"Yeah, but we have no way of knowing whether any of that has any bearing on your father's role."

"And we may never know unless we can see all those classified records and find out whether de Mohrenschildt knew of Oswald's effort to kill Walker and who de Mohrenschildt told, or at least who saw his reports."

Jim suddenly leaned forward, his eyes wide with excitement.

"I've got an idea."

"I'm all ears."

"I'll talk to Senator Gimble and ask him to make a discreet inquiry with Kay Brownstein, the CIA director. They're pretty close, and I think I could engineer it so that no one would know the underlying reason for the inquiry."

"I don't know, Jim. You remember what Harvey said. The more people we include, the greater the chance that something will go wrong."

"Sure. But we're not talking about anybody. We're talking about a United States senator and the director of the Central Intelligence Agency. And if anybody's in a position to help us, it's them."

"What about Teasdale's warning about sophisticated surveillance techniques?"

"Come on, Kelly. This is a meeting that'll take place in the United States Senate or the offices of the Central Intelligence Agency in Virginia. I'm sure Harvey's right when it comes to private homes and offices, but I can't believe that we need to have that concern here."

"Okay. You've convinced me. Should we tell Harvey?"

"No. I don't think so. It's not that I don't trust Harvey. I do. But let's take his advice. If we tell him, he might tell someone else inadvertently, and that might be a problem. So let's keep this to ourselves."

Kelly was still thinking about Jim's comment when the waiter brought their food. They debated it over and over again, and it was almost eleven-thirty when they emerged from the restaurant onto M Street and the humid summer air. The crowds had thinned out, and there were only small pockets of people on the sidewalk as cars now moved briskly up and down the street.

"I've got to get up early tomorrow morning to catch a plane to Minnesota," said Jim, "so don't think about asking me to go to another party in Potomac. Anyway, where's your Jeep parked? The least I can do is make sure you make it safely back to the 'burbs."

"Somewhere near 30th and P Streets."

"How could you do that, Kelly?" Jim asked with exasperation, knowing that the location was a residential neighborhood far from the main streets of Georgetown. "Parking all the way up there is not the smartest thing in the world. You knew you'd have to get the Jeep in the dark. Isn't there danger enough out there for you? Do you have to add to it?"

Kelly put her arm around Jim's shoulder and pulled herself close.

"I know you. And I had confidence you wouldn't let me walk there alone."

Jim returned the look in her eyes.

"I think you're starting to take me for granted," he quipped.

They walked down M Street and then turned up 30th Street, which was completely devoid of people and cars, chatting animatedly and totally absorbed with each other. Their focus on each other was so concentrated that they did not see the man emerge from the shadows.

"Stop right there," they heard the voice say.

Jim and Kelly turned around. Jim immediately recognized the assailant as the young black man who had been staring at them from the bar. He was a little taller than Jim, about twenty-five pounds heavier, and dressed in dark clothes. Both Jim and Kelly's eyes were drawn immediately to the handgun pointed at them.

Jim glanced at Kelly and saw that she was trembling.

"Just stay calm," he whispered to her under this breath. He then turned back to their assailant.

"What do you want?"

"Don't talk to me, motherfucker," the man responded in a clipped angry tone. "I'll do all the talking. Just give me your money. And don't try anything funny, or I'll blow your fuckin' heads off."

Jim and Kelly did as they were told, pulling dollar bills from their wallets. The man grabbed the money and stuffed it into his pants pocket.

He then looked at Jim.

"Back off, stud. I want you to lie face down on the ground. The bitch is coming with me."

The man then reached out with his left hand to grab Kelly's arm. As he took his eyes off Jim for that fleeting moment, Jim whirled around with lightning speed and kicked the man in the face with the back of his right foot. As the man stumbled backward and dropped the gun, Kelly kicked him in the groin. The mugger then bent forward and crumbled to the ground, moaning.

"Let's get out of here!" Jim yelled.

With that, they turned and ran toward Kelly's Jeep three blocks away. After they jumped into the Jeep and locked the doors, Kelly pulled out with the wheels screeching.

She then turned to Jim, almost breathless.

"I guess that kick was part of your Navy training."

"You bet. I'm a black belt in tae kwan do. Being a Navy SEAL does have its benefits."

"I guess so," said Kelly, her voice still trembling with fear.

Kelly turned to Jim as she drove through Georgetown's darkened streets. "Oh, Jim," she sighed. She said nothing more, but Jim understood at once. The fear that the mugger might not be just another criminal but an agent of someone trying to prevent the disclosure of her father's letter.

"What do you think?" Kelly asked, her eyes searching for an assurance that could not be given.

"I don't know, Kelly. I just don't know...."

CHAPTER 37

Geoffrey Gimble rolled over in bed and turned on the lamp on the nightstand. He looked at the digital clock, which glared two-twenty-seven in large green numbers. He propped himself up against the headboard with the pillows and then turned to his right.

Kay Brownstein looked up at him.

"That was wonderful."

"It always is." Gimble leaned over and kissed her gently on the lips. "I'm only sorry it took us so long to find each other."

"Well, I didn't spend much time in Minnesota," she said with a small laugh, "and so I couldn't bump into you at college or whatever. And I know you didn't hang around Boston much. So you couldn't have run into me."

As she mentioned Boston, Brownstein thought back to her youth. In retrospect, she realized now that she had led a charmed life in those early years, growing up with her brothers and sisters in that big white colonial off Brattle Street in Cambridge. There had been many highs and lows in her life since then. The excitement of the Foreign Service as a young professional. The tension of the Reagan White House during the Iran-Contra scandals. The risks and rewards of being special assistant to the secretary of defense and then as an assistant secretary of defense. And now, here she was, director of the Central Intelligence Agency, a position that exceeded even her considerable ambitions. And through it all, she proudly proclaimed to herself, she had maintained her appearance—no small achievement in a world where career demands often made exercise and sensible diets an unreachable goal. Her short sandy-colored hair had started to acquire some gray, which she deftly covered up with coloring, but her slender figure was not that much different than it was when she had attended Georgetown University decades earlier.

She glanced up at Geoff Gimble. A very accomplished guy, she said to herself. But also a wonderful man. Sensitive. Compassionate. And someone with unending intellectual curiosity, a trait that made their trysts that much more interesting.

Gimble returned her gaze.

"Life sure is full of surprises," he said. "Who would've thought that a country boy from the backwoods of Minnesota would someday become a United States senator and wind up sleeping with the Director of the Central Intelligence Agency?"

"We are people. Big titles don't mean we don't have emotions."

"Oh, I know. But it's more than that. I sometimes take a step back and ask myself, why is this wonderful woman interested in a slightly overweight, balding guy in his late fifties?"

"Oh, don't give me that bullshit," Kay said, laughing. "Your self-image is not that fragile. And, although I appreciate the compliments, you know I'm pushing fifty myself."

"Yeah, but no one would know it without reading your resume. Really. I run into people all the time who tell me how great looking you are. Of course, none of them knows of our relationship, and all I can do is nod in agreement."

"So what *do* you think, Geoff? Do you think we'll ever come out of the closet? After all, it's not like we're doing anything wrong. You're a widower and I'm divorced. And although I love coming to your townhouse here, I would like to make these visits without looking over my shoulder to make sure no reporter is around."

Gimble threw back the covers, stepped out of bed, and put on a pair of boxer shorts.

"That question calls for a drink. You want one?"

"At two-thirty in the morning?"

"It's better than seven o'clock in the morning."

"You're very persuasive. Okay."

He walked into the adjoining room and soon returned with two tumblers filled with scotch and ice. He handed one to Brownstein, who was now propped up against the headboard of the bed with the sheets up to her neck. Gimble settled into the black leather chair diagonally across from the bed. He took a long sip of the scotch and then looked up at Brownstein.

"I don't know. Once you make the relationship public, you invite gossip. Some of it'll be true and most of it won't. That's just how it is. For better or worse, that's what sells magazines and fills the nightly news on TV. And I don't know if I want to keep answering those kinds of questions. Nor do I want to have to wonder what people are really thinking. Especially since there are times when I have to get involved in legislation or other matters affecting the CIA." Gimble then paused, as if to give his next comment some emphasis. "I've spent a long time building my career, and I don't want people to start questioning my motives or my independence."

"I hear you. I really do. I obviously have some of the same concerns. But I just wonder whether there comes a time when you really do have to say, 'the public be damned.'"

"Maybe. But talking about getting involved with matters affecting the CIA, I forgot to mention something. One of my legislative assistants came to me today with a very unusual request, and it involves you."

"Oh?"

"Yeah. And he swore me to secrecy about it."

Brownstein's interest was aroused and she sat up straighter in the bed.

"You've got my attention."

"It concerns the assassination of President Kennedy. The father of a friend of his, a young woman, died and left a cryptic note saying that he had been involved in the assassination."

"You're kidding."

"No, I'm not. But it gets better. The father was a case officer in the CIA."

"Oh my God."

"Anyway, he left this letter with some clues as to how some investigator could determine who actually assassinated Kennedy."

Brownstein took a long sip of her scotch and placed the glass on the nightstand. She then stepped out of bed and put on the white terry cloth robe that was lying on the floor. She walked across the bedroom and settled into the other black leather chair across from the bed. She pulled the terry cloth robe closer, tucked her feet under her buttocks, and looked over at Gimble.

"Tell me more," she said.

"This CIA guy died a couple of months ago and left a letter that was given to his son, who was instructed to keep it to himself and to leave it to the JFK Records Board or some other appropriate agency after he died. But the son was killed in some terrible accident in Africa, and so the letter got passed on to the daughter, who is my legislative assistant's friend. Unlike her brother, the daughter couldn't leave well enough alone, and she started asking questions and trying to figure out what her father did in connection with the Kennedy assassination."

"Can't say that I blame her."

"No, I'm sure my curiosity would have driven me to look into it as well. The only problem is some other people weren't so happy about her looking into it, and my legislative assistant says that there have been several attempts on her life."

"Good Lord. That's horrible. Did they ever find out who tried to kill her?"

"No. Except that one guy was chasing her, and maybe the only guy, was ultimately killed in one incident. But he had no ID, and so the police haven't a clue as to who he was."

"So why is your legislative assistant coming to you? What does he want you to do?"

"He wants me—and you—to help figure out the father's cryptic clues."

"What are they?"

"Oh," Gimble said, "I'm not sure. I know one of the clues is a series of ten letters. But one of the other key things is some guy who helped Lee Harvey Oswald and was a CIA informant of some kind. My legislative assistant says they actually had some former CIA case officer look into it, and they were told that some of the CIA records on Oswald's benefactor are apparently missing. And so that's where you come in."

"I was afraid of that."

"Yeah. He wants to see if you can find those records and determine whether his friend's father had any kind of contact with Oswald's benefactor."

Brownstein put her empty tumbler down on the small table that separated the two leather chairs.

"Well, Geoff, you know I'd do anything for you. But I'm just wondering whether you really think this is worth pursuing. I don't have to tell you that there are countless theories about the Kennedy assassination and so many stories about coincidental deaths of witnesses. I'm just thinking that we'll be spinning our wheels here. Untold resources have already been devoted to trying to solve the assassination. I can't imagine we'll be able to solve it."

"You're probably right. But my legislative aide is a great guy who has done a lot for me, and I'd like to accommodate him. Up to a point at least."

"All right. Why don't you have your secretary call my administrative assistant, and we'll set up the appointment. I'm in town the next few days, so we can do it this week."

Gimble stood up and gave Brownstein a small kiss on the cheek. "I was hoping you would say that." He then took Brownstein's empty tumbler and walked into the adjoining room. Within a minute he was back, each of their glasses refilled with scotch. As he handed Brownstein her tumbler, Kay looked up at him.

"By the way, what's your LA's name?"

"Jim Roth. I think you may have met him."

"I think I have. I think he attended some of the meetings we've had on the Middle East."

"That's right. He did. He's very bright. Harvard Law grad and all that. A real solid guy."

Kay looked down at the tumbler and twirled the scotch around. She then looked over at the digital clock. It was almost three-thirty.

"And what about Roth's friend? Do you know her name?"

"Actually, I do. It's Roberts. Kelly Roberts. Her dad was Ted Roberts, who held some high positions at the CIA and State Department. You knew him, didn't you?"

Gimble could see Brownstein's eyes take on a faraway, vacant look.

"Yes," she said slowly, still staring at the scotch in her glass. "I did know Ted Roberts. In fact, I knew him quite well at one time. But," she added in slow measured tones, "that was a long time ago...."

Chapter 38

Dwayne Soggs looked out over the bow of his Catalina 30 sailboat as it sliced through the choppy seas of the Chesapeake Bay. The boat was making excellent headway toward St. Michaels on Maryland's Eastern Shore. He looked down at the tachometer, which showed that the boat speed was alternating somewhere between six and six-and-a-half knots. Not bad, Soggs said to himself, for a beam reach in these turbulent waters.

Soggs sat back in the cockpit with his hands on the large steel wheel he used to guide the boat. God, how he loved these days out on the water. There was something about the boat's movement that made it exhilarating and relaxing at the same time. And what made it particularly enjoyable was the minimal boat traffic. That was the benefit of having days off in the middle of the week instead of on the weekend. Almost everyone else, except the few on vacation, was back at work.

He also loved the idea of his being a sailor. He was especially proud of his ability to single-handedly sail his thirty-foot boat. There were not many police detectives who had sailboats of any size on the Chesapeake, or anywhere else for that matter. And even fewer black detectives who were sailors.

Soggs liked the idea of being an anomaly. A pioneer. That's what he was, he said to himself. He laughed at the thought. Growing up in the Southeast quadrant of Washington, DC, no one worried about being a pioneer. You just worried about making it out alive. But his parents had pushed him, and he had vowed to make good by using his brain and his athletic prowess. And more than that, he had vowed to give something back to the community. Which of course was why he had joined the DC police force.

It was not everything he had hoped it would be. There was the bureaucracy. The politics. And some of the guys he had to work with were assholes. But that was life. Nothing was perfect, he told himself. Balanced against the problems were the many pluses of the job. He liked and, more important, respected most of the guys—and women—he worked with. Most were dedicated professionals like him. And beyond that, there was, as he had hoped, a sense that you could do something to help people and make society a better place. Especially in his current line of work. Homicide. It was often heart-wrenching. But it was a challenge to investigate a murder and try to bring someone to justice. Because, at the end of the day, the victim almost always had a family who wanted closure. And if you could collar the perpetrator, you might make the world a little safer.

The job had its frustrations, though. The court system often made it difficult to make the collar stick. And sometimes it was not easy to track down the killer. Or even to know if there was a killer.

Soggs tacked the boat to keep his course, and he began to think about Bud Stamford's death. That was a great case in point, he said to himself. A wealthy guy in seemingly good health. No known enemies. No bad habits. A retired government employee with a stellar record. Who would want to kill him? Maybe nobody. Maybe medical science was not as sophisticated as we assumed and it was just some natural cause that escaped the coroner's examination. Certainly plausible, if not likely.

Still, something in Soggs's instincts told him otherwise, and he had learned to rely on his instincts—even when all logic and evidence pointed in the other direction. It was his sixth sense. Something most good cops acquired over time. Usually, however, there was at least some evidence to support his instincts. But in Stamford's case there was nothing. Absolutely nothing. Except that plastic tip from a hypodermic needle. Soggs had hoped that the plastic tip would lead to something, but his hopes quickly evaporated when Nogasaki, his friend in the medical examiner's office, had explained that Stamford was a diabetic who probably injected himself with insulin on a regular basis. Stamford's internist had confirmed all that. Even then, Soggs had left nothing to chance. He had returned to Stamford's apartment, found some unused needles in the medicine cabinet, and confirmed that they had plastic tips identical to the one he had found.

However much it all fit together, they were still left without any cause of death. And that bothered Soggs. Everything had a cause. He knew enough to know that. But they could not yet identify the cause of Bud Stamford's death.

Soggs's attention was brought back to his sailboat as the wind picked up and abruptly shifted direction. Instead of coming from the northwest, the wind was now coming from the southwest. The sails began to flutter, and the halyards made a clanging sound against the mast. The boat's speed dropped precipitously, and Soggs could feel the boat moving back and forth in the choppy seas, which remained unaffected by the change in wind.

Soggs's instinct as a sailor taught him to look at the source of the wind. He turned around and saw the cause of the wind shift. Large black clouds were moving quickly up from the southwest. It was obvious that the Chesapeake was about to be hit with another squall.

God fucking dammit, Soggs said to himself. I've just rounded Kent Point, almost in striking distance of St. Michaels, and now this. That was the only problem with summer sailing in the Chesapeake. Thunderstorms and squalls, some with considerable fury, frequently arose without warning. It reminded him of that common refrain about sailing—hours of boredom punctuated by minutes of sheer terror. Well, if he didn't do something quick, he would soon experience some of that terror himself. The wind had already picked up and was blowing at about twenty-five knots. The water, which had been a deep navy blue only moments before, was now a dark gray-green, and steep white-caps were relentlessly slapping against the boat's fiberglass hull. The boat was rocking back and forth as the wind and the waves worked at cross-purposes. Precautionary action was clearly needed.

The first priority was to minimize the rocking motion of the boat while he readied for the storm. He pulled in the jib, turned the boat into the wind, and locked the steering wheel in place.

Now what? He thought about his options and decided to bring down the mainsail and then use the diesel engine to run with the wind. But he wasn't about to climb out of the cockpit and deal with the mainsail without any protection. He put on his yellow foul weather gear, a life jacket, and a safety harness that he clipped to the steel rail. He was about to climb out of the cockpit onto the deck when he remembered the boat's diesel engine. Yeah. I'd better turn that on now, Soggs said to himself. The boat needs to be ready to move quickly after I tie the mainsail down.

He moved his hand below to the engine controls in the cockpit and turned the switch on. The engine started, gasped, and then died quickly. He tried it again. Same response. Goddammit, Soggs said out loud to no one but himself. What a hell of a time for this to happen.

He unhooked the harness from the steel rail and rushed down into the cabin and knelt down to lift up the housing underneath the cockpit to check the engine. Everything looked fine.

Soggs shook his head and put his hand on the low ceiling to brace himself against the boat's rocking motion in the rough seas. His mind raced through the possibilities. One cause seemed the most likely—air pockets in the fuel line. Air pockets could easily develop from the boat's stern moving in and out of the water. And if there was air in the fuel lines, the diesel fuel could not get through the engine.

There was only one way to test his hypothesis. He needed to bleed the fuel lines to eliminate any air locked inside, but that was not something he could do now. He would have to heave-to and hope that the placement of the sails would prevent the boat from being knocked down, or worse, by the storm.

As he bent over the engine in the cabin, Soggs thought about the nature of his predicament. It really is something, he said to himself, that a little bit of air could have such a devastating impact on the operation of this complicated machine.

It was at that moment that his mind wandered without command to Stamford's death. The thought hit him hard and quick and caused him to straighten his body—only to hear the dull thud and feel the immediate pain as his head hit the low ceiling. He brushed aside the pain at the exhilaration of realizing that he may have inadvertently discovered the cause of Stamford's death. It was a theory, but one that fit the facts. He now had an even greater incentive to hope that the storm would pass quickly. He had to call Nogasaki. He had to check out his theory. Maybe there was a way to tie up those loose ends after all.

CHAPTER 39

Jim descended the marble stairs outside the Russell Senate Office Building and walked quickly in a diagonal line across the parking lot toward the Senate side of the Capitol building. Although the morning sun was warm, there was a breeze that kept the humidity down and the temperature comfortable.

There was considerable activity outside the Senate building. Crowds of tourists were gathering at the foot of the broad marble stairs leading to the Senate chamber, and a group of Capitol police officers were trying to explain to people in cars that had turned off Constitution Avenue why they could not park in the Capitol parking lot.

Jim saw none of it as he walked by. His mind was totally absorbed by the meeting he was about to have with Senator Gimble and the CIA director.

He walked into the arched white-stone doorway below the marble stairs leading to the Senate chamber and flashed his ID badge to the Capitol policeman in front of the metal detector. As he proceeded down the hall past harried legislative aides and gawking tourists, Jim wondered whether Kelly should have come with him to the meeting. She wanted to, but she was afraid that her presence might inhibit the conversation. There could be questions about whether she was paranoid, whether her father's letter was genuine, and whether she had told the truth in describing phone calls and events. Those questions could not be asked freely— and the answers would not be given the same credibility—if she were present. So, after much discussion, Jim eventually agreed with Kelly that he should go to the meeting alone.

Jim also agreed with Senator Gimble that the meeting should not be held in his suite in the Russell Senate Office Building. Holding the meeting there would attract too much attention. The meeting would instead have to be in some secluded place where Brownstein could come and go without attracting the curiosity of the Senator's staff and other visitors to his Senate suite.

The senator's "hideaway" office in the bowels of the Capitol building was the perfect solution. Not every senator had one of those small interior offices in the Capitol building. As with almost everything in Congress, seniority and position were key factors in obtaining this perk. Some senators did not want or need the small office, but others treasured them.

The ostensible purpose of the hideaway office was to give the senator someplace to escape the unceasing demands of staff and constituents, a place to work on legislation or speeches in quiet and without disruption. Jim had heard other stories, however, of how the offices had sometimes been used by senators as a retreat to drink with their colleagues without drawing the attention and criticism of the staff. And other senators, Jim had heard, had used the offices for liaisons that also needed to be kept hidden from public scrutiny.

After walking for several minutes through the dimly lit hallways beneath the Senate chamber, Jim finally reached the office and knocked gently on the closed door. Within a few seconds, Senator Gimble opened the door and ushered Jim into the hideaway. It was hardly luxurious, and Jim marveled that Senator Gimble, or any senator, could relax in this windowless room with the musty smell of a basement. Jim looked around to see the spare walls with the bland light yellow paint, the relatively small desk with a few papers scattered about, the familiar bookshelves, and the green leather, government-issued couch. Not the kind of atmosphere one would imagine as the retreat for a powerful member of Congress.

As Jim entered the room, Kay Brownstein rose from a straight-backed chair covered in the same green leather that adorned the couch and extended her hand in greeting. After she and Jim exchanged a few words, Gimble mentioned that the CIA director had known Kelly's father.

"No kidding," said Jim with surprise. "It really is a small world."

"It certainly is," Brownstein said. "I am rather curious. What is his daughter like? She must be, what, late twenties?"

"That's right. Twenty-seven to be precise. Very independent. Lives out in Potomac at her parents' house and tends to her horses, teaching and riding and stuff."

"Let's get going," Gimble interjected. "Kay doesn't have a lot of time."

Brownstein returned to her chair, and Gimble retreated to the chair behind the desk with a motion for Jim to take a seat on the couch.

Jim looked over at Gimble behind the desk and remembered the first time he had met the senator. It had been about three years ago. Jim's tour with the Navy was about to end, and he had written a letter to the senator expressing his admiration for Gimble's record and Jim's interest in working for him. To Jim's surprise, Gimble's administrative assistant called shortly afterward to say that they had been impressed with his resume and that Gimble wanted to meet him.

The interview had gone well. But after about forty-five minutes, Gimble leaned back in his chair, picked up the scissors lying on his desk, and started absent-mindedly cutting threads from his tie. Later Jim would learn that picking threads from his tie was the senator's way of saying that the discussion was over. He would remember the lesson time and again after he started working for Gimble, realizing that there was no use in pressing a point in any discussion with the senator after he picked up those scissors.

Jim almost laughed to himself as he thought of the scissors. I can't imagine, Jim thought, that he'll have any use for them in this discussion. As if on cue, the senator reinforced Jim's intuition by taking charge of the meeting.

"Now, Jim," Gimble began, "I've shared your concerns and questions with Kay, but I think it might be useful for you to provide a summary of how we got here and, in particular, the details of Ted Roberts's letter to his children."

Jim then recounted the story of Jeff's death, the letter Kelly got from her father, and the ensuing events, including their discussions with Harvey Teasdale. Although he and Kelly decided that it would not be wise at this point to show the letter to Brownstein and Gimble, Jim did tell them about the three clues. He also reviewed the various questions and alternatives he and Kelly had considered. Gimble, and especially Brownstein, questioned him closely each step of the way, trying to understand what had happened and why.

"What it's come down to," Jim finally said, "is that Ted Roberts was apparently an honorable guy who went astray. But the key to figuring out what he did—and perhaps how and why Kennedy was killed—is to pursue the leads he gave us. We still don't know what the ten letters mean, but we do know about the 5412 Committee. The other element is this guy, de Mohrenschildt. I have to assume there's some connection between the 5412 Committee and de Mohrenschildt, something that may be locked somewhere in the CIA's records."

"Easy enough to assume," said Brownstein, "but far more difficult to verify and explain."

"Well, Kay," Gimble said, "can't you make a discreet inquiry into Ted Roberts's record, find out something about his activities on that 5412 Committee, and, perhaps most importantly, determine whether he had any contact with this guy de Mohrenschildt?"

"I can make inquiries, but that means someone else besides us is going to know about the inquiry—although I certainly won't tell them I know it came from Jim or that it involves Kelly or even that it concerns the Kennedy assassination. But it won't take much for anyone to make the connection between the inquiry and the Kennedy assassination. In any event," she continued, "I don't know what we'll do with the information, even if I find that Ted Roberts did have some kind of contact with de Mohrenschildt. We can't leap to conclusions about the Kennedy assassination merely because one of our case officers had some contact with a person who may have been some kind of informant for the agency."

"You're quite right, Kay," Gimble said, leaning forward and placing his clasped hands on the desk. "Finding answers to Jim's questions by itself may not be enough. But if we have enough information, we can go public with it. I could then go to Harris," he said, referring to Harris Wallingford, the Senate majority leader, "and seek the establishment of a special Senate committee to investigate the Kennedy assassination. The last special investigation of the assassination was conducted by the House of Representatives in 1978. We could take this new information to build on the record they developed—a record, I might add, that supports my own doubts as to whether Oswald did it by himself or even whether he did it at all."

Jim was buoyed by Gimble's response.

"I'm glad to hear that, Senator," he said, "because if a new Senate investigation is announced, it'll make it that much more difficult—and meaningless—for someone to chase after Kelly. The inquiry into Ted Roberts's role will be in the hands of Congress, and scaring or even harming Kelly will be of no benefit."

"Absolutely," said Gimble. "But remember, Jim, that any new congressional hearing into the Kennedy assassination based on Ted Roberts's letter could cause the kind of embarrassment and heartache I'm sure Kelly wants to avoid."

"True enough, and I'll keep that in mind. But I'd be interested in knowing why you have doubts about Oswald's role."

"Oh, I don't know. There are so many troubling aspects about any claim that Oswald did it and that he did it by himself."

Jim was not going to let Gimble off the hook so easily.

"Such as…?"

"I grew up with guns in Minnesota, hunting all kinds of things," Gimble began, leaning back in his chair. "And I find it hard to believe that Oswald, even as an ex-Marine, could fire three bullets within about seven seconds or so from a hundred yards, or whatever it was from the Book Depository, and hit a moving target with two of them. That's pretty remarkable shooting. Especially when you realize that he was using a World War II vintage rifle with a scope that was later found to be out of alignment. Which may explain why Oswald missed killing General Walker with the same rifle from thirty-five yards—even though Walker, unlike Kennedy, was sitting still."

"Maybe it was just dumb luck," Jim responded.

"Maybe. But then other things make it hard to believe that Oswald was involved at all."

"What do you mean, Geoff?" Brownstein asked, her curiosity obviously aroused.

"For starters, there's the Zapruder film."

"Oh, yes," Brownstein said. "I've seen the video. It's very graphic. The whole side of Kennedy's head was blown off."

"Exactly," said Gimble. "While experts argue about it, after looking at that video, it's hard for me to believe that the head shot came from the rear. You can clearly see Kennedy's head being thrown backward. So I have to assume the shot came from the front. And if it came from the front, it couldn't have been done by Oswald because the Book Depository was in the rear."

"In fact," Jim said, "there were lots of eyewitnesses on Dealy Plaza that day who said shots did come from the area in front of Kennedy's limousine. And even the 1978 House Committee concluded that one of the shots came from the front."

"True enough," said Gimble, "although I don't believe the House Committee said the shot from the front killed Kennedy."

"More than that," Brownstein said, "there are many people who've shown that the only explanation consistent with all the known facts is that Oswald did it. But I'm wondering, Geoff," she continued, her hands in her lap, "whether there's anything else that underlies your view about Oswald's role?"

"There is. Oswald's reaction after he was caught. He was incredibly cool and collected. I used to prosecute murderers years ago as the United States attorney in Minneapolis, and I can't remember any of those guys being as cool as Oswald was. Despite hours of interrogation without an attorney, he insisted that he had nothing to do with Kennedy's assassination. Which is also kind of strange if he was using the assassination to make some kind of political statement."

"I hate to be the skeptical one here, Geoff, but all of that has to be taken with a grain of salt. Oswald was an habitual liar. My recollection is that he denied owning any rifle, even though the one found in the Book Depository was his. He even had a false ID on him when he was arrested."

"That's all true. And I guess that does raise some question about these conspiracy theories. But then there's always Jack Ruby."

Brownstein stood up and wandered aimlessly over to the bookshelf by the senator's desk.

"Oh," she said with some weariness, "I've heard that too. People say he killed Oswald as an agent of the Mafia."

"Yeah, but consider this. Did you know, Kay, that Ruby was sweating profusely and pacing back and forth in his cell in the police station immediately after he shot Oswald. The police on duty said that he was like a caged, wild animal. And you know what finally calmed Ruby down?"

"What?"

"When they told him that Oswald was dead. It was as though he could finally relax, knowing that his mission had been accomplished."

"Well," Brownstein said to Jim, "you can see that your senator has a certain enthusiasm for this subject."

"I can indeed."

"I don't know if I can mount the same enthusiasm in my agency, but I'm willing to proceed to the next step. But please don't assume, Jim, that this will be simple and quick. Developing the facts—even to support a new Senate investigation—can take longer than we would like. Especially since we'll have to be careful. I'll start by picking one top case officer to examine Ted Roberts's record and to make an effort to find those missing de Mohrenschildt records. And we can go from there."

Jim almost bounded back to his office with excitement. He congratulated himself on the wisdom of going to Gimble and trying to get the CIA involved. Although he liked Harvey Teasdale, you couldn't have a better friend at the CIA than Brownstein.

Kelly was less enthusiastic when Jim reached her on the phone in the barn. She was, as Gimble anticipated, concerned about a new congressional investigation into the Kennedy assassination.

"I don't know, Jim. I keep thinking about what Harvey said. We're starting to get more people involved, and I'm scared that we'll lose control of this thing."

"But we talked about this already," Jim pleaded with some exasperation. "We agreed this was a good idea."

"I know, I know. But I'm just starting to have second thoughts. That's all."

Jim was crushed. He wanted, he needed, Kelly to agree with him.

"Look," he said, "why don't you think about this some more, and we'll get together tonight and talk about it."

"Getting together is always a great idea. Why don't you come out here around eight?"

Jim agreed and the conversation ended. As he hung up the telephone, Jim thought he heard a strange click. He looked at the receiver he was holding for a fleeting moment. His thoughts turned again, as they often did, to Teasdale's warning about sophisticated surveillance. He had tried to be careful in meetings and telephone conversations. But maybe, Jim said to himself, he had to be even more careful. Nothing of course could be done about the conversation that was now over. But it was something to keep in mind for the future.

CHAPTER 40

April 1998

Ted Roberts slowly walked into his library and started to absent-mindedly review the books on the shelves that lined the far side of the room. His eyes stopped at Thirteen Days, *Robert Kennedy's memoir of the Cuban missile crisis. Roberts placed his coffee mug on the desk and pulled the book out and started leafing through the pages. Memories of that time surged forward. The tension. The excitement. The frustration. He had had mixed feelings about the result. But he was there. A part of the Kennedy team. A part of history.*

It could have all ended so differently, he reminded himself. He could have worn that experience with the Kennedys as a badge of honor. But he had decided, as young men in a hurry sometimes do, that he had greater wisdom and insight than the people he worked for. And so he had continued to attend the meetings at Bruce's Georgetown home. The group remained at eight men, all of whom appeared to appreciate the enormity of their inquiry.

By the late spring of 1963 Bruce had decided that they should discontinue the meetings, at least for the time being, that it would be better if people assumed individual tasks to advance their project. Bruce would be the point person for everyone. No one objected. All recognized that no more discussion was needed to define their ultimate goal. And everyone trusted Bruce to do what was necessary.

Before they adjourned that last meeting, Ted gathered the courage to express reservations that had continued to suffuse his thinking.

"Shouldn't we take a step back and re-think this one more time?" he had boldly asked when Bruce asked if there were any further questions. "We all have our frustrations, and we all recognize the danger, but will history see this the way we do, as an unfortunate but necessary measure to protect our country? Or will we just be seen as a

band of conspirators who assumed power that never belonged to us and committed a deed that can never be forgiven?"

Although they had discussed the moral and historical ramifications of their inquiry innumerable times, Ted's question provoked considerable debate. As usual, Bruce sat quietly for a few minutes while others expressed their opinions—all agreeing that Ted's question was understandable but long since answered by the president's unforgivable conduct.

Everyone retreated to silence when Bruce began to speak.

"Your question is a good one, Ted, and one that we should never be afraid to ask ourselves again and again. But the truth is that we will never know beforehand how history will regard us. No one can have that kind of assurance. I have no doubt that some people, if they found out, would regard us as traitors and never forgive us. But we cannot be paralyzed by the risk. We have to do our duty as we see it. The only saving grace," he continued with everyone's rapt attention, "if saving grace it be, is that no one will ever know of our role. As we discussed from the beginning, we must each take a vow of silence, never to discuss this matter again as a group or with anyone. The secret must die with each of us. And anyone who violates, or even threatens to violate, that trust will be placing his own life at risk."

There was some nodding of heads as Bruce finished, and everyone left for the evening shortly afterward. As Ted started to walk through the dining room door, Bruce took his right hand in his and held it firmly for what seemed a long time.

"I appreciate your candor," he quietly said to the young case officer. "It took a lot of guts to raise that question in front of this group at this juncture. It's one of the reasons I'm comforted by your participation."

Bruce's comment endeared Roberts to Bruce that much more and was still uppermost in his mind when Lord telephoned Ted a few days later to remind Ted of his individual task. They agreed to meet the following Tuesday afternoon at Bassin's, the restaurant located around the corner from the White House on Pennsylvania Avenue.

As he sat back in his library chair, Ted thought back to that rendezvous at Bassin's. It was May and the weather was beautiful. The dogwoods and azaleas were in bloom and the sweet fragrance of flowers surrounded the White House grounds. Ted left a meeting in the West Wing sometime in mid-afternoon and walked the few blocks to the restaurant. Bruce was sitting at one of the outdoor tables when he got there, seeming to enjoy the mid-day traffic that traveled up and down the broad expanse of Pennsylvania Avenue to the Capitol.

Ted ordered coffee and, since he had missed lunch, a hamburger. Bruce nursed an ice tea. There was little small talk. Bruce was not the kind of person to indulge in idle discussion. He was almost always all business. They discussed Ted's individual project at some length. It was important to the group's plan, but Bruce's questions were curt and to the point. When Ted asked how the other parts of the plan were proceeding, Bruce did not worry about social amenities.

"It's best that you not know everything," was all he said. Although curious, Ted decided not to push the point. Maybe Bruce was right.

Finally satisfied that he had received what he needed, Bruce wrote a reminder to himself on a napkin and soon departed, leaving Ted to eat his hamburger alone. And now, as he recalled the scene more than thirty years later, Ted Roberts knew that Bruce had walked away with more than a napkin containing sensitive information. Bruce Lord had walked away with his peace of mind.

CHAPTER 41

Caleb Butler gathered up his papers from the counsel's table in the high-ceilinged courtroom of the United States Court of Appeals on the sixth floor of the United States Courthouse on Third Street and Constitution Avenue. As Butler was closing up his briefcase, the court clerk was already announcing the next case to be argued before the panel of three judges who sat stone-faced on the podium. Five attorneys dressed in dark suits rose from their seats in the polished wooden pews in the back of the courtroom and started to make their way to the counsel tables. Butler nodded to them as he moved through the aisle to the anteroom right outside the courtroom.

Small groups of attorneys were gathered just beyond the courtroom doors and engaged in hushed conversations underneath life-size portraits of former judges. After talking briefly with some of the attorneys, Butler left the anteroom and walked through the spacious corridors to the elevators. As he pushed the button for the first floor, Butler rehashed the arguments he had just made to the court and assured himself that he had handled the judges' questions well.

As he stepped off the elevator onto the main floor, Butler decided to check in with his secretary. Although his office was only a ten-minute walk from the courthouse, Butler had other pressing matters that might require his immediate attention.

He left the courthouse by the Constitution Avenue entrance and, as cars and taxis whisked by, pulled the small mobile phone from the inside breast pocket of his jacket and punched in the numbers for his office. Butler's secretary answered after two rings.

"Mornin', Laci darlin'. What's happening?"

"It's been pretty quiet, Caleb. Except that you did get a strange call from a woman named Jennifer."

"Does she have a last name?"

"That's the strange thing about it. I asked if she knew you, and she said no. But she wouldn't give me her last name. The only thing she would say is that it had to do with the lawsuit you filed against Barrington and Stone."

That response grabbed Butler's attention.

"What exactly did she say about the lawsuit?"

"Nothing really. Only that she had read about it somewhere and that it would be in your client's interest to talk to her. Something about information she thought you could use."

"Did she leave a number?"

"She sure did."

Laci then gave Butler the number. The 301 area code meant that the woman was located somewhere in a Maryland suburb of Washington, DC.

Butler ended the call with Laci and immediately punched in the number his secretary had just given him. After four or five rings, a woman answered. Her voice was vibrant and self-assured.

"Mornin', ma'am," Butler said in his charming manner. "This is Caleb Butler. My secretary left me a message that you had called."

"Yes, I did. I read in a travel magazine that you had filed a lawsuit against Barrington and Stone because someone got mauled to death by a lion on one of their safaris."

"That's correct, ma'am. We did file such a lawsuit."

"You may want to talk to Mary McGuire. She lives in Bethesda. She may be able to tell you something that may be useful in your lawsuit."

"Ma'am, it's obvious that you're tryin' to help my client, and I do deeply appreciate that. But can I ask your full name and what kind of information Mary McGuire might have for us?"

"My name really doesn't matter, Mr. Butler. All I know is that Barrington and Stone should learn the meaning of the word 'justice.' And maybe talking to Mary McGuire will help achieve that goal."

"Are you a friend of Mary McGuire's? Is that it?"

"The nature of my relationship with Mary McGuire isn't really important, Mr. Butler."

"Is your first name really Jennifer?"

"Actually, it's not. And, while I don't want to be rude, Mr. Butler, I think I've said all I want to say. Goodbye."

The dial tone signaled that the conversation was over. Butler immediately called Laci and asked her to find Mary McGuire's telephone number while he waited in the sunshine on the courthouse steps. Laci was back to him within minutes, and Butler punched in the numbers that his secretary gave him.

A woman's voice answered after a few rings. In contrast to "Jennifer," Butler sensed that the woman on the phone was older and more cautious, almost demure. The voice was soft, barely audible. Butler conjured up a small woman, fearful of something, or perhaps full of sadness.

"Mornin', ma'am. This is Caleb Butler, and I hope you'll pardon the interruption, but I was calling to tell you about a phone call I received that involves you."

"Oh?" said the woman, obviously intrigued. "Please go on."

"I should start by explaining that I'm an attorney in Washington, DC."

"Have I done something wrong?"

"No. Not at all," Butler responded in reassuring tones. "In fact, I'm hoping that you can help me to do something right."

"What might that be?"

Butler realized that the woman was not the kind to engage in long conversations with a stranger and that he had to get to the point quickly.

"I received a telephone call this morning from someone who knows you. She wouldn't give me her name, but she said that I should talk to you about a problem my client has."

Before he could continue, Mary McGuire cut him off.

"I'm not sure I know why you're calling, Mr. Butler, but it's not my practice to become involved in other people's problems. So I'm sorry you've gone to the trouble to call me. I do wish you success on your client's problem, whatever it may be, but I have to go now."

"Please don't hang up, ma'am," Butler pleaded in a stern but gentle manner. "I think I need to talk to you and I hope you'll at least give me a minute more."

"Just one minute, Mr. Butler."

"My lawsuit is against Barrington and Stone."

There was a long pause on the other end of the line and Butler's instinct told him that he had hit pay dirt of some kind. The only question was how much it was worth. Butler decided to take advantage of Mary McGuire's silence and to continue talking.

"You see, ma'am, my client is a young woman whose brother was killed by a lion on one of Barrington and Stone's photographic safaris. They've insisted they took all necessary precautions and are refusing to take any responsibility for this horrible incident. I'm led to believe that you may have information that would help me convince a court that Barrington and Stone should be held accountable for the death of my client's brother."

"I see," Mary McGuire said without emotion. There was another pause, and Butler could sense that she was trying to decide whether she should help him. Butler wanted to alleviate her obvious discomfort and make her realize that it was the right thing to do. But Mary McGuire was not making it easy for him.

"I'm not sure I want to talk about Barrington and Stone anymore," she finally said. "So I think I'll have to pass, Mr. Butler."

"Please, ma'am. Please. This is extremely important, and I would very much like your cooperation."

Butler knew that, if left with no other choice, he could subpoena Mary McGuire and force her to testify. But he didn't want to threaten her with legal process. Voluntary cooperation was almost always preferable.

"I don't want to appear presumptuous, ma'am," Butler continued, "but I'd like to make a suggestion. Could I meet with you at your home or wherever you would like for half an hour or so? That's all. I would very much appreciate it. And I have a feeling you'll feel better if we talk a little bit."

There was another pause as Butler waited for Mary McGuire to say something. He nearly jumped through the phone when he heard her response.

"When would you like to come out?"

Chapter 42

The white cordless phone rang a few times before it was finally picked up. The man put the phone to his ear and looked out the large window at the jagged brown mountains in the distance.

"Yes."

"We've got problems."

"What do you mean? I thought you had this thing under control."

"I thought I did."

"You told me that a message was sent to the girl and that she had been warned about pursuing the matter. You told me that did the trick."

"That's what I thought. But her boyfriend's gone to the senator he works for. Geoffrey Gimble. You know him. He wants the CIA to find some information so that Congress can open another investigation into the Kennedy assassination."

"This is not good."

"Don't worry. I can squelch the whole thing."

"I'd like to believe you, but my instinct tells me otherwise. Anyway, I'll be in Washington tomorrow. We'll talk about it."

The man placed the white phone back in its cradle and turned his eyes to the nearby mountains. They were losing control again, and he didn't like it. Why did life have to be so complicated? And why couldn't the dead rest in peace? No, he said to himself, it was not easy being the caretaker of a secret.

Chapter 43

The Monocle restaurant on Capitol Hill was unusually busy for a Thursday night. Almost every table was taken, and waiters were gliding noiselessly through the aisles with food and drink amid the quiet conversations of the patrons, most of whom were men in business suits.

Strategically located a few blocks from the Senate office buildings, the restaurant had long been a gathering place for Washington's power brokers, especially those having business with the United States Senate and its members. The subdued lighting and the spacing of the tables made the restaurant particularly conducive to those interested in a relaxed setting for the conduct of business.

In one of the far corners of the restaurant, Geoffrey Gimble put his coffee cup down on the white tablecloth and looked up at his dinner companion. Ari Stein, Israel's ambassador to the United States, was placing his napkin on the table.

"That certainly was a satisfying meal," said Gimble.

"Couldn't be better. And I'm glad we had this opportunity to review the situation. We really need those appropriations, and I'm hopeful we've mapped out a strategy that will help you get the president's bill through the Senate."

"It won't be easy, but we've got a good shot. I think other pressures, including the need to get it done before the summer recess, will help."

"I place our fate in your hands for the next few weeks. But tonight my fate lies in my wife's hands, and it's time for me to return to the embassy."

Gimble looked down at his watch. The hands showed that it was ten-twenty-two. He placed his napkin on the table as the two of them stood up. They walked to the front door, talking animatedly about the results of the recent Wimbledon tennis tournament. The maitre'd' bowed slightly as they passed and then opened the door for them.

Gimble and Stein were greeted by warm air as they stepped out onto D Street in the Northeast quadrant of Washington. Stein nodded in the direction of the black limousine on the other side of the street. The chauffeur was standing by the rear door, obviously waiting for his passenger.

"Can I give you a lift back to your home?"

"No thanks, Ari. It's a beautiful evening, and the short walk will do me good after that meal."

"Till tomorrow then. Shalom, my friend."

"Good night, Ari. It's always a pleasure."

As Stein walked toward the limousine, Gimble started down D Street and then turned left on First Street. He felt good as he moved briskly down the street. The night air was suffused with the pleasant smells and noises of summer. It all brought back fond memories of his childhood in rural Minnesota, a time, Gimble was sure, when life was much simpler.

He glanced at the Washington landmarks that he passed as he continued down First Street. The United States Supreme Court. The Library of Congress. And, on the other side of the street, the majestic facade of the Capitol building itself. All bathed in warm lights that made the white marble that much more radiant.

Yes, he assured himself, I have done well. Washington's a great city, and even better if you're a United States Senator. There were, to be sure, some costs. The hours are lousy. Hearings most mornings. Debates that last well into the night, primarily to allow constituents to see their senators on C-Span. And then there was the ridiculously low salary. An income of a hundred fifty thousand dollars or so might seem plentiful to some. Most of his constituents certainly thought so. He laughed to himself as he thought about it. His constituents probably thought he lived a life of luxury, being driven everywhere in a limo. He knew better. Washington was an expensive town. Only senators with great wealth or a modest living style could survive on their salaries.

Although considerable, the costs paled beside the benefits. You can't beat the drama and beauty of your surroundings, he said to himself in his silent monologue. For people like him, it was also a grand opportunity, frustrating at times, to do some good. And that certainly helped to offset the meager earnings.

The meeting earlier in the day with Kay Brownstein and Jim Roth was a case in point, he said to himself. Here he was, a country boy from Minnesota, talking with the CIA director, who also happened to be his lover, and a harried but talented legislative aide, reviewing the Kennedy assassination, one of the country's most enduring tragedies. And more than that, he was in a position to do something about it. He had generated further investigation by the CIA. He might initiate new congressional hearings. And, who knows, he might even play a role in finally solving the mystery.

Before he knew it, Gimble was on the Southeast side of town and beyond the office buildings of the House of Representatives. A few minutes and he would be back in his townhouse. He would call Kay and then see if there was a movie he could watch on television. Something to distract him and put him to sleep.

His musings amidst the quiet of the night were suddenly interrupted by the sound of footsteps on the pavement. Quick footsteps. Someone coming up behind him. Fast.

Gimble stopped and turned around. The dimly lit streetlights revealed nothing. No one was there. Gimble stood, looking for a few seconds. Maybe he was mistaken. Maybe it was someone moving in the opposite direction. He turned back and continued his walk home.

The footsteps resumed again. Someone walking quickly. Someone coming up from behind him.

Gimble's heartbeat accelerated. Was he being stalked? He turned around again. Nothing. He felt like shouting out but resisted the impulse. He looked around. Most of the townhouses on the street were dark. But if someone assaulted him, surely he could shout and catch at least one homeowner's attention.

He turned around and started walking again. The footsteps on the pavement started up again.

Gimble picked up the pace and was almost trotting. His mind raced over many things. Crime in the nation's capital was still a problem. Even for senators. He remembered the story he had heard about John Stennis, an older senator from Mississippi who had been shot many years ago by a youth in a robbery attempt right outside Stennis's home in a fashionable neighborhood off Connecticut Avenue. If it happened to Stennis, Gimble said to himself, it could happen to me.

The footsteps continued, but Gimble did not stop or turn around. He was, he admitted to himself, too scared. He was approaching his street. Gimble reviewed his options. There weren't many, and he picked one that seemed to offer the best refuge. I'll turn left and duck into the alley between the townhouses immediately around the corner, he said to himself. I won't be seen, and I can wait there in the shadows. Wait for what? he asked himself. Time. Ten minutes. Fifteen minutes.

Enough time to make him feel secure that the danger, if danger it was, had passed.

Gimble turned the corner and, as planned, quickly moved into the alley. He went back a few yards and just stood there in the darkness, not moving, as still as he could be. There were no sounds except for his rapid heartbeat, which sounded like it was coming through his chest.

The footsteps stopped. He strained to hear some movement. He wanted, he needed, to hear something, a noise that would alert him to what was happening—or what might happen. But the only thing he heard aside from his heartbeat and his heavy breathing was the rustle of the leaves in the trees from the light breeze.

He stood there in silence for what seemed like hours but was probably only minutes.

The voice came from behind and almost made Gimble stumble backward.

"Hiding from something?"

Gimble whipped around. Although his eyes were accustomed to the dark, it was still hard to see the man clearly. But the figure appeared to be a man wearing a suit and tie and holding what appeared to be a handgun with a silencer.

"Why are you following me?" Gimble blurted out finally. "What do you want?"

"No more investigations."

"What're you talking about?"

Gimble never heard the assailant's response. Three muffled shots rang out in quick succession and pierced Gimble's heart. The senator silently collapsed in a crumpled heap on the alley's broken pavement.

The assailant took off his gloves and slowly unscrewed the silencer from the handgun's barrel. He placed the silencer in his jacket pocket and returned the gun to the shoulder holster underneath the jacket. He fished Gimble's wallet out of his jacket, took the dollar bills, and pulled Gimble's pants pockets inside out. He then turned around and quietly left the alley from the other end.

Chapter 44

Jim was looking at the mirror in his bedroom and tying his tie when the phone rang. He looked at the clock radio by his bed. Seven-thirty. He knew it was his father. No one else called him so early in the morning.

Jim walked over to the nightstand by the bed with his tie still askew and picked up his mobile phone.

"Hi, Dad."

There was no immediate response. All he could hear was sobbing. Uncontrolled sobbing.

"Dad?"

"Jim, he's dead."

"Becky? Who's dead? What're you saying?"

"He's dead," she repeated in between sobs.

"Who, Becky? Who?"

"The senator," she finally said. "He was killed last night."

"Oh my God," Jim moaned as he sat down on the bed.

A thousand thoughts crowded Jim's mind. He then remembered that Becky was still on the phone.

"What happened?" he asked.

"Nobody knows for sure. He was found in an alley a few blocks from his home. It was apparently a robbery. His pants pockets were turned inside out and the money from his wallet was missing."

"Where are you now?"

"I'm home, but I got the call from Helen," she said, referring to the senator's confidential secretary, "and I'm leaving for the office. Helen's already there."

Jim was silent as Becky's message sank in. Her voice brought him out of his daze.

"Jim, you've got to come to the office right away."

"I'm leaving now."

Jim put the phone back on the nightstand and got up from the bed. He was stunned. People were assaulted and sometimes killed in robbery attempts in Washington all the time. But he never anticipated that it would happen to someone he knew. And especially not Senator Gimble.

He walked back to the mirror and stared blankly at his image with his tie askew. His thoughts drifted back to the meeting with the senator and Kay Brownstein yesterday. And then to the click he had heard on the phone when he finished his call with Kelly.

"It can't be," he murmured to the image in the mirror. And then he paused. "Can it?"

He walked over to the edge of the bed and sat down. He wanted, he needed, answers, but all he could do was think of questions. What had really happened to the senator? Was it really just another street crime? Or had someone murdered the senator because of his willingness to open new congressional hearings on the Kennedy assassination? And, if it was a planned murder, was Jim the one responsible for the senator's death? After all, there would have been no promise for new congressional hearings if Jim had not asked for the meeting in the first place. The horror of that possibility gripped Jim, and he leaned over, placing his head in his hands.

Logic pushed Jim to think of the future. If a United States senator could be disposed of so easily, what about him and Kelly? Were they next? These assassins had already failed in two attempts on Kelly's life, but Jim knew now that Kelly's survival was nothing but dumb luck. He could not take any more chances.

Jim picked up his mobile phone and punched in Kelly's number. She answered with an echo that signaled her presence in the barn.

"Kelly," Jim asserted, almost demanded. "Don't ask any questions. Just listen. The senator's been killed and I need to talk with you. I have to go to the office for a little bit, and then I want you to meet me at Fletcher's Boathouse down by the canal at noon. And wear something fitting for a canoe ride. We have to be alone where no one can overhear us."

Within hours Jim and Kelly were in a canoe moving slowly down the Potomac River toward the Key Bridge that connected Georgetown with the northern Virginia community of Rosslyn. They slowly drifted under the bridge, past Theodore Roosevelt Island, and toward the commanding white stone structure of the Kennedy Center.

"I just can't believe it," Kelly repeated. "It's all so terrible."

Jim sighed. He was numb from it all. He had gone from a high the day before, knowing that Kay Brownstein was now going to help them, to feeling helpless and stupid and, worst of all, naive. And now, he was sure, he had set in motion a chain of events that had led to Senator Gimble's death.

He had recounted his feelings and thoughts to Kelly, who had listened with rapt attention, her eyes reflecting the sadness and terror she now felt. And then Jim explained his plan. They had to get away after Gimble's funeral, to think it through in peace, to decide what to do. Until this morning, he would not have suggested that he and Kelly go away together. Their relationship had not ripened to the point where that kind of suggestion could be made. But that was yesterday. Today was different. There was no time for niceties. Kelly understood and agreed at once. She knew they had no choice.

Chapter 45

Dwayne Soggs walked quickly down the wooden pier in the late afternoon sun after tying up his sailboat at Mears Marina on Spa Creek in Annapolis. Although his mind was preoccupied with the call he had to make, Soggs could not help but notice the rows of boats tied up in their slips. Most of them were sailboats, and almost all of them were of fairly substantial size. No matter how many times he had walked down that pier, Soggs always enjoyed the sight of those sailboats, now rocking gently in the light wind and salt air and creating a clanging sound as the halyards hit the tall aluminum masts.

As he walked through the near-empty marina in his shorts and T-shirt, Soggs's memory retraced the sail back from St. Michaels. It had been as exhilarating as he could have expected. Fifteen to twenty knot winds from the west, minimal chop on the seas, and clear skies. A real contrast with the trip to St. Michaels, which had been interrupted by several long-lasting squalls. He thought back with pride how he had finally maneuvered his boat into the St. Michaels's harbor without his engine. No small feat with a thirty-foot sailboat. All of which made the trip back to Annapolis that much more enjoyable. An engine that worked and no rough weather to master. Still, the return trip had sapped his strength, and he was looking forward to a cold beer on the deck of his boat. After that, he would clean up the boat and then wander across the bridge to town to get an early dinner at one of the early American pubs by the Annapolis Dock.

That was all yet to come. His first priority was to reach Nogasaki. The medical examiner had been out each time Soggs had called, and Soggs had not yet talked with him.

Although Soggs had his cell phone with him, it was not working each time Nogasaki had returned the call, obviously a reflection of the isolated places Soggs had visited around St. Michaels.

As he reached the end of the pier, Soggs saw the men's lockers. He parked himself in the shade on the bench right outside, pulled out his cell phone, and punched in Nogasaki's number. Within seconds the phone was ringing. Soggs was about to hang up when he heard Nogasaki's voice. He sounded breathless, like he had been out running.

"What're you up to, man?" Soggs quipped. "It sounds like you've been jogging around the cadavers."

"Almost—but not quite—true. I'm trying to get out of here, and I made the mistake of picking up the phone. If I'd known it was you, I would've let it ring."

"You're too kind. Hey," Soggs said, changing to a more serious tone, "I got some questions for you about that Stamford case. You remember him, don't you?"

"Sure, the dude with the great health report who died for no reason. You figured that one out?"

"I'm not sure. But I've got some new thoughts. They came to me when my engine shut down in the Chesapeake Bay in the middle of a thunderstorm."

"You certainly picked an interesting time to come up with new thoughts. Why didn't you wait until you were on land and your life wasn't at risk?"

"I think better under pressure."

"Okay, okay. So let's hear it. What're your new thoughts?"

"Check this out," Soggs began. "I go down into the cabin to find out why my engine shut down, and I realize it's because of an air pocket in the fuel lines. A tiny bit of air shut down the whole goddamn engine."

"I don't know much about sailboat engines, but I am curious to see how you make the connection to Stamford's death."

"Patience, man. I'm just getting into gear."

"All right."

"So I thought to myself, 'why couldn't the same thing happen to a person?' I mean, if air could prevent the fuel from flowing through a tube and getting into the engine, maybe air could prevent the blood from flowing into some vital organ. You get it? Maybe somebody injected air into Stamford's veins and prevented blood from going through his pipes the way it should."

"I stand corrected," said Nogasaki. "You're a lot smarter than I thought."

"I could've told you that."

"Anyway, you're right."

"I am?" Soggs responded with excitement.

"Hard to believe, huh?" Nogasaki replied with a laugh. "Yeah, air can block blood flow and kill a person. And if there's enough air injected, it could kill someone almost instantaneously."

"You're kidding."

"Not at all. It's called an air embolus."

"Tell me more."

"Okay. You have to go back to the basics of anatomy."

"Make it simple," Soggs said. "I'm no physician and my brain's a little mushier than usual because I just got off the boat."

"You have to think of the blood flow through the body. The blood in your body contains oxygen. The blood with oxygen, or the oxygenated blood, is supplied to the body through the aorta. The veins then take the used blood—which has been depleted of oxygen—back to the heart for a new injection of oxygen."

"How does that happen?"

"I'm getting to that. You have to remember that the heart is nothing more than a glorified pump."

"I can see you're taking my request for simplicity to heart."

"I'll let that pun go by without comment. Anyway, the blood from the veins goes into the right atrium of the heart, which is like a chamber, and then to the right ventricle, a different chamber. And from there the blood leaves the heart through the pulmonary artery, which goes to the lungs. I'm really simplifying it here but, in essence, the pulmonary artery takes that blood and allows it be injected with oxygen."

"So far so good. I understand what you're saying."

"Here's the critical part. If you inject air into someone's vein, it could—if there's enough air—prevent the blood from going into the pulmonary artery or, the more likely scenario, it could stop the blood once it's in the pulmonary artery. Either way, you're a dead man."

"Is this like a heart attack?"

"No, no. Not at all. A heart attack, at least what I think you're referring to, focuses on the blood that's going to the heart muscle itself. When people talk of cholesterol and clogged arteries, they're talking about the blood the heart needs to keep on pumping."

Soggs paused to digest the medical examiner's explanation. One question immediately loomed large in his mind.

"Let's go back to the injection of air into the veins. Would there be any signs of what happened if there was an autopsy?"

"It depends."

"On what?"

"On when the autopsy occurs, for one thing. Let's go back a step. Take your ordinary surgery. Surgeons are always concerned about air getting into the veins when they do surgery, and if something like that happened while they're operating, they could probably see some kind of action that would alert them to what was happening. Some gurgling of blood in a cavity. But if you do an autopsy a day or two or more after it happens, it would be more difficult to detect. And unless you knew what you were looking for, you wouldn't even consider it."

"How long was Stamford dead before you did the autopsy?"

"I can't remember without looking at the report, but I'm sure it was at least a couple of days. And I have to be honest. I wasn't looking for an air pocket in the pulmonary artery. I don't know if I would've found anything if I had thought about it. But I'm telling you, I know I didn't think about it. It's not something you see very often. In fact, I don't know that I've ever seen it."

"Why not? I know that sounds stupid. But wouldn't more people bent on crime think about it?"

"Probably not. It sounds like a pretty sophisticated means of killing someone. Most of the murders I see are by people who don't have the brains or the time to be sophisticated about it."

Soggs was silent for a moment as he absorbed Nogasaki's comments.

"So what now?" the medical examiner asked. "Stamford's been buried, you know."

"Yeah, but this is a real possibility. It would explain why the guy otherwise appeared to be in good health."

"It certainly would," Nogasaki replied.

"Do me a favor. Go back to the autopsy report, and I'll do the same tomorrow morning. Maybe there's something else in there that would bring this all together."

"You got it. Now I'm out of here. Catch you tomorrow."

Soggs closed the phone and looked out over the boats tied up at the docks and gently rocking in the light winds. Life sure was unpredictable. One phone call and everything had changed. Maybe he could tie down those loose ends after all.

CHAPTER 46

Jim and Kelly stood on Nebraska Avenue in the Northwest section of Washington. The rambling campus of American University was to their backs, but their attention was focused on the imposing stone facade of the Metropolitan Memorial United Methodist Church across the street. They watched in silence as large crowds of people in suits and other business attire gathered in pockets on the manicured church grounds.

God, Jim thought to himself, I never thought I'd be attending Senator Gimble's funeral. At least not at this stage in my life. I'm supposed to be in the Senate today, working on some important piece of public business. Instead, I'm saying goodbye to the man who's done more than anyone to shape my career.

Jim looked up at the sky. Thick dark clouds moved slowly overhead. The rain seemed imminent but had held off all morning. A sudden surge of sadness overwhelmed Jim and he grabbed Kelly's hand. She responded by gently squeezing his hand.

"What's with the traffic?"

Kelly's question brought Jim back to reality.

"What're you talking about?"

"There is none."

Jim looked around and noticed that the section of the street in front of the church had been blocked off at both ends by large black sport-utility vehicles with red lights flashing in the windshields. Similar vehicles were parked on the sides of the street, and there was an abundance of police cars and officers swarming all over the church grounds. Even more noticeable to Jim's eye were the numerous men in dark glasses with earplugs. The Secret Service.

"The president's obviously coming," Jim replied. "I'd heard rumors that he might give one of the eulogies if he returned from Europe in time. I guess he made it back."

Jim gave a sigh. Nothing was going to change by staying on the opposite side of the street.

"Come on," he said to Kelly. "We might as well go over."

They walked across the street, and Jim began to spot many familiar faces. Senators. Cabinet members. Some colleagues from the various Senate staffs.

As they moved through the crowd toward the church entrance, Kelly stopped without warning. Jim turned around and saw her eyes wide with fear. Or was it anger? He wasn't sure. He turned back to see a tall, fashionably dressed man with silver hair looking at Kelly from a short distance. The man stared at Kelly for a few seconds and then abruptly pivoted to walk away from her and Jim.

"Who was that?" Jim asked.

"The asshole congressman I used to work for."

Before Jim could ask anything more, they were distracted by a familiar voice saying hello to them. They turned around to see Harvey Teasdale.

"Well, this is a surprise," said Jim.

"It shouldn't be," said Teasdale. "As I mentioned at our first meeting, I had many meetings and other encounters with Senator Gimble when I was with the agency. And I always had great respect for him. So I wanted to come to pay my respects."

"That's really good of you," said Jim.

"Not at all. It really is a tragedy. It's one thing to die in battle. But these senseless killings are really heart-wrenching."

"You can say that again," Kelly chimed in.

"Did they find the guy who did it?"

"No," said Jim. He knew they never would, but he could not tell Teasdale—at least not now—what he really thought. That the murder was anything but a random street crime. Maybe later he would convey his suspicions to Teasdale. But for now it was something he had to keep to himself. So he pretended that he believed what everyone else did—that it was just another killing on Washington's streets. "We've been hounding the police department," Jim explained, truthfully, "but they've come up with nothing. Absolutely nothing."

"Well, look," said Teasdale, "I'll let you go. I just wanted to come over and say hello. And I'm sure we'll be in touch again soon."

As Jim and Kelly resumed their approach to the church, they saw Kay Brownstein coming toward them. Jim's attention was immediately drawn to her eyes.

They were dull, lackluster. For some reason, Jim wondered if she had been crying.

Jim shook Brownstein's hand and introduced her to Kelly. Brownstein gave Kelly a warm greeting, holding her hand for a long moment.

"It's so good to meet you," she said to Kelly. "I'm just sorry that it has to be under these circumstances."

"I'm glad to meet you too. Especially because I wanted to thank you for meeting with Jim the other day. It was so good of you to take the time and, more importantly, to offer your help."

"You're quite welcome. It seemed like a good cause. I had hoped that Geoff would be here to guide us in dealing with these matters." As she made that remark, she gave Jim a forced smile. She then turned back to Kelly. "But my offer still stands, and I'm hoping we'll have something to tell you sometime soon."

The conversation was interrupted by the arrival of a young man who mentioned to Jim that the pallbearers were needed at the church. Jim excused himself and walked off with the young man. Brownstein and Kelly watched them leave, caught in a seemingly awkward moment without anything to say to each other. Brownstein broke the silence.

"Kelly, I'd like to talk to you about a few things. Would it be possible for you to come by my office in the next day or so?"

"I'm going out of town tonight for a few days. But I'll talk to Jim and I'm sure we can arrange something after I get back."

"I think the world of Jim, and I know Geoff did too. But I'd rather talk to you alone."

Brownstein's proposal caught Kelly off-guard. Why would she want to exclude Jim? Other questions popped into her mind, but she suppressed them all.

"Not a problem. It's not every day the director of the CIA wants to meet with me."

"If it's convenient, what about this afternoon? I think I could clear my calendar for some time."

"Sure."

"Good. Here's my card. Call my office and ask for Amanda. She'll set it up."

Kelly scrutinized the card closely and then looked up at Brownstein. She had a strange look in her eyes. But there was no time to dwell on that.

"Come on," said Brownstein. "I think it's time to go inside."

CHAPTER 47

Jim leaned back on the chair in his condo and gazed out the window at the Washington Monument. The rain had finally come and had then given way to sunshine and less humidity. Under other circumstances, there would have been many things he could have done on such a pleasant afternoon. But not now.

He twisted off the top on the bottle of beer and took a long swallow. He had hoped that the funeral would provide a release from the tension and the grief, but it had proved to be a false hope. He still could not reconcile himself to the senator's death. For three years the senator had been the central focus of his activities and thoughts. It was hard to believe that the man had been with him one day and gone the next. Jim recalled something Norman Mailer had written about John Kennedy's death. Jim couldn't remember the exact words, but it was something to the effect that tragedy was like an amputation. The nerves of one's memory, Mailer had said, go back to the limb that's no longer there.

Jim didn't know much about Norman Mailer, but those words captured exactly how he felt. With one exception. Jim was not only wrestling with the emotional trauma of the senator's loss. He was also plagued by guilt. The police insisted it was nothing but a standard mugging. But Jim could not shake the possibility, if not likelihood, that Gimble had been stalked and killed by someone who knew of the meeting with Brownstein. Someone who feared the consequence of the CIA's investigation and a possible congressional inquiry into the Kennedy assassination. In other circumstances the notion would have seemed preposterous. Not anymore. Kelly's brush with death had demonstrated that her father's concerns had been well founded. Somebody was fearful of the truth and was apparently willing to use any means—including murder—to prevent its disclosure.

Jim's mind could have continued the pursuit of unanswerable questions, but the phone was ringing. He picked it up after a few rings.

"Jimmy, my boy. How're you doing?"

His father's voice had its customary buoyancy.

"As well as could be expected, Dad."

"I saw the funeral on television. They showed some of the president's speech. He's quite a speaker."

"He sure is. Even I was pretty touched by what he said."

"I feel very bad for you, Jimmy. I really do. I know how hard this must be for you."

"I'll get through it. It'll just take time. But how's by you? How are you feeling?"

"Oh, I'm doing okay. I've gotta use this goddamn wheelchair much of the time. But it's motorized and your mother's getting a fair amount of exercise trying to keep up with me when we go for a walk, if you want to call it that."

Jim had to give the old man credit. He was tough. He's probably nearing the end and still showing a fighting spirit. Jim caught himself as he thought of his father's death. He couldn't imagine how he would deal with that.

"So, Jimmy," his father continued, "what now? What'll you do? You do have to work, you know."

Jim took another swallow of beer and looked out the window toward the Washington Monument.

"I know. But I'm not sure what I'm going to do. I could probably get another job in the Senate. Maybe I'll try practicing law. I don't know. I'm going to take some time off. In fact, Kelly and I are going to go away for a few days, take in some sun and try to figure things out."

"You and Kelly? I knew you were friends but I didn't know things had progressed that far."

Jim thought back to his conversation with Kelly in the canoe and their plan. There was only so much he could afford to tell his father over the phone.

"To tell you the truth, Dad, I don't know how far things have progressed either. But I need a break, and God knows she does too. So we just said, the hell with it. Let's just go. It was kind of spontaneous."

"Hey, Jimmy," the elder Roth interjected, "whatever happened to that lawsuit she filed?"

"Oh, it's still going on. Her lawyer's supposed to meet with someone who may be able to give them some information to break the case wide open. And from what I know about this lawyer, he's a real tiger. So if there's anything out there to help Kelly, I'm sure he'll find it and make good use of it."

"I know some lawyers down in Washington besides you, you know. What's this guy's name?"

"Butler. Caleb Butler."

"That's some name. Sounds like it's right out of a novel."

"No," said Jim with a smile, "I think he's from Kentucky. But he's a character. A real character. If Jim Croce had ever written songs about lawyers, he would have done one on Caleb Butler."

Jim's reference to Croce was not accidental. He knew that his father had been a long-time fan of the mustachioed singer with the curly hair and the songs about funky characters.

"Well, in my book," his father responded, "that's the best compliment you can give a lawyer."

Jim took another swallow of beer and realized that the best antidote for his troubled mind at this point was his father. Jim felt distracted, relieved. And he decided to let the conversation continue, enjoying his father's down-to-earth observations and wry humor. And knowing that this too would pass one day.

Chapter 48

The posted speed limit on the George Washington Parkway on the Virginia side of the Potomac River was fifty, but Kelly kept the Jeep at sixty miles an hour. She didn't want to be late for her three o'clock appointment with Kay Brownstein. She was working on a tight schedule, and there was no room for delay.

Kelly had never been to the CIA before, and Brownstein's assistant, Amanda, had been careful to explain the route. Kelly finally saw the signs for the CIA exit and made the right turn through the tall trees. After a couple of turns, she found herself on the road leading to the CIA headquarters. Within minutes she arrived at the visitor's center. A young woman in uniform inspected her driver's license, gave her a visitor's badge, and advised her to proceed up the winding driveway to the main buildings.

The CIA headquarters was different than Kelly had expected. Instead of a colorless structure in a drab setting, the main building sat on top of a rolling hill surrounded by pine trees and large boulders. A large satellite earth dish and barbed-wire fencing around the perimeter gave some suggestion of the CIA's mission, but, overall, the complex seemed to be more of a corporate park than the housing for the federal government's intelligence operations.

Kelly parked her car in the visitor's lot and walked up to the main building. She was finally here. Thank God, Kelly said to herself. I don't know if I could've taken the tension much longer.

At first it had been curiosity. Kelly had wondered what Brownstein wanted to tell her. Maybe something that would unlock the mystery of her father's letter and his role in the Kennedy assassination. But Kelly's initial curiosity had been eclipsed by a stronger and more troubling emotion. There was something cryptic, even unsettling, about the CIA director's comments at Senator Gimble's funeral. Why, for example, did she not want Jim to come? What kind of secrets could she tell her that could not be shared with Jim? And then there was that look in Brownstein's eyes. A faraway, almost misty, countenance. Something more was at work than her father's letter, Kelly convinced herself, but she had no clue as to what it was.

Kelly's focus shifted to her surroundings as she drew closer to the canopied entrance of the main building of the CIA headquarters. She was particularly taken by the large bronze statute of the Revolutionary War hero Nathan Hale at one side of the entrance. He had a scarf around his neck, his feet were bound, and the inscription at the base contained the all-too-familiar words: "I only regret that I have but one life to give my country."

Kelly strode into the cavernous lobby. It was an impressive introduction to the CIA. Dozens of stars had been chiseled into the marble on one side in memory of CIA employees who had died in service to their country. The other side of the lobby had the Gospel According to Saint John chiseled into the marble: "And ye shall know the truth, and the truth shall make you free." I guess that's why I'm doing this, Kelly said to herself. I'll have to remember those words.

Kelly walked up to the security guard stationed on the right side of the lobby. After confirming the appointment with the director, the guard told her to walk through the metal detectors. She was then escorted by another young woman in uniform to the VIP waiting room on the right side of the lobby. No one else was there. Kelly waited for about ten minutes before a tall, thin woman with short gray hair walked up to her and introduced herself as Amanda.

"Come on," said Amanda. "The director's waiting for you."

They walked in silence to the left side of the lobby, climbed a short flight of stairs, and stopped at a closed elevator door. Amanda inserted a key, the elevator door opened, and they walked inside. Amanda pushed the button for the seventh floor, and within seconds Kelly entered a small but tastefully furnished waiting room. Amanda guided Kelly through the empty waiting room, past a conference room, and into the director's spacious office. Kay Brownstein was seated behind the desk and talking on the telephone. Amanda excused herself and then closed the door behind her.

Brownstein, still in mid-conversation, smiled and waved Kelly over to a comfortable chair in front of the desk. Kelly sat down and glanced around the office. There were the government-issued leather couches and chairs, but the office showed the touch of someone who knew something about decorating. Large oil paintings, plants, and strategically placed lamps conveyed an aura of elegance and power.

After a few minutes Brownstein finished her telephone call. She returned the phone to the cradle, turned in her chair to face Kelly, and placed her clasped hands on the desk.

"I'm glad you were able to make it."

"Not at all," Kelly responded. "As I mentioned, I'm just grateful for your assistance."

"You're more than welcome. As sad as I am about Geoff's death, life must go on. Your inquiry could have consequences that extend far beyond you. And that was one of the reasons I was anxious to talk with you."

"You mean there's something else?"

Kelly realized that her anxiety was all too evident, but Brownstein gave no recognition of it. She simply nodded and leaned slightly back in her chair.

"I have some preliminary information from our investigation," the CIA director began, "that I can pass on to you."

"Great!"

"Let's start with Oswald. The agency kept track of him pretty closely, or as closely as we could, after he defected to the Soviet Union in 1959 and then after he returned to the United States in 1962. The files on Oswald were routed to quite a number of people, and your father was one of them."

"Was that because he worked with this 5412 Committee?"

"Precisely. The Special Group, as it was known inside the agency. In any case, your father was given access to the files because he was involved in Cuban operations. After he returned to the United States, Oswald surfaced as a player in various activities involving Cuban refugees. I should add, though, that it was never entirely clear whether Oswald's sympathies were for or against Castro."

"I thought Oswald distributed leaflets in New Orleans for the Fair Play for Cuba Committee, or whatever its name was."

"He did. But we also had information, much of which is already out in the public domain, that he was offering to help Cuban refugees who wanted to overthrow Castro. Oswald was, and remains, an enigma. But we don't have to know the truth of his mindset to get to your father's possible role in the Kennedy assassination."

"Thank God for that."

"In any event," Brownstein continued, "since your father was spending considerable time on Cuban affairs, he was also on the classified circulation list for the contact reports that George de Mohrenschildt prepared on Oswald. Whether your father read them or not, I have no idea. There's no document we can find in the records where he discusses de Mohrenschildt or the contact reports. But we do know that he had access to them."

"So where does this lead us?"

"We believe that de Mohrenschildt knew of Oswald's attempt to assassinate General Walker in early 1963."

"Yes," said Kelly, "I do remember that assassination attempt from earlier conversations."

"Oswald failed miserably, but that's not the issue here. Jim asked me to look for the de Mohrenschildt contact reports that deal with Oswald's effort to kill Walker. For the moment, we have still been unable to locate them. However, we believe those reports were prepared and did exist at one time. We also suspect that those files may have been purged from our records. In plain language, we suspect that someone intentionally destroyed those records concerning the Walker assassination attempt."

"Why would anyone do that?"

"We don't know for sure. But here's one possible scenario." Brownstein shifted in her chair and then paused for emphasis. "Anyone who knew of Oswald's effort to kill Walker would also know that Oswald was prepared to commit murder for political reasons. And, if you believe in conspiracy theories about the Kennedy assassination, someone with that knowledge could try to recruit Oswald to kill President Kennedy."

Kelly said nothing, but Brownstein could see that Kelly was trying to place the information into some kind of context that would explain her father's role. Brownstein had no interest in rushing a response.

"Would you like some coffee or soda or something else to drink?" she asked. "I'm so sorry. I should have asked when you first arrived."

"Actually, I think I would like some coffee."

Brownstein pressed the button on her phone and asked Amanda to bring in the coffee along with some tea for herself. She then leaned forward again, her hands resting on the desk and her eyes focused on Kelly.

"Let me give you some thoughts on how this may bear upon your father."

Kelly nodded in anticipation.

"Let's assume that your father did read de Mohrenschildt's reports on Oswald's attempt to assassinate Walker. Or suppose your father knew de Mohrenschildt and had learned about the attempt directly from conversations with de Mohrenschildt. In either case, your father would have been in a position to suggest to someone—maybe a conspirator—that Oswald be recruited to do the deed. Assuming of course that there was a conspiracy to kill Kennedy and that Oswald did do it."

"I do understand the significance of all this. But we're still left with the question as to whether my father even knew de Mohrenschildt, let alone whether they talked about Oswald's attempt to kill Walker. And there's no record to indicate that my father read any reports that de Mohrenschildt made on Oswald's attempt to assassinate Walker. So, basically, we don't really know what my father knew, let alone what he did. That's where we really are, isn't it?"

"All of that's true. But..."

"But what? There's something more?"

"Yes. Yes, there is something more. It may be just a coincidence. But I think you should know it."

"Please. Tell me."

"You know, of course, that your father was involved in the mission to train Cuban refugees in early 1961 so that they could try to recapture Cuba."

"Yes. Jim and I met with Harvey Teasdale, who was friends with my father in the CIA, and he explained all that. That was the mission that eventually led to the Bay of Pigs invasion in the spring of 1961, right?"

"Correct. And, as Mr. Teasdale may have told you, he and your father made quite a few trips to Guatemala in early 1961 in conjunction with that mission."

"You're not going to tell me..."

"Yes, I am. We have information that de Mohrenschildt was in Guatemala at the same time. And although de Morenschildt was not tracking Oswald's activities at the time, he was a CIA contact and making reports. It's possible—and I just mean possible—that your father met de Mohrenschildt when the two of them were in Guatemala."

"But we're still left with speculation, aren't we?" Kelly asked, almost pleaded. "We still don't know for sure that my father knew de Mohrenschildt, let alone that de Mohrenschildt later told him anything about Oswald."

"That's true, Kelly. These are all just suppositions. But Jim did describe your father's letter to me, and that letter does, I'm sorry to say, give some credibility to this speculation. Because your father was not one to make up things like that."

Kelly's eyes widened as Brownstein made that last remark. What did she know about her father's propensity to make things up? Her curiosity drove her to ask the obvious question.

"Jim did mention that you knew my father. How well did you know him?"

Before Brownstein could respond, Amanda walked in with the coffee and tea on a tray.

"Why don't we relocate to the couch?" Brownstein suggested. "It'll be a lot more comfortable."

Brownstein then directed Amanda to place the tray on the coffee table in front of the couch. Amanda seemed to have anticipated the suggestion. Before Kelly could move from the chair, the coffee and tea were already waiting on the coffee table, and Amanda had already departed, again closing the door behind her.

As she settled into the couch, Kelly suddenly, and for no apparent reason, felt a certain informality, almost intimacy, that made her relax. Brownstein reinforced the feeling by asking Kelly about the house, the horses, and how she liked living in Potomac. The conversation put Kelly at ease and gave her a sense of control. No guesswork in answering those questions.

After a few minutes, Kelly mustered the strength to ask about the other matter Brownstein wanted to discuss. The CIA director put her teacup back on the tray and looked into Kelly's eyes. In a way, it almost scared Kelly. Maybe she wasn't prepared for what Brownstein had to say. But the CIA director hesitated only for a few seconds before responding.

"I'm not sure I know where to begin. So maybe it would be best to tell you something of my early education and how I met your father."

"Sure," said Kelly warily, not knowing what to expect.

"I grew up in Cambridge, Massachusetts. My father taught at Harvard, and it was, especially as I look back on it, a wonderful time in my life. From there, I went to Wellesley and then to Georgetown's Foreign Service School in Washington."

"How'd you choose that career path?"

"In retrospect, I think it was because of my father. He had served in the State Department during the Kennedy administration, and his recollections of that experience always conveyed a sense of excitement in foreign affairs. I adored my father, and I guess my career choices were shaped by his views."

"I can certainly relate to that, because I adored my father too."

"Yes. I know you did."

Something in Brownstein's response took Kelly by surprise. What would she know of her feelings for her father? She wanted to put the question to the CIA director, but she restrained herself. She had a sense that Brownstein would reveal the answer in due course.

"Washington was certainly an exciting city for a young girl," Brownstein continued. "Especially if you had visions of some day being part of the Foreign Service and making American policy in international relations. I was naive, of course, but those heady visions contributed to the excitement I felt at the time."

"I know my father loved his work in international affairs. So it's easy for me to understand the excitement you felt."

"I'm sure you can. And I'm sure you can imagine how excited I was when I landed a fellowship in Paris in my first year in Georgetown. Nothing could have been better. Paris is such a wonderful city. It's not only an international meeting ground. There are the restaurants, the architecture, the culture. And it's also a very romantic city."

Kelly was starting to get a sense of where Brownstein was going, and she was not sure she liked it. She was starting to feel uncomfortable. She was even starting to feel anger, and she felt the need to say something.

"That's where you met my father? Is that it?"

"Yes. I thought he was with the State Department because I met him at a meeting sponsored by State. Later I found out that he was working for the CIA. But to a young girl of twenty-two, those were minor details. Ted Roberts was unlike any other man I had ever met. He was quite a few years older than I was, but that didn't matter to me. He was remarkably fit, incredibly charming, and very smart. And there was something more. He had a certain way, a certain magnetism, that distinguished him from anyone I had ever met before."

Brownstein could see the troubled look in Kelly's eyes.

"I know this may be difficult for you, Kelly. But, believe it or not, it's even more difficult for me. I wouldn't be telling you this if I didn't feel I should."

"I'm not sure I agree with that. I don't mean to be rude, but I can see that you want to tell me that you fell in love with my father. Is that it?"

"That's certainly part of it."

"I'm sorry, Ms. Brownstein. I really am. But I don't need to know all the details about the affair you had with my father while he was still married to my mom."

Brownstein immediately sensed the defiance in Kelly's voice. But she could not let the matter drop.

"I recognize how hard this must be for you, Kelly, and, like I said, I wouldn't be telling you all this if I didn't feel I had to. Unfortunately, there's more to it than my feelings for your father."

"What more could there be?"

Brownstein averted her eyes from Kelly's for the first time. The roles seemed reversed to Kelly, and she could see that Brownstein was now biting her lip to control her emotions, obviously in the grip of some distant memory.

It had been a clear and chilly December day in Paris. She remembered it vividly. The mixture of elation and anxiety she felt in anticipation of the State dinner to be held at the American Embassy that evening. And the conversation she needed to have.

To ease the tension she had taken a long walk along the Seine, passing the many stone bridges and the towering facade of the Cathedral of Notre Dame. It was a wonderful time, thinking about what could lay before her. The hopes. The possibilities. And, of course, the risks. She could not know what would happen. But there was no turning back now.

The beginning of the dinner was all she could have hoped for. Ted looked ravishingly handsome in his formal cutaway attire with the white bow tie and ruffled shirt. They sipped champagne and danced close, so close she could feel the warmth of his body and the beat of his heart. It was a magical moment. And then he took her, almost gliding, to introduce her to the short heavyset man with the thick glasses and the gravelly voice. He was surrounded by the usual entourage of security and diplomatic personnel. But Ted was able to cut through effortlessly, a sign, she said to herself, of the high place he occupied in government circles.

"Mr. Secretary," Ted said to Henry Kissinger, "I'd like you to meet Katherine Brownstein, one of the rising stars in the Foreign Service." Ted looked back at Kay with that broad smile, the one that had first attracted him to her. And so it went, dancing and drinking and eating and enjoying the gala, the kind of evening she had dreamed of as a young girl in Massachusetts.

As the end of the evening drew near, she knew she could defer it no longer. As they danced that last slow dance, holding each other close, she told him. It came out quickly without fanfare. Not that any elaboration was needed. Ted stopped and looked at her. His surprise was obvious. Beyond that, it was difficult to gauge what he was thinking. As she later learned, he himself did not know what to think. And so it dominated their conversations for that last week in Paris. The strain. The options. The decision.

Kay Brownstein now looked at Kelly. She had to tell her what else there was to the affair with her father. She could keep it inside no longer.

"I had an abortion."

Kelly's mouth dropped open and, for the first time in her life, she understood what it meant to feel speechless. Thoughts formed in her head, but her mouth suddenly became very dry and she didn't think she could actually say anything. So the two of them just sat there, looking at each other, neither knowing what to say. Or being able to say it. Kelly finally broke the silence.

"I don't understand," she demanded, almost shouted. "Why are you telling me this? What possible benefit can it have now?"

"I don't want to hurt you, Kelly. I really don't. But you need to understand the connection I have to your father." She then paused. "And to you."

"What connection? How you tried to ruin my father's marriage and our family?"

"You can't look at it that way, Kelly. Your father was an incredible man. He loved your mother very much. But he was away in Paris for extended periods, and I was a naive young girl who was totally infatuated with him. I didn't appreciate the consequences. And then, when I found out I was pregnant, I told him. I won't lie. I wanted him to leave your mother and start a life with me. But he would have none of that. So I had an abortion."

Kelly had a stunned look on her face.

"I can't believe this," was all she could muster.

Brownstein leaned forward with an imploring look in her eyes.

"Our relationship ended when my fellowship expired and I returned to Washington. I talked to your father on occasion, and he was instrumental in helping to move my career along. But we never saw each other except when we might be attending the same meeting. In the meantime, I promised him that his family would never know of our relationship."

"So what changed your mind now?"

"Oh, Kelly," Brownstein moaned. "Your father always spoke of you and how much you meant to him. And so I felt, in some strange way, an affinity for you too. And then I met with Jim and Geoff to discuss your situation. It made me realize that those feelings for you had never disappeared, and I wanted to do whatever I could to help you."

Brownstein put her hand to her temples and rubbed them slowly.

"When Jim explained how close you had come to being killed." Brownstein paused. "The pain was something I had never experienced before. I felt the need to call you, to comfort you. And then that horrible tragedy with Geoff. He and I had been so close." She looked at Kelly with soulful eyes. "And then he was gone. Just like that. I was totally beside myself. I needed you. And I convinced myself that you needed me too."

"I don't know what to say," Kelly said at last. "I'm not sure what I think or what I feel. I just don't know."

"There is one more thing."

Kelly picked up her head and looked at Brownstein. What more could there be?

"It was my last conversation with your father," Brownstein continued, almost in a whisper. "It was a strange conversation. He called me unexpectedly. I hadn't talked with him in I don't know how long. He made me promise again, begged me, never to reveal my relationship to him. I asked him what had prompted him to call. He just said that there was a chance he might not be around much longer, and he wouldn't be able to rest unless he knew that I would keep my word."

"What did he mean by that? Why did he think he wouldn't be around much longer?"

"I had no idea. I asked him if he felt okay, and he said he felt fine. I tried to press him, but it was clear he wouldn't tell me anything. And then he just said goodbye."

Kelly listened with her mouth half-open, her mind trying to make sense of it all.

"Why do you think he did that?"

"I'm not sure. But it was as though he had a premonition that his death was imminent. It was frightening. And it reinforced my desire to keep my promise to him. Especially when I learned shortly afterward that he had died unexpectedly."

"Oh my God," Kelly groaned. "Do you think…?"

"I don't know, Kelly. I don't know. But it is something you need to keep in mind. I'm more than happy to help you figure out the clues in your father's letter. But there may be some risks involved. Some deadly risks. And I don't want anything to happen to you because of something your father did. Something, I should add, that can't be undone."

They sat there in silence looking at each other. Brownstein watched Kelly's face closely. After a few minutes Kelly took Brownstein's hand in hers.

"I understand. I think I understand," she said quietly.

And then they embraced and held each other for a long time.

CHAPTER 49

Dwayne Soggs sat at his desk in the second district headquarters, rolling the plastic tip he had found in Bud Stamford's condo around in his fingers. He kept staring at the tip, hoping that his effort would somehow produce a brilliant new thought that would help him unlock the mystery of Stamford's death.

"What're you doing, Soggs?"

Soggs looked up and saw one of his colleagues. Another detective named Greg Harmon. He and Harmon went back a long way. They were complete opposites in appearance and background. Soggs was stocky, black, and stretching to reach five-feet eight-inches in height. Harmon had that preppie look. A sturdy, six-foot two clean-cut Caucasian with sandy hair and blue eyes. He had grown up in Germantown, Maryland, a distant suburb, but had wanted the challenge of working on a metropolitan police force. The District of Columbia was the obvious choice. He and Soggs had ultimately been assigned to a patrol car together and had worked their way up the ranks together.

The bond between Soggs and Harmon was deep, and they often talked about their cases, using each other as a sounding board and sometimes looking for new ideas when all other leads had grown stale.

"You want to know what I'm doing?" Soggs said with resignation. "I'll tell you what I'm doing. I'm waiting for this plastic tip to solve a mystery for me."

"Wow, Soggs. If you're reduced to that, I'd say you've hit rock bottom."

"I always knew you had an astute mind, Harmon. You pick up on things fast."

"That's my nature."

"But I'm telling you. If this plastic tip could talk, I think we'd have some insight into one of the more clever murders I've seen in some time."

"What makes you say that?"

"Mostly instinct. But there are some facts that support my theory."

"Like what?"

"An older but healthy guy with a lot of money named Bud Stamford is found dead in his condo. He lives alone, so it's a few days before he's discovered. Nogasaki does an autopsy, but he can't pinpoint the cause of death. As far as he's concerned, the guy should still be alive."

"I'll give you credit, Soggs. It's starting to get interesting." As he made that remark, Harmon pulled a chair from the next desk and sat down, putting his feet up on Soggs's desk.

"Trust me," Soggs responded, leaning back in his chair. "It gets better. I find this plastic tip in the condo. It's from a hypodermic needle, so naturally I think the guy's been injected with something. Now I've got the case solved. At least so I thought. But Nogasaki tells me that he didn't find any toxic substances in the guy's body. Nogasaki also tells me that the plastic tip means nothing because the guy was a diabetic and probably had needles around to inject himself with insulin. I go back to the condo and confirm that the plastic tip is in fact identical with some needles in the guy's medicine cabinet."

Harmon folded his arms across his chest and tightened his lips, obviously trying to make sense of it all. There was an obvious gap in his colleague's explanation.

"So what makes you think he's been murdered?"

"People don't die when they're healthy. And, aside from a mild case of diabetes, everything about this guy's autopsy says that he's healthy. So that means there must have been some foul play."

"You got me there," said Harmon.

Soggs pulled a box of Marlboros from the top drawer of his desk, lit a cigarette and took a long drag.

"You keep smoking that shit," said Harmon, "and you won't have to worry about this guy Stamford's death. You'll be keeping him company."

"I appreciate your concern for my long-term plans. But if you were any kind of buddy, you'd try and help me figure this thing out now before I'm overtaken by cancer."

"Okay. I hear you. What else you got?"

"I think this guy Stamford died from an air embolus."

"An air what?" Harmon asked with raised eyebrows.

"An air embolus. It hit me when I was out sailing on the Chesapeake. An air pocket blocked the fuel lines on my boat, and I figured, hey, why can't air block the flow of blood in a guy's veins? Nogasaki confirmed that my hunch was right. He said if you inject enough air into a person's veins, they can die immediately."

"You're kidding."

"Trust me, Harmon. I'm in no kidding mood right now."

"So what makes you think this guy died of an air embolus?"

"Don't you see? If somebody dies from an injection of air, there's no toxic substance to be found. Nor is there any sign of trauma or damage to any organ. After a few days, the air pocket can disappear. At least that's what I thought when I was out on the boat. And so it doesn't matter if this plastic tip is identical to the ones in the guy's medicine cabinet. The perps could've used one of Stamford's own needles to get the deed done."

Harmon nodded, again trying to assess Soggs's explanation.

"What'd Nogasaki think about your theory of how Stamford died?"

"When I got back from my sail, I called him from the marina. He said he would check it out, and he did. He called me back the other day and said that it's possible—'certainly possible' were his words—that Stamford died from an air embolus."

"What made him say that?" Harmon asked.

"To begin with, he said his autopsy findings were consistent with it."

"That means nothing. Pain in your temples is consistent with a temporary headache. It's also consistent with a fatal brain tumor."

"You should've been a lawyer," Soggs quipped.

"I've seen enough to have some of it rub off."

"Anyway," Soggs continued, "in addition to the consistency you don't much like, Nogasaki noticed some mild abrasions on Stamford's wrists. Before he gave it no notice. But that too is consistent with an air embolus. The abrasions could mean someone was holding Stamford down while somebody else injected him with the air."

"Well, I guess if you have enough consistencies, it can add up to something."

"So that's where I am," said Soggs, leaning forward in his swivel chair. "What's your advice, Doctor?"

Harmon paused for a moment and stared at the ceiling. He then turned back to Soggs with a determined look.

"What about the fingerprints on that plastic tip you're holding? In fact, I was going to ask you. Don't you feel a little stupid playing with evidence without wearing rubber gloves?"

"I'm not as stupid as you think. There were no fingerprints on the plastic tip."

"None?"

"What's the matter, Harmon? Has your hearing gone bad? I said none."

"Don't you find that a little strange, Dwayne? I mean, if Stamford pulled the plastic tip off a needle to give himself an injection, wouldn't it include at least his fingerprints?"

Soggs gave Harmon the surprised look of discovery.

"I'm going to have to take back some of the things I've said about you, Greg. I think that is an astute observation. In fact, I feel a little stupid that I didn't think of it."

"Don't feel bad. Just accept the fact that you're a man of limited capabilities."

"Very funny. Anyway, the absence of fingerprints is certainly consistent with my notion that there's a murderer running around Washington who knows how Bud Stamford died. What else you got, buddy?"

"I presume you've talked to his friends and neighbors and all that stuff."

"Yep."

"What about a diary or something like that?"

"Funny you mention that. He did have a diary, and I looked at it the other day. We had looked at it before. It's got some notations in it that I don't understand. We've asked Stamford's sister, his neighbors, and everybody else we could think of. Nobody had a clue."

"Anybody else you could ask?"

Soggs shook his head and then turned in his chair to face the wall. Harmon could see that Soggs was mentally reviewing his interview list, trying to decide if someone might have been omitted. After a minute or so, he turned back to Harmon.

"Well, now that I think of it, there is one other person I could ask."

"Who?"

Soggs crushed out his cigarette and looked at Harmon.

"A young woman who saw Stamford a night or two before he died. An old family friend who hadn't seen him in a long time. So it didn't seem like she would be in a position to decipher these diary notations."

"You never know."

"Maybe you're right."

"Of course I'm right. I'm paid to be right. But don't call her now," Harmon said, standing up and putting his chair back in its place. "I didn't come here to help you solve a case. I need you to come with me."

"What for?"

"We got another jogger killed over in Foggy Bottom. It's going to get a lot of publicity, and the chief says he wants the two of us on it."

"All right," said Soggs. "Let me take this plastic tip back to the evidence room, and I'll meet you by the car."

Soggs really wanted to take care of the Stamford matter first. It was a challenge that was starting to consume him. But there was no rush. Stamford wasn't coming back. The call to Kelly Roberts could wait.

Chapter 50

Dear Dad,

This has probably been the hardest week of my life. Painful is probably the best word. And part of the pain is that you're not here to talk to me about it.

I met with Kay Brownstein this afternoon. It was not the highlight of my day, to the say the least. I couldn't believe what she told me. I didn't want to believe what she told me. I know you understand. Otherwise, you wouldn't have insisted that she keep her relationship with you a secret.

But here's the hard part, Dad. That was your secret too. All those years, all that time. I still can't believe that this actually happened. I don't want it to change how I feel about you, but I have to be honest, Dad. It made me angry. And worse, I was incredibly disappointed. Other girls' fathers made mistakes. Not my dad. At least that's what I always believed. Maybe I was too naive. But you were the glue that held me together even in the roughest times. Even when you weren't here. Your memory was always, or almost always, enough to carry the day. Now what?

My mind's a jumble. I can't think straight. And more than that, I'm scared. I'm constantly looking over my shoulder and checking locks. I don't know what to do. Should I continue this search and maybe place my life at risk? Kay—she said I should call her that—says I can't change the past and that I should put an end to it. I'm not sure. But I do know I need to find someplace far away that will be safe and give me a chance to figure this all out. So Jim and I are going to sneak out of here tonight and go to the Cayman Islands. I've never been there, but it sounds exotic. And maybe the warm Caribbean air will clear my head.

By the way, I know what you're thinking. Jim and I are not a thing. At least not yet. But I have to tell you, Dad. He's the closest thing I've found to you. He's smart, witty, and caring. What more could a girl want—right?

That's it for now. But we'll talk again later.

Love, as always,

Kelly

CHAPTER 51

A silver Camaro pulled into the sloping parking lot of the Irish Inn at Glen Echo, a large Victorian house with white siding. In earlier days, the house had been a biker hangout, but in more recent times it had been converted into a stylish restaurant for the residents of Bethesda, Potomac, and other nearby Maryland suburbs. Situated just above the Chesapeake & Ohio Canal that paralleled the Potomac River, the restaurant offered an intimate setting for candlelight dinners or drinks at the wooden bar.

Becky, her long blond hair flowing behind her, stepped out of the driver's side of the Camaro, just as a male companion, a former colleague from Senator Gimble's office, emerged from the passenger side. The man, sporting a mustache and a wide-brimmed hat pulled low over his eyes, walked around the front of the car to grab Becky's hand, and the two of them ambled up the steps to the restaurant amidst the last glow of the sun setting behind the tall trees that surrounded the house.

Within ten minutes, Jim's Mazda Miata turned sharply into the parking lot and parked a few cars down from Becky's Camaro. Jim and Kelly got out of the car and walked up the steps into the Inn, looking straight ahead and taking no notice of the other couples parking their cars and drifting into the restaurant.

An hour later the Inn was shrouded in darkness, save for the few spotlights that cast rays of light onto the parking lot that encircled the restaurant. As one couple moved up from the parking lot toward the entranceway, Kelly, now wearing a wig of long blond hair and Becky's top, stepped out of the restaurant with Jim, who had a fake mustache affixed to his face and the wide-brimmed hat of Becky's companion on his head. From all appearances, they could have easily been mistaken for Becky and her male companion. Especially to anyone who might have been watching from a distance.

The two of them moved quickly toward Becky's Camaro, opened the doors, and, within seconds, had exited the parking lot onto MacArthur Boulevard, the street in front of the restaurant. After a short distance, the Camaro made a left-hand turn and eased onto the access road that would put the car on the Beltway heading south into Virginia.

Two hours later, Jim and Kelly were sitting on a plane en route to the Cayman Islands. They looked at each other with obvious satisfaction.

"I still can't believe we did that," said Kelly. "I think we've taken this cloak-and-dagger stuff to new heights."

"Maybe so, but it was worth doing. I can't believe anyone could have overheard us on the canoe ride, but we can't be too careful. I'm tired of people showing up unexpectedly. And I think it was great of Becky to go along with it. Even though I couldn't tell her why we were doing it or what was going on."

"And you're sure no one heard you discussing it with her?"

"Positive. We were in the hallway outside the senator's office. It's inconceivable that anyone could have put a bug there."

Content with that explanation, Kelly leaned back in her seat and stared out the window. She was lost in her thoughts, and she and Jim talked only intermittently over the next couple of hours.

After a while, the pilot announced on the intercom that the plane was flying over Cuba. Kelly looked out the window. Even in the bright reflection of the moon, all she could see were specks of light that suggested an agrarian and largely dispersed population.

"It's hard to believe that this little poverty-stricken island could have caused such turmoil in the Kennedy years," she said, almost to herself as much as to Jim.

"I know what you mean. But back then, people were finding communists under every rock, and they no doubt were concerned that the Russians would be on America's doorstep if communism got a foothold in Cuba."

"Oh, I know. But I can't help but wonder how my father's life—and maybe mine as well—would have been so different if people had taken a more realistic view of what was going on."

Jim looked at Kelly. Her eyes had a vacant look.

"How're you feeling? Still thinking about Kay Brownstein?"

"I guess."

Kelly then turned to Jim, her eyes focused on his. There was a sadness that Jim detected, something he had never seen before. He thought he understood the reasons for that look, but Kelly's next comments caught him off-guard.

"I guess her experience proves what I didn't want to believe. That all men are assholes who will do anything to get into a woman's pants. Even my father," she said with a shake of her head. "It makes me sick. It really does. And, try as we might, there's not much women can do about it."

Jim suddenly recalled the angry look Kelly had given him at her house when they had first opened the envelope containing her father's letter and he had asked about her move back to Potomac. Jim could not help but wonder whether there was some kind of connection.

"Does this have anything to do with why you left your job on the Hill?"

Kelly did not respond immediately. She just stared at Jim, her mind racing back to the memory she had tried so hard to bury.

"Kelly," his secretary said, "I have the congressman on the line. He's at the airport and wants to know if you can come by his townhouse around six tonight to go over tomorrow's testimony. He has some workmen coming over and can't make it down to the office."

All Kelly could feel was elation. She was quickly moving up the food chain. After starting as a lowly legislative correspondent, she had impressed the congressman with her diligence and insight, had been elevated to become one of several legislative assistants, and now, here she was, being singled out to meet with him at his residence. She was obviously emerging as an important person on his staff, and she promptly assured the congressman's secretary that she would be there at the appointed hour.

It was actually a few minutes before six when Kelly knocked on the black door of the narrow townhouse down the street from the Cannon House Office Building. The congressman, dressed casually in jeans and a blue work shirt, opened the door and led Kelly up the stairs to the second floor, which housed the kitchen and living room.

"Where are the workmen?" Kelly asked.

"They got finished early, but I thought it would be best to meet here anyway. Fewer distractions."

Kelly took no notice of the comment as the congressman directed her to the upholstered couch in the living room and asked if she wanted a drink. Kelly looked at him with surprise, not sure what to say.

"Why? Are you having one?"

"Sure. If we have to work late into the night, we might as well make it enjoyable. I'll make us both a Bloody Mary."

Kelly was not sure that having a drink was the best way to delve into the work that lay ahead, but she was not about to argue with her boss. She sat down on the couch, pulled out the draft testimony from her leather case, and set the document on the coffee table in front of the couch.

Within a few minutes the congressman was sitting next to her on the couch, talking to her about the testimony while they both sipped their drinks. He spoke with high energy about the issues addressed in her draft, complimenting her work, and assuring her that she had a bright future. At first Kelly found it strange to be talking about these matters while seated next to the congressman on the couch, but she was not all that familiar with his working style and scolded herself for being too prudish.

The more they talked about the testimony, the more comfortable she became. See, she said to herself, no cause for alarm. Just two congressional colleagues dealing with serious public issues.

Before too long, the glasses were empty, and the congressman excused himself to get refills. Within minutes he returned with new Bloody Marys for each of them. By now she had accepted the notion that her congressman, perhaps like others on the Hill, liked to enjoy a drink with work. She could deal with it. In fact, there was really nothing to it. But then, while reviewing one of the points in the testimony, the congressman gently placed his hand on her knee, just below the hemline of her skirt. The gesture startled Kelly and made her feel uncomfortable, but she was not sure what she should do about it. She didn't want to embarrass the congressman by taking his hand off her knee or asking him to do so.

Still, while he rattled on about the testimony, Kelly's thoughts were totally preoccupied with what seemed to be happening. She had had enough experience to know about the wily ways of men, and, in any other circumstance, she would have had no trouble concluding that the congressman was trying to hit on her. But this was a senior and respected member of Congress who had a wife and children back in Oregon. And although stories of congressmen with wandering eyes were rampant, she could not believe that of her boss. He was too warm, too nice, and too genuine to be one of those philanderers. At least that's what she wanted to think. But her confidence was shaken by his next remarks. He turned to her, looked directly in her eyes, and put his hand on her shoulder.

"You know, Kelly," he whispered, "you and I could be much more than colleagues at the office."

Before she could think of what to say, his lips were on hers and he was pushing her back on the couch. She began to resist, trying to push her hands against his chest, but he was much bigger and stronger than she was, and he was already starting to pull off her skirt in a frenzy of emotion. She continued to cry out in protest and struggle, but he placed one hand over her mouth to quiet her and then continued to rip off her clothes and his pants in rapid, almost frantic, motions. She writhed under the weight of his body in an effort to escape the assault, but it proved to be hopeless. It was over in a matter of minutes.

"I can't believe this," said Jim. "It's worse than anything I would have imagined."

"Tell me about it."

"Why didn't you do anything about it? He's one asshole who should have been put in jail."

"Believe me, I tried. More than anything, I wanted him to suffer the way I did. But it wasn't going to happen. Jeff and I met with prosecutors in the United States Attorney's Office. We told them what happened and asked, demanded really, that they throw the book at the guy. They were sympathetic and all that, but they were not optimistic about succeeding. How would it look to the jury, they said, when the congressman testified, as he certainly would, that we had been drinking and that it had been consensual sex. What could I show to prove otherwise? It would be my word against his, and that wouldn't be enough."

Jim thought about Kelly's response for a few seconds and then nodded.

"I would like to say you made a mistake, but I think you probably did the right thing by dropping it."

"I'm sure I did. Because, win or lose, there would also be the publicity. I would be a natural target for the media. The case would be all over the newspapers and television news broadcasts. And if I lost, I would carry that stain for a long time. Maybe forever. It was a risk I didn't want to take."

There was a pause, and Jim's mind searched in vain for something meaningful to say.

"I'm sorry," he finally said. "I truly am sorry."

Kelly placed her hand on his.

"I know," she said softly. "I know. Anyway, getting up early and reliving all that has suddenly made me real tired. So, if you don't mind, I'm going to take a nap."

Kelly then leaned back in her seat and closed her eyes. Jim picked up a book and tried to read, but his thoughts continually returned to Kelly's sordid tale of betrayal and rape.

By the time Kelly woke up, the big Boeing 757 was pulling up to the tiny terminal building on the Grand Cayman Island. As Jim and Kelly reached the open door to exit the plane and walk down the stairs, they were hit by a waft of tropical air wrapped in the pleasant fragrance of blooming flowers. It felt warm and soothing on their faces, and they looked at each other.

"This is going to be hard to beat," said Jim.

Kelly said nothing. She just grabbed his hand and followed him down the stairs.

It took almost two hours for them to clear customs, get their bags, and rent a Jeep for the trip to the Westin Casuarina Resort on Seven Mile Beach. Within twenty minutes Jim and Kelly pulled into the circular driveway of the Westin, a collection of adjoining white buildings of several stories with light blue roofs. The valet, a young man with a smile and a British accent, greeted them, and a bellboy seemed to appear from nowhere to take their bags out of the Jeep. While the valet drove the Jeep away, Jim and Kelly strolled into the Westin's large lobby behind the bellboy and their bags.

The hotel had a much more informal atmosphere than Kelly had anticipated. The slate floor, the palm trees, the comfortable couches, and the cavernous ceilings conveyed a sense of affluence that was somehow unpretentious. Kelly was not sure why, but the hotel made her feel relaxed. And secure.

After they registered, Jim and Kelly walked hand-in-hand out the rear of the lobby and onto the decking with assorted pools. They stood there in silence for a few minutes, soaking in the star-lit night and the gentle breezes. For the moment, nothing seemed more important than to become acclimated to their new surroundings. All of which appeared to be equal to their expectations. It was spectacular. Their gaze extended immediately beyond the pools to Seven Mile Beach, a broad expanse of seemingly soft white sand and scattered casuarina trees with thick foliage.

"I like this already," said Jim. "We may never go back to Washington."

"You won't have to convince me."

It was almost two o'clock by the time Jim and Kelly got to the hotel room. The only light in the room was from a lamp with a low-wattage bulb. Although it was hard to think of a hotel room as romantic, to Jim the subdued lighting gave the room an intimacy and warmth that it no doubt lacked during daylight hours.

Jim and Kelly walked out to the small balcony and looked out over the Caribbean waters gently rolling onto the beach in a never-ending motion. The black sky sparkled with stars and had a clarity that Jim could never remember seeing in Washington. He looked around. There were no glaring lights or activities to compromise the beauty of the night. Most of the Westin's other hotel rooms were dark, and the lighting from other hotels and condos appeared in the distance to be nothing more than yellow dots.

Jim looked at Kelly. Nothing needed to be said. They turned back toward the water and watched the undulating waves lap against Seven Mile Beach. Kelly broke the silence after a few minutes.

"I noticed you were thoughtful enough to get a room with two double beds."

"We have to keep our options open. And remember, this is a time to decide how to reduce the pressures—not increase them. You've been through enough already."

"No pressure needed. You wait here. I'll be back in a minute."

Kelly returned to the balcony within a few minutes wearing one of the white terry-cloth robes provided by the hotel.

"You certainly look relaxed," said Jim. He hesitated for a few seconds. "And beautiful."

As he finished speaking, Jim put his right arm around Kelly's waist and pulled her close, kissing her gently on the lips. Kelly responded in kind, and they stood there for minutes, kissing and holding each other. They paused briefly, and Jim took Kelly by the hand and led her back into the room.

They stood and looked at each other and then embraced, holding and stroking each other. Jim slipped his arm inside Kelly's robe and pulled her closer. She was wearing nothing underneath, and Jim felt a rush as he touched Kelly's bare skin. Kelly sighed as the robe slipped off and they both fell down onto one of the beds. She glanced up at Jim with half-closed eyes and slowly pulled off his polo shirt.

It was the moment they had both anticipated and they intended to make the most of it. The night could not last too long for either of them.

Chapter 52

Caleb Butler drove his black 745 BMW sedan through the late morning traffic on Bradley Boulevard in Bethesda, Maryland. Large maple and oak trees bordered the street's two lanes, and beyond the trees were homes of various styles and vintage. Some of the homes were older and modest, but many others were large and stately.

When he reached Wilson Lane, Butler made a right turn. He drove another few blocks and then made a left onto Mary McGuire's street. He pulled the car in front of her house and stepped out into the warm summer air. George Kruger, who had been sitting in the front passenger seat, exited at the same time and put on his suit jacket.

Like Bradley Boulevard and Wilson Lane, Mary McGuire's street was dominated by large trees. Butler and Kruger walked down the cement sidewalk and turned into the path leading to her house.

Mary McGuire's home was like many others on the street. A relatively small colonial with white siding, black shutters, a charming front porch, and a white picket fence. Butler guessed that the house was probably built in the 1950s.

He knocked gently on the front door. After a few minutes it was opened by a petite woman with short white hair. Butler guessed that she was in her late fifties or early sixties.

"Ms. McGuire?" Butler asked.

"Yes."

Butler held out his hand.

"I'm Caleb Butler, ma'am, and this here is my colleague, George Kruger."

Mary McGuire extended her hand and gave each of them a firm handshake.

"Please come in," she said in a soft voice.

She then escorted them through the foyer to a small library to the left of the center hall stairs.

Butler scanned the room. Shafts of sunlight from the large window on one side made the room very bright. But the room did not appear to enjoy much use. There were two walls of books that looked untouched, a small desk that was devoid of papers, a fireplace that was remarkably clean, and a corduroy couch with a couple of hardback chairs circled around a barren coffee table made of glass and chrome.

As he surveyed the room, Butler's eyes were immediately drawn to the framed photograph on the end table by the couch. It showed President Kennedy shaking hands with a much younger but balding man in a setting that Butler recognized as the Oval Office. There was a scrawled inscription on the photograph that Butler assumed was Kennedy's handwriting.

Butler's curiosity was aroused. The length of the inscription indicated that Kennedy had known the man. Butler wondered what the relationship was between the two men. He also wondered whether the man was Mary McGuire's husband. Whoever the man was, the picture was obviously of some importance to her. It was the only photograph in the room.

Mary McGuire directed Butler to the couch, and he settled his broad girth into the end by the window. Kruger placed himself at the other end, and Mary McGuire sat on one of the hardback chairs across from Butler.

"First of all, ma'am," Butler began in his courtly manner, "I want to thank y'all for agreeing to meet with us. I know this is an imposition on your valuable time, but I think this may be very important to our client, and I know she'll appreciate it as well."

Mary McGuire said nothing. She just gave a small smile and nodded. This is not going to be easy, Butler said to himself.

"In any event," Butler continued, "it may be useful to explain the situation. My client's brother went on a photographic safari with Barrington and Stone in Africa. Jeff was his name. Jeff was not a hunter and, in fact, knew nothing about guns. He just wanted to take some pictures of the wildlife and the scenery. Jeff knew of course that wild animals in Africa can be dangerous. But Barrington and Stone never explained that there was any risk to life on these photographic safaris. Quite the contrary. They had promised that appropriate precautions would be taken to make sure that there was no risk like that."

"But that wasn't done. Is that it?"

Mary McGuire's comment startled Butler.

"No, you're quite right, ma'am. They were not given adequate protection. I'll spare you the details, which are not pretty. But the end result is that Jeff was attacked by a large lion in the middle of the night and dragged from his tent. He never had a chance of survival."

Mary McGuire placed her hand over her mouth in obvious dismay when Butler described Jeff's demise. But she didn't say anything, and Butler decided to continue.

"Jeff and his younger sister, who's in her twenties, were very close. Both of their parents are dead, and they just had each other. She's not married and lives alone not far from here in Potomac. Needless to say, she was distraught over Jeff's death."

"Oh, that poor child," Mary McGuire sighed.

"Under the circumstances," Butler said, "we felt that Barrington and Stone should do something for the sister to make up for her tragic loss. But so far they have refused to offer anything, and we felt that we had no choice but to file a lawsuit to seek some kind of justice in the courts. And I should add," Butler remarked with some emotion, "that this is not just any case to us. Because Jeff was a lawyer in our firm, and, if fate had not intervened, he would have had a great career in the law."

Butler watched Mary McGuire closely as he described the lawsuit, but she gave no indication of what she was thinking. She sat stiffly in the chair, her emotions and thoughts well camouflaged.

"As you might imagine," Butler went on, "it would be of some significance if we could find an earlier instance of an attack by a lion or some other wild animal on a Barrington and Stone safari. That would show that Barrington and Stone had clear notice of the dangers confronting their clients. The courts place some limitations on the use of that kind of information, but, at a minimum, it would show that Barrington and Stone was negligent in failing to do more to protect Jeff and the other clients. If nothing else, Barrington and Stone should have at least warned their clients of the potential danger."

Butler was hoping that Mary McGuire would volunteer some information or other response, but she continued to sit in silence. He had no choice but to go on.

"As you know," he said, looking at Kruger and then back to Mary McGuire, "I received this telephone call from a woman named Jennifer. Now this woman acknowledged that her real name is not Jennifer, but she said that you might have some information that would help us and, if I recall her words correctly, teach Barrington and Stone the meaning of the word 'justice.'"

When Butler finished, Mary McGuire dropped her head slightly and stared at the floor in front of her. Butler could see that she was overcome with emotion.

"Ma'am?" Butler inquired. "Are you all right?"

"Do you need some water?" Kruger asked.

Mary McGuire picked up her head and looked at Kruger.

"Thank you, no. I'm fine."

Butler saw his opening and decided to take the plunge.

"I don't want to be presumptuous, ma'am, but I have a sense that your family had an experience with Barrington and Stone, and I'm thinking that you might feel better if you talk to us about it."

There was a long pause as Butler and Kruger watched Mary McGuire try to regain her composure.

"I'm so sorry," she finally said. "This is not easy for me."

"That's all right," Kruger replied with obvious sympathy. "Caleb and I don't want to make it hard for you. But we're hoping that talking to us may be a release for you as well as helpful to our client."

There was another long pause as Mary McGuire continued to struggle with her emotions. She then opened her eyes wide and looked directly at Butler.

"My husband died unexpectedly not too long ago," she began. "It was not a good time for me. It was also very difficult for our son, Barry. He was an only child and he was very close to his father. They were best friends. They played tennis together. They went skiing together. And they talked a lot. Even when Barry was away at school."

Butler was a seasoned lawyer who had become hardened to tales of woe. It was, he thought, part of his growth as an attorney. A good lawyer needed a detached perspective to provide objective advice to people whose thinking was clouded by emotions. But there was something very touching about Mary McGuire, and sadness started to envelop Butler as he listened to her story.

"For weeks after my husband's death," Mary McGuire continued, "Barry could do nothing. He was a young man in his late twenties. He had a bright future. He had a job as a stockbroker on K Street downtown and a condo on Connecticut Avenue. But he would come here often in the evenings and on weekends. And he would sit in this room for hours. Because this was my husband's favorite room. The one where he and my son spent so many hours talking about so many things."

Mary McGuire then paused again, and Kruger asked again if she wanted any water. She shook her head and proceeded with her story.

"Barry finally decided he needed a drastic change of environment. Something, he told me, that would help him overcome the terrific pain he felt."

"So what did he do?" Kruger asked.

"He took a job with Barrington and Stone."

"What kind of job?" Butler gently asked.

"Oh, I'm not exactly sure. The nature of the job wasn't that important to Barry. It was just a way to get to Africa. He had always loved animals. We always had a dog, and even as a little boy he loved going to the zoo. A friend had told him that Barrington and Stone was a very reputable company that took people on photographic safaris, and Barry just followed up. It all happened very quickly, and within weeks he was writing me from a tent somewhere in Africa. He was excited about being in Africa and his spirits seemed to soar."

"I can imagine," said Butler. "Africa can certainly be an exciting place. Especially if you love animals."

"Yes, it can be. But," she added slowly, "like a lot of things in life, it wasn't as good as it seemed."

"Why? What happened?" Kruger anxiously asked.

Barry McGuire sat at the wooden table, joking with Nancy Crossing, one of the more striking, and certainly one of the more enjoyable, clients on this three-week trip. In her early thirties, Nancy had an effervescent personality and a well-shaped body that had attracted Barry from the moment he had met her at the Nairobi airport. Her husband, Ron, was a serious photographer and often left her back at camp, where Barry had charge of the logistics. So it was not unusual for Barry to find time in the afternoon to sit with Nancy, as he was now doing, to share a beer along with good conversation.

As the afternoon sun started to dip lower on the long grass plains of Tsavo National Park, Barry excused himself. Nightly chores waited. Although experienced in these private tented tours, the staff still required supervision, and that was Barry. As he rose and turned back to the main tent, Godfrey Chambers, the safari director, approached him with a somber look and a rifle that Barry immediately interpreted as trouble.

"Barry, my good man," Chambers began in his clipped British accent. "We've encountered a bit of a dilemma here, and you, for better or worse, have been selected to be our savior."

Chambers then proceeded to explain that the ranger, the "great white hunter" as Barry jokingly called him, the one man with expertise in firearms and best able to protect the camp against the dangers of unwanted animal attacks, had come down with malaria and was being taken by helicopter to a Nairobi hospital. Barry was not entirely surprised. The ranger had complained of headaches and a slow-growing fever for the last couple of days. Everyone had wanted, even expected, that it would pass, but Chambers now made it clear that those had proven to be false hopes.

"As you know," Chambers continued, placing his hand on Barry's shoulder, "we're a little short-handed, and I was hoping you could fill in until someone else can reach us. But that may not be for a day or so."

Barry's first reaction was fear. Hunting and guns had never been his strong suit. In fact, growing up in Bethesda, Maryland, he had never fired anything other than rifles used for skeet-shooting, and even that was only a very occasional experience. Still, he had gone on short excursions with the ranger and had had some practice with the ranger's powerful .454 Winchester. He was no expert, Barry said to himself, but nothing ever happened on these trips anyway. He could deal with it for a night or two. In fact, it might be fun. A break from the normal routine. So Barry nodded his head in silent agreement and took the rifle from Chambers.

Hours later, the clients were all nestled in the tents pitched in a circle, the only real light coming from the camp-made fires in the center that burned throughout the night. A few of the staff, all local black men, sat around a small fire by one of the client tents and talked quietly amongst themselves. Otherwise, the camp was devoid of human sounds.

Barry sat near the camp's main fire in a wooden chair, the Winchester rifle cradled across his arms and on his lap. He looked at the stars glowing in the blackness of the night. It was a beautiful sight, one that he could enjoy amidst the intermittent animal sounds that had now become a recognized and comforting cacophony. He was glad to be in Africa.

He had no idea what time it was, but he knew it was very late because his eyelids were starting to feel very heavy. Better get up and walk around, he said to himself. Get that blood pumping. So Barry stood up and began a slow trek around the perimeter of the tents, the rifle crooked across his right arm. As he skipped over a small stream near one of the tents, he thought he heard a rustling in the tall grass and bramble bush. He turned toward the noise, his heart suddenly beating very quickly. He picked up the barrel of the rifle slowly with his left hand and put his right index finger around the trigger. He stood there for a minute or so waiting, his ears straining to hear anything else. But there was nothing. Indeed, as he thought about it, even the mixture of nightly animal sounds suddenly seemed strangely muted. No matter. He was happy to hear nothing new.

Barry started to retreat from his position, backing up slowly, his rifle held tightly and his eyes focused on the location where he thought he had heard the rustling noise. After going backward like that for about ten yards, he felt relieved. It was probably one of the small animals that seemed to be everywhere, he said to himself. He was sat-

isfied that this night, his first night as the great white hunter, would end as unceremoniously as all the other nights on all the other safari trips he had taken.

He walked slowly toward the tents and the security of his wooden chair. He hadn't gone more than another twenty yards when he heard it. The growl. A deep-throated growl that belonged to something very large. A growl that made his heartbeat accelerate beyond measure.

He turned quickly. The first thing he saw were the eyes. They shined with an eerie glow in the reflection of the large fire behind him. But there was no time for contemplation. The large lion was charging at breakneck speed. Barry instinctively raised the rifle to his right cheek, his arms and fingers trembling with unspeakable fear. He tried to steady the rifle and keep the barrel sights on the lion, quickly closing the distance to him. Time was short, he knew, and there was no margin for error. Now or never he screamed to himself. Now! His shaking index finger pulled hard on the trigger and he waited for the explosion of gunfire that would stop the predator dead in its tracks.

All he heard was the empty click of a misfire. It echoed in his ear, his last conscious thought.

Mary McGuire looked at the two lawyers sitting across from her on the couch.

"That's what happened," she said stoically.

Butler and Kruger looked at each other, shaking their heads. They then turned back to the sad woman in front of them.

"I'm just wondering, ma'am," Butler asked. "How did you find out what had happened? Who contacted you?"

"That's the funny part of it. Some official-sounding person called me from Barrington and Stone and said only that there had been a tragic accident. That person made it sound like it was just one of those things that they couldn't control. But a few weeks later I got a call from the hunter—the one who wound up in the Nairobi hospital. He told me what had really happened. Somebody had obviously told him. And he said that they had made a terrible mistake and that they never should have given the rifle to Barry. The hunter knew what it takes to be a gunman, and he knew that Barry didn't have the skills or the experience to do the job. He said that to me. He knew. They all knew."

Butler and Kruger noted the anger in Mary McGuire's voice as she made the last remark.

"Do you remember the name of the hunter?" Kruger asked.

"I'll never forget it. Remington. Mike Remington."

"I'll be damned," said Kruger under his breath. "I'll be damned."

"Who's Jennifer?" Butler asked. "Do you have any idea who she is and why she called me?"

"I'm not sure. I imagine it was my niece. She's very protective of me, and she was very frustrated with me because I refused to file my own lawsuit."

"Why didn't you?" asked Kruger.

"I didn't need any money to live on, and nothing I could do in court would bring Barry back. And I didn't want to spend any time reliving the details of my son's death. I didn't think I could endure that."

"I can certainly appreciate that," said Butler. "I truly can."

With that, Butler and Kruger rose from the couch.

"You've been very kind, ma'am," said Butler, "and we've already taken too much of your time. I'm very grateful for your willingness to tell us about your son. I know it hasn't been easy."

"You're most welcome," said Mary McGuire, extending her hand. "I do feel a little better having talked about it, and I'll be willing to help you if you think it would be useful. So you can feel free to use this information in any way that will help your client."

"I thank you for that, ma'am," said Butler, "because I think your story will be helpful. This is precisely the kind of information we needed."

As they walked toward the front door, Butler asked about the framed photograph in the library.

"That was my husband. He was a long-time government servant who spent some time in the Kennedy administration."

"What part of the government was he in?" Kruger asked.

"The Central Intelligence Agency. It was a wonderful career. At least most of it was."

Butler decided not to pursue that cryptic comment. The woman had already endured enough in telling them about her son. Butler did not want to stir up other emotions that might be equally unsettling.

As she stood, holding the front door open for them, Mary McGuire could not resist asking her own question of the two lawyers.

"By the way, what is your client's name? I guess I should ask since she's almost a neighbor."

"Kelly Roberts," Butler responded.

There was a look of recognition on Mary McGuire's face.

"Kelly Roberts? You mean Ted Roberts's daughter?"

"The one and the same," said Kruger. "Do you know her?"

"No. I don't know Kelly. But I did know her father and I knew he had two children. And, as strange as this may sound, for a long time I'd been thinking of calling her and her brother. But I never did. I wonder. Would it be possible for you to ask Kelly to call me? I would very much like to talk with her."

"Not at all, ma'am," said Butler in his smooth drawl. "It would be my pleasure."

As they walked to the car, Butler turned to Kruger.

"It all fits. We asked Remington at the deposition whether he had known of any attacks on Barrington and Stone's clients. Barry McGuire was an employee. We didn't ask about employees."

"We'll certainly ask now," said Kruger.

"We certainly will. We certainly will."

Chapter 53

Jim and Kelly strolled down Seven Mile Beach hand-in-hand in the warmth of the late morning sun. Jim reveled in their new surroundings. It felt good to be with Kelly and wearing nothing but a baggy swimsuit and walking on soft sand underneath bare feet. He felt more relaxed than he had since Jeff's death.

They passed the Governor's Residence and a few scattered people sunbathing on the beach outside the condos that looked out over the water. Jim soon saw their destination. A collection of sailboards stacked underneath a group of casuarina trees about twenty-five yards from the water's edge.

As they approached the sailboards, Jim saw the person responsible for their rental. A small bearded man wearing shorts and a T-shirt and sporting large sunglasses. As Kelly stood nearby surveying the water with its different shades of turquoise, Jim explained to the bearded man that he wanted to rent one of the boards to go windsurfing for about an hour or so.

"Wind's blowing pretty hard," the man observed. "Maybe fifteen or twenty knots. It's not a time for beginners. Have you ever done this before?"

"Many times. So you don't have to worry. I'll be okay. I actually like it when the wind blows this hard."

The man noticed that Jim was carrying lime green windsurf gloves. They lent credibility to Jim's expressions of confidence.

"All right. Just sign this release form and I'll set you up."

As he was signing the form, Jim asked the man the same question he always asked people when he went windsurfing in seawater.

"Any problems with sharks here?"

"Nope," said the man in a matter-of-fact manner. "Never. No sharks out there."

Jim knew otherwise. He had learned from his Navy experience that sharks are just about everywhere in salt water. Especially warm salt water. And they were not confined to deep water. Sharks often cruised close to beaches populated by bathers. But Jim was not about to argue with the man. Even if they were close to shore, the likelihood of contact with a shark would be remote. And besides, in this wind his sailboard would move faster than any shark.

Within ten minutes Jim found himself leaning back on the sailboard as the wind pushed against the board's sail and carried him swiftly away from the beach and Kelly, who had agreed to wait on the beach and soak in the sun. Ever mindful of dangers that could lurk anywhere, no matter how careful their plans, Jim had extracted a promise from Kelly that she would remain right there in full view and surrounded by other people. Only then, said Jim, could he leave her alone for the hour-long excursion that he planned.

As he sailed farther and farther from the beach, Jim felt exhilarated. The wind coming across his back. The spray from the two- or three-foot swells splashing on his bare feet. It was hard to beat. And difficult to think of anything else. There was something about open water that allowed your mind to drift without a care. Even their concerns with assassins seemed manageable on the water.

Before he knew it, Jim was about three hundred yards from the beach. He looked back toward land over his right shoulder. The entire span of Seven Mile Beach could be seen clearly. The almost white sand and turquoise water, the trees, and the Westin and the other hotels and condos. It looked like a wide-lens picture from a postcard.

Jim decided to tack and return toward the beach. He was moving too quickly out to the open sea, and Jim did not like to be beyond sight of the beach. Especially when there were no other windsurfers in sight.

Jim dropped the sail and turned the board around. He had done it countless times before. But it was not an easy maneuver in the choppy seas. Before he could complete the task, his feet slipped on the slick board and he fell over backward into the clear navy blue water. Jim quickly pulled himself back up on the board, stood up and, with feet firmly planted, picked up the sail with the board pointed toward the beach.

Jim leaned back and let the wind fill the sail. The board quickly picked up speed and he started to relax. It was a momentary respite. Before he had gone twenty yards, a rogue wave hit the board sideways and he slipped off again into the warm water. He quickly pulled himself back on the board. This is going to be more difficult than I thought, he said to himself. He straddled the mast and pulled the large sail out of the water.

A dark movement in the water caught Jim's eye as he tried to steady himself on the board. What was that? A shark? No, Jim reminded himself. No likelihood of that. But he needed to see what made the movement to satisfy himself that it was nothing.

His eyes scanned the undulating seas. Trying to discern anything was made that much more difficult by the shadows of white cumulus clouds racing across the blue skies.

Jim stood there for at least a minute, bobbing up and down on the board and holding the line for the sail, which remained half-submerged in the water. No other movement. It was time to move on. Jim picked up the sail and the board accelerated toward the beach.

It happened without warning. Jim glanced behind the board and saw the black fin emerge from the water. Fear gripped him. His heart started pounding so hard he could almost feel it in his mouth. All that knowledge of sharks was meaningless in the face of grim reality. Especially now. There was no one to call to. No one to lend assistance. He would have to deal with it alone.

This is no time to fall in the water, Jim said to himself. He tightened his hands around the wishbone bars that encased the sail. He bent his legs a little more and leaned back a little more to increase his speed. "I've got to get out of here," he said out loud to himself. He tried to say it with confidence, but his fear persisted, and he began to wonder whether he would ever see Kelly again.

The board picked up speed quickly but the black fin kept pace with him. Oh my God, Jim said to himself. This thing is racing with me. I can't believe this is really happening. Not here. Not now. Not to me.

But what was so strange about it? He knew about windsurfers being attacked by sharks in the Mediterranean and the open ocean. And he certainly knew that shark attacks were common among surfers in Florida, California, and Hawaii. Why couldn't it happen in the Cayman Islands? It didn't matter where they were. Sharks apparently viewed the sailboard or surfboard as a fish that could satisfy their endless hunger. It's nothing more than that, Jim said to himself. I'm just another piece of food.

Although he was positioned well, Jim could feel his hands trembling, and he started to worry that the slightest bump from a wave could jar him loose and throw him back into the water. He could not let that happen. He had to hold on tight and keep his speed up.

He felt the wind shift slightly, and he adjusted the sailboard accordingly. This was no time for mistakes. And then it happened. A sudden explosion of energy and water that almost turned the sailboard on its side. A large porpoise leaped out of the water alongside Jim and then dove back underneath his sailboard.

A sense of relief washed over Jim. It was not a shark. He should have known that. Sharks cannot move as fast as his board was moving. Only porpoises could race like that.

He watched as the porpoise made several more leaps ahead of him. It was a thing of beauty. And a welcome release from the tension.

Jim decided to tack again and head back toward the open seas away from the beach. He now felt secure that no sharks were about. Porpoises and sharks are mortal enemies, he said to himself. The porpoise will be my protection.

As the sailboard started to pick up speed, Jim heard the sound of a motorboat in the distance. His eyes scanned the water and saw the boat coming toward him from the south. It was not a large boat, but it was moving very quickly. Jim kept his course. His large sail was easy to see, and the boat would have ample room to avoid him. Or so he thought.

The boat was rapidly becoming larger and larger. Jim kept waiting for the boat to change direction, but it continued to head right toward him. Fast.

Jim reviewed his options. They weren't many. A sailboard could not outrace a motorboat. Keep the course, he told himself. Maybe the guy's just out for a cheap thrill. Trying to scare a lonesome and vulnerable windsurfer.

It did not take Jim long to realize that something more was at work. The boat gave no indication of changing course. It continued to speed directly toward him.

When the boat was within twenty-five yards or so, Jim knew that staying on the sailboard was no longer an option. In seconds the boat would be crashing right into him. No choices were left. As the boat closed the distance Jim released his grip on the sail and dove into the water, going down as deep as he could. He looked up from below and saw the boat rip the sailboard into two pieces.

Jim quickly moved to the surface and gulped down some precious air. He grabbed onto one of the floating pieces of the sailboard and looked around. The motorboat was making a wide turn and apparently coming back for another pass at him. Jim searched the seas for another person. A windsurfer. A sailboat. Anything. But it was futile. There was no one else in sight. He decided to wait until the boat was near him before making another dive.

The boat picked up speed and headed right toward him. As the boat closed the gap to twenty-five yards or so, Jim took another dive to the side. He looked up again and watched the boat crash through one of the floating pieces of sailboard.

I don't know how much of this I can take, Jim said to himself. He then raced to the surface again for another breath. He looked for a piece of sailboard to support him, but the wreckage was now scattered about and not within easy reach. He would have to rely on his own resources.

As he was treading water, his eyes scanned the water in search of the boat. It did not take long to find. The motorboat was making a wide turn behind him. Jim watched closely, now breathing heavily from the deep dives he had made. His legs were feeling tired and there was a pain in his chest. How long do I have to do this? he asked himself. How long *can* I do it?

As the boat bore down on him, Jim took another plunge into the water. He did not, maybe could not, dive as deeply as he had before, and the sound of the boat's engine was more audible than it had been before. Too audible. He knew then that this was not just a teenager with a morbid sense of fun. This was a planned attack. Whoever was driving that boat had a clear interest in doing him harm.

As he broke through the water for the third time, Jim was gasping for air. And scared. However fit he was, there was only so much he could take. In this test of wills, he was destined to lose. And then he saw his refuge. Two young men on jet skis. They were laughing. Enjoying their vacation. Not knowing that they could save a life. My life, Jim said to himself.

Luckily for him, a piece of sailboard drifted by as he saw the jet skis. He grabbed the sailboard piece with one hand and waved his other hand as high and as strenuously as he could. He yelled as well, but he knew his voice was not likely to be heard above the engine noise.

As the men approached, they could see the torn pieces of sail and board scattered about. Their watercraft slowed down, and they finally saw Jim waving his hand.

"Hey, man," one of the men said as he pulled alongside Jim. "What happened to you?"

"I wish I knew. Please. Can you give me a lift back to the beach?"

"Hop on board," the young man replied, helping Jim onto the back of the jet ski.

Never had a jet ski felt so good. Jim turned around to look for the motorboat. It was nowhere to be seen. His momentary relief quickly turned to fear. Kelly. Was she safe? Had an attempt been made on her life while Jim indulged his passion for windsurfing? Although the craft sped quickly through the blue waters, it could not move fast enough for Jim. His eyes scanned the beach, searching for Kelly in her black bikini. Jim could feel his heart pounding as his eyes yielded nothing. And then, as the boat approached the breaking waves, Jim saw Kelly strolling down the beach to greet him, a look of concern on her face.

Within minutes Jim was walking with Kelly on the soft sand back toward the Westin. She had been lying on a towel with her eyes closed and had seen nothing. But now she could see the terror in Jim's eyes as he described what had happened. As they walked back in silence, Jim still trembled. The experience had shaken him. The Cayman Islands had not been the escape he had envisioned. Could he ever go windsurfing again? Maybe. But not this week. I'm confined to land for the remainder of the stay, he said to himself.

The phone was ringing as Jim and Kelly entered the hotel room.

Jim picked it up.

"Hello."

"You were lucky out there, man."

It was a man's voice. Surprisingly gentle in tone. A slight British accent. Jim somehow knew it was the driver of the boat. And his pent-up anger erupted.

"What the fuck were you doing, asshole? You could've killed me!"

"Never mind what I was doing," said the voice in a slow cadence. "Go to the deck at the Hell's Post Office on Botabano Road. Be there at nine o'clock tonight and wait. And bring the girl. It's a matter of life and death. *Your* life or *your* death."

"What?"

"The deck at Hell's Post Office. Botabano Road. Nine o'clock. And bring the girl."

Jim heard a click. The conversation was over.

"What'd he say?" Kelly asked with obvious concern.

"He wants me and you to go to the Hell's Post Office deck on Botabano Road at nine o'clock."

"Where's that?"

"I don't know. But that's the easy part. I'm sure we can find out where it is. Whether we go is the more difficult question."

"Was that the guy who tried to run you down?"

"I'm sure it was."

"Then why should we go? He's obviously out to get you. Maybe us."

"I know," said Jim, sitting down on the edge of the bed. "But let's reason it out. If we don't go, he can still try and get us. If we call the police and bring them with us or have them nearby, he can obviously see that, and he'll never show up.

And beyond that, we have no proof. I never saw his face, and I'm sure he knows that. Anyway, none of this really matters. He said it was a matter of life or death, and, given what I've been through, I think we have to take him at his word."

"I don't get it," Kelly said with mounting anger and frustration. "Why couldn't he tell us whatever he has to say over the phone? Why make us go to some place we've never heard of?"

"Maybe our phone's tapped. And maybe this guy doesn't want somebody else to hear what he wants to say. Anyway, I don't think we have a choice. We've got to do it."

Kelly looked at Jim, but the tone of his voice left no room for argument.

CHAPTER 54

Hell's Post Office, it turned out, was a favorite tourist spot. Although the concierge at the Westin seemed confident that they would have no trouble finding it at night, Jim and Kelly took a drive out in the afternoon to make sure.

Hell was apparently a town of some kind a few miles from the Westin in a sparsely populated part of the Grand Cayman Island. The post office, which included a gift shop, had a wooden deck in the back that looked out over an expansive field of black lava rock. Obviously, Jim said to himself, this is what someone imagined hell to be like.

In the daylight hours the black rock seemed innocuous. Especially with numerous visitors milling about. But when Jim and Kelly returned a little before nine o'clock that evening, all of the other visitors were gone and the black lava rock had an ominous appearance in the darkness of night.

Jim and Kelly stood there in the corner of the deck, talking by themselves, waiting for the "voice" to appear. And hoping that they had not made a mistake in coming to Hell's Post Office by themselves. By nine-thirty they began to feel that nothing would happen.

"Let's go," said Kelly. "This place gives me the creeps. I wanted to enjoy this trip, and trust me, this is not enjoyable."

"I guess you're right," Jim responded with resignation. "Let's give it five more minutes."

Their conversation was then interrupted by another voice. *The* voice.

"Don't look down or around. And don't ask questions. Just listen."

"We are listening," Jim insisted.

"Someone paid me a lot of money to kill you this morning. But you got lucky. We would not be talking now if those jet skis had not shown up. The person who paid me knows I did not succeed," the man's voice continued in unemotional tones. "I was prepared to make another attempt through other means. It would've been easy. But for some reason I was told to give you a message instead."

"What's the message?" Kelly demanded.

"Leave well enough alone."

"That's it?" Jim exclaimed in astonishment. "That's the message that we came here for?"

"I'm told you would know what it means. And also that you now know what can happen if you don't heed the message."

Jim and Kelly looked at each other. They knew what the message meant.

"Well," said Jim, "your patron has a way of making his point."

"I did not say it was a he."

Jim and Kelly looked at each other with surprise.

"It's a woman?" Kelly asked.

"It doesn't matter whether it's a man or a woman. Just heed the message."

"Can't you tell us anything more?" Jim persisted.

He waited for a response, but nothing came. He waited a few seconds.

"Are you still there?" Jim asked.

There was no response. After about five minutes of silence, Jim and Kelly walked slowly from the deck to the Jeep parked on the road. Neither said a word, but the grim reality of the afternoon—coupled with the earlier experiences in Washington—made conversation unnecessary. They each knew that they were no longer in control of their own lives. They had survived at the mercy of some unknown person. Or persons.

As they got into the Jeep, Jim turned to Kelly.

"We're playing with fire here."

"We sure are. My father knew what he was talking about. Maybe I should put the genie back in the bottle."

"Maybe you should. Especially if you want to live a long life."

It was a quiet ride back to the Westin.

Chapter 55

April 1998

Ted Roberts put Robert Kennedy's book back on the shelf and walked over to the cathedral window on the far side of the library. The rain was coming down harder and had created a heavy drumbeat against the towering trees that dominated the rear of his property. He stood there, motionless with his arms folded across his chest, for what seemed like hours, looking but not seeing, thinking of all that had happened. And what he assumed had happened. Because he did not know everything. Not that it was that difficult to piece together.

Some of it had become clear to him in November 1963. But the final moment of truth had come on that blustery afternoon in March 1975. Roberts remembered that he had just left a meeting in the Old Executive Office Building, the stately and ornate government building across the street from the White House, and was walking through Lafayette Park to buy shoes at one of the fashionable men's clothing stores on Connecticut Avenue. Thick clouds of gray moved quickly in the fading sunlight as he absent-mindedly crossed the park. The familiar voice startled him and brought him out of his reverie. He looked up to see Johnny Roselli.

Roselli looked dapper in his expensive-looking suit, his tinted glasses, and his silver hair combed straight back. As he recalled the scene now, some twenty-three years later, Ted Roberts could not help but think of Roselli's fate. Months after that chance meeting in Lafayette Park, Roselli, or rather the body parts of Johnny Roselli, were found in an oil drum floating off the Miami coast. The price one paid for being in the Mafia—at least if there was a fear, as there was in Roselli's case, that someone might tell the government more than he should.

As a young CIA case officer in the early 1960s, Ted Roberts did not fully appreciate that side of the Mafia. He only knew that the organization, and more particularly Sam Giancana's Outfit in Chicago, had agreed to help the CIA assassinate Fidel Cas-

tro and other Latin American leaders whom the CIA regarded as a threat to American security. Roselli was one of the CIA's contacts, maybe the principal contact, for the Mafia. It all seemed so clear in those early days. The good guys and the bad guys. By helping the CIA deal with Castro, the Mafia was part of the good guys. At least so he thought. Now Roberts was not so sure.

He did not know Roselli all that well, although he had seen and talked with him numerous times in meetings with more senior CIA officials in the early 1960s. Still, Roselli was charming and engaging when they met on that afternoon in early 1975. There was the usual small talk. Matters of family and health. In due course Roselli mentioned the investigation that President Ford had recently ordered on the CIA's assassination attempts in earlier years and the separate investigation that the Senate was gearing up on its own initiative. All a product of the new post-Watergate environment in Washington.

"They'll find out a lot," Roselli observed, "but they'll never get near the 'big one.'"

Roberts nodded in agreement. He had never discussed the Kennedy assassination with Roselli and, in accordance with Bruce's strict instructions to compartmentalize everything, Roberts never knew whether Roselli knew anything either, let alone whether Roselli had been involved. But it didn't take much to know then that the "big one" was Kennedy's assassination. And at that moment, Roberts somehow sensed, even knew, that the Mafia was involved in some way.

"It'll be interesting to see what develops from the investigations," Roselli continued in that long-ago conversation. "They've already talked to a lot of people, and they'll certainly talk to more. They may even want to talk to you."

Roberts agreed that he could be, and probably would be, one of those people the investigators would interview. He also knew the investigators could skirt close to the truth about the Kennedy assassination. But, like Roselli, he did not anticipate that the truth would come out through those investigations. Not that he wanted it to remain a secret forever. Because he had already begun to realize that he and his cohorts had made a terrible and unforgivable mistake. And he had also begun to believe that posterity had a right ultimately to learn the truth. And so, after shaking Roselli's hand and resuming his trek to the clothing store, he began to wonder, seriously for the first time, how the truth could be disclosed.

He knew enough to know that he would not do it. At least not then. He had two small children he was crazy about, a wife he adored, and a life he loved in Potomac. Disclosure of what he knew and what he suspected would lead to his imprisonment and untold social abuse from an angry nation. And, if he was right about the Mafia's involvement, he might have ended up the same way Roselli did. And even if the Mafia wasn't involved, others—people who had already killed at least once—would have had the same motivation to silence Roberts any way they could. He was not prepared to take that risk.

Things were different now. His wife was gone and his children no longer needed him as they once did. And he had decided that the secret should not die with him. Something had to be done. Easy to say, he told himself, but difficult to accomplish. Because he knew that some of those people were still out there. And they would still have the same motivation to silence him, or anyone, who proposed to tell the truth.

Without knowing exactly what he would do, Roberts walked over to his desk and settled into the chair. He pulled out some stationery to write. What would it be, he asked himself? He looked up from the desk and gazed out the window. A letter. Yes. A letter to his children. They would have to be the guardians of his secret. And they would have to be the ultimate messengers. It was the only way to serve history and protect his family.

As he looked out the window, he could see that the rain had stopped and that the sun was beginning to peek from behind the clouds. Ted Roberts pulled a black felt-tip pen from the desk drawer and began to write.

Chapter 56

Kelly walked past the shops on Woodmont Avenue in Bethesda, Maryland in the late afternoon amid the bright sunlight and the appealing scents of grilled meat from nearby restaurants. The ostensible purpose of her trip was to buy some clothes, but the real reason, she knew, was to get out of the house and mix among strangers so that she could think through all that had happened. And, more importantly, to decide what she should do.

She had hoped that the trip to the Cayman Islands would provide the escape she had needed. And to some extent it had. But it had all been tarnished by the attempt on Jim's life and the message they had received from his assailant. Jim insisted that she could not live her life like this. Curiosity about her father's past was one thing, he said. But it was only worth so much. She should not have to sacrifice her life—or Jim's—to pursue her father's ghost. But Kelly had difficulty letting go. She knew enough to know that her father's letter would plague her forever if she failed to discover the truth of his involvement in the Kennedy assassination.

While she wrestled with the dilemma, Kelly's body turned down Elm Street without conscious thought and entered the large public garage where her Jeep was parked. The garage was still packed with cars—a product of the short supply of parking spaces to meet the needs of the throngs that crowded Bethesda's restaurants and stores. She trudged up the ramp toward the top level without taking any notice of her surroundings—or the unusual absence of other people.

It was then that she heard footsteps. Brisk footsteps behind her. She stopped and turned around but saw no one. Fear gripped her. She remembered all too well what had happened to Senator Gimble. Was her indecision about her father's letter now causing concern for her predators—whoever they might be? Was she about to experience another assault?

She was not going to let that happen. She picked up the pace toward her Jeep as the steps behind her continued, echoing loudly in the cement structure of the garage. They had an ominous sound. She pulled out her key, hit the remote, opened the Jeep, and jumped in. She could not have turned the ignition on any faster, and the wheels screeched as she backed out and quickly moved the Jeep down the ramp, passing a young woman who, like her, had been walking up the ramp in shoes that had created the echo—and generated the fear that now made Kelly's decision easy.

As the Jeep moved out of the garage, Kelly knew there was nothing left to debate. She could not live her life constantly looking over her shoulder and wondering whether a stranger in a garage or some other public place was an assailant. There was only one thing left to do, she said to herself, and she quickly punched in Teasdale's number on her cell phone. After identifying herself to the receptionist, Kelly only had to wait a few seconds before she heard Teasdale's familiar voice.

"Hello, Kelly. How are you? I haven't talked to you in a while."

"I know." Although she wanted to sound calm, Kelly could hear the tremor in her voice. "Jim and I went away for a few days and we just got back."

"Sounds great. You guys certainly deserved a break from all that's happened. Where'd you go?"

"The Cayman Islands."

"Great choice. There are few places as nice as the Cayman Islands. But I have to say, Kelly, you don't sound good. Is everything okay?"

Kelly took a deep breath. She was not changing her decision.

"No, unfortunately, everything is not okay." Kelly then explained what had happened to Jim and their meeting with the mysterious messenger at Hell's Post Office. "So," she continued, "I've come to the conclusion that I can't do this anymore. To myself or to Jim."

To her surprise, Teasdale did not try to dissuade her.

"I have to agree, Kelly. Especially because I don't see any clear path to finding the answers you're looking for. And on that score, I'm sorry to tell you that I have not been able to come up with anything really helpful about your father. The only thing I do know is that we are obviously dealing with people who can, as your father warned, be a danger to you. Maybe it was the mob. Maybe not. But their identity is of no difference to you right now. Whoever these people are, they are not people to fool with. And I too believe that your continued pursuit of this matter is going to place you in danger. A danger, as you've already seen, that no one can protect you against."

"I couldn't agree more, Harvey. So let's put it on ice for now. But I do want to thank you for all your time and everything you've done. You've been great, and, if nothing else, I'm just glad we had the chance to meet."

"Believe me, Kelly, the feeling is mutual. And I hope you'll let me know if you change your mind or if there's anything more I can do for you."

After she closed the call, Kelly felt more relaxed than she had in a long time. Articulating her decision to Teasdale helped to put the seal on it. Only one more conversation was needed. She punched in Jim's number at Senator Gimble's office and he picked up after the second ring.

"Hi, Jim. How does it feel to be back at work?"

"I'm not sure. My body's here, but I think my mind is still back in the Cayman Islands."

"What're you doing?"

"Some transition work for the new senator appointed by the Minnesota governor to take Gimble's place. I'm still thinking about what I'll do next. I got an offer this morning to be a counsel on the Judiciary Committee. But I don't know. Maybe I'll take the committee job. Maybe I'll stay here for a bit. I'll see. But no final decision yet."

"I can't say the same about me. I made the decision."

"Don't keep me in suspense."

"I'm letting go. You're right. I can't live like this. I even called Teasdale, and he agrees that I'm making a mistake by pursuing this. Whether the Mafia was involved or not, he doesn't know. But he just doesn't see any way to escape the danger."

"You know I agree with him, Kelly. You've got to let go. And you've got to do it now."

"I'm glad to hear you say that. I was worried you might have changed your mind."

"Not a chance."

"Then you've made my day."

"So how about dinner tonight?" Jim quickly added. "We can celebrate our new lease on life."

"Great idea. And then you can go with me to see Mary McGuire."

"Mary McGuire?"

"Yeah. Remember? I told you about the voice mail I got from Caleb Butler. He talked to her about my case, and she said she wanted to see me. I arranged to see her tonight."

Jim agreed, and they scheduled an early dinner so they could get to Mary McGuire's house at a decent hour. As she hung up the phone, Kelly took a deep breath. The decision had been made. No more questions. No more discussions. It was finally over.

Chapter 57

The buzzer resounded in Caleb Butler's spacious office. The senior attorney put down the red pen he was using to edit a brief and punched his secretary's line.

"Yes, Laci."

"Darren Feldstone's here."

"Good. Please escort him to the small conference room on the eighth floor and ask George Kruger to meet me there."

Butler got up from his chair and ambled down the firm's internal staircase to the eighth-floor conference room. By the time he got there, Kruger and Feldstone were sitting at the small rectangular table, drinking coffee and talking about something other than the case.

Butler poured some black coffee into one of the firm's logo mugs and sat in the chair diagonally across from Feldstone.

"Darren, my boy," Butler began, "we can spare ourselves any need to posture today. This meeting is off the record. I asked you over here in the hope that we can put an end to this foolishness and do something that's right and that'll make everyone feel good."

"I don't know, Caleb. That sounds like posturing to me."

"No, Darren. That's just your knee-jerk lawyer response. The fact is I really don't want to posture. I want to settle this case."

"We can settle it, Caleb. We offered you a hundred thousand dollars. You turned it down. Don't talk to me. Talk to your client. That's more than she would get from any jury under the circumstances. Her brother's death was obviously a sad event. But no one—and certainly no one as smart as he was—could have been blind to the danger of living in a tent on the African plains."

Butler leaned across the table to bring himself closer to his adversary.

"Come on, Feldstone. That's lawyer talk. The guy saw those fancy brochures that your client produces. You know what I'm talking about. The brochures with color pictures of all those happy clients in their safari gear. Clients standing on the African plains without a care in the world. Clients being served dinner under candlelight by waiters dressed in white jackets. Jeff Roberts didn't see any photos of lions crashing through tents. And he didn't expect to see any photos like that. Because he thought he was dealing with an experienced and reputable company that knew how to control wild animals. Or at least keep them out of his tent at night."

"I hate to sound cold-hearted, Caleb, but you're trying to paint this Harvard-educated lawyer as some naive soul who believed every advertisement he read in a magazine or saw on television. That's crazy."

Butler watched Feldstone become more agitated as he warmed to his argument.

"I'm sure," the Barrington and Stone lawyer went on, "that Jeff Roberts never assumed he would meet the woman of his dreams at some chosen vacation spot simply because he read a brochure that had a picture of a gorgeous blond in a bikini. Why would he assume that animals in Africa are only dangerous when they're outside the campsite? The guy had to know what he was facing. And he had to know that no safari company could give him any guarantees as to what a five-hundred-pound lion would or would not do at night. Wild animals are, by definition, unpredictable. So your position just doesn't make sense."

Butler leaned back in his chair.

"Who's being unrealistic now? It's precisely because wild animals are unpredictable that we're sitting here. Barrington and Stone had to know, just as city slickers like you know, that wild animals are unpredictable. And since wild animals are unpredictable, Barrington and Stone had to do whatever was necessary to protect their clients. Or at least warn their clients about the risks—before the trip began."

Feldstone absent-mindedly picked up one of the many sharpened pencils that were set in a tray next to some legal pads in the center of the table and began twirling it with his fingers.

"I don't know where we're going with this, Caleb. We've been down this road. You know our position, and my client feels very strongly about it. We did everything that seemed appropriate. The safari had a professional hunter with them. They had campfires. Barrington and Stone had no reason to believe that any lion would be charging through the campsite under those conditions."

It was the opening that Butler wanted. He leaned forward in his chair again, bringing his face within inches of Feldstone's. He waited a few seconds and then began to speak in a whisper.

"Save that bullshit for the jury, Darren. There's still a big question in my mind as to where that professional hunter was when that lion sneaked into Jeff Roberts's tent. But let's put that question aside." Butler paused again and locked eyes with Feldstone. "What if I was to tell you that Barrington and Stone knew that all of its precautions would be insufficient? What if I was to tell you that a Barrington and Stone safari had experienced a fatal lion attack in a campsite only a short time before Jeff Roberts's death? I take it your position might be a little different."

"What're you talking about, Caleb?" Feldstone fired back. "You took Remington's deposition. He couldn't recall any such incidents, and I'm certainly not aware of any."

"I remember Remington's deposition very well. You're right to this extent. Remington couldn't remember any incidents involving Barrington and Stone *clients*. But we didn't ask him about attacks on Barrington and Stone *employees*."

Feldstone just gave Butler a blank stare.

"Employees? I'm not getting your point."

Butler then told Feldstone the story of Mary McGuire's son.

"So, Darren," the Kentucky lawyer concluded, "you might want to take off your lawyer hat for a minute and look at this from the perspective of a juror. A juror who might want to take a photographic safari in Africa someday. Or better yet, a juror whose son or daughter might someday decide to go on a safari. I think that juror would find it very interesting that Barrington and Stone didn't take any new measures or provide any warnings even though they had had a lion attack only a short time before Jeff Roberts's death."

Butler paused for effect while Feldstone digested the new information. Butler then decided to try to close the deal.

"Come on, Feldstone. If you were a juror, wouldn't you find all of this pretty important?"

Feldstone placed the pencil back in the tray.

"I see where you're going, Caleb," the Barrington and Stone attorney said, rising from his chair and gathering up his papers. "You have some new information, but I don't think it's going to get you where you want to go. I'll pass your comments on to my client, but don't hold your breath for a higher settlement offer."

As Feldstone left the conference room, Kruger turned to Butler.

"Well, that was unproductive. I guess he didn't appreciate the significance of Mary McGuire's story."

"Oh, no. He understood the significance of her story. He was just posturing. So don't worry. He'll be back."

CHAPTER 58

The wind whipped down Mary McGuire's street as Jim and Kelly emerged from Jim's Miata. The weather was warm and humid, almost balmy. Thick clouds hung in the night air and seemed to promise rain any minute. It was, Kelly thought, like those tropical evenings in the Cayman Islands. Only now they were in Bethesda, Maryland.

"So why do you think Mary McGuire wanted to see you?" Jim asked Kelly as they walked toward the house.

"I don't know. She never gave Caleb any real explanation."

They had only a short walk from Jim's car to the front door of Mary McGuire's house and had no reason to notice the white van parked on the opposite side of the street about thirty yards down from Mary McGuire's house. From all appearances, the van looked just like another neighborhood vehicle—except that, unlike the other parked vehicles, the van was not empty.

Kelly knocked on the front door while Jim stood behind her. After a few seconds, Mary McGuire opened the door wide. She didn't wait for introductions.

"You must be Kelly," she said with her hand extended. "I'm so glad to meet you. And so glad that you decided to come over."

"Not at all. It's my pleasure."

Kelly then turned to Jim.

"This is a good friend of mine, Jim Roth. I hope you don't mind, but I asked him to come along."

"Of course that's fine," said Mary McGuire as she took a look outside, up and down the street. It struck Jim and Kelly as strange, as though she were fearful of something. But they said nothing, and the moment quickly passed, with Mary McGuire inviting them inside.

As she closed the door behind them, Mary McGuire knew immediately that she had made the right decision in arranging for Kelly Roberts's visit. There was something comforting about Kelly's personality and demeanor. Something that made Mary McGuire sense that Kelly would understand her situation and help her resolve the questions that had plagued her for so long.

Mary took Kelly and Jim into the library and took a seat on one of the hard-back chairs as Jim and Kelly settled onto the couch. Centered on the coffee table in front of them was a pot of hot water and tea bags along with some sugar wafers. And on the far corner of the table was a nine-by-twelve-inch brown envelope with no markings.

"Can I offer you something to eat or drink?" Mary McGuire asked her guests. Both Jim and Kelly shook their heads.

"Thank you, no," said Kelly. "We've already eaten dinner."

There was a moment of silence, and Jim began to feel awkward, not knowing how the conversation would proceed. He felt a sense of relief as Kelly took the initiative.

"Caleb Butler told us about your son. What a horror. It must have taken a lot for you to get through that."

"It did. In fact, I'm still not over it, and I don't know that I ever will be. The grief of losing a child is something I had read about and could easily understand, but the reality is far worse than anything you can imagine. But," she added with a soulful look at Kelly, "it's not much different than the pain you've had to endure. What happened to your brother is also an unspeakable horror. Incidents like that take your breath away and make you realize how fragile life can be. In a moment, your whole life can be turned upside down without warning."

"You can say that again," Jim interjected. "I was enjoying life working for a great senator. And then he was killed one night in an apparent robbery on Capitol Hill."

"Oh," Mary McGuire sighed, "I'm so sorry to hear that. I guess each of us has his own story to tell."

"You're so right," said Kelly. "And I think those tragedies, or just the knowledge that they could happen to you, are the kind of things that can bring people together. 9/11 showed us that as well."

"It's interesting you should say that." There was a pause, and Kelly could not help but sense a certain fear in Mary McGuire's voice, and it piqued her curiosity as to what lay behind the request for the visit. "Because it's that common bond,"

Mary McGuire finally added, "or at least the possibility of that common bond, that accounts for you being here tonight."

Jim and Kelly looked at each other with surprise.

"I'm not sure I know where to begin," Mary McGuire continued. "I don't want you to think I'm crazy, but there are certain things about my husband's death that still puzzle me. If I tell you what they are, you'll see why I think they may also involve your father, Kelly. And I was hoping that maybe you could help shed some light on all this."

"Tell us about it," said Kelly.

Mary McGuire shifted in her chair and folded her hands in her lap.

"I guess the best starting point is to tell you that my husband—Dale was his name—served for many years in the Central Intelligence Agency. He was a little older than Ted, but they became fast friends. This would have been around 1959 or 1960, I would guess. And they wound up spending a lot of time together, working on projects and even traveling together."

"It really is a small world," said Kelly.

"It gets even smaller, Kelly. But I didn't appreciate it all until recently."

Jim and Kelly stole another quick glance at each other, and then Kelly turned back to her hostess.

"Why do you say that?"

"It began after your father died, Kelly. Although he and Ted had not seen each other that much in the last few years, Dale still had a deep affection for Ted as a friend, and he was very upset to learn about Ted's death. But as time went on, it became clear to me that Dale was concerned about more than the loss of a friend. There was something about your father's death that troubled Dale. Something that Dale thought might affect him."

Kelly leaned forward in her seat and looked at Mary McGuire closely.

"I don't mean to interrupt, Mrs. McGuire, but I'm not sure I understand what you're saying. Did your husband think there was some foul play in my father's death?"

"I don't know for sure. But, yes, I guess that's the concern that I have. I didn't think so at the time, but now...." She paused and shook her head ever so slightly. "I just don't know. It was all so strange, so mysterious."

"Dale, are you doing anything important this morning?"

Dale McGuire looked up from the papers on his library desk and saw his wife standing in the doorway, her hands on her hips and a determined look on her face. He knew she was up to something.

"Why?" he asked with a grin. "What activity do you have planned for me now?"

"Golf. It's too nice a day to stay cooped up in the house."

McGuire understood his wife's choice. The weather had turned unusually warm for early April, and what better alternative could there be for an early spring day with abundant sunshine? The Bethesda Country Club was a short drive away, and there would be little competition for a starting time on a weekday morning.

McGuire leaned back in his chair and considered his wife's suggestion. It was not a bad one. Indeed, he had taken her up on it many times since his retirement from the CIA. There was, to be sure, something relaxing about being on Bethesda's golf course, with its large trees, long fairways, and well-manicured greens. And more than that, he knew that the serenity of the setting, coupled with the sweet smell of freshly cut grass, could be an effective antidote to the dark thoughts that had plagued him since Ted Roberts's death.

He had tried to push those thoughts to the back of his mind. Confronting them was an exercise in frustration. Because he did not know, and was sure he would never know, what had really happened to Ted. He only knew that his death was unexpected and untimely and one that inevitably raised questions whether it was, as everyone said, of natural causes. But McGuire knew what others did not. That certain people feared Roberts. Not so much as to who he was, but for what he could disclose. And if those unspoken fears had resulted in Roberts's death, McGuire knew it might be only a matter of time before he suffered a similar fate.

It was an anxiety McGuire had to bear alone. It was unthinkable that he would share it with his wife. The burden, and risk, would be too much for her. But she knew he had been troubled by Ted Roberts's death. And she knew that he was eager to make the most of whatever time he had left. From McGuire's perspective, it was a small way to repay his wife for those many years of work when long hours and extended travel were part of his routine. So he wanted to play golf with her whenever he could. Because she loved the game, and he would do anything now to make her happy.

Still, he could not accept his wife's suggestion that morning for a round of golf. He had financial papers that had sat on his desk for too long and that had to be settled. Everything had to be tidy for his wife if the unexpected should happen to him as well. So he turned down his wife's invitation and persuaded her to go without him. He promised to be there when she returned.

About an hour after his wife had left, he was still sitting at his desk, working his way through tax returns and investment statements, when the doorbell rang. He looked out the window and saw a large familiar brown truck. UPS, McGuire said to himself. He got up and opened the door to find a heavyset man in a brown uniform holding a small carton.

"Mr. McGuire?" the man pleasantly inquired.

"Yes," he said hurriedly, reaching for the package.

"This is for you. But I have to collect seventeen dollars for it."

"Not a problem. Let me get my checkbook," McGuire responded, turning his back to the delivery man and walking toward the library. As he did so, the delivery man stepped inside, followed by another man wearing a brown uniform who had been standing on the side of the doorway and had not been visible to McGuire. They quietly closed and locked the front door.

As soon as he emerged from the library into the foyer, McGuire realized what was afoot, but it was too late. The two men grabbed him and tried to wrestle him to the floor. McGuire instinctively called upon the martial arts he had learned at the CIA and tried to block the heavyset delivery man's effort to place a cloth with some evil-smelling substance over his mouth. Although now in his sixties and a little overweight, McGuire's punch found its mark in the large man's stomach, and he crumpled with a moan. The other man, now wearing a black ski mask, was thinner and quicker. Within seconds he had stepped behind McGuire and, by placing an arm lock around his neck, was able to cover McGuire's mouth and nose with the cloth. Within seconds McGuire was lying motionless on the floor. The two men completed their task quickly and then picked McGuire up, carried him into the library, sat him in the chair, and gently placed his head and arms on the desk. By the time they left, everything looked as it should.

Mary McGuire knew something was wrong as she approached the house a couple of hours later. The presence of the fire truck and ambulance with lights flashing, coupled with the small pocket of neighbors huddled on the lawn nearby, left no doubt that something had happened to her husband.

She turned sharply into the driveway and jumped from the car, leaving the door wide open, and ran to the front door where firemen and a medic were standing. Before she could reach them, she was confronted by her neighbor, a large woman who threw her arms around Mary McGuire.

"Mary, Mary," she wailed, holding her close. "It's too late. He's gone."

Mary McGuire pulled herself from the embrace and looked into her neighbor's eyes, searching, hoping for something that was not there. Mary felt herself go limp and could do no more than mouth the words, "no, no," over and over again.

The neighbor then explained that their son Barry had come home to have lunch with his father and had found him slumped over the library desk. "Obviously a heart attack or something," the neighbor opined. "At least that's what the medics think."

Jim and Kelly listened with rapt attention as Mary McGuire finished explaining what she had found and how she had felt.

"So you never knew for sure what killed your husband," Jim asked Mary McGuire.

"No. Not really. I never had an autopsy performed. It seemed pointless at the time. There was no forced entry or other signs of wrongdoing. And the medics assured me that it was a heart attack or perhaps a cerebral hemorrhage. I don't know," she said, almost to herself, shaking her head. "I didn't have the stomach to pursue it. But as time went on, I kept remembering over and over again the vague suspicions that Dale had raised. And so I decided to go through his papers."

Mary McGuire stopped for a moment, poured some hot water from the pot on the coffee table, and made herself a cup of tea. She gently placed the saucer and cup on her lap and then took a long sip. Kelly and Jim waited in silence, not yet knowing what to say.

"There really wasn't that much that I could find in Dale's papers," Mary McGuire continued. "But I thought that, whatever troubled him, it must have involved something that he and Ted had done together, something at work that was extremely sensitive. Which would explain it all. Because Dale really was very close-mouthed with me when it came to the classified things he did. He always said it was better if I didn't know."

"I can understand that," said Kelly.

"There was nothing I could find in the papers that would explain anything. Except maybe this."

She picked up the nine-by-twelve-inch brown envelope that had been lying on the coffee table and pulled a piece of paper from it. The paper reflected the yellow tint of age. Mary McGuire handed the paper to Kelly. Mary McGuire could see from the astonished look on her face that the paper had some meaning for Kelly.

The paper was a handwritten note dated April 30, 1961. Kelly read the words in silence and then handed the note to Jim. He could feel his heartbeat accelerate as he digested the short message:

Dale—

I was very sorry to read about the disaster at the Bay of Pigs. I know how much effort you and Ted and the others had put into its success. It's unfortunate that the president would not stand behind you.

I'll be traveling down here a good part of the spring and then probably to Dallas. I'll try to hook up with you next time I'm in Washington. Or let me

> *know if you ever make it to Dallas. In the meantime, give my best wishes—and condolences—to Ted.*
>
> *George de Mohrenschildt*

Jim and Kelly looked at each other. The note established one fact that had eluded them until now: Kelly's father had known George de Mohrenschildt since at least 1961. There was still some uncertainty as to what her father did, but he clearly would have been in a position—especially if he read de Mohrenschildt's subsequent CIA reports about Oswald—to know about Oswald's existence and perhaps Oswald's willingness to be an assassin for the right cause.

"This certainly is an interesting letter, Mrs. McGuire," Kelly said after re-reading the note a third time, "but I'm not sure I understand why you think it's important."

Mary McGuire didn't hesitate in responding to Kelly's question.

"You should know, Kelly, that Dale was initially a great fan of President Kennedy's. At least up until the Bay of Pigs fiasco. Although I never knew exactly what Dale did, I did know that he had some involvement in planning that invasion of Cuba. I know, for example, that he took some trips to Guatemala where they trained the Cuban refugees and others who formed the invasion force at the Bay of Pigs. And I also know—because he was so vocal about it afterward—that the president's failure to provide needed air support for the invasion was a great disappointment to Dale. He felt that the president had not only broken his promise but also, and perhaps most importantly from Dale's perspective, endangered the lives of all those men who participated in the invasion."

"I can imagine his disappointment," Kelly responded. "Jim and I talked to one other CIA case officer who was involved, and he had a similar reaction."

Mary McGuire resisted the temptation to ask Kelly the identity of that other CIA employee. She had no right to ask the question, she said to herself.

"Anyway," Mary McGuire said, "I too was disappointed with President Kennedy. Mostly because Dale was. But I continued to be a Kennedy supporter. I had been at social functions at the White House. And, to be candid, I was mesmerized by John Kennedy. He had a magnetism that few people can generate. There was something about his charm and wit. And when he took your hand to say hello, it seemed that his interest was focused totally on you. I know that sounds naive, but that's how I felt. And I wasn't alone in feeling that way."

"I do know what you mean," said Kelly. "Even now, when I see old film clips of Kennedy, you can see that smile and all that charm. He really did seem to be a dashing figure."

"He certainly was," Mary McGuire responded. "Especially because the public knew nothing about his womanizing and all those other stories that came out in later years. So I was extremely upset when Kennedy was assassinated. I remember standing on line for hours to pay my respects when his casket was put on display at the Capitol Rotunda. I also took a great interest in the investigations of his assassination. I read newspaper reports. I read books. Anything I could get my hands on."

Mary McGuire took a deep breath and paused for a moment. It was clear that she was glad to finally be discussing her feelings with someone.

"In the course of my reading, I learned that this gentleman, George de Mohrenschildt, was Lee Harvey Oswald's friend. So when I found this note after Dale died, it made me wonder whether Dale's strange behavior at the end was somehow tied to Kennedy's assassination. And the possibility scared me. Because it meant that other people could have been involved too—people I don't know but who might know me or what I might find."

Jim and Kelly were silent for a moment while they pondered Mary McGuire's speculation. It had a ring of truth to it. The only question was whether Jim and Kelly should disclose the existence of Ted Roberts's letter. To Jim, it was an easy call. But he knew that only Kelly could make that decision.

For her part, Kelly wanted to tell Mary McGuire about her father's letter, but she could not help but remember Teasdale's warning: the greater the number of people who knew about the letter, the greater the difficulty in trying to keep the letter a secret—especially from those people who were obviously watching her. And beyond that, she had decided that the search was over. No more questions. No more meetings. And, hopefully, no more attempts on her life or Jim's. She wanted to allay Mary McGuire's fear—but only if it would keep the matter closed. So, after a minute of consideration, Kelly decided she would not tell Mary McGuire about her father's letter.

Kelly looked directly at Mary McGuire and tried to finesse the issue.

"You may be on to something. Quite frankly, I've had my own concerns as to whether my father's death had any connection to Kennedy's assassination. So there's a certain irony—and maybe tragedy—in your raising the question with me. But I can't give you a definitive answer. Because I don't know anything myself."

Jim could see that Kelly was becoming overwhelmed by emotion. Tears started to well in her eyes, and she was starting to bite her lip. The emotion was equally obvious to Mary McGuire.

"I'm so sorry, Kelly," she said, "if I've caused you any pain or suggested something that hurt you. I hope you realize that I would not want to do anything to make you feel bad."

"Oh, I know that, Mrs. McGuire. But sometimes the truth—or a possible truth—does hurt. And sometimes there's nothing we can do about it."

"Maybe I should suggest something," said Jim, leaning forward on the couch and looking from Kelly to Mrs. McGuire. "Being an outside observer of sorts, I can't help but wonder if you'll both be driven crazy searching for something that will be very difficult, if not impossible, to find. People have been investigating and writing about the Kennedy assassination for decades. Each of you seems very resourceful, but let's be honest with each other. Trying to find the truth of the assassination—which is what you'll need to know to answer these questions you've raised—is a monumental task. I think each of you will be better off to let the thing drop. Who knows what really happened? Whatever it is, we know one thing for sure. Neither Kelly's father nor Mr. McGuire is coming back. I hate to turn to clichés, but maybe you'd both be better off letting sleeping dogs lie."

Kelly was grateful for Jim's suggestion. While the de Mohrenschildt note to Dale McGuire was intriguing—and maybe critical to understanding her father's role in the Kennedy assassination—she didn't want to change her decision. She wanted to be off the case.

"I think Jim may be right," Kelly said. "I know this has bothered me as well, and I've spent a lot of time thinking about it and looking into it. But I'm not sure my time has been productively spent or that I'm any better off for the effort. So I think Jim's advice may be the best course. For both of us."

Mary McGuire sat in silence, staring at the de Mohrenschildt note. After a minute or so, she looked up at Jim and Kelly.

"This thing has haunted me for too long. It's made it difficult for me to do anything. I've even been afraid sometimes to do the simplest things for fear of being confronted by someone who knew something. So I agree with you. I think it's time to let go."

When Jim and Kelly finally left Mary McGuire's house, the white van turned on its lights and moved slowly down the street. Neither Jim nor Kelly gave it any notice. They were too absorbed by the note from de Mohrenschildt. Although satisfied with the advice they had given to Mary McGuire, they could not easily cast the note aside. It was too disturbing.

"I guess," Kelly said to Jim as they reached his car, "it really is a small world. Maybe smaller than I would have liked."

Chapter 59

Dwayne Soggs maneuvered his late-model Chevy cruiser down the long driveway leading to Kelly Roberts's house. The late afternoon sun cast brilliant rays through the branches of the pin oaks that framed the driveway and swayed slightly in the westerly breeze. The shifting branches made the rays of sunlight almost dance on the driveway.

As he approached the house directly in front of him, Soggs cast a glance to his left. The setting was serene. White stables made radiant by the sunlight. Horses grazing in the nearby pasture with the smell of hay swirling in the air. No sounds except for the isolated chirping of a few birds. Nothing like the District, Soggs said to himself. Quiet. Maybe too quiet. But I could get used to this. At least for a little while.

Soggs pulled the car to a stop at the edge of the circular driveway immediately in front of the house. He put the gear into park and stepped out into the warm air. As Soggs closed the car door, Kelly, dressed in her familiar jodhpurs and a large navy blue T-shirt, came out through the front door.

"Detective Soggs?"

"Yes, ma'am."

Kelly walked down the porch and extended her hand in greeting. With his dark brown eyes, shaved head, and stocky build, Soggs gave Kelly the impression of being a tough cop. The two of them stood there talking aimlessly about matters other than the purpose of the detective's visit. Before too long, the last rays of sun were beginning to disappear over the Potomac River, which could be seen through some of the trees at the rear of the house.

"Would you like to come inside?" Kelly asked. "I know it seems like the country to you, but we do have chairs out here in Potomac. And I could get you something cold to drink."

"No thanks. If it's all right with you, I'd just as soon sit out here on your porch. I spend half of my life cooped up in a small office and the other half rummaging around apartments and townhouses, most of which are cramped for space. So I'd rather look at your trees and horses if you don't mind."

"Not at all," said Kelly, sitting down on the top step of the porch. Soggs placed himself on the porch step right below Kelly and leaned against the wooden railing.

"So here's where we are, Kelly," he began. "You remember how we spoke some weeks ago. I couldn't figure out why or how Bud Stamford died. But I did have a suspicion that it might have been the product of foul play."

"Yes. I do remember all that. And, to be candid, I found it all a little upsetting. Bud was such a sweet guy. It was hard to imagine anyone would've wanted to do him harm."

"The world's a tough place. Sometimes nice people like Mr. Stamford find themselves in bad situations. And, while I know you think he was a sweet guy, who knows what he was really like or what his friends were like. I hate to sound like an old cynic, Kelly, but the world's full of surprises. People are not always what they appear to be."

"Oh, I know. But I'd known Bud almost my entire life. And trust me. He was what he appeared to be. A sweet, generous man."

"Well, Kelly, I'm convinced that Mr. Stamford knew some people who were not so sweet and generous."

"You really think he was murdered?" she said hesitatingly.

"Yeah. I think he was murdered. And by someone he knew. Someone who had some pretty sophisticated notions about how to kill someone. I guess what I'm saying, Kelly, is that this was not a robbery gone bad. You know, where a guy walks into his apartment and finds the robber, who then panics and kills the homeowner in desperation. That's not this case. This was planned. By someone who wanted to make it seem like Mr. Stamford died of natural causes."

As Soggs explained his theory, Kelly's thoughts drifted to Mary McGuire. She could have expressed the same suspicions about her husband's death. Who knew? Strange as it seemed, maybe there was a connection between Bud's death and Dale McGuire's. After all, both men had served in government around the same time. And both men were friends of her father. It was all something to think about, but not now. There were still some lingering questions about Bud's death.

"Why do think it was someone Bud knew?" Kelly asked the detective. "And what do you mean by sophisticated methods? What exactly did this killer do?"

"Here's what I think, Kelly. I think Bud Stamford was killed by someone who used a hypodermic needle to inject a lot of air into his veins."

"What? I've never heard of that. That can kill someone?"

"You bet. And if it's enough air, it can kill instantaneously. It's called an air embolus. It prevents the blood from going into the heart muscle or into the lungs. In either case, you're a dead man."

"Oh my God," said Kelly. The thought of someone injecting air into Bud's veins with a needle was horrifying. It meant that someone had to hold him down, or at least inject him with air when he was sleeping or unconscious.

"And here's one of the troubling aspects to this kind of murder," Soggs continued. "Unless you know what you're looking for, it's hard to know that the person's been murdered. If you don't do an autopsy, it might seem that the person died of a heart attack or some other natural cause. And if the autopsy is not done quickly enough, it could still escape your attention."

"And you're sure Bud didn't die of natural causes?"

"Positive. There's nothing in the autopsy that would explain his death. Except some mild abrasions on his wrists, which indicate that someone may have been holding him down while someone else injected the air. And then there's this plastic tip I found in the apartment. It belonged to a hypodermic needle. Now Bud Stamford was diabetic, and he could've dropped the tip along the way when he injected himself with insulin. But then his fingerprints would've been on it."

"And there weren't any fingerprints," Kelly guessed.

"Right. No fingerprints at all. Which suggests the tip was taken off the needle by someone wearing gloves. Or someone who was careful enough to wipe it clean afterward. Either way, it wasn't Mr. Stamford's needle. Or at least not one he used to inject insulin."

Kelly's thoughts again turned to Dale McGuire and her father. For all she knew, either or both of them could have suffered the same fate as Bud. Only there was no way to know for sure. At least she didn't think so. But she was too afraid of the thought to mention it to Soggs. Telling him would require disclosure of her father's letter, and she could not forget Teasdale's warning that the police were probably incapable of protecting her.

"Here's where you come in, Kelly," the detective went on. "There are some handwritten notations in Mr. Stamford's daily calendar that I can't figure out. They might give us some valuable information as to the people he saw in his last days or hours. Someone who might be a suspect. Or someone who could lead us to the perpetrator. And I was hoping you might know something that would enable us to understand those notations."

"Fire away."

Soggs then ran down a number of names and initials that had no meaning to Kelly. She wanted to give him some answer that would solve the riddle, but her mind came up blank in every instance.

By now, the sky had begun to darken and the fading sunlight was supplemented by the glow of spotlights on the house and barn. The wind had also picked up and another thunderstorm seemed to be in the offing. Streaks of lightning could be seen in the west beyond the river.

The shrill ring of a cellular phone interrupted Soggs as he was asking his last question. The detective pulled the phone out of the holster on his pants belt, had a mumbled conversation, and then looked up at Kelly as he replaced the phone to its holster.

"Well, Kelly. Time for you to go inside and for me to take off. I do appreciate your time. Unfortunately, you're not going to be our savior here. But it really was a shot in the dark. I knew you hadn't seen Mr. Stamford much in recent years, but I figured, hey, nothing ventured, nothing gained. Right?"

"I'm sorry too, Mr. Soggs. I wish I could have told you something that would be helpful."

"I know, Kelly. I know. Anyway, it was worth the trip. It's not often I get a chance to see a place as nice as yours."

They both stood up and shook hands, and Soggs slowly walked toward his car. Kelly stood on the porch and watched him. When he opened the front door of the car, Soggs turned back to Kelly.

"Hey, there's one thing I forgot to ask. What about the initials AT or HT? We couldn't be sure of the letters. But it appears that Mr. Stamford had planned dinner with someone with those initials shortly before he died. Maybe the day he died. The initials had the restaurant Sam and Harry's marked down next to them."

Kelly knew about Sam and Harry's, the pricey steakhouse downtown, but she didn't have an immediate reaction to the initials. AT? HT?

"No. I'm sorry. They don't ring any bells."

"Okay. I'll call you if I have anything else. Have a good evening."

Within seconds, Soggs had turned the car around in the driveway and Kelly watched the red taillights disappear into the darkness.

As she walked through the front door, it hit Kelly hard, so hard she spoke the words audibly to herself.

"Of course. HT. Harvey Teasdale. How could I be so stupid?"

But what good would that do? Kelly asked herself. The murderer couldn't be Harvey Teasdale.... Could it?

Kelly stood there in her foyer for minutes, recollections and thoughts racing through her mind. Suddenly it all came together. The pieces of the puzzle seemed to fit. Fear started to envelop her body. "Oh my God," she murmured. Without thinking, she ran to the mobile phone lying on the kitchen counter.

Jim was sprawled out on the couch in his condo, sipping a bottle of beer and watching Will Smith and Martin Lawrence in *Bad Boys II* when his cell phone rang. He stopped the DVD and picked the phone up on the third ring. He immediately sensed the terror in Kelly's voice.

"Jim," she almost yelled into the receiver. "It's Teasdale. It's Teasdale who's behind all this."

"Slow down, Kelly. What're you talking about?"

"Okay. Okay. I'll try to slow down. I just can't believe it."

"First of all, where are you?"

"I'm at the house. Detective Soggs just left."

"Oh, that's right. I forgot you were supposed to meet with him this afternoon."

"Well, I did, and he just left. He seems pretty sure that Bud was murdered."

Nothing surprised Jim anymore.

"I guess we should have anticipated that," was all he said. He waited for Kelly to explain, and she didn't waste any time. She related her conversation with Soggs, the possibility of Stamford dying by an air embolus, and the initials AT or HT written next to a restaurant in Stamford's daily calendar.

"Don't you see?" Kelly almost screamed. "Teasdale's the one person who connects with everyone and everything. He knew my father and he knew Bud. I'm willing to bet he knew Dale McGuire too. Bud tells him about our inquiry and he gets scared that someone will disclose something. So he kills Bud. The same way he killed McGuire, I bet. And..." Kelly paused, as though the words were stuck in her throat. "I wouldn't be surprised," she continued, "if my father's death was also his doing."

Jim sat up on the couch. His response was quick and to the point.

"I'm not buying into Harvey being a serial killer, Kelly. I guess it's possible, but we've seen Harvey, we've talked to him, and he seemed to really care about your father and you. I just can't believe he's that good of an actor. Why would he do all this?"

"Think about it. Teasdale and my father and McGuire are upset with Kennedy after the Bay of Pigs and all those other things. You heard Teasdale tell us how disappointed they all were. They all do something to arrange Kennedy's assassination. And then—years later—my father start's feeling guilty. Maybe he wants to disclose it to the world. Perhaps after we're all gone. But he wants to disclose it. He tells Teasdale. Harvey doesn't want any disclosures. Even after he's dead. So my father's got to go. Same with Dale McGuire."

"Oh, come on, Kelly. All you have are suspicions. No facts."

"Stop being such a fucking lawyer, Jim," Kelly almost yelled, pacing around the kitchen with the phone held tightly to her ear. "Please listen. Teasdale thinks he's got the thing under control. And then he gets this call from Bud."

"Yeah, but remember, Kelly, Bud said he wouldn't tell Harvey about your father's letter."

"Don't you see, Jim? He doesn't have to. Harvey was an undercover agent. He knows how to penetrate secrets. He probably has a sixth sense that tells him what's going on. After all, why would Ted Roberts's daughter suddenly be interested in talking to some stranger about her father's career?" As she mouthed the words, Kelly's thoughts immediately turned to her brother. He had the letter before her, and who could say—maybe Caleb Butler's suspicions about his death were well founded. And maybe she had been under surveillance from the moment Blackhorn had handed her the letter at the funeral. Before she could think through those questions, Jim's voice brought her attention back to the immediate problem.

"Kelly, you there?"

"Yeah, yeah. I'm here. Just thinking about something," she said, almost absent-mindedly.

"I don't know, Kelly. It's got a ring of plausibility to it, but I'm not prepared to accept all of this. Harvey's been such a good guy to us, and especially to you."

"Of course he has. Because he wants to keep tabs on us."

There was a long pause, and Kelly assumed Jim was trying to decide whether she was right. So his next comment startled her.

"Kelly," he said slowly, "we should not be discussing this on the phone. Especially if you're right. If we've learned nothing else, we should have at least learned that."

Kelly's response was quick. "Not to worry. I'm not using the house phone. I'm using my cell phone. I can't imagine that's tapped."

Jim was not sure that was a satisfactory response. Kelly's house could be bugged. But if so, it was too late. Too much had already been said.

There was a long pause as they both considered Kelly's frightening suggestion. Kelly's instincts told her she was right. But she had to agree with Jim. Her theory was based almost entirely on supposition. No hard facts.

"Maybe you're right," she finally said, the hesitation in her voice unmistakable. "But don't you think we should at least tell Soggs what we're thinking? I remember Harvey saying the police couldn't protect me, but I'm not sure we should buy into that anymore. Especially if we're right. He might have been saying that just to protect his own ass. Anyway, I don't think we can sit here and go on like nothing happened."

Now it was Jim's turn to think of the alternatives. He understood what would happen if they started spilling their guts to the police. The circle of people who would know about Ted Roberts's letter would expand considerably, and they could then find themselves in the very kind of danger he thought they had avoided by deciding to drop the matter. And even if they could be protected against the danger, the publicity would create a tremendous emotional strain for Kelly. But he had to agree with her. It was difficult to sit back and do nothing.

"Okay. Let's tell Soggs. But let's do it together. And let's do it now."

"That's easy. To tell you the truth, I don't feel comfortable staying alone in the house right now."

"Come on over."

"Let me change out of these jodhpurs and I'll be there within the hour."

Jim took a long swallow of beer and leaned back on the couch. It seemed like it was starting all over again. Just when he thought it might be over.

Chapter 60

Caleb Butler finished the call and placed the phone back in the cradle and caught a glimpse of the Capitol in the growing darkness. As he did so, he could see that his other line was ringing. Butler glanced at his Rolex watch. Eight twenty-five. Laci had long since gone. No secretary meant that Butler would have to answer his own phone.

"Caleb Butler," he announced in his slow drawl.

"Caleb, it's Jerry Kraft."

Butler's curiosity was immediately piqued. The private investigator would not be calling him so late unless he had something interesting to report.

"Jerry, my good man. To what do I owe this pleasure?"

"Remember how you told me to keep an eye out for anything I learned about this guy Jeff Roberts? Anything, you said, that could help his sister's lawsuit."

"I certainly do remember."

"Well, here's something. I'm not sure it's helpful, but I leave that up to you."

"I'm all ears."

"I just happened to see Dwayne Soggs over at Friendship Heights," said Kraft, referring to the area on the western side of the District next to the Maryland border. "Dwayne and I used to be on the Metropolitan Police Department together. Except he's still there. He's now a detective in the homicide division."

Butler sat up straight in his chair.

"And?"

"And he tells me he just left Kelly Roberts's place out in Potomac. Says he's checking out the death of some family friend of hers."

"I know nothing about that. What happened to the family friend?"

"I don't know, but that's not the reason I'm calling. Soggs says the Roberts's place is really beautiful. The only thing that marred the beauty, he says, is some PEPCO van at the entrance to the place. Says he saw it just sitting there as he was leaving."

Butler did not understand the significance of Kraft's disclosure. PEPCO was the local electrical utility, and its vans were a frequent presence in the Washington, DC metropolitan area.

"I'm not sure I get it, Jerry. Why is that important?"

"You know me, Caleb. Always checking things out. Dwayne says—in passing of course—that it looked like an *abandoned* PEPCO van. I guess because he couldn't see any PEPCO workers. That struck me as a little strange. So I called my buddy at PEPCO to see if they had any crews out on River Road in Potomac. And he checked the computer and said no. So I'm thinking, maybe it's nothing. But maybe something's going down that you should know about."

Butler's curiosity now turned to concern. PEPCO was a large utility. Record keeping might not be what it should be, and the information Kraft got from his contact could have been wrong. Or maybe not. And if not, Kelly might be in some kind of danger. Somebody could be using a PEPCO van as cover for some sinister purpose. He didn't know, but he knew he needed to check it out. The first order of business, though, was to call Kelly. Immediately. He needed to advise her of the van and to ask that she remain in the house until he could determine the reason for its presence.

"Thanks, Jerry. You done good. I'll take it from here."

Butler pushed the button to end the call and then punched in Kelly's phone number.

CHAPTER 61

After hanging up with Jim, Kelly went over to the barn and put some feed into the horses' bins. Although she didn't want to take the time to attend to daily chores, she had a feeling she might not be back to the house until the next day—or maybe later. She then ran back to the house, bounded up the steps to her second-story bedroom, and proceeded to throw her T-shirt and jodhpurs on the floor while pulling jeans and a cotton sweater out of her large walk-in closet. Her movements were quick, almost mechanical. Her thoughts were completely focused on Soggs's visit and her new perspective on Bud Stamford, Dale McGuire, her brother, and, most especially, her father. It was surreal, almost impossible to believe. But she had a compelling sense that her suspicions about Harvey Teasdale were well founded.

After changing clothes, Kelly almost ran down the stairs. She turned on the living room lights, grabbed her keys, and was about to dash out the door when the house phone rang. She didn't want to answer it, but who knew—it might be Jim. She walked quickly over to the kitchen and picked up the phone. The display screen showed a Washington, DC telephone number that Kelly immediately recognized. Caleb Butler. Kelly stared at the phone for a few seconds while it continued to ring and tried to decide whether she should answer it. She shook her head and placed the phone back in the wall unit. This was no time to talk about the lawsuit. Whatever it was, it could wait until the morning.

Kelly quickly exited the house and settled into the driver's seat of her Jeep. The headlights came on automatically as Kelly turned on the ignition. She turned the car around in the circular driveway and headed toward River Road, the headlights illuminating the entire width of the driveway.

Kelly saw the huge log when she was about twenty yards from River Road. It lay across the entire width of the driveway. She stopped the Jeep and put it into park, leaving the engine idling.

Kelly instinctively became suspicious as she stared at the log. What was it doing there? Had someone thrown it across the driveway to block her exit? She looked around, her hands wrapped tightly around the steering wheel, and saw nothing except the tall trees bending in the stiff breeze. She turned back to the log and tried to assure herself that it was no cause for concern. Falling trees were a common phenomenon on her property. Especially in heavy winds. And, she reminded herself, the winds had increased considerably within the last hour or so as the storm approached. So maybe it was just one of those things. Anyway, it really didn't matter. She had to leave the house, and the driveway was the only way out. The Jeep may be great in rough terrain, but it was not going to make it over that log. It had to be moved.

Kelly jumped out of the Jeep. She could roll the log to the side and be on her way.

It was dark and her eyes were focused on the log. She didn't notice the white PEPCO van parked on the side of the driveway entrance. Nor did she see the two men dressed in black who came up from behind her. Her last conscious thought was bending down to move the log.

Chapter 62

Jim looked at his watch. It had been more than an hour-and-a-half since Kelly had called. She should have been there by now. He picked up the phone and called Kelly's mobile phone. All he got was the voice mail. That was strange. Maybe her phone wasn't working. Or maybe she had forgotten to turn the power on.

He walked over to the refrigerator and pulled out another beer. What to do? What *could* he do? He'd just wait. At least for a little while. And then what? Drive out to Potomac to get her? That didn't make sense, and he quickly dismissed the thought. He wasn't sure exactly what route she was taking to his place, and, in any case, he could easily ride right by her. No, that was a stupid idea.

Jim trudged back to the couch and picked up the DVD remote. Watching *Bad Boys II* was out. His thoughts were too jumbled. He clicked on CNN. He needed some noise to keep him company. His eyes glazed over as he looked at the television screen. Kelly's theory about Teasdale had startled him. Maybe she was right. Maybe not. Either way, it was all very troubling. The problem was that they had no hard facts. Only assumptions. Perhaps logical assumptions, but they were still assumptions.

He looked at his watch again. Where was she? He got up and started pacing around the room. Sitting quietly in front of the television was impossible. Thinking was impossible. He had to do something. But what?

The ringing of the phone brought him back to reality. He almost leaped across the couch to pick it up after the first ring.

"Kelly?"

The gravelly male voice that responded made it clear that Jim had guessed wrong. The voice had a slight whistle, as though the man was talking through a gap in his teeth.

"It's not Kelly. And don't expect her any time soon. She's going on a little trip."

"Who is this?" Jim demanded. "What've you done with Kelly? Where is she?"

"Listen, and listen carefully. You and Kelly have not taken our messages seriously. Maybe you'll take them seriously now. We've got Kelly. She's okay for now, and she'll be okay as long as you keep your mouth shut. Don't think about calling the police or anyone else. And don't underestimate our ability to know who you're talking to. I hope you've learned that by now. So, if you want to see Kelly again—alive—you'll pay attention to this message. We'll be in touch."

"Who is this?" Jim screamed into the phone. "What do you want?"

There was no response. Only the click of the phone to indicate that the conversation was over.

Jim slumped back in the couch. His worst fears had become a reality. It was going to be a long and sleepless night.

Chapter 63

Kelly opened her eyes slowly. She felt groggy, and her head throbbed with a dull ache that cried out for aspirin.

Where was she? What had happened? She tried hard to remember what she was doing in her last waking moments. Going to Jim's place. That's right. The log. Yes, she was going to move the log. That was the last thing she could remember.

She was lying on her back on a bed, looking straight up. Her eyes brought into focus a cathedral ceiling made of logs. How ironic, she thought. She moved her eyes slowly down from the ceiling to the walls. They were made of the same kind of logs.

Bright sunlight poured through a large window on her right side. There was a maple nightstand on her left with a small lamp in the shape of a wagon wheel.

She pushed herself up and leaned on her elbows. The door was directly in front of the bed and closed. The room had light brown hardwood floors and a large Indian rug underneath the bed. The room was otherwise barren. No other furniture. Not even a picture on the walls. Nothing to enliven the room—or give her some indication of where she was. Not that it should have been a surprise. The musty smell made it clear that the room was seldom used.

She looked at her clothes. She was still wearing the same jeans and white cotton sweater she remembered putting on to go to Jim's place.

What had happened to her? She swung her legs to the right and sat at the edge of the bed. She was not chained down or restricted in any way. But something was obviously wrong. Somebody had brought her here. Somebody who had kidnapped her. The thought overwhelmed her and she started to shake with fear.

She was obviously in the custody of killers. The only thing she didn't know was who they were. Or did she?

She stood up and walked over to the window. Her legs felt a little wobbly. She looked at the windowpane. It was very thick. She also noticed that there was no way to open it. It looked like it was sealed shut.

Kelly stared out the window. The topography looked like a desert, with scattered trees and small scrubby bushes. About thirty yards or so from her was a small stable, also made of logs, with five quarter horses milling about in a corral next to the stable. Beyond the stable loomed large brown mountains and a bright blue sky. The position of the sun indicated that, wherever she was, it was early morning.

Under other circumstances, Kelly would have enjoyed the view. But not now. Not today. She knew she had been taken to some place far away. Mountains like this didn't exist in Maryland or any place east of the Mississippi.

Kelly tried to imagine where she was. California? Arizona? Maybe Nevada. She couldn't tell for sure, but she knew it was somewhere out West.

The sudden opening of the door startled her. She turned around and saw a large heavyset man standing there. Maybe six-two or six-three. Close-cropped brown hair. Not too old. Somewhere in his thirties and badly in need of a shave.

"Have a good rest?" the man asked. He had a slight whistle to his speech and a sarcastic manner that made an innocent question seem sinister.

"I've had better."

"No doubt."

Kelly's eyes followed the man closely. There was something about him that made her skin crawl. He did not look directly at her, but she sensed that he was checking her out, almost undressing her with his eyes.

In other circumstances, Kelly would have walked away. That option was obviously not available to her. In fact, she didn't know if she had any options. For all she knew, she was a moment away from rape or a violent death or maybe both. The possibility seemed very real. People with good intentions don't kidnap other people, Kelly told herself.

"Where am I?" she asked.

"That really doesn't matter much," the man answered in a patronizing voice. "But I think you can see that it's the desert. A very isolated desert. So I wouldn't give any thought to trying to go anywhere. You'd get lost and die before anyone could find you. Not that you'd have much luck escaping. That window is made of non-breakable glass and, as you might have noticed, it doesn't open."

"I don't mean to pry," said Kelly with obvious sarcasm, "but who are you and why did you bring me here?"

"That's not for me to explain. Sit down and I'll bring you some breakfast."

The man abruptly turned on his heels and closed the door behind him. Kelly could see the bolt lock engage. She was not leaving the room.

She surveyed her surroundings again and was thankful to see a bathroom in the far left-hand corner. She walked over and inspected it. The bathroom was clean and appeared to have everything she could need. Even a shower. But no windows. The heavyset man knew what he was talking about. She was not going anywhere.

Within a few minutes, he returned with a tray and put it on the nightstand next to the bed. Kelly looked at it. Scrambled eggs, sausage, toast, orange juice, and coffee. Just looking at it made Kelly realize that she was hungry. Very hungry. She tried to think of the last time she had eaten. Probably yesterday's lunch.

Kelly looked up at the man with no name. He had a smirk that accentuated Kelly's discomfort. He then turned around without saying a word and left the room.

Kelly stared at the breakfast tray. Was the food poisoned? There was no way to know, and maybe it didn't matter. She really had no choice. She had to eat and there were no alternatives. Kelly sat down on the bed next to the nightstand and drank the orange juice. It tasted good. She was usually a slow eater, but she was too famished for niceties. She scarfed down the food like it was her last meal. Who knew? Maybe it was.

After finishing the breakfast, Kelly pulled out a pillow from underneath the pale orange bedspread and used it to support her back against the headboard. It was her only option. Unless she wanted to sleep or stand.

As she sat on the bed, Kelly tried to imagine what had happened. Somebody had obviously decided that she had gone too far. Or was about to go too far in figuring out what had happened to her father and the role he played in the Kennedy assassination. The only thing that mystified her was why she was still alive. Not that she was complaining. But somebody could have just as easily killed her, she surmised. Just like they killed Bud. Maybe Dale McGuire too. And maybe even her father.

She sat there for what seemed like hours, her head against the backboard, looking out the window, trying to put it all together. She then heard footsteps approaching the room. She wondered what the heavyset man was bringing her now. Or what he would tell her. She steeled herself for another uncomfortable encounter and watched the door closely. The lock disengaged, the door swung into the room, and there before her stood someone new. A small wiry man with thinning gray hair and dressed casually in beige slacks and a purple golf shirt.

His eyes locked on to Kelly's and the two of them stared at each other for a minute or so. The man finally broke the silence.

"Good morning, Kelly. I am sorry that we had to meet under these circumstances, but you left me no choice. My name is Bruce Lord. I was a colleague of your father's at one time."

Kelly did not respond immediately. So this was the famous, or maybe infamous, Bruce Lord. Her father's mentor. Her kidnapper. Many thoughts swirled in her mind, but it all came down to one basic proposition.

"How could you do this to me?" she finally said. "I thought you were my father's friend. And you should have been my friend too."

"In a funny way," Lord remarked as he took a few steps toward the bed, "I am your friend. The only reason you're not dead right now is because you're Ted's daughter." He then paused for a moment. "But who knows what the future holds."

"What does that mean?"

Lord gave her a cold stare.

"You're tough, Kelly. But that's one of the things I like about you. You're not afraid to confront reality. Most people are different. They try to camouflage their fears and avoid uncomfortable facts. Not you. You want to get it out in the open and deal with it." Lord smiled broadly. "You would have made a great operative in the Company."

"Thanks for the compliment. Unfortunately, it doesn't do much to lift my spirits right now."

Lord walked to the edge of the bed and sat down. He looked directly at Kelly.

"Believe me," he began. "I didn't want this to happen. In the worst way, I hoped it never would happen."

"What changed your mind?"

"You changed it. I thought I had everything under control. You spoiled that. You started asking dangerous questions and talking to the wrong people. I became angry and resentful."

"Is Harvey in on this with you? Is that how you know what I was thinking and doing?"

"Actually, Harvey is not part of this. I know you think he is, and, believe me, he has played a useful role. But, no, Harvey is not here, and he doesn't know that you're here."

"I don't get it. How do you know so much then? And how do you know what I think about Harvey?"

"Come on, Kelly. Harvey warned you—correctly—that surveillance techniques are very sophisticated. You should have heeded his warning. Your meetings with him provided a useful tool to keep tabs on you. And Harvey, being the skilled operative that he is, gave you sound advice to lie low so that your life would not be endangered. It was the one thing that made it unnecessary to eliminate him. He played right into our hands without knowing it."

Kelly reflected on Lord's comment. Some of it didn't make sense.

"Wiretaps on telephones I understand. But how did you know about our trip to the Cayman Islands? Or the conversations on my cell phone?"

"Trust me. It didn't take much to keep an eye on you and Jim. Even when the two of you resorted to a canoe trip on the Potomac River. Very clever," Lord remarked, "but hardly enough to avoid our oversight. And the surveillance on your cell phone was not much of a challenge either. We don't have to rely on wiretaps all the time. Bugs are equally effective."

"So you knew I was going to Jim's place yesterday. Right?"

"Right."

"And you knew we were planning to call Detective Soggs."

"Right again."

"And you were afraid of what might happen if Jim and I told Soggs what we thought."

"Bingo."

"But why? We were not going to point the finger at you. We thought Harvey was the culprit."

"I know. But once you told the police what you thought and disclosed your father's letter, everything would start to unravel. Questions would be asked, leads would be followed, and it would not take long for people to come looking for me. It would only be a matter of time."

Kelly paused for a moment as she thought about Lord's responses. There was an obvious gap.

"Okay. So you knew what I was thinking and all that. How'd you get to my house so fast and put that log on the driveway?"

"We knew that Soggs was coming out to visit you. And we knew we had to be ready to take action quickly. Especially if we had to bring you here."

"That's another good question. Where am I? I know it's pretty far away. Is this your place? How'd I get here?"

"Some questions will have to go unanswered, Kelly, but I will tell you this. We used a drug like chloroform to put you out for a while. A long while. We then took you to an isolated airstrip in Virginia where my plane is parked. No one around. And we took a long trip. We thought it best to bring you here. It's a nice spot, but you wouldn't want to be out there alone. Especially at night."

"Who's the waiter?"

Lord laughed.

"I'm glad to see you haven't lost your sense of humor, Kelly. That's Tom. A strange fellow. But he does perform valuable services for us. And he's available to cater to your needs. Which I think will be pretty limited for the time being."

Kelly turned to the window. She wanted to cry, but she didn't want to show Lord any weakness. He was a traitor. And he made her angry. She turned back to face her captor.

"You killed President Kennedy. That's what this is all about, isn't it? You don't want the world to know that you were involved."

Kelly watched Lord's facial expression change and his cheeks turn red. She could see the anger welling up inside him.

"That's not quite right," he responded in a low and hostile voice. "But after all your effort, and given your predicament, I guess you deserve to know. Especially since no harm can come from it."

"Thanks for the offer."

Lord got up from the bed and walked to the far side of the wall and then turned back to Kelly, his arms folded against his chest.

"You have to remember that I worked undercover for our government. I was skilled in many things. Including killing people. But I believed, and I mean this sincerely, that I was a patriot. If I did kill, it would be for our country's good."

"I'm sure," said Kelly, disguising her skepticism.

"And I was prepared to die for my country too. On many overseas assignments I carried cyanide pills everywhere I went. And if I was captured, I was prepared, or at least I thought I was prepared, to take those pills and end my life rather than disclose my country's secrets."

Kelly knew that Lord wanted to gain her sympathy, but all she felt was revulsion.

"Things changed to some extent," he went on, "when John Kennedy was elected president. He was truly inspirational. Although I know you weren't born yet, Kelly, you may remember reading how Kennedy said in his inaugural address, 'Ask not what your country can do for you. Ask what you can do for your country.' I took those words to heart. My hopes soared and my dedication to the CIA intensified. I was more eager than ever, if that's possible, to do good. And more than ever I was prepared to sacrifice anything, even my life, for my country."

"So what happened?" Kelly cried out. "How'd you go wrong? I can't believe that you would've killed Kennedy because you didn't like some of his decisions. We can't go around killing our leaders just because we don't like them. We live by the rule of law. We're not barbarians."

"To some extent you're certainly right, Kelly. But much more than that was at stake."

"I don't understand. What more could be at stake?"

"We certainly were surprised and disgusted when Kennedy canceled the air support for the Bay of Pigs invasion. I thought he allowed himself to be bullied by Khrushchev, the Soviet premier, at their summit meeting a couple of months later. I was stunned by his weak response to the Russians in the Cuban missile crisis. And I was appalled by his willingness to sign a test ban treaty with the Russians and then to sell them wheat to help them escape the failures of their communist system. As bad as those events were, I agree with you, Kelly, that they alone would not have justified the president's elimination."

"So what am I missing? What else is there?"

Lord instantly recalled the first moment when he recognized the danger.

They are in the wide corridors of the private residence on the second floor of the White House. It is the spring of 1961. The pleasant fragrance and warm weather on the outside contrast sharply with the crisis atmosphere inside the White House. The situation in Laos has reached a boiling point. The Joint Chiefs of Staff are talking about sending thousands of American troops to fight a ground war in Southeast Asia, a prospect that frightens many of the liberal advisers who surround Kennedy. The president, however, has said in his speeches that he will use any and every weapon in the country's arsenal to stem the advance of communism, and he, for one, is prepared to take the president at his word.

He is there to brief the president with Ted Roberts and McGeorge Bundy, the national security adviser. The president, they know, often takes naps in the afternoon, a habit said to be common among great leaders like Winston Churchill, a means of preserving the president's ability to manage the affairs of state from early morning through late at night. And so they have been directed to meet the president in the personal residence at four o'clock. They are then told that he is using the Lincoln Bedroom down the hall and will meet with them there.

They engage in small talk while waiting. Most of the conversation is confined to Ted and himself. Bundy is an austere man of few words, and, while they have worked with him on numerous matters, neither Ted nor he is close to the national security adviser. He glances anxiously at his watch. It is now almost four-thirty. He and Ted pace in small circles while Bundy sits sphinx-like in one of the ornate chairs against the wall. Bundy has done this a hundred times already. For him and Ted, it is not a common experience.

Suddenly there is a commotion down the hall by the door to the Lincoln Bedroom. Bundy rises from his chair, and the three of them slowly move down the hall toward the historic room. The omnipresent Secret Service agents are there, and, as the door of the Lincoln Bedroom opens, two women quickly emerge, both stunningly beautiful, one a brunette, the other a blonde, and both laughing and trying to adjust clothes that look rumpled. Two grim-faced Secret Service agents with ear pieces are escorting the women to elevators that will take them to the White House entrance. Another Secret Service agent is standing by the open door to the Lincoln Bedroom. "The president will see you now," he says without emotion.

Lord remembers that scene, as he did a thousand times before, and looks at Kelly with cold eyes.

"John Kennedy," he says slowly for emphasis, "was a walking time bomb waiting to explode. We knew—as the public did not at the time—that he couldn't keep his pants on. The womanizing was constant and, more than that, it was reckless. Any woman he could find. Security meant nothing to him. I'm sure you've heard about Judith Exner. She had a relationship with Sam Giancana, the head of the Chicago mob, at the same time she was sleeping with Kennedy. He didn't care. Even when the FBI director told him to stop, he couldn't. He continued to talk to her."

Kelly could see that Lord was becoming more agitated as he recounted his perspective on John Kennedy. He was obviously obsessed with the subject. And he could not be turned aside.

"Exner was just the tip of the iceberg," Lord continued. "The women were everywhere, and they presented a mortal danger to our nation's security. It's as old as the Bible. Samson and Delilah represent just one of the more famous encounters. Enemies use women to infiltrate their adversaries' inner circles. We had a real concern that Marilyn Monroe might blab to the press about classified information she acquired from her affair with the president, but she died under suspicious circumstances before anything happened. I don't think she was a spy, but there were other women, and who knew where they came from or what they might do with the information they acquired. Right before he died, the Senate was investigating Kennedy's relationship with a German woman who was married to a Washington diplomat and, more importantly, was reputed to be a communist spy."

"Was she?"

"I don't know. But I do know that the mob or the Russians or some other crazy despot could have compromised our nation's security at any time by sending a beautiful woman to Kennedy. He would have accepted her with an open zipper, no questions asked. The public may have been ignorant," he went on, "but some of us in the CIA, like some of the guys in the Secret Service detail and the FBI, we all knew what was going on. We had even listened to tapes of some of these affairs. It was a horrifying experience to learn that our president was so vulnerable. So we were scared. Very scared."

Lord's revelations were not entirely surprising to Kelly. She had read about Kennedy's womanizing. There were tales of pool parties with naked women and prostitutes being brought to the presidential suite. It was part of Washington lore that would periodically show up in the press and in books. But Kelly had never considered the danger that Kennedy's womanizing posed to the country's security.

"I see your point, but still," she pleaded, "this is totally wrong. That's not enough. There had to be alternatives."

"I wish there had been alternatives. We certainly explored them. But it was a different time, Kelly. Public disclosure would have been helpful. But newspapers were not prepared to publish accounts of the president's womanizing. Even if they could document it. The press didn't like to talk about personal things like that. For God's sake," he added with a shake of his head, "in the early 1960s the television networks wouldn't show a man and wife in bed together—even with their pajamas on. Can you imagine the press talking about the president's unrestrained habit of sleeping with anything that wore a dress? In fact, at one point the publisher of the *Washington Post*, who was a Kennedy friend, had a nervous breakdown at a newspaper editors' convention and gave a rambling speech in which he mentioned the president's affairs. And still nothing was said in the press."

"I understand what you're saying. But that's no justification for assassination."

"It was to us, Kelly. Because the danger was not just theoretical." Lord paused and glanced up at the cathedral ceiling as his mind searched for the long-ago memory. "'Pay any price, bear any burden, oppose any foe to assure the survival of liberty.'" Lord looked back down at Kelly. "Those were Kennedy's words in his inaugural speech. I remember them clearly. And I remember when Kenny O'Donnell, his closest aide, told me in the summer of 1963 that Kennedy was going to withdraw all our troops from Vietnam after he was re-elected in 1964. I was sick inside. Because, strange as it may seem today, we were then locked in a deadly struggle with communism almost everywhere around the world. A withdrawal from Vietnam in 1964 would have been like pulling America's thumb out of the dike in the fight against communism. So O'Donnell's comment only confirmed what I had already seen: that Kennedy's promises of fighting any foe and bearing any burden in defense of freedom were all lies. The man was going to sell us down the river." Lord paused and looked directly at Kelly. "His womanizing made the prospect that much more probable. He could fall for some strategically placed woman and put the country in a situation where our nuclear superiority would mean nothing."

Kelly sat there on the bed, now cross-legged, thinking about Lord's revelations. She could understand the fear and frustration that he and his colleagues must have felt at the time. But none of that, she said to herself, could justify murder. Because that's what this was, plain and simple. Murder.

"Oh, this is not right," Kelly said. "You assumed the right to decide whether a president elected by the American people should live or die."

"It's easy to take a high moral ground decades after the fact, Kelly. Those of us who lived it at the time knew our country could not afford the risk that Kennedy represented. Unfortunately, it was a risk that no one really could prevent." Lord then paused again. "Unless the man was eliminated."

Kelly now understood, and her thoughts turned to her father.

"Was my father part of this group that talked about 'eliminating' the president?"

"Yes, he was. Ted attended the meetings and played a critical part in our plan. He knew George de Mohrenschildt and learned about Oswald. I can't remember now whether your father read some contact report by de Mohrenschildt or whether de Mohrenschildt told him directly. Either way, your father knew that Oswald was some strange guy who was alienated from society and had tried to kill General Walker."

Lord remained motionless for a few moments, his arms again folded across his chest, as he thought back to the time when the decision had been made. After a few moments, Kelly saw his eyes come into focus. He then put his hands in his pockets, looked at Kelly, and said what was now obvious.

"Oswald was the perfect foil for our plan."

"Was de Mohrenschildt part of the plan too?

"No. I certainly never had any conversations with de Mohrenschildt about the plan, and I'm sure that your father didn't either. We wanted to restrict the number of people involved. For obvious reasons. They had to be people we knew extremely well and could trust with our lives. People who could be counted on to abide by the oath of secrecy we gave to each other. De Mohrenschildt didn't fall into that category. Telling him would have exposed all of us—not to mention the plan—to unacceptable risks. So, no, your father did not enlist de Mohrenschildt to be part of our plan. In fact, I'm sure de Mohrenschildt never knew his connection to the whole sequence of events."

"So Oswald was the guy who killed Kennedy?"

"Oh, no. Oswald really was a patsy, as both Oswald and de Mohrenschildt later said. Oswald was told that he would be part of a plot to kill Kennedy, and he brought his rifle to the school depository for that purpose. But we had our own contacts through the Mafia. After all, we had already been working with them in trying to eliminate Castro and other leaders. We knew that they had people on call who were, to be blunt, a little more skilled at this type of thing than Oswald. People who could be counted on to do the job right. And we also knew that they would be only too happy to assist our endeavor. Albeit for different reasons."

"I've read that certain people in the mob didn't like the Kennedys, but I still have a hard time believing that they would participate in a plot to assassinate the president. That would have been a high-risk gamble. They would have been wiped out if their role was publicly disclosed."

"I'm sure they considered all that," Lord said in his matter-of-fact tone. "But you have to remember three things, Kelly. First of all, their hatred of the Kennedys was deep. Giancana had played a pivotal role in Kennedy's election by giving him the votes to win Illinois. Giancana and the others thought that their assistance would be rewarded in some positive way. Instead, all they got were wiretaps and indictments from Bobby Kennedy's Justice Department. They were understandably disappointed. And people who disappoint the mob," he said, "usually pay a heavy price. The second point is equally important. It was not the mob's decision. It was ours. And so things were worked out in a way to give them deniability, if you want to call it that. Not that any of this mattered from a practical perspective. And that's the last point, Kelly. No one was going to find out. Because the people we engaged were professionals. They knew how to do this stuff without leaving a trace."

Lee Harvey Oswald stood in the southeast corner of the sixth floor in the Book Depository and watched a fellow worker take the elevator down to lunch. He was now alone. He looked at his watch. It was about ten minutes to noon. He quickly walked stone-faced over to the staircase next to the elevator on the north side of the large open room and knocked gently on the door leading to the stairs. The door was pushed open and a young man with short dark hair slithered through, casting quick glances toward the open part of the room. He had a black leather case strapped to his back.

"No one else here?" the man quietly asked.

Oswald shook his head.

"Let's go," the man commanded in the same quiet manner.

Oswald followed the stranger in silence. He didn't know his name. In fact, he knew nothing about him. Other than that he would be at the staircase door by eleven fifty. He studied the man as they walked to the southeast corner of the sixth floor. Like Oswald, he was of medium height with a slim build but, in the short-sleeved shirt he wore, Oswald could see that the man was much more muscular. He presumed that the stranger was an American, but he had a slightly olive complexion that made Oswald wonder whether he might be Italian or Cuban.

When they reached the southeast corner of the floor, the stranger took the leather case off his back and gently placed it on the floor. He then pulled white latex gloves from his pants pocket, stretched the gloves over his hands, and looked up at Oswald with a nod of his head. Oswald didn't have any latex gloves, but that was of no moment to him. After all, he worked at the Depository, and there would be no surprise if his fingerprints were identified afterward. And besides, no one was going to find him after the deed was done. He would disappear from view. In the meantime, he knew what had to be done. Without exchanging words, the two men quickly stacked cartons of books to create an impenetrable wall by the window. They made sure, however, to leave an unobstructed view of Elm Street and the rest of Dealy Plaza.

No sooner had they finished stacking the cartons than they heard the elevator door open on the north side of the floor. They both squatted quickly behind the stacked cartons to avoid being seen. Oswald peeked through a crack in the cartons and saw a fellow worker, a young black man named Bonnie Ray Williams, step out and sit down to eat his lunch of fried chicken and soda.

Oswald looked over at his nameless companion. The stranger was like a stone figure. He stared straight ahead in silence at the cartons, frozen in his squatting stance. Within a few minutes, Williams, having finished his lunch and obviously believing he had been alone, got up and took the elevator down. Oswald looked anxiously at his watch. It was five minutes after twelve. He and his companion waited a few seconds in their frozen stances to make sure there were no other noises and, more importantly, no other visitors.

Satisfied that they were alone again, the stranger opened the black case he had brought. Oswald saw that it was a Mannlicher-Carcano bolt-action rifle like the one Oswald had brought to the Depository that morning in brown-paper wrapping. Like his gun, Oswald saw that the stranger's gun included a telescope. But unlike his gun,

Oswald could see that the stranger's rifle was polished and had the general appearance of being new. A man who devotes substantial time to the care of his weapons, Oswald thought. A professional at work.

Working in silence, the stranger quickly assembled the gun, screwing in the barrel and affixing the telescope. The man was extremely proficient, completing the task in a minute or so. Before the stranger had finished the assembly, Oswald pulled out his similar but much more worn Mannlicher-Carcano rifle from the brown-paper wrapping. He was not sure what the stranger's plans were, but Oswald needed to be ready.

Oswald and the stranger then stacked a few cartons in front of the window on the southeast corner to be used as a resting place for their rifles. They then looked out the window to assure themselves that their view of Elm Street remained unobstructed.

The stranger then looked up at Oswald and softly said two words: "The elevator." Oswald, remembering his instructions, understood at once. He walked quickly over to the elevator on the north side and pushed the down button. The elevator was there in less than a minute. Oswald pulled the wooden gate open and used a short metal bar supplied by the stranger to make sure the elevator remained open on the sixth floor. He then retreated to the nest of cartons on the southeast corner and looked down at his watch. It was twenty-five minutes after twelve.

Within minutes, the approach of the president's motorcade was signaled by growing activity on Dealy Plaza. They looked out the window and saw the procession of black limousines and police motorcycles moving slowly up the street, all the while attracting hordes of people from all directions who were watching in awe or waving excitedly at the president and his elegant wife.

Without a word, the stranger gently put his hand on Oswald's shoulder and motioned for him to squat behind the stranger. Oswald immediately realized the import of the maneuver. There was only going to be one actor in this play.

It was over in a few minutes. The stranger worked with his expected proficiency and in silence, firing three shots in rapid succession. Oswald could not be sure, but he thought he heard the pop of another gunshot as well. In other circumstances and with a different person, Oswald might have asked whether there was another shooter. But not now. Not with this man.

The presidential motorcade had sped off, and the crowds had quickly dispersed as frightened people tried to understand what had happened. Sirens seemed to blare from every direction, and, as Oswald glanced down to the street, police seemed to be everywhere. None of it seemed to faze the stranger. He turned around while still kneeling and motioned for them to leave. Oswald dropped his rifle in between stacks of cartons while the stranger rapidly disassembled his rifle, replaced it in the black leather case, and then slung the case over his back. The two of them then ran without a word to the open elevator on the north side. They allowed the elevator to drop halfway down the floor. The stranger jumped on top of the exposed elevator. It was, Oswald thought, a masterful way for the stranger to escape unseen through the interior of the building. The stranger looked at Oswald from the top of the elevator and said only, "Remember the pickup point." Oswald responded with a knowing nod. He then threw the metal bar down the elevator shaft, pushed the elevator's down button, and exited through the staircase door.

Kelly sat there cross-legged on the bed, listening with her mouth half-opened as Lord finished his explanation of how the assassination was accomplished. Her mind was numb with the startling nature of the revelations. What could she say? There was only one obvious question.

"What was the pick-up point?"

"Jack Ruby's house."

Kelly now understood.

"But he never made it. Did he?"

"No. He never did. And the rest, of course, is history."

Kelly sat there in silence, overwhelmed by everything that had been said. Everything had now been answered. Everything, that is, except the one question that mattered most. She didn't want to ask it for fear that the answer would be devastating. But she could not back down now.

"Why did you kill my father?"

Kelly could see that the question caught Lord off-guard. He walked over to the window and the sunlight shaped the outline of his figure. He stared outside for a minute or so and then turned toward Kelly, his hands on his hips. He had a troubled look on his face.

"I like your direct approach, Kelly. That was one of your father's great attributes as well."

Kelly remained silent. She wanted to hear the answer. In that respect, at least, Lord did not disappoint her. He did not mince words.

"It was probably the most difficult decision of my life, Kelly. Even harder than the decision we had made about President Kennedy. Because I could rationalize that decision in light of the national interest. I couldn't make the same justification when it came to Ted. At least not to the same extent. But he wanted to tell the world what we had done, and, quite frankly, I didn't think he had a right to disclose something that had been told to him in confidence and that involved actions that he knew had been taken to protect the nation's security. And more than that, he had taken an oath of secrecy—an oath that we all agreed to honor. He was going to violate that oath."

Kelly exploded with unrestrained anger.

"Those are just words. You didn't kill my father to protect some honor code. You did it to save your own ass."

"I don't think I would put it as crudely as that, Kelly. But I guess you could say that I was afraid of the personal consequences if your father disclosed what he knew. And as he got older, the risk of disclosure became greater because his guilt got worse. He kept calling me and saying that we had to tell the truth for the sake of history. I didn't agree. Ironically, I came to the point of view that he had expressed earlier. I wasn't sure that history would look kindly in retrospect on some government officials who took such power into their own hands. So Ted became an unacceptable risk."

"What about Dale McGuire and Bud Stamford? Did they also become unacceptable risks?"

"I'm afraid so."

Kelly began to realize that Lord was a man with no moral compass. It made her sick inside, and she wanted to end the conversation. But another question needed to be answered.

"What about my brother? Was that your doing too?"

Lord shook his head.

"I'd like to believe I'm a talented operative, Kelly, but controlling wild animals is not among my skills. So, no, I had nothing to do with your brother's death. That was a true accident of nature. But we had him under surveillance too. We suspected that your father might have written something down or told your brother something, and so we watched him closely after your father's passing. And we watched your brother's law partner closely too." Lord paused and looked directly at Kelly. His blue eyes were cold and heartless. "The lawyer," Lord repeated. "We knew he was going to be a problem after Jeff died. But that was a problem we took care of."

Kelly now understood. Blackhorn did not die of a heart attack. He had suffered the same fate as the others. Everything had now become clear. Everything except her own fate.

"So where does that leave me? Am I just another unacceptable risk that has to be eliminated?"

Lord did not respond immediately. The question seemed to hang in the air, suspended by Lord's apparent indecision. He slowly paced around the room with his head down as though he were giving careful thought to the question. He then looked up at Kelly, his hands back in his pants pockets, and shrugged his shoulders.

"I must admit that life might be easier for us if you weren't around to spill your guts, so to speak. On that score, I must tell you that we are disturbed by the disruption you've already caused, and can continue to cause, to our lives. But…." His voice trailed off and he looked at Kelly intently.

"But what?" Kelly interjected.

"There is one thing that might make a difference to us."

Kelly was not sure who the "we" and the "us" included, but that was now secondary. Her survival was of paramount importance.

"What is it?"

"The letter. The letter your father wrote. Where is it? We would like to have it. We don't want that letter showing up somewhere else. So if you give us the letter, Kelly, or tell us where it is, that would weigh heavily in your favor here. You can trust me on that."

Sure, Kelly said to herself. Just like my father trusted you. And all those other friends who have now been silenced. But in her anger, Kelly now understood why she was still alive. Lord and his cohorts needed to get the letter. They couldn't take a chance of the letter surfacing after her death. The letter was now the key to her survival.

"I'll give it some thought," she replied with a bravado that surprised even her. "But don't hold your breath."

Lord nodded impassively.

"I would urge you to give it serious consideration, Kelly. As things stand now, you're not in a good bargaining position. In the meantime, I should tell you that we took the liberty of taking some additional clothes from your house in case you want to change. I'll ask Tom to bring them in and also to give you some of the old paperbacks we have here. Something to keep your mind occupied. And maybe we'll talk later."

He then left the room and locked the door behind him.

Chapter 64

Jim's first sensation was pain. The headache he felt was worse than anything he had ever experienced. He opened his eyes to the morning sun and found himself sprawled on the couch wearing the same clothes he had on last night. The television was still on.

Jim glanced around the room and saw the four empty bottles of beer on the coffee table. In other circumstances, he would have suspected that his headache was nothing more than a hangover. But he knew the source of his headache lay elsewhere—the unremitting tension he had endured from the moment he had received the telephone call from that stranger.

Jim looked at his watch. Eight twenty. He had been asleep less than three hours.

His thoughts quickly turned to Kelly, and he again asked himself the same questions that had plagued him throughout the night. Who had taken her away? Where was she? Was she okay?

The last question was the most disturbing. He had no idea whether she was still alive. The alternative was too horrible to contemplate. He had to think positively.

Okay, big shot, he said to himself. What now? Nothing imaginative materialized in his mind. There was no alternative except to revisit the same options he had exhaustively reviewed the previous night.

Call Soggs? Jim quickly dismissed that idea again. True, he was prepared to call Soggs with Kelly when they were going to pass on information concerning Stamford's possible murder. But things were different now. Kelly had been kidnapped, and Jim was willing to take Kelly's kidnapper at his word that only harm could come to her if the police were told. So Soggs was out. At least for the time being.

Kay Brownstein. The CIA certainly had plenty of experience with kidnappings, and Brownstein had considerable resources at her disposal. Resources that could be used to locate and hopefully rescue Kelly. And beyond all that, he was certain that Brownstein would be upset and willing to help.

Then again, Jim said to himself, the CIA was a large government agency, and if Brownstein was told about Kelly's kidnapping, someone else in government could learn about it as well. Someone who might pass the information on to Kelly's kidnapper.

That was no small risk, Jim decided. Brownstein wasn't going to rescue Kelly herself. She would have to tell someone else. Someone in the CIA or some other governmental agency. And who knew what relationships existed there? Jim wasn't sure whether Teasdale was behind Kelly's disappearance, but that didn't really matter. Whoever it was, the kidnapper was probably Ted Roberts's former colleague in the CIA or some other governmental agency, and there was a good chance the kidnapper still had contacts in the government. If Brownstein learned about the kidnapping, the kidnapper might also learn what she knew. So Jim decided to shelve the idea of telling Brownstein. At least for the time being.

What were the other choices? He couldn't bear the idea of just sitting around and doing nothing. That would require the kind of patience he never had. He needed to do something. But what?

Call Teasdale? Jim had seriously considered that alternative last night and he toyed with it again while looking at the television screen. Calling Teasdale continued to have some appeal for him. Jim still wanted to believe that Harvey was their friend and that Kelly's suspicions were misplaced. The guy seemed to have a genuine respect for Ted Roberts. And it was clear to Jim that Harvey liked Kelly. But what if Kelly was right about Teasdale? That too was a real possibility, and Jim certainly wanted to know the answer to that question. If he called Harvey's office and was told that Harvey was out, that might indicate that Teasdale was behind the kidnapping. Or it could indicate nothing. Teasdale might have a legitimate appointment outside the office.

What if Harvey was in his office? That would prove nothing, Jim told himself. Teasdale could have locked Kelly away somewhere in the Virginia hills and still be in his office by the next morning.

Either way, if he told Teasdale about Kelly's disappearance, Jim faced the same problem that he had with Brownstein. Even if Harvey was clean, there was no way Jim could be sure that no one else would learn about the kidnapping.

And if Harvey were involved in the kidnapping, Jim's call would alert him to Jim's willingness to tell someone—something that might also endanger Kelly's life. So calling Teasdale was out.

Jim felt powerless, and he didn't like it. He liked to think of himself as a person who seized the initiative, and this was hardly the time to change course. He got up from the couch and went to the bathroom and threw some water on his face. He then walked over to his desk and pulled out the handwritten notes he had made of the clues in Ted Roberts's letter. He studied the clues carefully. Maybe they contained something that would resolve his dilemma.

After a few minutes, Jim realized that it was hopeless. No matter how long he looked at them, the notes gave him no guidance. He was on his own.

Jim put the notes down on the desk. He didn't know what he should do. But he knew one thing for sure. He had to talk to somebody. Just to hear himself talk out loud might focus his thoughts and help him formulate an action plan. That was all well and good, but who could he call?

It didn't take Jim long to come up with an answer to that last question. There was only one person whose opinions he respected and who could be trusted completely.

Jim needed to make that call. But he couldn't take the risk of calling on his phone. It was probably tapped. He also had to assume that he was being watched. How could he make the telephone call? He couldn't even use the public phone on the street. Someone could see him using it. There was one possibility. But it would put his acting skills to the test.

Jim looked down at his watch again. It was after nine o'clock. Most ambitious lawyers in the Capital would be glued to their desks by now. He picked up the phone and called a friend at a nearby law firm. His friend picked up after the fourth ring.

"Peter. It's Jim."

"Jim. How are you? What're you up to these days?"

"I'm still trying to figure out my future." Although the comment was true, it was nothing more than a smokescreen to elicit the right response from his friend. "I've got some offers in the Senate," Jim continued, "but I'm wondering if I should pursue something in private practice."

"I can certainly relate to that dilemma. But, as you know, I felt life would be better by limiting the amount of time spent in public service."

Jim breathed easier. The conversation was moving in the right direction.

"I know. I remember that you decided to leave the Senate after being there only two years. Which is why I'm calling. I was wondering if I could come by and talk to you for a few minutes. I've got to give a response to one of the Senate offers today," Jim lied, "and I'd like to bounce some thoughts off you before I do."

"No problem. When do you want to come by?"

"How about now?"

"Sure. Come on by. I'm working on a brief and the break would be good for me."

Jim hung up and went to his desk and stuffed the notes of Ted Roberts's letter into his pants pocket. He might need them in his phone call. He then rushed to the elevator and took it down to L Street. He reached his friend's law office within minutes.

Jim's friend didn't need any discussion to see that Jim's mind was preoccupied with something other than job offers in the Senate. His unshaven face and crumpled clothes complemented the strained look on his face.

"Please don't ask any questions, Peter," Jim pleaded. "I'll be straight with you. I needed to get out of my condo to make a telephone call. I think my phone is tapped, and making calls from there carried too much risk. So I was hoping you would have an empty conference room or office I could use for a few minutes."

"No problem. But listen. If there's anything I can do, please, let me help you."

"I appreciate that, but there's nothing to do right now. Except keep this to yourself."

Peter led Jim to a small conference room and closed the door behind him as he left. Jim sat at the conference table, picked up the phone and punched in the number.

"Jimmy. What a pleasant surprise."

Jim had never been so glad to hear his father's voice.

"Dad, listen, I need to talk with you about something important."

"Oh. What's the matter?"

"First of all, Dad, you have to promise to keep this a secret. Don't even tell Mom. It'll just make life more difficult for you and me."

"That's tough, Jimmy. I don't like to keep things from your mother. But if you ask me that, it must be pretty important. So you've got my promise."

"It's Kelly, Dad. She's been kidnapped."

"What? What're you talking about? Why would anyone want to kidnap Kelly? She's such a fine girl."

"That's not the point, Dad. It's real complicated, and I don't have time to tell you all the details."

"Give me something, Jimmy. I'm a pretty smart guy, and I used to be pretty good at solving problems. But I can't help you solve this problem unless I know more than what you've told me so far."

Jim then told his father everything—Ted Roberts's letter, Kelly's efforts to figure out the role her father played in the Kennedy assassination, and the various attempts made on her life and his. He ended with the kidnapper's warning to remain silent and Jim's explanation of why he couldn't tell the police, Kay Brownstein, or anyone else.

There was a long pause after Jim finished.

"Dad, are you still there?"

"Yeah, Jimmy. I'm still here. I'm thinking. You didn't bring me an easy problem."

"Tell me about it."

"Tell me about that letter again, Jimmy, and those three clues Kelly's father left."

Jim recited the three clues—the reference to the 5412 Committee, de Mohrenschildt, and the ten letters.

"Why? What are you thinking, Dad?"

"Well, it seems to me that there's something there. After all, Kelly's father was saying that you could use those clues to find the bad guys. And I have to presume that those same bad guys are behind Kelly's kidnapping."

"That's what scares me. But that's not going to tell us where Kelly is."

"I don't know. Maybe not. But maybe there's something in those ten letters."

"Oh, I don't know, Dad. I've looked at those letters a thousand times. Nothing comes to mind."

"Let's think about this. What are they? They're not an acronym for some governmental agency. They're some kind of code. They're a door to something else. You have to look at those letters as a communications vehicle of some kind. You know, Jimmy, an access line to the bad guys' identity or location."

The answer exploded in Jim's mind. He stood up and pulled the notes out of his pants pocket and looked at the ten letters again.

"That's it, Dad. That's it."

"What? What're you saying, Jimmy? What is it?"

"It's a telephone number, Dad," Jim said with rising excitement. "Don't you see? It's a telephone number."

"So what's the number?"

Jim looked at the telephone he was using and transposed the ten letters. He wrote them down on one of the legal pads on the conference table and recited the ten numbers to his father.

"Here's what I get, Dad: 7628795985."

Jim's father wrote the number down and looked at it.

"I don't know, Jimmy. I never heard of a place with a 762 area code. Hold on."

Jimmy could tell that his father was pulling out a telephone book to find out where, if anywhere, there was a 762 area code. He was back within a minute or so.

"Nope. No 762 area code anywhere. You sure you read those letters right?"

Jim looked at the letters again and checked his transposition. He could not see any errors and started to get the sinking feeling that their only hope had just vanished. But as he stared at the letters, a thought came to him. A desperate thought perhaps, but one that could be right.

"It could be, Dad," he said, "that the letter "O" is really a zero. Let's try that."

"Then it would be a 702 area code. I know that one by heart. Las Vegas. Let me look."

His father's confirmation came within a few seconds.

"Yup. 702 is Nevada."

"I'm going to try it."

"And then what, Jimmy? What if you're right?"

"Then I'm going to Nevada to get Kelly back."

"That's crazy, boy. Totally crazy. To begin with, how do you know that's where they took Kelly? And even if they did take her there, so what? These people are dangerous. You can't go there by yourself."

"If we're right, I've got to believe that's where they took her. The kidnapper said they were taking her on a trip. And as far as doing it myself, well, what can I say, Dad? I'm between a rock and hard place. I have to do it."

"Get serious, Jimmy. I know you were a Navy SEAL and all, but you can't do this alone."

Jim stood there, the excitement of discovery swirling in his mind. He needed to get moving.

"Here's where your promise comes in, Dad. You've got to promise me you won't tell anyone about this. Please, Dad. Please. Promise me."

"Oh, Jimmy. That's really asking a lot."

"Okay. I'll tell you what. Give me three days. Just three days."

"Oh, I don't know," Jimmy's father pleaded. "Three days. A lot of bad things can happen to you in three days' time. That's too long."

"No, it's not, Dad. Think about it. Even if I left for Nevada this afternoon, I wouldn't get there until tonight. I couldn't plan on doing anything until tomorrow, and anything I do is not going to happen immediately. I need at least one full day to do something."

"All right," said his father with obvious reluctance. "But then what? What do I do after three days?"

"Call Detective Soggs with the Metropolitan Police Department in Washington, DC. He'll know what to do. I don't know his telephone number, but it's the Second District Headquarters. I'm sure you can find it."

"Thanks for the vote of confidence."

"I'll be talking to you, Dad."

"This troubles me, Jimmy. You need help."

Jim ignored his father's comment. There was no time for debate.

"Dad..."

"Yeah, Jimmy."

"I love you."

Jim's first instinct after hanging up with his father was to call the ten-digit number. If Teasdale answered, he said to himself, it would confirm what he suspected. The phone could also be answered by the man who had called to tell him about Kelly's disappearance. Jim was sure he'd recognize that voice as well. And if someone else answered, he could ask for Teasdale. If the person indicated that Teasdale was there or that he knew who Teasdale was, that too would confirm Jim's suspicions. It would all be that simple.

Jim started to punch in the number and then slowly put the receiver down. No, he cautioned himself, this won't work. Even if I hang up as soon as someone answers, Jim warned himself, that person—if it was one of the kidnappers—would become suspicious. Suspicions would also emerge, Jim continued his silent monologue, if someone else answered and he asked for Teasdale and then hung up. Either way, the call could endanger Kelly's life. No, he concluded, calling this way is not the right approach. So now what? The question lingered in his mind, longing for an answer that would not come. He sat there at the conference room table, trying to sort it through. Somehow he had to call that number without raising the kidnapper's suspicions.

As he sat there, lost in his thoughts, Peter knocked gently on the conference room door and poked his head in.

"Everything okay, Jim? Anything I can do for you?"

It was then that the answer came to Jim.

"Yeah," he replied, standing up and waving Peter into the room. "There is something you can do."

"Tell me."

"I want you to make a telephone call with me and ask for someone."

"Who?"

"I don't know. We'll have to make up a name." Jim paused for a moment. "Jorgenson. Robert Jorgenson. Yeah, that's it. Ask for Robert Jorgenson."

Peter gave Jim a small smile and a quizzical look.

"What is this? A practical joke of some kind? You want me to call some number and ask for a fictional person we know is not there?"

Jim shook his head, and his somber countenance made Peter realize it was anything but humorous.

"I wish it were just a practical joke, Peter. And I wish I could explain it all to you. But I can't. I really can't. I'm going to call a number, but I'm not going to say anything. Instead, I would like you to use the other phone and pretend to ask for a client named Robert Jorgenson. The person will say he's not there, and you can say something like, 'I'm sorry, I've got the wrong number.'"

"Suppose he asks me what number I'm calling? What do I say?"

A good question, Jim said to himself. He could give Peter a telephone number that was close to the number he now had. But Jim did not want to give Peter any information that could somehow lead to the right number. Somehow he had to keep it all a secret. At least for now. So his response to Peter was quick and cryptic.

"Tell him your secretary placed the call and you'll have to check with her."

"And what're you going to be doing all this time?" Peter inquired with obvious curiosity.

"I'm just going to listen in. I need to know if someone is at this number, but I don't want that person to know I'm calling. But I'll recognize his voice, if in fact he answers. I know it's a little strange, but, please, bear with me. It's real important," he added in a strong voice that conveyed the desperation he felt.

Peter nodded and walked over to the other phone on the conference room credenza.

"Let's go for it."

Jim punched in the number and nodded for Peter to pick up. The phone was answered on the third ring.

"Hello."

"Robert Jorgenson, please."

"No Robert Jorgenson here. You must have the wrong number, buddy."

Jim immediately recognized the voice of the man who had called him about Kelly. The whistle in the voice was unmistakable. It still left unanswered the question of whether Teasdale was involved too, but at least Jim knew that the phone number housed the kidnappers—whoever they were.

As Peter gave his apologies and hung up, Jim congratulated himself on the maneuver. Even if the phone had caller ID, the man could not know anything other than the call came from a Washington, DC law firm with more than a hundred lawyers. There would be no way to make a connection to Jim.

As he walked back to his condo, Jim tried to formulate a plan of action. The starting point seemed obvious. The kidnappers' house was in Nevada. He also had to assume that Kelly had been taken there. So the first step was easy. Take a plane to Nevada. But what city in Nevada? And where exactly would he go once he got to a particular city? He had a telephone number but no location.

The solution was easy. He would call his contact from SBC. After all, they were the local telephone company out there, and his contact used to lobby him all the time in the Senate on telecommunications legislation. He would certainly be able to find the location with the telephone number. And then Jim would know where to go.

Getting there, of course, would be easier that figuring out what to do afterward. His father was right. Getting Kelly out would be no easy matter, and it would certainly be difficult to do it alone. But he was trained in undercover operations, and he was confident that those skills would be of great use. Especially because the kidnappers would not be expecting him. The element of surprise would be another advantage in his favor.

The only open issue was the number of kidnappers. That could make a difference in what he could do—and whether he could be successful. He wasn't sure of the number, but he couldn't believe that there were a lot of people involved. Anyway, it didn't matter. He couldn't worry about the likelihood of success. He now realized how much he cared for Kelly. How much he needed her. He had to go to Nevada. It was not a question of whether it was the best choice. It was the only choice.

CHAPTER 65

Jim listened carefully as the pilot announced on the intercom that Las Vegas was less than fifty miles away. Jim stared out the plane's oval window and saw the last vestige of the day's sunlight bouncing off rugged brown mountains and crystal blue lakes that became larger and larger as the plane continued its descent.

In other circumstances, Jim would have dwelled on the beauty of Nature's pageantry. But not now. Kelly was in danger—if she was still alive. And Jim was, he confessed to himself, scared. Sure, he had some background in undercover operations, but success would be uncertain even if he had years of law enforcement experience and a well-conceived rescue plan. He had neither. All he had was an aching heart and an unwavering commitment. He was not going to abandon Kelly. He knew that might not be enough. But it was all he had for the moment.

Within a short time, the neon lights of Las Vegas came into view against the early evening sky. As the plane dropped its landing gear for the touchdown, Jim tried to imagine how Kelly had been brought to Nevada. He assumed it had been on a private jet of some kind. He didn't know the details, but he had other information that would be critical in shaping any rescue plan.

Jim's contact at SBC had been able to determine that the kidnappers' house was situated somewhere near Indian Springs in some desolate foothills about fifty miles northwest of Las Vegas. The telephone people could not verify the precise street, only its general location off the main highway. The streets, Jim was told, such as they were, were often no more than unfinished dirt roads. Nor could they give Jim any useful information about the owner of the house. The phone was listed under a name that Jim did not recognize.

Still, Jim had enough information to pull out an atlas and determine that the Nellis Air Force Testing Range was located nearby and that auxiliary airfields, both private and public, were common to the area. The kidnappers had no doubt used one of those airfields to transport Kelly to Nevada.

There was probably a certain logic to the kidnapper's hideaway, Jim mused. He had convinced himself that the kidnappers included Teasdale or at least one of Ted Roberts's colleagues from the CIA, and they were probably familiar with the area from their government service. The kidnappers also had to know that most of the nearby area was off limits to the public. Much of that nearby land area was devoted to classified military activities that had to be shielded from public scrutiny. That was no small benefit for the kidnappers, Jim realized. It gave them the freedom to move in and out without fear of detection.

Jim's idea was simple. He would start by renting a Jeep to be sure that he could handle any rough terrain he might encounter. He would drive up to the area early in the morning, park the Jeep in a protected spot nearby, and walk the last half-mile or so to where the house should be. It would be best to have the Jeep nearby, but Jim feared that he might be discovered if he parked the Jeep too close to the kidnappers' house.

In any event, the rest would depend on what he found. He would try to get a sense of the routine, if any, that people were following. Maybe there would be times when Kelly was outside and alone. That would make any rescue effort that much easier. Especially because he didn't know how many kidnappers there were or whether they would be armed.

The possibility of a quick rescue was enticing, but Jim knew the reality would probably be different. Seeing Kelly alone outside the kidnappers' hideaway, he told himself, is probably a pipe dream. He guessed that she was probably confined to a room inside the house. If so, Jim knew that he would have to find the precise room where Kelly was being held. Hopefully she was in a room that had a window that he could open during the night to engineer Kelly's escape.

Whatever. He had some training in undercover operations, Jim reminded himself again. And he was motivated. He would figure it out when he had more information.

Within an hour, Jim was cruising in his rented Jeep toward the Strip. The heart of Las Vegas. Theme hotels dominated the thoroughfare. New York, New York, with its rendition of the New York City skyline. Excalibur, with the turrets and castle facade. The Luxor, with the huge pyramid shape. The Paris hotel, with its imposing renditions of the Eiffel Tower and the Arc d' Triomphe. And others, each more extravagant than the next, and all adorned with flashing neon lights of various sizes and colors, most announcing the particular entertainer who headlined the hotel's show.

Jim passed Caesar's Palace and pulled into the circular drive of the Mirage. He brought the Jeep to a halt in front of the hotel's wide glass doors with the multicolored palm trees embossed in the middle of each glass door. The uniformed valet opened the door and Jim stepped out of the Jeep. He looked around. The hotel consisted of tall, adjoining white structures surrounded by tropical plants and trees with moats and water fountains in perpetual motion. In any other city, the Mirage would have stood out. In Las Vegas it was one of the nicer hotels, but nothing exceptional. If anything, the Mirage seemed more understated, and in Jim's eyes, more polished, than many of the other hotels. No matter. He was not there to gamble or enjoy the sights. He was on a mission, and all he needed was a good place to stay for a short time. Hopefully a very short time.

Jim took his duffel bag out of the Jeep and walked through the hotel's front doors. He turned to the right and walked up to the expansive registration desk. It was longer than anything he had ever seen in Washington, DC. He approached one of the desk clerks, a beautiful young woman with long dark hair who smiled broadly and asked if he wanted to register.

"I sure do."

As the woman took information from him, Jim scanned the enormous fish tank behind the front desk. It was unlike anything he had ever seen before. Large and multi-colored fish glided from one end to another. The tank also included sharks, some of fairly substantial size. Jim wondered why the sharks did not seem interested in the other fish. No doubt, he thought, because the sharks were well fed and didn't need the other fish to satisfy their endless hunger.

He was about to meet some sharks of a different kind, Jim said to himself. The human kind. Hopefully, those sharks would be just as relaxed and inattentive. His life—and Kelly's—might depend on it.

He took the key card from the hotel clerk and asked her to wake him at six o'clock in the morning. Not that he planned to get much sleep. That was a luxury he might not enjoy for a while.

CHAPTER 66

Kelly stared at the plate of eggs and sausage that had long since grown cold. She knew she had to eat, but her appetite had deserted her. She tried to sip the lukewarm coffee as she stared out the window from the bed, her heart racing as she contemplated her situation. It was not good. There seemed to be no way to escape, and she felt that the end was closing in on her. The more she thought about it, the more fearful she became.

Not that Kelly was a stranger to fear. She could recall the panic she had endured on numerous occasions while riding on the back of a horse. But that was different. In each of those instances, the danger could be defined, and, to some extent, controlled. At some point, she knew, the horse would stop and she would get off. The fear she felt now was constant and completely beyond her control. She continued to hold out hope that she could survive as long as she kept the whereabouts of her father's letter a secret. But she was no fool. Lord could use torture or other sordid techniques to force the information from her. After all, she reminded herself, these guys were not gentlemen. So who knew? Any day might be her last.

Jim was also a constant presence in her thoughts. What did he know? What was he doing? Kelly assumed that Lord or perhaps Tom had told him something. Otherwise he would run to the police. Or maybe he would tell Kay Brownstein. Neither result would be good for Lord and his cohorts. So, Kelly reasoned, somebody must have told Jim something to make sure he didn't tell anyone. That of course didn't mean that Jim would keep it a secret. Maybe he would tell someone anyway. Or would he? Kelly couldn't be sure. She tried to think through what she would have done if Jim had been kidnapped and she had been warned to keep silent. What would she do?

These and other questions ran through her mind as she stood by the window, watching the horses in the nearby corral. Her thoughts were interrupted by the opening of the door. She turned to see Lord standing there, dressed in blue jeans and one of the golf shirts he seemed to favor.

"Have a good breakfast?" he inquired.

"The food's not bad. But," she added with an air of defiance, "I'd enjoy it a lot more if I was back in Potomac, Maryland."

Lord ignored Kelly's comment and walked toward her.

"I just wanted to see how you're doing this morning and to make sure everything is to your satisfaction."

He can be charming, Kelly thought. But she knew him for what he really was.

"Come on. Let's be straight with each other. None of this is to my satisfaction. You killed my father. You've kidnapped me and you're holding me here against my will. How could anything be to my satisfaction?"

"Oh, Kelly," Lord replied in a patronizing voice. "You fail to recognize how different it all could be. You could be dead. Or you could be in some other environment that would be a lot less attractive than this one. I know you'd rather be somewhere else. But you have to stop thinking like that. You'll find the time more enjoyable if you realize how much better off you are than you might have been with someone less caring than me."

"I'll try to keep all that in mind the next time I look out the window from my locked room."

"Anyway, I did want to bring you up-to-date with our thinking here."

"I'm listening."

"We do want to make a decision soon, you know. My colleague has some reservations about this situation and wants to find some way to work this out so that you can go back to Potomac."

Kelly was eager to know who the unnamed "colleague" was, but she didn't interrupt Lord. She wanted to hear the rest of what he had to say.

"To be honest," he continued in his matter-of-fact tone, "I disagree. We've already eliminated other people, and one more is not going to make any difference. You are Ted's daughter, and that does trouble me. But we've given you every opportunity—and warning—to leave well enough alone. You disregarded all the advice and all the warning signs, and I am fairly certain you'll continue to make trouble for us if we give you back your freedom. However, as I told you before, there is one thing that would make me look at this a little differently."

"The letter?"

"Yes. Your father's letter. Have you made any decision on that?"

Kelly shook her head. She had no intention of telling Lord where the letter was and she was eager to tell him that. But she knew that candor would be counter-productive. So she masked her true feelings.

"I have given it some thought. But I still need some more time."

"I'm not sure how much time you have, Kelly. So, again, I would urge you to come to a decision, and hopefully the right decision, very soon. Things may be heating up. We're a little concerned that Jim may be a problem."

The comment about Jim piqued Kelly's curiosity.

"Why? What's he done?"

"I don't know that he's done anything yet. He's been told to lie low and I hope he'll have the good sense to follow those instructions. We don't think he's told anyone. Which would be good for you. Because we don't like to operate under pressure, Kelly. But we're not sure where he is now. And if he has done something foolish, it could force us to do something that we might otherwise want to avoid. So we're trying to figure out exactly where he is and whether he's done something he shouldn't have."

"If it's any consolation, I haven't heard from Jim since I've been here. So I don't know where he is or what he's doing."

"You certainly are feisty this morning, Kelly. I'll have to ask Tom what he's putting in those eggs."

"You do that. But make sure it's all edible."

"Anyway, Kelly, we'll be back to you. Very shortly, I might add."

As Lord turned to leave, Kelly could not resist asking the question that Lord's earlier comments had triggered.

"By the way, who's your 'colleague'?"

Lord gave Kelly a blank stare.

"I think we'll let that one lie for a while, Kelly. Maybe in due course. But not now."

He then turned around and walked out of the room, closing the door behind him. She was alone again and more frightened than ever. Time was running out.

CHAPTER 67

Jim drove the Jeep off the side of the dirt road and pulled it alongside a huge sandstone-colored boulder. He put the Jeep in park and stepped outside. The morning sun made him feel warm and comfortable. The heat also confirmed the wisdom of his decision to wearing nothing more than a T-shirt and jeans.

So far, so good. He looked at his watch. It was not even eight o'clock. Plenty of time to find the kidnappers' place and survey the situation.

The first steps had gone forward without a hitch. He had awakened early, wolfed down a blueberry muffin, and took his coffee with him. He was on the road shortly after six o'clock. He had then taken the hour or so drive up US 95 to Indian Springs, the largest town near the kidnappers' hideaway.

Calling Indian Springs a town was something of an exaggeration. There was a motel complex that had a general store and a casino. There was also a post office and a few other buildings. But there was nothing else that bore any resemblance to the towns Jim was used to in the Washington, DC area.

The clerk at the motel's store was able to give Jim directions to the road where the house might be. The clerk did not know Teasdale by name and had no recollection of seeing anyone with Teasdale's description. But there was apparently a younger and much larger man who occasionally came to the motel's store to get supplies, and the clerk believed that the man occupied the house, or cabin as he called it, that Jim was trying to find. Jim assumed that the younger man was the one who had called him the evening Kelly had disappeared.

Jim locked the Jeep, gathered up his backpack, now stuffed with the sandwiches and bottles of water he had purchased at the motel store, and pulled out the light jacket he had brought with him. Although the daylight hours could be warm, Jim knew enough about the desert to know that the evenings could be much cooler, and he had to be prepared to be on the scene after nightfall. He also took out the binoculars he had purchased in Washington before his departure. He knew they could prove critical to whatever he did. They would enable him to survey the scene from a distance and avoid being detected.

Jim tied the sleeves of the jacket around his waist and started walking up the dirt road to where the cabin might be. The terrain consisted of gravel and sand punctuated with large boulders and scrubby bushes. Large brown mountains, like the ones Jim had seen from the plane's window, could be seen nearby.

As he walked along the road, Jim realized that he could be easily seen by anyone driving up or down the road to the cabin. I should've thought of that earlier, Jim scolded himself. The adjustment was easy. He moved about twenty-five yards from the road and tried to follow a path parallel to the road. The boulders and sloping terrain near the road did shield him from view but also made the walking that much slower. No matter. He had time on his side. With luck, he should be at the cabin within an hour or so. That would leave him with plenty of daylight hours to assess the situation.

The walking proved to be far more tiring than Jim had anticipated. Part of the problem was the terrain. As he walked along, the boulders became larger and the hills became steeper. Traversing them often took a substantial amount of time and energy.

The walking seemed endless. The sun moved higher in the sky and the sweat made the T-shirt cling to Jim's body. The discomfort of the heat was compounded by frustration. He walked down several dirt roads that led nowhere and was forced to double-back. But he could not, would not, give up.

Eventually he came to a large rising hill that towered above the road. He trudged up the hill and looked down below. There it was. Off the road was a long dirt driveway that led to a cabin in a small valley. Jim guessed that the cabin was about a hundred yards or so from his position.

Jim maneuvered about ten yards down the side of the hill and nestled behind some boulders that, he hoped, would prevent him from being seen. He pulled out the binoculars and brought the scene into focus.

The single-story cabin appeared to be made of cut logs with a black roof. Although it was impossible to gauge its size with precision, Jim thought the cabin had about three thousand square feet of living space with a small porch in front. A Mercedes sedan, a Jeep Wrangler, and a pickup truck were parked on the far side of the cabin. Off to the other side closer to Jim, was a small stable with some horses in a corral. Now there's a twist, Jim said to himself. Kelly's been kidnapped by horse lovers.

There was no human activity that Jim could discern. He decided that he would have to wait. To move any closer in daylight would expose him to the risk of being seen. Obviously a bad move.

The wait gave Jim time to focus on a rescue plan. He was fortunate that the cabin was only one story. He could easily open or break a window. The cabin's proximity to hills and boulders also made a closer approach—especially at night—equally possible. The only question was Kelly's location in the cabin. He also needed to confirm the number of kidnappers and to make sure they were otherwise occupied when he made his rescue attempt.

Jim watched closely when the cabin door opened after he had been there about an hour. A small balding man in jeans and a golf shirt briskly walked to the Wrangler, got in, and drove away in a cloud of dust. Jim didn't recognize the man but guessed that he was in his sixties.

The man's appearance and departure raised the obvious question in Jim's mind—who was he? It was not Teasdale, and it did not appear to be the younger man described by the motel clerk. That left one of two possibilities. Either Teasdale was not involved, or he was involved and the man leaving was a third kidnapper. Jim hoped that Teasdale was not involved. Because if there were three kidnappers, the odds of Jim's success would be that much less.

As he considered the various problems and possibilities, Jim heard an unfamiliar noise. He glanced absent-mindedly at his immediate surroundings and froze in fear. There, not more than a few feet from his right foot, was a large rattlesnake curled in an attack position with its tail vibrating. He knew little about rattlesnakes except that they were poisonous and that, without treatment, a bite could be fatal. Which is what his situation would be if he got bitten out in the middle of nowhere.

The snake seemed to stare at Jim defiantly, its forked tongue moving in and out of its mouth. An attack seemed imminent. Jim assumed the bite would be unable to penetrate his skin if the snake bit his hiking boot. But what if the snake struck his unprotected leg above the boot? That seemed equally possible. So now what? There was no time for long reflections. Jim decided that his best bet was to back away.

As he slowly pushed off his heels in a backward motion, Jim heard the sound of leather scraping against the boulder behind him. He turned to identify the source of the unexpected noise. All he saw was a blur. And then everything went black.

Chapter 68

Jim opened his eyes to see Kelly leaning over him and dabbing his forehead with a wet cloth. He was lying on his back on a bed in an unfamiliar room. He felt disoriented, and he could see the look of concern on Kelly's face.

"Oh, Kelly," Jim mumbled, as he tried to push himself up on his elbows. "I'm so glad to see you. You have no idea."

As soon as he uttered the words, Jim felt the throbbing pain on the back of his head and slumped back on the bed. He went to rub the sore spot and immediately felt the lump. It was very tender.

"You jerk," Kelly said. "What were you doing? Trying to be a one-man rescue squad?"

"I missed you," said Jim with a painful grin. "I had to do something."

"Calling the police or the FBI would have been useful. They've been through this before."

"Maybe so. But then you'd be dead by now. At least that's what they told me."

Kelly stared into Jim's eyes.

"Well," she murmured, tears welling up in her eyes, "I appreciate what you tried to do. I just…." The words trailed off and Jim could see the emotion in Kelly's face. He wanted to say something, but the words would not come. Instead, he sat up and threw his arms around Kelly, and they held each other tight. After a few minutes, they released each other and Jim looked into Kelly's moist eyes.

"What happened? How'd I get here?"

"They saw the reflection of the sun off the binoculars you had. So they sent their big gofer, a guy named Tom, to take care of you. He sneaked up behind you and knocked you out with a nightstick."

"Wow. He did a good job. I don't remember a thing."

Jim then told Kelly about the telephone call with his father and the efforts he had gone through to find her. When he finished, Jim eased himself off the bed and walked over to the window. Aside from the pain in his head, he felt fine.

He stared out at the stables and the horses he had seen from his hiding place. He then turned around and looked at Kelly sitting cross-legged on the bed. Aside from red eyes, she appeared to be in good physical condition. Still, Jim had to satisfy himself.

"I've been so worried. How're you doing? Are you okay?"

"Physically I'm okay. But I'm terrified. For both of us. We're living on borrowed time at this point."

Kelly then recounted what had happened since her last conversation with Jim. The log in her driveway. The discovery that she had been kidnapped. The long conversation with Lord about President Kennedy's assassination. The possibility of her elimination, and Lord's repeated requests for her father's letter. Jim listened intently and in silence, all the while leaning against the wall next to the sealed window.

"So what do we do now?" he asked when she had finished, more to himself than to Kelly.

"I don't know that we have a choice."

"I'm not sure that's right. There's got to be something we can do."

"Sounds great. But what?"

Before Jim could respond, they heard an unexpected noise. Jim and Kelly turned around and, to their astonishment, saw Tom holding the door open while Lord stood in the doorway next to Kay Brownstein. Jim and Kelly's mouths dropped open, and for a few seconds no one said a word. Kelly finally broke the silence with her eyes focused on Brownstein and the anger in her voice was unmistakable.

"I don't understand. What are you doing here? How can you be a part of this?"

Brownstein took a few steps toward Kelly, her hands clasped behind her back and a somber look on her face.

"I didn't want to be a part of anything that would cause you harm, Kelly. I really didn't. I meant everything I said when we met. I do feel a connection to you through your father, and I did want to help you."

"You have a strange way of doing that."

"Not really. I did everything I could to dissuade you from pursuing this. Because I knew what could lay ahead if you persisted."

"But why? Why would you want to stop me? Why would you care if I did persist and the truth was told about Kennedy's assassination?"

Lord interrupted before Brownstein could say anything.

"I think it would be best if you sat on the bed with Kelly," he said to Jim. "I don't want you to get any funny ideas about trying to escape."

While Jim did as he was told, Brownstein walked over by the window and turned to respond to Kelly's question.

"It's my father," she began. "He was part of Bruce's group. Like the others, he was in the Kennedy administration, and he too saw a need to do something about the danger that Kennedy represented to the country. In time, he began to have second thoughts. Like your father, Kelly, my dad was overcome with guilt as he got older, and he told me all about it right before he died. Who was involved, why they did it, and even how they did it—at least as much as he knew. It was a heartbreaking confession done literally on my father's deathbed. He broke down in tears right before he slipped away."

Brownstein paused and sighed before she continued.

"At first I didn't know what to do about it. But I finally decided that the truth should die with him and the others. Because my father was an honorable man who devoted much of his life to public service, and I was not going to let his reputation be tarnished by something he thought, rightly or not, would be good for the country. And I told Bruce that I would help him in any way I could to make sure that the truth was never disclosed."

"You can't possibly believe," said Jim, "that you can get away with this. Killing us is not going to help you. People will know we're missing. People who care about us. People who will do something and expose your role in this."

"I'm not sure that's right," Lord responded. "If we did eliminate you, I'm confident that our involvement would never be discovered. There would be two bodies buried in the vast desert out there. If they were ever found, I'm certain the deaths would be attributed to natural causes."

Kelly understood at once. The same technique that had been used to silence Bud could be used on them. But there would be no Detective Soggs to uncover the mystery of their deaths. No one to tell the world what really happened.

"There's another thing you should know," Brownstein added. "This is not just about my father. My career is at stake here too. If the truth about my father's role were exposed, I have no doubt that I would feel the repercussions. It would be unseemly for the government's CIA director to be the daughter of someone involved in Kennedy's assassination. I admit that entered into my thinking as well."

Jim could not let the irony—and tragedy—of the situation escape notice.

"Don't you find it a little hypocritical to commit more murders in order to preserve a reputation and a job that are tied to a high moral standard? Anyway," Jim continued, turning toward Lord, "I don't care what method you use to kill us. The government will discover the truth sooner or later."

Brownstein started to say something, but Lord held up his hand to indicate that he wanted to respond to Jim's comment.

"You should not have any illusions about who we are or what we can do. I was willing to die for my country when I served in the CIA, and Kay is no different in that regard. The two of us are prepared to die now, if necessary, to take this secret to the grave. Each of us carries cyanide pills to preserve that option. I've also got this cabin wired to blow up if we think it's necessary. We're not anxious to die. But we will if we have to. So," Lord concluded, looking directly at Jim, "there's no fear here about being pursued by the FBI, the police, or any other law enforcement agency you can think of. We have the capacity to deal with government investigations. We've stopped them before and we could do it again."

Kelly could see that Lord's comment triggered an immediate and hostile reaction in Jim. He stood up from the bed and took a few steps toward Lord, his eyes wide and his fists clenched.

"You killed Senator Gimble too. Didn't you?"

Tom stepped in front of Lord, pulled out the handgun stuck in his belt, and pointed it at Jim.

"Shut the fuck up and sit down."

Jim recognized the whistle in the voice. He slowly backed up and returned to his sitting position on the bed. Lord said nothing, but Jim interpreted the silence as an admission.

"There was no mugging," Jim continued. "No robbery. It was you. You murdered him in cold blood because you were afraid he would open another investigation of the Kennedy assassination. Tell me I'm wrong. I'd love to hear it. But I know I won't. Because I'm right, aren't I? You killed Senator Gimble. Just to protect your secret."

"It's not my secret," Lord answered. His manner was patronizing. "It's the country's secret. And it should remain secret. No good can come from re-opening an investigation of President Kennedy's death. Better to let it just wallow in the unknown. Senator Gimble didn't understand that. He had to be stopped."

Kelly listened to the exchange intently, and her gaze instinctively moved to Brownstein, who was standing by impassively. The horror of the situation was difficult for Kelly to comprehend.

"You told me that you and the senator were so close. How could you stand by and let him be killed?"

Brownstein did not hesitate to respond. It was obviously something that she had already reconciled in her mind.

"We *were* close and I did care for Geoff. But he was determined to pursue this matter with investigations and hearings and all kinds of publicity. I knew, as he did not, the damage that would do to me and to my father. And I was not about to sacrifice my father's reputation or my career for our relationship. I know it sounds cold-hearted, Kelly, but I've learned the hard way that no man is worth it. My disappointment with your father taught me at least that. But he also showed me how to use sex to my advantage. Your father opened doors that would have remained closed if I had tried to do it on my own. And I was not afraid to use relationships with other men—including Geoff—to get what I wanted. Geoff was a good man, but he was expendable."

Ironically, Kelly could sympathize with Brownstein's perspective on how men took advantage of women. She had had her own experience to draw upon, but she was not about to share that experience with Brownstein. The woman had become as evil as Bruce Lord.

"This conversation has already dragged on too long," Lord interjected. "We came here only to tell you that we're going to review the situation and make our decision on your future by tomorrow morning. We can't let this go on forever."

"Which is why I finally decided to come here, Kelly," Brownstein said. "Bruce told me that you've been unwilling to tell him where your father's letter is. Please, Kelly. I know how much you loved your father. But don't be foolish. It may be the one thing that can save you and Jim."

Kelly nodded but said nothing. She looked over to Jim, whose face was flush with anger and frustration.

"Well," Jim said, "in the meantime I may need some medical attention. This lump at the back of my head hurts like the blazes. If I've got to go, I at least want to enjoy my last evening without this incredible pain."

"That's not a problem," said Lord. "Tom will get you some aspirin. And if you need some more, you just have to ask him. He'll be outside your door, day or night, to provide anything you need, including aspirin. But you should also know that Tom is prepared to do anything—and I mean anything—if you try to escape or do anything else foolish. I hope and trust that you won't put him to the test."

With that said, the three of them left Jim and Kelly to think about their future—if indeed they had one.

CHAPTER 69

Howard Roth sat in his wheelchair and stared at the telephone on the end table in the family room of his Toms River, New Jersey, home. The late afternoon sun streamed through the half-opened blinds and made the use of lamps unnecessary.

In other circumstances, it would have been a perfect time to read. But Roth could not indulge his passion for reading on this sunny afternoon. To enjoy books required him to concentrate on the words he was reading. That was not possible now. His mind was totally distracted by his younger son's plight. He had not heard from Jimmy since they spoke yesterday. He remembered Jimmy's warning that he might be out of touch for sometime and that his father should wait three days before contacting anyone. But three days was a long time. A lot could happen in three days. A lot of bad things. Things that could be irreversible.

Howard Roth was torn. He had promised his son that he would wait the three days. He wanted to keep his promise. He had always admonished his sons—drilled them really—with the notion that a man's word was his bond and should never be broken.

Still, every rule had its exceptions. And Howard Roth's promise to his son seemed to cry out for some kind of special dispensation. Howard Roth had great faith in his son's talents, but rescuing a kidnap victim by himself was not one of them. His son's life, and Kelly's too, might depend on his willingness to get help from the proper authorities.

What to do? Howard Roth needed to talk to someone. Just like his son needed to talk to him. How ironic, he thought. Maybe the apple doesn't fall far from the tree. Jim's father felt that he too would feel better if he could explore his dilemma with someone he could trust, someone who would care, and, most especially, someone who might be in a position to help.

Under other circumstances, his wife would be the obvious choice. But talking with her now would only complicate the situation. She would be understandably concerned and would press her husband to do something. He knew her well enough to know that. And then he would be back where he was now—trying to decide whom to contact. Except then he would also have to worry about consoling his wife. No, better his wife should remain in the dark. At least for the time being.

Who else was there? He obviously couldn't call that Detective Soggs. He knew enough to know that the police would be obligated to do something, and then he would have to accept the risk that he called them too early.

Who else could he call?

The idea slowly emerged from his intense concentration. A lawyer. He needed to talk to a lawyer. He wouldn't have to worry about premature disclosures because lawyers are obligated to keep their clients' confidences. But which lawyer? He knew many lawyers from his professional career, but he was not sure they had the right experience for this problem. He needed a lawyer who knew something about kidnappings. Or one who knew the world of Washington politics.

It was then that he recalled an earlier conversation with Jimmy about Kelly's lawsuit. She had a lawyer in Washington, DC. Sure, he wasn't retained to investigate her kidnapping, but he was a lawyer in the nation's capital and he had her best interests at heart. At least he was supposed to. Yes, the senior Roth said to himself, I should call Kelly's lawyer. He would understand the dilemma. And he would be in a position to know what to do.

What was his name? Howard Roth searched his memory. Nothing came to mind. He looked out the window at the trees bending in the stiff breeze. He furrowed his brow as he strained to recall the conversation with Jimmy.

Butler. That was it. Butler. That was a start. But there must be dozens of Butlers in the Washington area. What was his first name? God, Howard Roth said to himself, old age sucks. In earlier times, his memory would have been sharper and the name would have come to him within seconds. Now remembering anything was too often a struggle. But he would do it. If he remained patient, the name would come to him.

Rhett? Rhett Butler? No, he chided himself. That's the hero in *Gone with the Wind.* But he was on the right trail. He remembered Jimmy saying something about the attorney being from the South. Somebody who could have been the subject of a Jim Croce song. It was a biblical name. Not something you often run across in Toms River.

Caleb. That's it, he congratulated himself. Caleb Butler. He's Kelly's attorney. He's the guy to call.

Howard Roth wheeled himself over to the telephone on the end table, picked it up, and punched in the number for information in Washington, DC.

CHAPTER 70

Jim looked at his watch. Two-thirty. He glanced over at Kelly, who was standing by the window.

"It's really eerie out there," she whispered. "There's no light except for the moon."

Jim could detect the fear in her voice.

"I know. But we've talked this through. We've got no choice. We won't survive even if we tell them where your father's letter is. These people are killers. They're not going to thank us for the information and send us on our way. They'll take care of us the same way they took care of your father. And Senator Gimble. Don't forget that."

How could she ever forget that? Here she was, holed up in some cabin with the man who had murdered her father.

"Are you ready?" Jim asked in a hushed voice.

She had steeled herself for this moment.

"Yeah. As ready as I'll ever be."

Jim knocked firmly, but not too loudly, on the locked door to the room.

"Tom," he called in a soft voice. "Are you there?"

There was no response. Jim waited a minute or so and then repeated the procedure.

Jim heard some shuffling feet.

"Tom?"

The response came from behind the closed door.

"Yeah, asshole. Wadda you want?"

"This pain at the back of my head is still killing me. I need some more aspirin."

"Jesus Christ."

There was a long pause.

"What do you think?" Kelly asked Jim in a whispered voice. "You think he'll get it?"

"I don't know. Let's see."

Jim stood near the closed door while Kelly waited by the window. After a few minutes, Jim heard the shuffling noise of Tom's returning footsteps. The lock disengaged and the door opened slowly. Tom took a few steps inside the room. The gun was stuffed inside the top of his pants, and he was holding some aspirin in a hand that he held out to Jim.

Jim took a few steps toward Tom's outstretched hand so that he was within inches of his face. With lightning speed Jim jabbed his index and middle fingers, held stiffly together, into the middle of the hollow where Tom's neck met his chest. Tom instantly crumbled to the hardwood floor without a sound.

"I can't believe it," Kelly exclaimed in a whisper. "It worked."

"I told you. This tae kwon do stuff is for real. Now let's get out of here! He'll come to pretty soon and wake the others up. We don't have a lot of time."

Jim threw on his jacket and Kelly grabbed a sweater. They stepped out of the room into what appeared to be a large open family room with a cathedral ceiling and high-paneled windows. The moon cast enough light in the darkened room for them to quickly find the front door. They rushed to the door, opened it quietly, and then ran to the stables where the horses were standing noiselessly in the corral.

"We don't have time for saddles," Kelly reminded Jim in a soft voice as they hurried into the stable. "Just see if you can find some bridles hanging on the walls."

They rushed around the interior of the stable, guided only by the light of the moon, trying to see or feel the presence of any bridles. Jim could feel his heart pounding. The bridles were, he knew, essential to their escape.

"I found them," Jim finally whispered excitedly.

Kelly dashed over to where Jim stood and saw the pegs with the hanging leather bridles. She grabbed two of them and ran out of the stable toward the corral.

Jim looked at the shelf immediately above the bridles and saw some foot-long flares. He had already scolded himself for not taking Tom's gun. It was too late to go back to the house now, but who knew? Maybe some flares would come in handy. He took two and stuffed them into the inside pocket of his jacket.

By the time Jim emerged from the stable, Kelly was putting a bridle on the second horse, a small pinto. A slightly larger appaloosa was standing next to the pinto with its bridle on and the reins hanging limply on its neck.

"How the fuck do I get on this thing?" Jim asked.

"I told you. Grab the mane. The horse has no sensation there. And pull yourself over his back. Come on."

By the time she finished speaking, Kelly had already pulled herself onto the back of the pinto. Jim grabbed the appaloosa's mane, pulled himself up, and took hold of the reins.

"I never thought I'd begin my riding career like this," he whispered to Kelly. "What do I do?"

"Just remember what I told you. Squeeze his sides with your thighs and keep your center of gravity as close as you can to his back.'

With that Kelly jerked on the reins and led her horse through the corral gate that she had already opened. Jim was right behind, holding the reins with one hand and the horse's mane with the other.

As soon as they trotted out of the corral, the lights in the house came on.

"He's up," Jim said excitedly. "Let's get moving."

Guided by the light of the house, the two of them steered their horses toward what appeared to be a trail between two large boulders. The trail led up the side of the mountain.

"Lean forward on the horse's neck when you climb," Kelly instructed Jim.

As they moved up the mountain, Jim and Kelly could hear hurried footsteps on the wooden porch of the house that echoed in the stillness of the desert night. The footsteps were accompanied by excited shouts that signaled the discovery that Jim and Kelly were gone.

As they climbed higher into the mountains, Jim turned back and looked at the house, aglow with lights, in the valley below. He could see figures running around the corral.

"They're saddling up their horses," Jim shouted to Kelly. "Keep it going."

Jim and Kelly followed what appeared to be a well-worn trail. It took them back and forth between large boulders, past scrubby bushes, and into higher elevations.

Kelly remained in the lead. Jim amazed himself by staying on the horse, which appeared to have an even disposition.

When they reached a plateau, they turned sideways and looked back toward the valley. They could see three lights moving slowly up the mountain behind them.

"This is not going to work," Jim said. "They've got flashlights, and I'm sure they know these trails. It won't take long for them to overtake us. Especially since we really don't know where we're going."

"So what do we do? Wave a white flag and surrender?"

"No. But we've got to do something."

"You'll have to come up with a plan more specific than that. They're gaining on us."

"I'm trying."

"I have an idea," said Kelly excitedly. "Let's get off the horses, slap them, and hope that they go at least a little farther up the mountain. Lord and his crew will probably continue to follow the horses up the mountain. In the meantime, we go down the mountain. And we stay off the trail so they can't see us."

"Yeah. And then what?"

"What about your Jeep?"

"Too far away. And besides that, I don't have the keys. Remember? Tom took them from me when he knocked me out."

"Yeah, I do remember. Forget about the Jeep. Let's go back to the cabin. Maybe we can find the keys to one of their vehicles."

"Good idea. And don't forget. I've got these flares. I have no idea what we want to do with them, but at some point we may want to set them up somewhere. Maybe as a beacon to attract attention."

"Let's worry about that later. Come on."

They slid off their horses, slapped them in the rear, and watched the horses lope up the trail.

Jim and Kelly then started making their way down the mountain, back toward the cabin. They took care to stay far enough away from the trail they had just left to make sure they could not be seen by their captors. Jim remained thankful that the night was clear and that the moon was almost full. Its light enabled them to move quickly down the rough and unfamiliar terrain.

As he looked down the other side of the mountain, Jim could see two lights and make out the figures of two riders in the distance moving up the trail.

"Hey," he whispered to Kelly. "There are only two of them now. What happened to the third rider?"

"I don't know." Kelly took a long look. "We can discuss it later on the drive back to Las Vegas."

They moved quickly, scaling the large boulders and running down the sides. They avoided the small trees and bushes and jumped from rock to rock whenever possible. After a short while, they came to a small clearing surrounded by boulders. Without saying a word, they stopped for a moment to catch their breath.

"I thought climbing up a mountain would be difficult," Jim whispered in short breaths. "It never occurred to me that it would take so much energy to go *down* a mountain."

"You'll have to take up a more rigorous workout schedule when we return to Washington."

"All right. But we don't have time to lollygag about now. We've got to keep moving."

As they moved to the other side of the clearing, Jim and Kelly each took a quick look down the mountain at the cabin with the light pouring out from the windows.

"Not too much longer," Jim said.

As he finished speaking, a large mass suddenly appeared from above them and knocked Jim to the ground. It was Tom. He pounced on Jim's prostrate figure and punched him across the jaw. Kelly could see the blood instantly flow from Jim's mouth. She ran over and jumped on Tom's back, but he pushed her against a large boulder with a backward swipe of his heavily muscled left arm. Kelly hit the rock hard, and she immediately felt a numbing pain in her back that made her feel light-headed and dazed.

Tom turned his attention to Jim.

"Hey, asshole," Tom growled, "it's payback time."

He cocked his right arm to hit Jim across the jaw again. As Tom's arm came down, Jim raised his left arm to block the blow and simultaneously hit Tom hard in the stomach with the curled fist of his right hand. Jim knew he had hit the mark when he heard Tom exhale with a sputtering cough and saw him lean forward, grabbing his stomach with his left hand.

Jim took advantage of Tom's momentary pain by pushing him backward and freeing himself from the large man's grip. Jim bounced to his feet and adopted a tae kwon do defensive stance with legs spread apart and arms at the ready. Tom staggered to his full height and rushed at Jim. But Jim was ready for the assault. He spun around and hit Tom high in the chest with his right foot. Tom fell backward and hit his head hard against one of the large boulders. Kelly, still leaning against the boulder she had hit, heard the thud and knew immediately that the damage was severe. Tom slumped to the ground.

Jim was breathing hard and watching Tom closely. He was taking no chances. When Tom did not move after a few seconds, Jim inched closer.

"He's out," he whispered to Kelly. "Maybe for good."

Jim took a few more steps until he was standing over Tom, who had remained motionless the entire time. He then moved closer to the inert figure.

"Is he dead?" Kelly asked in a hushed tone.

"I'm not sure."

Jim started to bend over Tom. Suddenly Tom's arm darted out and grabbed Jim's leg. Jim fell backward, and Tom started to struggle to his feet. The large man was still feeling the effect of his encounter with the boulder. Jim was faster. He jumped to his feet and gave Tom, not yet standing completely upright, a swift kick under the jaw with his right foot.

Jim knew the kick was well placed and saw Tom fall over backward, again hitting his head hard against the nearby boulder. He rolled over on his back with arms spread out and feet spread wide.

"You've got him now," Kelly said.

Jim knew he had to be more cautious. He maintained his tae kwon do stance and watched Tom closely. He slowly counted to ten and then inched closer. He kicked Tom hard in the side. No movement. No reflex. The man was out. Maybe this time it was for good. He leaned over Tom and tried to find his pulse. There was none.

"He's dead," he said softly to Kelly. "He's really dead."

"I can't believe it."

"Me either. I've never killed anyone before."

Kelly could hear the guilt in Jim's voice.

"Come on, Jim. This is no time for remorse. It was self-defense."

"I know. But still...."

Kelly could see that Jim himself was a little dazed. She needed to take charge. She pulled herself up and almost pushed Jim down the mountain.

"Come on. Let's keep it moving."

The rest of the trip down the mountain was a blur to Jim. Before he knew it, he and Kelly were running as hard as they could to the well-lit cabin. They rushed to the three vehicles parked on the far side and opened the doors to see if the keys had been left inside. They came up empty-handed and ran back into the cabin through the front door.

"Check the family room," Jim yelled to Kelly. "I'll look in the bedrooms."

Jim ran into one of the bedrooms on the other side of the family room. It was a large room with a king-size bed, built-in bookshelves, a large wooden dresser, and a cabinet with a television and CD player. Jim looked at the top of the two nightstands on either side of the bed, rummaged through the drawers of the nightstands and the dresser, and ran his hands down the bookshelves. Nothing.

He raced into the other bedroom, which had a similar layout and comparable furnishings. Jim turned everything upside down but found nothing. He ran into the family room.

"Nothing here," Kelly said without a prompt.

"The kitchen," Jim yelled. "Let's try there."

"Hurry, Jim. Hurry. We don't have much time."

"Why? I'm sure we have a little time. They're probably still chasing our horses."

"I doubt it. Those horses are not likely to stray too far up the mountain. They're just as likely to start coming back down the trail and to the security of the stable."

"I hear you. Let's give ourselves five minutes. If we don't find the keys by then, let's just make a go for it and hide in the hills. Maybe we can make it back to Indian Springs in the morning."

They hurried into the large kitchen. Like the rest of the house, it was made of cut logs.

Jim rummaged through the drawers, throwing the contents on the floor in the desperate search for a set of keys. Jim could feel the sweat gathering on his forehead. The pressure was enormous. He glanced at Kelly. She was no less frantic, hurriedly pushing her hands through drawers and opening cabinets.

"Two minutes," Jim shouted out to Kelly. "That's all we've got."

After a minute or so, Jim looked at his watch. It was hopeless. They would never find any of the keys to the cars. At least not within the time they had. They had to leave. Jim's thoughts were interrupted by Kelly's shout.

"I found them! I found them!" she screamed with excitement, holding up keys on a chain that had a Jeep Wrangler logo.

"Come on," Jim yelled. "We're out of here."

They ran through the kitchen door and stopped dead in their tracks. Standing before them in the middle of the family room were Brownstein and Lord, who was wearing a wide leather belt with a holster and holding a pistol pointed directly at Jim and Kelly.

"I'm glad you found the keys," Lord said in his patronizing, matter-of-fact manner. "Unfortunately, I don't think it's a good time to go for a drive. So just put those keys on the coffee table by the couch and sit down."

Kelly sat down at one end of the large L-shaped leather couch. Jim sat at the other end. Lord and Brownstein moved to the other side of the large slate coffee table so that they were standing just a few yards from Jim and Kelly. Lord kept his gun pointed at the two captives.

"We found Tom on a plateau," Lord said in a voice filled with disgust. "He's not doing too well. In fact, I don't think he's coming back at all."

"It wasn't intentional," Kelly responded. "Tom attacked Jim, and Jim just tried to defend himself. Jim didn't try to kill him. Tom fell and hit his head against a rock."

"That's not important right now," said Lord. "Tom's death only complicates our lives that much more and makes the decision as to your future that much easier."

Brownstein looked from Jim and then to Kelly.

"I'm afraid Bruce is right. To report Tom's death to the authorities would only invite questions that we don't want to answer."

"So what're you going to do now?" Jim demanded. "Just shoot us here like this? You think you'll be able to avoid questions from the authorities that way?"

"Please, Jim," Lord responded with feigned light-heartedness. "You disappoint me. I would've thought by now that you would realize that we are much more sophisticated than that. We're not barbarians. We do things carefully. And we don't leave tracks. But, sad to say, it's irrelevant to you how we do it. The bottom line is that you've left us no choice. I can promise you this much, however. Like the others who have gone before you, you won't feel any pain."

The reference to others confirmed Kelly's suspicions as to what Lord had in mind. Their captors obviously planned to inject them with air and leave them somewhere in the desert, victims of some cause that would never be determined.

It was then that Jim heard the fluttering sound. It was faint at first, and he seemed to be the only one who heard it. He knew immediately that it was not a natural sound of the desert night.

The sound became progressively louder and caught everyone else's attention as well.

Kelly turned to Jim.

"What is that?"

By then Jim knew what the sound signified. But he saw no need to explain and just shrugged his shoulders.

The two of them turned their attention back to their captors, who remained standing in front of them across the coffee table. Lord and Brownstein gave each other a knowing glance.

"Those are helicopters," Brownstein commented curtly.

"Yeah," Lord echoed. "At least two. And they sound like big ones. Maybe Hueys."

Everyone remained silent as the noise of the helicopters became louder and louder. Within minutes, it was clear that the helicopters were coming directly toward the cabin.

Jim immediately thought of his father. Thank you, Dad, he murmured to himself, for breaking your promise.

Lord and Brownstein looked disturbed but gave no indication of any desire to change course. Not that it was any surprise to Jim. He couldn't imagine that Brownstein would want to face the public humiliation of being arrested as a kidnapper—something that would far eclipse any shame in being the daughter of one of Kennedy's assassins.

Within a short time, they could all see the outlines of two huge helicopters hovering in front of the cabin with large spotlights focused on the cabin. The silence was finally broken by a magnified voice from one of the helicopters. The incredibly loud voice came in a slow staccato style that, in Kelly's mind at least, seemed to reflect the power that lay behind it.

"THIS IS THE FBI. PUT DOWN YOUR WEAPONS AND EXIT FROM THE FRONT DOOR WITH YOUR HANDS ABOVE YOUR HEADS."

Lord and Brownstein gave each other a long look. After a few moments, they just nodded their heads. Jim sensed that they had already developed an escape plan in anticipation of the helicopters' arrival. A secret passageway that would provide an escape? Or just a determination to fight to the death?

Lord kept his gun pointed at Jim and Kelly while Brownstein moved into the kitchen. Within a minute or so, all the lights in the cabin went out. When they did, Lord pulled out a small flashlight and shined it on Jim and Kelly.

"We don't want to make it too easy for our visitors," Lord said in a casual manner that Kelly found frightening. To Kelly, it not only signaled a refusal to cooperate with the FBI. Lord's comment also meant that she and Jim would not be released to the FBI's custody.

Brownstein returned to the family room with two small candles. She placed them in front of Jim and Kelly and lit each one. Lord turned off his flashlight, and then he and Brownstein receded to a corner of the family room away from the front door and the large windows.

Jim recognized the benefit of the ploy immediately. From the helicopters' vantage point, the only people who could be seen would be Jim and Kelly. Even with the helicopters' spotlights, Lord and Brownstein would be hard to pinpoint.

The voice from the hovering helicopters echoed into the cabin again.

"THIS IS THE FBI. PUT DOWN YOUR WEAPONS AND EXIT FROM THE FRONT DOOR WITH YOUR HANDS ABOVE YOUR HEADS. NO ONE WILL BE ABLE TO LEAVE THE CABIN IN ANY OTHER WAY."

Lord looked directly at Kelly and Jim from the far corner of the family room, his gun now pointed directly at them.

"I'm afraid that the plans for your future have changed once again. I meant everything I said when I talked about dying for our country. And," he added slowly, "dying to preserve our secret. We do not intend to be arrested and interrogated and held up for public ridicule for something that preserved the country's security. The only problem for you is that you now have to die with us."

"Why?" Jim exclaimed. "Let us leave. You can stay here and die if you want."

Lord did not mince words in rejecting that alternative.

"That's unacceptable. We're not going to let you live and tell what you know. If I have to die, I at least want to preserve what I can of my reputation. And so does Kay. By the time the FBI gets in here, we'll all be burned beyond recognition. People will be left only with guesswork as to what happened—or what brought you here."

"That's not true," Jim interjected. "There are people out there who do know why I'm here. That's why those helicopters are outside your house."

"Nice try," Lord retorted, "but no dice. Our plan is irreversible."

"I don't get it," said Kelly. "What're we going to do? Wait here until the FBI destroys the place?"

"Oh, no," Brownstein replied. "I've already triggered the timer. This place is going to blow to smithereens in five minutes. It'll be quick and painless for all of us."

Jim and Kelly exchanged looks of fear and desperation.

"You can't be serious," said Jim. "Don't you think people will ultimately figure out what you did and why you kidnapped Kelly?"

"Not really," said Brownstein.

"Anyway," Lord added, "it doesn't matter. That's our decision, and, for better or worse, you'll have to live with it. Or, should I say, die with it."

Kelly fell back on the couch, her heart pounding furiously.

Jim's mind continued to race through the alternatives. There had to be some way to avoid this suicidal pact. It was then that the idea came to him.

He cleared his throat and leaned over in an apparent effort to tie the laces on his hiking boots. As he did so, he caught Kelly's attention and let his jacket drop over the boots. Jim knew that Lord and Brownstein were at an angle of vision to his right that prevented them from seeing what he discreetly showed Kelly—the flares in the inside pocket of his jacket. Jim raised his eyebrows and moved his head slightly toward the front door to indicate that Kelly should make a movement away from him to distract Lord and Brownstein.

Kelly seemed to catch on immediately. At least Jim hoped that she did. They didn't have any other choice. Or much time.

Jim sat up on the couch. As he did so, the loud voice from the helicopter pierced the silence once again.

"THIS IS THE FBI. THIS IS YOUR LAST WARNING. PUT DOWN YOUR WEAPONS AND EXIT FROM THE FRONT DOOR WITH YOUR HANDS ABOVE YOUR HEADS."

"Kiss my ass," Lord responded in a soft voice that could be heard only by those in the family room.

As soon as Lord made his comment, the large high-paneled window was punctured by a canister that landed in the middle of the family room and immediately began to emit a gas. Kelly jumped up from the couch and moved farther away from Jim.

"Hey," Lord yelled. "Get back on the couch."

It was the distraction that Jim needed. He had already removed the plastic caps from the tops of the two flares. He quickly pulled the flares out of his jacket pocket and, in one swift movement, used both hands to place the tips over the lit candle in front of him. Fiery red flames instantly erupted from the flares.

By the time they realized what Jim was doing, Lord and Brownstein saw the two flares flying toward them.

Jim leaped over the coffee table and ran to the front door.

"Come on," he yelled to Kelly.

Jim saw Kelly rush through the gas that was quickly filling the family room. The two of them reached the front door almost simultaneously. Opening it was no easy matter in the haze of gas. As they struggled with the doorknob, Jim and Kelly heard shots as Lord and Brownstein tried to stop them. Thank God for the gas and the darkness, Jim said to himself. We're not very visible targets. Still, the door wouldn't budge, and Jim knew that little time was left. Desperate for an alternative, he saw the small wooden table by the door. In one swift movement, he picked it up and heaved it at the large window with everything he had. Shattered glass was suddenly everywhere, but the hole made by the gas canister was now made large enough for him and Kelly to jump through with ease.

They ran in the direction of the huge helicopters. The noise was deafening, and the wind generated by the helicopters' blades was stronger than anything Kelly would have imagined. But no matter. They were out of the cabin.

As they raced toward the security of the helicopters, Jim and Kelly were thrown to the ground by a booming explosion that immersed the cabin in a towering fireball of flames and debris. Jim scrambled on top of Kelly and covered her head with his head and hands as fragments of the cabin landed all around them. When the shower of wreckage stopped, Kelly picked up her head and looked back in the direction of the cabin. It was totally engulfed in flames that seemed to reach into the sky.

"Oh my God, Jim," Kelly sighed. "I can't believe they did it."

She waited for Jim to respond, but there was no answer. His body lay inert on top of her. She then looked down and saw that her shirt was covered in blood. Fear gripped her. Was it hers? Or Jim's? She didn't know but she felt herself get weak.

"Jim?" she called again in desperation. Still no response. She gently pushed him off of her, and his body fell over limp. It was only then that she saw the mass of blood gushing from the side of his head.

"Jim!" she cried in anguish.

As Kelly struggled to her feet, her clothes saturated with blood, she looked around in search of help while the helicopters landed nearby. The whirling blades were brought to a standstill and the helicopter doors slid open. In what seemed like an instant, the ground was swarming with men in jackets and hats emblazoned with the FBI logo. In the rush of people and commotion, Kelly suddenly saw a familiar face.

"Detective Soggs," she yelled. "Oh my God, I'm so glad to see you."

"Kelly," he responded with obvious concern. "Let me help you."

Kelly pushed the detective away as he grabbed her elbow and excitedly pointed to Jim's motionless body. Soggs leaned over the body and immediately called out to an FBI medic. While the medic administered to Jim, Soggs stood up and placed his arms around Kelly, who was now sobbing uncontrollably. The detective tried to comfort her as best he could, all the while watching as the flames slowly brought the log cabin to the ground.

Chapter 71

Jim and Kelly sat in the chairs across from Harvey Teasdale and waited in silence while he finished the telephone call he had received shortly after they had arrived at his office. Jim, his head swathed in a large white bandage, glanced over at Kelly. She looked radiant. And more than that, she looked relaxed. A look Jim hadn't seen on Kelly for some time.

Jim felt as relaxed as Kelly. He noticed the change in his own mental state after he had returned to Washington the day before. Only then did he realize how much pressure Kelly's search had created in his life. And how relieved he was to know that the dangers to their lives had been removed. They could now pursue their careers—and their relationship—without looking over their shoulders. At least he hoped it would be so.

After a few minutes, Teasdale placed the telephone back in the cradle, leaned forward in his chair, and placed his clasped hands on the desk. A smile slowly emerged.

"That was a friend of mine at the FBI. One of the associate directors. He was gloating over the manner in which the situation was handled."

"Wasn't he disappointed that Lord and Brownstein were not brought back alive?" Kelly asked.

"Sure. It would have been of tremendous value to be able to question them. But there was nothing more that could've done. He presumes that they perished in the cabin's explosion, but…."

Jim and Kelly looked at Teasdale, their eyes wide with anticipation.

"But what?" Jim asked anxiously.

Teasdale shook his head in disbelief.

"They couldn't find any bodies in the rubble of the cabin."

"Nothing?" Kelly persisted.

"Nothing. Which of course is strange. Because, no matter how forceful the explosion, and it was powerful, they should have been able to find something. So I just don't know. I don't have an answer. And neither did he."

"Could there have been a secret passageway or something else that they used at the last minute to escape?" Jim asked.

"Maybe. The cleanup has not been completed, and I'm sure they'll keep looking. Who knows? Maybe something will be found to show that the two of them did die as we think they should have. But, in the meantime, I guess this will be just one of those things that adds to the whole mystery of the Kennedy assassination."

"By the way," Jim inquired, "were you surprised to learn of Bruce Lord's involvement?"

"Not entirely. There was always something unnerving about him that made me wonder what he was really about. A charismatic and very accomplished operative who always seemed to be pushing the edge of the envelope."

"You mean operating outside the law?" Jim asked.

"More than that. Most of us in the Company—especially in the 1950s and early 1960s—knew that the agency did not have to abide by the same rule of law that governed the other agencies. But still, we knew there were limits. At least I thought so. But for Bruce, I often suspected that he knew no limits—only what he thought was right. And he obviously took it to an extreme that I did not know about."

"Well, you must have known he didn't like what Kennedy was doing as president," Kelly suggested.

"Sure. I knew he was disappointed with Kennedy's performance. We talked about it all the time. And like the others, I knew about Kennedy's womanizing. But I did not sense the danger that Bruce did. And I had no idea he would have taken it as far as he did. The rest is easy to understand. Having made that decision to eliminate Kennedy, he could have easily enlisted others to help. He had a talent for recruiting top prospects out of college. And once they joined the agency, those college recruits developed a bond with Lord that transcended the usual bureaucratic lines of command. We were known inside the agency, with some respect and perhaps a little humor, as Lord's Angels. I guess the only reason I wasn't included in the Kennedy plot was because he knew I had reservations about the legality of some of his techniques."

"How'd he wind up in Nevada?" Jim asked.

"He retired from the agency many years ago, and he built that cabin near the Nellis testing site. He became very familiar with the area through his work in the Company and obviously found it to be an attractive place to retire."

"I'm still amazed," Kelly said, "at the FBI's speed in organizing that rescue effort. We wouldn't be sitting here if it had taken any longer."

"It's just fortunate," Teasdale responded, "that Detective Soggs happened to be in his office when Caleb Butler called. The telephone number supplied by your father, Jim, was also pretty helpful. And, of course, as my friend at the FBI remarked, the proximity of the Nellis Air Force Base proved to be critical. Once the FBI devised its action plan, it didn't take long to get the right people assembled and boarded onto those helicopters."

"I'm just curious," said Kelly. "How did Detective Soggs get there so fast?"

Teasdale smiled.

"He's one dedicated detective. He just wanted to be there for the finale. As soon as he talked with Butler and pulled in the FBI, he caught a plane to Las Vegas and made the FBI agree to his request to be included in the team that boarded the helicopters."

"So what now?" Kelly asked. "Will the FBI open some kind of formal investigation into the Kennedy assassination to finally determine what happened and who did what?"

Teasdale leaned back in his chair.

"No. I don't think so."

"That'll be tough to resist," said Jim, "given the widespread publicity concerning Kay Brownstein's death. It's all over the news, and I've got to believe that the press is going to push for some answers as to what happened and why."

"I think that's all true. But the press doesn't really have much to go on. Right now, the public knows nothing other than that the CIA director and a former CIA case officer have died in a mysterious explosion. The FBI can't add much to that—at least not in public. All they have is Lord's explanation and a copy of Kelly's letter, all of which they've agreed to keep under tight wraps. There are no other witnesses or documents, and I'm told the president is opposed to opening another investigation into the Kennedy assassination unless he knows in advance something definitive will be proven."

Jim looked at Kelly.

"That's not all bad, you know. It means that, at least for the time being, your father's letter will remain known only to a select few. And maybe that's as it should be."

"I certainly feel that way. And I certainly was not going to give in to Lord's request for it."

"That was pretty gutsy of you under the circumstances," Teasdale interjected. "But I am curious. Where *did* you put it?"

Kelly winked at Jim and then turned back to Teasdale.

"It was in the safe in Brownstein's office."

Teasdale gave Kelly a puzzled look.

"It was in her office? I don't understand. How could that be?"

"I had initially hidden it in an old cereal box in the pantry of my kitchen. But when Jim and I decided to go to the Cayman Islands, I knew I couldn't leave it there any longer. I was too afraid that someone would break into my house and turn everything upside down looking for it."

"What about a safe-deposit box in a bank?" Teasdale asked. "I would think that would have been a safe place."

"Maybe for other people, but not for me. These people seemed to have too many connections. And who knew what they could do? So I didn't think I could even trust a bank. I needed to put it somewhere that I knew would be well protected. And Brownstein was the obvious choice at the time. She already knew about the letter and, stupid as it was in retrospect, I trusted her. So, when I went to meet her right before we left for the Cayman Islands, I asked Amanda, her assistant, if she could hold an envelope for me. I didn't tell her what it was—other than that it related to something Brownstein was looking into for me. I asked her to keep it very confidential, and I guess Amanda proved to be a better guardian than I could have expected. She obviously didn't tell Brownstein about it."

"I'll be damned," Teasdale whispered under his breath. "I'll be damned."

There was a pause as they all enjoyed the irony of the situation. Kelly finally broke the silence.

"Well, Harvey, I can't thank you enough. You've been great to me, and I'm more than a little embarrassed to think that I began to question your sincerity."

Teasdale responded with a broad smile.

"Not at all. It's good for you to carry a little skepticism in life."

He turned toward Jim.

"In the rush of everything, I forgot to ask you about the head wound. We were all a little concerned at the time that you might not make it. But it looks like you've got it all under control now."

"Yeah, it's healing nicely, and the stitches should come out in the next few days. I was fortunate. I'm still not sure what hit me. Whatever it was, it made a deep laceration and knocked me out. But the doctors say it should have no permanent effects."

"Well, then," said Teasdale, standing up and walking from behind his desk. "I can see that all's well that ends well." Jim and Kelly had also risen from their chairs, and they all walked to the door. As they stood there saying goodbye, Teasdale turned to Kelly.

"By the way, what happened with your lawsuit? Your connection to Caleb Butler has already served you well, but I was wondering whether there are any other benefits here."

"Oh," said Kelly, her eyes wide with excitement. "It got settled. The safari company gave me two million dollars. Two million dollars. Can you believe it?"

"Good for you," said Teasdale. "That's wonderful. What're you going to do with all that money?"

"I'm talking to Harvard Law School about creating some kind of scholarship in Jeff's name. Something that will keep his memory alive for a very long time. Because it's really not my money. It's his."

"So," Teasdale observed, "you've had two big victories in a week."

He then turned to Jim.

"And what about you? What's next on your agenda?"

"I'm probably going to leave the Senate and try my hand at writing screenplays, maybe novels. It's something I've always wanted to do. And these last few weeks have made it clear that I shouldn't defer my dreams. Life's too short. So I'm going to give it a shot. And if it doesn't work out, I guess I can return to law or public service."

"That sounds like a sensible plan," Teasdale responded. "Something I wouldn't mind doing," he added with a laugh. "But, unfortunately, I've got to go over to the White House for a six o'clock meeting. So I'll have to say so long for now." He took Kelly's hand in his and gave her a long look. "And I hope you'll let me know if I can ever help again. As I told you in our first meeting, there's nothing I wouldn't do for Ted Roberts's daughter."

"I appreciate that. I really do." She gave Teasdale a hug, and then she and Jim walked down the narrow stairs to the front door. When they reached Jefferson Street, Kelly turned to Jim.

"You know, there's an inscription on the wall in the CIA lobby that I can't forget: 'And ye shall know the truth, and the truth shall make you free.' I never realized how much truth there is in that saying."

"Why? Do you now feel free?"

"I sure do. Knowing the truth about my father has taken a great weight off my shoulders. In some strange way, the unknown was a tremendous burden. I now feel so relieved. I feel like I have the freedom to do whatever I want to do. I can focus on the future. Except...." And now she gave Jim a fearful look. "What do you make of the possibility that Lord and Brownstein might still be alive? Do you think we have to be worried about that?"

Jim shook his head.

"No, I really don't think so. They have to believe that you've disclosed whatever your father told you and whatever you know. So there's no longer any incentive for them to spy on you or do you harm."

Kelly thought about Jim's response and then nodded.

"I think you're right. I really do."

"So what now?" Jim asked, looking at his watch. "It's almost six o'clock on a beautiful summer evening. What to you want to do with your new-found freedom?"

Kelly looked up at Jim's hazel eyes and put her arm through his.

"Something that comes to mind is a relaxing dinner at my house with a good bottle of wine. The only thing that might be missing is someone to share it with. Got any plans?"

"As it turns out, I'm free tonight. So I'll be glad to take you up on that offer."

They then took each other's hands and walked down Jefferson Street toward Kelly's parked Jeep.

###

ACKNOWLEDGMENTS

This is, first and foremost, a work of fiction designed to entertain rather than inform. That said, I have tried to make the historical references consistent with the abundant literature available on John Kennedy's presidency and to make the discussion of the assassination consistent with known facts. That has been no easy task because, as any scholar of the assassination knows, there is considerable disagreement in the literature concerning almost every aspect of the assassination, including whether Lee Harvey Oswald was involved and, if so, whether he acted alone. I have staked out one theory in this book but make no pretense to have solved the mystery of Kennedy's assassination.

Whatever the merits of my theory, I am indebted to the many people who have investigated Kennedy's assassination and provided ample fodder for my imagination. I am also indebted to many others who generously gave me the benefit of their professional expertise and, in some cases, a thorough reading of the manuscript. One person requested anonymity, but he knows who he is and how much I appreciate his contribution. Others include Dr. Harry Agress, Dr. Charles Citrin, and Roger Zuckerman.

Several others read portions or all of the manuscript with a critical eye and provided many useful suggestions. Those readers include Joanne Alafoginis, Richard Curtis, Jerry Gross, Shelly Kale, Evyan Koenig, Robert Koenig, Hank Paper, and Cathy Singleton. Two readers deserve special mention: Tony Edens and Doug Katz. Each devoted untold hours to reading and re-reading the manuscript and then discussing their ideas and proposals. To them, I am especially grateful.

Thanks also go to the team at Seven Locks Press, especially Jim Riordan. Their dedication to producing a quality product and their patience in responding to my many questions went far beyond the call of duty.

Special thanks also go to my daughter Lindsay and my son Brett, whose support and suggestions were a constant source of encouragement.

And then there is my wife Jan. She is the glue that held the project together over many years, providing endless encouragement and showing extraordinary patience in my repeated requests for her to review every page of the manuscript, no matter how many times it was re-written. Her insights and proposals were invaluable but, in the end, any shortcomings or mistakes in the book are my responsibility alone.

ABOUT THE AUTHOR

Lew Paper is a graduate of the University of Michigan and the Harvard Law School and holds a masters degree from Georgetown Law School. He has held a variety of positions in the private and public sectors, including service as a Fellow at Georgetown Law School's Institute for Public Interest Representation, Legislative Counsel to United States Senator Gaylord Nelson, and Associate General Counsel of the Federal Communications Commission. He has written three previous books: *John F. Kennedy: The Promise and the Performance*, *Brandeis: An Intimate Biography*, and *Empire: William S. Paley and the Making of CBS*. His articles and book reviews have appeared in *The New York Times*, *The Washington Post*, *The New Republic*, and numerous other publications. He currently practices law in Washington, DC.